Advance Praise for *The Tudor Conspiracy*

"A fascinating tale of young Elizabeth in danger at her sister's court. Fast-paced and exciting, with beautifully researched historical details and a most engaging hero, this story is so vivid you feel you are there!"
—Diana Gabaldon, author of the Outlander series

"In C. W. Gortner's skillful hands, plots and counterplots come to seething life . . . Lovers of Tudor history and suspense fiction will be riveted by this swift-paced, sexy, enthralling novel."
—Nancy Bilyeau, author of *The Crown*

"C. W. Gortner has done it again! Intrigue at the Tudor court never looked more lethal than in his capable hands, as forbidden desires and deadly rivalries turn sister against sister and plunge our bold hero into a labyrinth of deceit. Full of breathtaking action, dark twists, and unexpected revelations, this is an unputdownable read!"
—Michelle Moran, author of *Nefertiti*

"Suspense, intrigue, betrayal, and deadly rivalry: What more can you ask for? From the serpentine halls of the court to the vicious back alleys and stews of Tudor London, Gortner has brewed a swashbuckling, perilous adventure that you simply can't put down!"
—M. J. Rose, author of *The Book of Lost Fragrances*

"C. W. Gortner has an unmatched talent for bringing the past to life. *The Tudor Conspiracy* is historical fiction at its best: a compelling story masterfully told, vivid characters fully drawn, and an accurate depiction of [the] history of the time. A novel not to be missed!"
—Tasha Alexander, author of *Death in the Floating City*

"*The Tudor Conspiracy* weaves a suspenseful, tangled skein of intrigue. It is a vibrant historical mystery and crime-thriller with an A-list cast of characters. Here are Elizabeth Tudor and her Robert Dudley in a light you've seldom seen them."
—Margaret George, author of *Elizabeth I*

Praise for *The Tudor Secret*

"Gortner handles action with aplomb, adding a riveting, fast-paced thriller to the crowded genre of Tudor fiction."

—*Publishers Weekly*

"Even Tudor fans who know the main players and historical backdrop will be captivated by Gortner's storytelling and his engaging hero. . . . Grabbing reader interest [with] the quick pace and lush historical references. This novel is both entertaining and thoughtful."

—*Romantic Times*

"Brilliantly executed plot and three-dimensional characters . . . highly recommended."

—*Historical Novels Review*

"An exciting, vividly rendered story of intrigue and espionage."

—*Book List*

"If you're looking for a book that will pull you back into the Tudors, this one is a good choice."

—*Bookreporter.com*

"Filled with real-life spies, intrigue, danger, and royal secrets, Gortner has created a book that will delight fans of history for years to come."

—*Night Owl Reviews*

Also by C. W. Gortner

The Tudor Conspiracy

C. W. Gortner

St. Martin's Griffin
New York

THE TUDOR CONSPIRACY. Copyright © 2013 by C. W. Gortner. All rights reserved. Printed in the United States of America. For information, address St. Martin's Press, 175 Fifth Avenue, New York, N.Y. 10010.

www.stmartins.com

Library of Congress Cataloging-in-Publication Data

Gortner, C. W.
    The Tudor conspiracy / C. W. Gortner.—First edition.
        p. cm
    ISBN 978-0-312-65849-6 (trade pbk.)
    ISBN 978-1-250-04277-4 (hardcover)
    ISBN 978-1-250-01095-7 (e-book)
    1. Mary, Queen of Scots, 1542–1587—Fiction. 2. Scotland—History—Mary Stuart, 1542–1567—Fiction. 3. Espionage—England—Fiction. I. Title.
    PS3607.O78T83 2013
    813'.6—dc23

                                                            2013004023

St. Martin's Griffin books may be purchased for educational, business, or promotional use. For information on bulk purchases, please contact Macmillan Corporate and Premium Sales Department at 1-800-221-7945 extension 5442 or write specialmarkets@macmillan.com.

First Edition: July 2013

10 9 8 7 6 5 4 3 2 1

For Erik

She has a spirit of enchantment.
—SIMON RENARD, referring to Elizabeth Tudor

Cast of Characters

IN ORDER OF APPEARANCE

1. **Brendan Prescott:** Spy in service to Elizabeth; works under the alias Daniel Beecham
2. **Kate Stafford:** Lady-in-waiting to Elizabeth
3. **Peregrine:** Brendan's squire, former stable groom at Whitehall
4. **William Cecil:** Former court secretary, adviser, and spymaster
5. **Katherine Ashley:** Princess Elizabeth's governess and household matron
6. **Robert Rochester:** Comptroller to Queen Mary
7. **Mary Tudor:** Queen of England
8. **Jane Dormer:** One of the queen's wards and attendants
9. **Susan Clarencieux:** Queen Mary's favorite lady
10. **Sybilla Darrier:** One of the queen's ladies
11. **Simon Renard:** Ambassador of the Hapsburg emperor, Charles V
12. **Margaret Douglas, Countess of Lennox:** Cousin to Mary and Elizabeth

13. **Edward Courtenay, Earl of Devon:** Cousin to Mary and Elizabeth
14. **Elizabeth Tudor:** The queen's sister and heir to the throne
15. **Scarcliff:** Courtenay's body servant
16. **John, Ambrose, Henry, and Guilford Dudley:** Robert's brothers
17. **Jane Grey:** Daughter of the duke of Suffolk, a prisoner in the Tower
18. **Robert Dudley:** Elizabeth's close friend, a prisoner in the Tower
19. **Nan:** A tavern maid
20. **William Howard:** Lord Admiral

The
Tudor
Conspiracy

WINTER 1554

———◆◆◆———

There comes an inevitable time in every life when we must cross a threshold and encounter that invisible divider between who we are and who we must become. Sometimes, the passage is evident—a sudden catastrophe that tests our mettle, a tragic loss that opens our eyes to the bane of our mortality, or a personal triumph that instills in us the confidence we need to cast aside our fears. Other times, our passage is obscured by the minutiae of an overcrowded life until we catch it in a glimpse of forbidden desire; in an inexplicable sense of melancholic emptiness or a craving for more, always more, than what we already possess.

Sometimes we embrace the chance to embark on our passage, welcoming it as a chance to finally shed the adolescent skin and prove our worth against the incessant vagaries of fate. Other times, we rail against its unexpected cruelty, against the sharp thrust into a world we're not ready to explore, one we do not know or trust. For us, the past is a haven that we are loath to depart, lest the future corrupt our soul.

Better not to change at all, rather than become someone we will not recognize.

I know all about this fear. I know what it is to hide a secret and pretend that I can be like any other man—ordinary, commonplace, unremarkable; my days regimented between dawn and dusk, my heart given to one alone. I craved to be anyone but who I was. I felt I had seen all I had to see of vicissitudes and broken innocence, of the savageries perpetuated in the name of faith, power, and lust. I believed that in denying the truth, I would be safe.

I am Brendan Prescott, former squire to Lord Robert Dudley and now in service to Princess Elizabeth Tudor of England.

In that winter of 1554, my deception found me.

—◆◆◆—

Chapter One

"Cut and thrust! To the left! No, to *your* left!"

Kate's shout resounded within Hatfield's vaulted gallery, punctuated by a metallic hiss as she lunged toward me on soft-shod feet, brandishing her sword.

Ignoring the sweat dripping down my brow, my shoulder-length hair escaping its tie and plastered to my nape, I gauged my position. I had the advantage of my weight and height, but Kate had years of training. Indeed, her experience had come as a complete surprise to me. Kate and I had only met five months before in the palace of Whitehall, during the time of peril when I served as a squire to Lord Robert Dudley, son of the powerful Duke of Northumberland, and she acted as an informant for our mistress, Princess Elizabeth Tudor. During our time at court, Kate had displayed rather unusual skills for a woman, but when she first offered to instruct me it never occurred to me that she'd be so adept with a blade. I'd thought to call her bluff, thinking at best all she could manage was a few thrusts and parries. She soon proved how wrong I was.

I now averted her lunge, her sword slicing the air. Twisting around, pivoting on my shoes' soft leather soles, I watched her stalk to me. I let her approach, feigning weariness. Just as she prepared to strike, I leapt aside, slashing down with my blade.

The smack of steel against her gauntleted wrist clapped in the hush like thunder. She let out a startled gasp, dropping her sword to the floor with a clatter.

Taut silence fell.

I could feel my heart pounding in my throat. "My love—oh my God, are you hurt? Forgive me. I didn't mean it. I didn't . . . I didn't realize . . ."

She shook her head, peeling back her gauntlet. I saw a slice in the red cloth lining where my sword had bit through. My stomach somersaulted. "But how . . . ?" I gaped. I ran my finger over the keen edge of my blade. "My sword, it—it's not blunted. The tip: It's always supposed to be blunted. The nub must have fallen off!"

I started to check the floor, paused, in sudden understanding. I looked at the long-limbed youth standing as if petrified in a corner.

"Peregrine! Did you blunt my sword as I told you?"

"Of course he did," said Kate. "Stop yelling. Look, I'm fine. It's just a scratch." She extended her wrist. That tender white skin I'd kissed countless times had begun to darken into what promised to be a magnificent bruise, but to my relief there was no visible wound.

"I'm a brute," I muttered. "I shouldn't have struck so hard."

"No, that's exactly what you should have done. Surprise and disarm your opponent." She leveled her honey-colored eyes at me. "You'll need a better instructor. I've taught you everything I know."

Her praise gave me pause. Though it gratified me to hear, I

found her compliment a little too opportune to take at her word. I leaned down to the sword at her feet. My jaw clenched. "I should have known. Your nub seems to have fallen off as well." I paused, taking in her expression. "God's teeth, Kate, are you mad? Why would you do such a thing?"

I felt her set a warning hand on my arm, but I ignored it as I swerved back to Peregrine. He didn't shift a muscle. His green-blue eyes were wide, framed by the dark thicket of curls falling about his face. He didn't know his day of birth but believed he neared his fourteenth year, and though he hadn't grown much in height, his features were starting to lose their elfin childishness, revealing the handsome man he would become one day. The clean air and plentiful food here in Elizabeth's manor of Hatfield had transformed him, erasing all trace of the malnourished stable hand who'd first befriended me at court.

"You should have checked," I said to him. "That's part of being a squire. Squires always double-check their master's gear."

Peregrine stuck out his lower lip. "I did check it. But—"

"You did?" Though I heard the sudden anger in my tone I couldn't stop it. "Well, if you did check, you did a poor job of it. Maybe you're not ready to be a squire. Maybe I should return you to the stables. At least there no one can get hurt."

Kate let out a cry of exasperation. "Brendan, honestly! Now you *are* being a brute. Peregrine is not to blame. I took off the nubs before you got here. I'm also wearing enough quilting under my jerkin to weather a storm at sea. I wasn't in any danger."

"No danger?" I turned to her, incredulous. "I could have cut off your hand."

"But you didn't." She sighed and raised herself on tiptoes to kiss me. "Please don't make a fuss. We've been practicing every day for weeks. Those nubs had to come off sometime."

I growled, though I knew I shouldn't berate her. It had taken me some time, and many bruises, to recognize that while outwardly a vehicle to teach me the intricacies of swordplay, our practice sessions were, in truth, our way of directing our frustrations that we'd not had the opportunity to ask leave to wed before Princess Elizabeth departed for London to attend the coronation of her half sister, Queen Mary.

Given the circumstances, Kate and I had reluctantly decided not to burden Elizabeth with our request to marry. In the days leading up to her departure, the princess had kept a firm smile on her face, but I knew she was apprehensive over her reunion with her older sister, whom she had not seen in years. It wasn't merely the seventeen-year difference in their ages. While Elizabeth had been raised in the Protestant faith, a result of her father King Henry's break with Rome, Mary had cleaved to Catholicism—and it had almost cost her everything in the final days of their brother King Edward's reign.

I knew all too well about the dangers the princesses had endured. Like Elizabeth, Mary had been targeted by John Dudley, Duke of Northumberland, who ruled in Edward's name. While the young king lay dying, Northumberland had schemed to capture the Tudor sisters and set his youngest son Guilford and daughter-in-law Jane Grey on the throne instead. He might have succeeded, too, had I not found myself thrust into the midst of his plans, unwittingly becoming one of the architects of his demise. It was how I'd first met Kate and come to serve Elizabeth; now, with Northumberland dead, his five sons imprisoned, and England celebrating Mary's accession, Elizabeth had had no choice but to obey her sister's summons, though, to my disconcertion, she insisted on returning to court without us.

"No, my friends," she said. "This is hardly the time for me to appear with an entourage. I'll attend the coronation as a loyal subject and be back here before you know it. It's not as if Mary *wants* me to stay. She has enough on her platter. I'd only be a burden."

Elizabeth had chosen only her trusted matron, Blanche Parry, to accompany her. I didn't like it. The night before she left, I asked her again, in vain, to let me go with her, citing my fears for her safety in the cesspool of intrigue at court.

She laughed. "You forget I've breathed the airs of that cesspool my entire life! If I could survive Northumberland, surely there isn't much to fear. However, I promise you that if I find need of protection, you'll be the first person I send for."

She left Hatfield as autumn gilded the land. With her gone, the household settled into a quiet routine. As I fought off my disquiet over her safety by dedicating myself to my studies, my sword practice, and other chores, I came to realize it wasn't that Elizabeth had not wanted me with her, but rather that she'd known me better than I knew myself and acted in my best interests.

The truth was I wasn't ready to return to court. I still needed time to heal.

Remembering this, I regretted my tone with Peregrine, who had helped me through so much. Keeping an arm about Kate's waist, I motioned to him. "Come here," I said.

He sidled forth. He had become my shadow, following me everywhere—"like an adoring pup," Kate had remarked—as evidenced now by the appeal in his wide-eyed gaze.

"I ought to send you off to empty the bilge pit or something equally unappetizing," I grumbled. "Haven't you learned it's never wise to trust a woman?"

Kate jabbed me in the rib.

"Yes," said Peregrine. "I mean, no."

"Well?" I arched a brow. "Which is it: yes or no?"

Kate let out a laugh. "You are impossible! Let the lad be. He has years yet to learn about the wiles of the fairer sex." Stepping away from me, she undid the snood at her nape, releasing her auburn hair. I ruffled Peregrine's curls. "I am indeed a brute," I said to him. "Please, forgive me."

Peregrine was opening his mouth to reply when Kate exclaimed, "Papa, what a surprise!" and I froze where I stood, staring toward the gallery entrance in disbelief.

Coming toward us was the last person I'd expected to see—a dapper figure in a black cloak, a satchel strapped to his shoulder. As he removed his flat black cap from his balding pate, I thought William Cecil looked younger than his thirty-three years and healthier than the last time I'd seen him. Even his russet-colored beard was free of any telltale white, and his bronzed face was a sure sign that, like me, he'd been spending much-needed time outdoors, tending to a garden or herb patch or whatever it was he did when not manipulating other people's lives.

"I trust I do not intrude?" he said in his smooth tone. "Mistress Ashley told me I would find you here, taking your exercise."

"You always intrude," I heard Peregrine mutter, and I set a hand on his shoulder. Cecil's light blue eyes glinted in amusement as he looked in the boy's direction before he turned to Kate, who appeared uncharacteristically flustered. Though she feigned surprise, I had the distinct impression Cecil's arrival here was not unexpected.

"My sweet Kate, it's been too long." Cecil embraced her. "My wife, Lady Mildred, was most concerned you might have taken ill. We were relieved to get your note."

Note? I shot a sharp look at Kate as she hugged Cecil in return. She had every right to, after all. She had become his ward upon her mother's death, raised in the Cecil household by him and his wife. Why shouldn't she have written to him? Only, she had not mentioned it to me, though she knew how I felt about this man. She had not contended with him as I had, when he had served Northumberland as his private secretary and lured me to spy against the Dudley family. She had not learned that her beloved guardian had several faces, none of which could be fully trusted.

"I'm so sorry to have worried you and Lady Mildred," Kate now said. "I've wanted to visit, but—" She turned to me, taking my hand in hers. Cecil glanced down with apparent indifference at our clasped fingers, though he could hardly have missed the inference. "Time just got away from us," Kate went on. "Didn't it, Brendan?" She smiled at me. "Lately it seems we haven't enough hours in the day. The house always need so much work."

"I can imagine it," Cecil said. "And I don't wish to be an imposition, though I was hoping to stay for supper. I brought a meat pie and jar of honey. I left them with Mistress Ashley." He smiled warmly at Kate. "I remembered how you used to love honey from our hives when you were a girl."

"Oh, how kind of you! Yes, I'll see to it at once." Kate glanced again at me; my stomach knotted. It took all I could muster to say dryly, "Indeed. How could we refuse?"

Cecil met my gaze. He hadn't missed the undertone in my voice. I already knew there was more to his visit than mere worry over Kate's health.

"A moment, if you will," I said to him, and I guided Kate a short distance away, leaving Peregrine to glare at Cecil. In a taut voice, I asked her, "What is this about? *Why* is he here? And why didn't you tell me he was coming?"

"Just heed him," Kate said. "It's important."

I went still. "Is it about . . . ?"

"Yes." She put a finger to my lips, preempting my eruption. "You can berate me later, but for now I'll leave you two alone so I can see to supper. Try not to hit him, yes?" She turned about with a bright smile, gesturing to Peregrine. As she herded him out, Peregrine glared over his shoulder at Cecil.

"Judging by the look on your face, and your little friend's reaction, I assume you'd rather I wasn't here," he remarked.

"And I see you haven't lost your acuity. What do you want?"

He smiled, moving to the window seat. "You're looking fit," he said. "You've put on weight. The air here at Hatfield suits you, it seems."

"Better than the court," I replied. I concentrated on keeping an impassive stance. Cecil was an expert dissimulator; he knew how to get under my skin. I could already sense him gauging me, assessing how this time of seclusion, of early mornings and earlier nights, had transformed me so that I no longer resembled the callow youth he'd lured into informing against the Dudleys. "You haven't answered my question," I said.

"I came to see you." He sat. "Kate sent me a note, but I wrote to her first. I told her I had important news to impart. She returned word that I should present myself."

"You could have written to me."

"Yes, I could have. But would you have replied?"

"Depends." I eyed him. "You still haven't answered my question."

To his credit, Cecil looked discomfited. "I would not have come were it not a matter of urgency, I assure you. I've no desire to cause you any more trouble than I already have."

"Is that so?" I asked, and as we faced each other for the first time since the tumultuous events that had first brought us together, I reflected on the irony that two such antithetical men could hide such powerful secrets about each other. For only I knew how ruthlessly Cecil had acted to destroy his former master, Northumberland, and protect Elizabeth, just as only Cecil knew the truth of who I was.

I tensed as Cecil shifted aside the pile of books on the window seat and perched on the cushions. He picked up one of the volumes, perusing it. "I see that besides your swordsmanship, you've taken to studying Spanish and French. Quite a formidable endeavor, if I do say so myself. One might think you're preparing for something."

I had to school myself to meet the impact of his pale blue eyes. Enough had gone between us for me to know I'd always be on the short end of the mallet when it came to Cecil. Even now, as he stood poised against the window embrasure as if he were still holding audience in his London manor, his power and influence vast, though rarely exercised in public, I felt a shudder pass through me as I contemplated everything he was capable of.

I clenched my jaw. "Lest you forget, I now serve Princess Elizabeth. I am not your informant anymore, so get to the point. What is this urgent matter?"

He inclined his head. As usual, his matter-of-fact air didn't do justice to the exigency that must have propelled him to Hatfield. Still, his opening volley took me off guard.

"Have you any word from Her Grace?"

I felt a chill that had nothing to do with my sweat-dampened chemise. "Not recently. We had a short letter from her a month or so ago, saying she was staying on at court through Twelfth Night. We assumed the queen had invited her to stay."

Cecil arched his brow. "Oh, she is staying, but not because she was invited. Mary has ordered her to remain at court." He paused. "Do I have your interest?" He reached into his satchel to remove a sheaf of papers. "These are reports I recently received from an informant. I assumed that under the circumstances, you wouldn't take my word for it."

I crossed my arms with deliberate nonchalance, hiding my disquiet.

"Elizabeth is in danger," he said. "Grave danger, according to these reports."

I took a moment to meet his gaze. I found no deception there, no conniving. He looked both troubled and sincere. Then again, he was a master at hiding his motives.

"In danger?" I repeated. "And you have an informant at court who told you this? Who is it?"

He shook his head. "I don't know." He untied the leather cord binding the sheaf. "These reports started arriving a month or so ago—all anonymous, all in the same hand." He extended one of the papers to me; as I took it, he added, "That's the last one. It arrived about a week ago. You can see the paper is a common grain, like the others, but I believe the man who wrote these reports must be employed at court. His information indicates proximity to the events he describes. Look at the handwriting: It's orderly but not overly literate; a secretary or notary, perhaps."

I scanned the report. The writing reminded me with a jolt of the neat lettering I'd often seen in the castle account ledgers kept by Archie Shelton, the Dudley family steward. Shelton had trained me to be his apprentice. He also first brought me to court to serve as a squire to Lord Robert Dudley, plunging me into danger.

I tore myself away from the memory. "I don't understand," I said, looking up at Cecil. "This is an account of Queen Mary receiving a Spanish delegation to offer the Emperor Charles V's congratulations on her coronation. Why is that unusual? The emperor is a fellow sovereign."

"Turn it over," he said. "The page. Turn it upside down, and hold it up to the light."

I went to the windowpane and pressed the paper against it. I had to focus, but then I began to see them: translucent white lines, surfacing like ghosts between the inked ones.

There was another letter, hidden within the letter.

I squinted. "I can't make it out. The words are too faded."

"The special ink he used is activated by lemon juice," Cecil explained. "It's a familiar ploy, and I'm ashamed to admit it took me a while to figure it out. Clearly this is not the work of a trained spy. At first, I thought someone was playing a trick on me, in rather poor taste, sending me reports of seemingly innocuous events at court. But as they kept arriving, I started to get suspicious. Fortunately, Lady Mildred always keeps on hand the juice of preserved lemons from our orchard." He met my stare. "I have transcribed everything for you here, on this paper. What that invisible letter says is that unofficially, the Spanish delegation brought Charles V's secret offer of marriage to his son, Prince Philip."

"Philip?" I started. "As in, the prince of Spain?"

"The same. And the emperor is more than a fellow sovereign: He is the queen's first cousin, whom she's always treated as a family confidant. She relies on his advice. Should she accept his offer of marriage to his son, one of the terms of the betrothal will be returning England to the Catholic faith. Charles V will tolerate nothing less. It also goes without saying that a rapprochement with Rome would be calamitous for every Protestant in this realm, and most of all for Elizabeth."

He picked up the page on which he'd transcribed the

invisible words from the reports. "See here. 'Her Majesty heeds exclusively the imperial ambassador, Simon Renard, who deems Elizabeth a bastard and heretic, and menace to the queen.'" He glanced up at me. "They're all in this vein: two or three secret lines per report, yet taken together they present an undeniable picture."

My heart started to pound. Cecil might be a liar, but when it came to Elizabeth he was nothing if not thorough. She meant everything to him; she was the reason he persisted, the beacon that guided him through the shoals of his disgrace, as the fall of Northumberland had been his fall as well, for Queen Mary had exiled him from court.

"Her Majesty doesn't strike me as someone who is easily swayed by others," I said.

"Yes, she is like her father that way; she makes up her own mind. But she is also the daughter of Catherine of Aragon, a princess of Spain, and Simon Renard represents Spanish interests. He has served the Hapsburg emperor Charles V for many years, and she takes his advice seriously. If Renard is advising that Elizabeth poses a threat to her faith and her desire for a Hapsburg marriage, nothing could be more calculated to rouse her suspicions. After all, religion is the queen's lodestone. She believes God himself guided her through her vicissitudes to the throne. Elizabeth is a Protestant; she stands in direct opposition to everything Mary hopes to achieve, including returning England to the Catholic fold."

Alarm went through me. "Are you saying this man Renard seeks the princess's arrest?"

"And her death," replied Cecil. "It can mean nothing else. With Elizabeth out of the way, the succession is to Prince Philip and Mary's future child. An heir of Hapsburg blood to rule England and unite us with the empire, thereby encircling the French—it is Charles V's dream. Renard is a career civil servant; he knows whoever delivers that dream stands to gain a great deal."

I stared at him, aghast. "But the queen would not harm her. Elizabeth is her sister and . . ." My protest faded as I took in Cecil's expression. "Dear God, do you think he has any proof against her?"

"Besides accusations whispered in the queen's ear? No, not yet. But that doesn't mean he shan't be long in obtaining it. Make no mistake: Simon Renard is a tenacious opponent. When he sets his mind to something, he will not stop until he achieves it."

I clearly heard the soughing of the evening wind rising outside. I took a moment to collect my thoughts before I said quietly, "What is it you want from me?"

He smiled. "What else? I want you to go to court and stop Renard. You earned Queen Mary's trust when you risked yourself to help her escape Northumberland's coup. She would welcome you. Gain a post in her service and you can beat Renard at his own game."

I let out a terse laugh. "Just like that? I return to court and the queen grants me hearth and board, and a post to boot?" My mirth faded. "Do you think me a complete fool?"

"On the contrary, I think you have a flair for this work, as previous events have shown." He glanced at the pile of books by his side, now overlaid by his reports. "I do not believe this rural life can satisfy you for long, not with so much important work yet to do."

His unexpected insight stung me, more than I cared to admit. I didn't relish his knowing things he had no right to. I didn't want him inside my head.

"The last time I accepted an assignment from you," I said, "I almost perished."

"Yes." Cecil met my regard. "A spy does run that risk. But you prevailed, and rather well, I might add, all things considered. This time, at least you'll be prepared and know who your foe is. You will also return to court under the alias I gave you when you first met Mary. You will be Daniel Beecham, and his return is unlikely to arouse much interest."

He rose from the window seat, leaving the reports on my books. "You needn't answer me now. Read the reports and consider whether you can afford to ignore them."

I didn't want to read his reports. I didn't want to care. Nonetheless, he had already lured me to his bait. He stirred something in me that I could not evade—a restlessness that had plagued me ever since I had left court for this safe haven.

Cecil knew it. He knew this terrible craving in me because he also felt it.

"I still must talk to Kate about this—" I started to say. I stopped, noting his impatient frown. "She already knows, doesn't she? She knows you want to send me back to court."

"She's no fool, and she cares for you—rather deeply, it would seem. But she also understands that in matters such as these, time is often the one commodity we lack."

I clenched my jaw. I thought of Kate's enthusiastic cajoling of me to master the sword, her determination for me to excel. She must have suspected a day would come when I'd be compelled to return to court in defense of Elizabeth.

"I should wash up before supper," said Cecil. "I assume you'll have more questions after you read these. I can stay the night, but tomorrow I must return to my manor."

"I haven't said I agree to anything."

"No, not yet," he replied. "But you will."

Chapter Two

Outside the window the gray sky leached into the colorless winter landscape, blurring the demarcation between air and land. Gazing toward the forest, where bare trees swayed in the snow-flecked wind, I felt this haven, this place of refuge for me, begin to fade away inexorably, like a brief, idyllic dream.

We can guide her to her destiny—you and I. But first, we must keep her alive . . .

I turned to the window seat and took up the reports. There were six total, and though I pressed each one to the glass, in the ebbing afternoon light it was difficult—impossible, in some cases—to decipher everything written between the inked lines. Cecil's concise transcription, however, confirmed what he'd told me: It appeared the Spanish ambassador Simon Renard had sowed fear in the queen regarding Elizabeth's ultimate loyalty to her, using the princess's Protestant faith to tarnish her reputation and implicate her in something dangerous enough to warrant her arrest. What that something was, the informant did not say, probably because he didn't know. There were various mentions of one Edward Courtenay, Earl of Devon, a nobleman who apparently had befriended the princess. I made a mental note to ask Cecil about this Courtenay.

I didn't realize how long I'd been sitting there, reading, until I heard Kate's footsteps on the creaking floor. I looked up to find the gallery submerged in dusk. She stood before me in a sedate blue gown. As she took in the papers strewn about me, she said quietly, "Supper is almost ready."

"You knew about this," I said.

She sighed. "Yes. Cecil wrote to say he had urgent news concerning Her Grace; he didn't give any details, just insisted he must speak with you. What was I supposed to do?"

"You could have told me."

"I wanted to, but he said he wanted to show you something in person." She glanced again at the papers on the window seat. "It looks serious."

"It is." I told her about the reports and what Cecil had extrapolated from them.

When I finished, she wet her lips. "God save us, danger follows her like a curse." She exhaled a worried breath. "I've been dreading this day, hoping against hope it wouldn't come to pass."

I stood and took her hands in mine. She had strong hands, bronzed from working on her treasured herb garden, her nails cut short, with a hint of dirt under them. All of a sudden I ached at the thought of leaving her.

"If these reports are true, she needs me," I said. "What I don't understand is why she hasn't written to us directly. Surely she must know by now that she is in danger."

"If she does, it's not a surprise that she hasn't written," Kate said. I looked at her, frowning. "There was a time before I served her," Kate added, "when she was sixteen years old. She became implicated in a treasonous plot hatched by her brother Edward's uncle, Admiral Seymour, who was beheaded for it. Elizabeth was harshly questioned, our own Mistress Ashley taken to the Tower for a time. When Elizabeth told me about it, she said it was the most frightening time of her life. She vowed she'd never willingly put a servant of hers in danger again. She hasn't written because she's trying to protect you. You must think me very selfish for wanting to do the same."

"If you wanted that, you'd have burned Cecil's note and bolted the door."

"Guilty as charged." She let out another sigh. "When must you go?"

"Soon," I said softly. "I must talk to Cecil again after supper, but I assume he'll want me to leave as soon as possible. He said time was one commodity we lacked."

"He does have a way with words, doesn't he?" She managed a faint smile. "If you're going to leave, however, then I think it's time for you to do something important for me."

Around us, without warning, the unspoken stirred. She reached under the neckline of her bodice and withdrew an object strung on a leather cord—a fragmented golden artichoke leaf, tipped by a tiny chipped ruby.

"Will you tell me what this is?"

My mouth went dry. "I—I did tell you. It is my troth, a pledge of my love for you."

"Yes, but what does it *mean*? I know you acquired it during that awful time when we were fighting to save the princess from the Dudleys. That woman who raised you, Mistress Alice, gave it to you. Why? What is its significance?" Kate paused, her voice softening as she took in my silence. "It has to do with your past, doesn't it? Cecil knows, too. If you can trust him with it, why not me?" She reached out to caress my face, the jewel dangling at her breast. "Whatever it is, I promise I will never betray you. I'd die first. But if you must return to court to risk God knows what dangers, you can't expect to leave me behind with this secret between us. I must know the truth."

I couldn't draw enough air into my lungs. I looked into her eyes, so steady, so determined, and was overcome by my secret, which I'd vowed to never tell another soul.

"You cannot understand what you ask," I said quietly. "But I do trust you, with my very life." I guided her to the window seat. "You must swear that you'll not tell anyone," I said, taking her hand in mine, "especially not Elizabeth. She must never know."

"Brendan, I already said I'd not betray your confidence—"

I gripped her hand. "Just swear it, Kate. Please, for me."

"Yes," she whispered. "I do. I swear it."

I nodded. "I've never told Cecil about that jewel. The only other man who knows about it is Archie Shelton."

"Shelton? The Dudley steward who brought you to court? He knows?"

"He *knew*. He's dead now. He must be. He couldn't have survived that night we were trapped in the Tower after London declared for Mary. It was chaos. The gates closed on us. Northumberland's supporters were clawing at each other to get out. I saw Shelton disappear in the crowd, trampled underfoot. He died, and the secret of the jewel died with him. Cecil knows who I am, but he doesn't know I have evidence to prove it."

I paused, faltering. I saw myself again as a lost child, scrambling to hide as the Dudley brood hunted me, walloping for the foundling without a name. I remembered my beloved Mistress Alice, bathing my bruises, murmuring that something special set me apart. That something had set loose a chain of life-shattering events, and as I thought of everything that had happened to me, everything I had discovered, I realized I couldn't keep it to myself any longer. I had to share this terrible burden.

In a low voice, I told Kate my story, starting with how I'd been brought as a babe to the Dudley household and raised to be their servant, neglected and disdained until I was summoned to serve Lord Robert, the most dangerous Dudley of all.

"When he came to the castle to escort me to court, Shelton warned me to do as I was told, to be a faithful servant and never betray the family on whom I depended for my survival. He said my fealty would be rewarded. But then I met Elizabeth. Then I was hired by Cecil to spy on Lord Robert and help her, and everything changed. I unraveled the mystery of my birth. After twenty-one years of believing I was nobody, I discovered that I had royal blood in my veins." I went silent for a moment. Then I said haltingly, as Kate drew in an incredulous gasp, "My mother was Mary of Suffolk, Elizabeth's aunt. I am a Tudor."

I had never said these words aloud, and I saw the impact of my revelation spread across Kate's face. She raised a trembling hand to her chest, touching the jewel. "How—how did Shelton find out?" she finally uttered. "How is this jewel connected to it?"

"Shelton delivered the jewel to Mistress Alice." I came to my feet. I couldn't stay seated anymore. "He had served the Suffolk household long before he entered the Dudleys' service. That leaf is part of a larger jewel, which was broken apart after my mother's death; she bequeathed its leaves to those she thought she could trust. But Mistress Alice had already fled with me to the Dudley castle and let it be known I was a foundling. Shelton must have spent years searching for her. And when he found her, she told him about me."

"But why would she have told *him?*"

I forced myself to shrug, though her question pierced my soul. "My mother had concealed her pregnancy from everyone save Alice; when she died, Alice took me away to hide me. I believe she did it to protect me and my mother, to keep secret that a Tudor princess had given birth to a bastard."

"Dear God. And you've known this, all this time. You've kept it all to yourself."

"I had no choice. Don't you see, Kate? That jewel may prove my birthright, but it's too dangerous to reveal—for all of us. A bastard is of no account, but if anyone thought I was legitimate . . ." I shuddered, turning away from her.

"Do you think Shelton knew who your father was?" she asked softly.

"If he did, I'll never know now." I cleared my throat. "I never wanted any of this. If I could, I'd undo it all. I'd rather be a foundling than this . . . this creature of shadow."

"You are not a creature." I heard her skirts rustle as she stood. I felt her hand on my shoulder. Desolation filled me.

"I do not ask you to live with this," I whispered. "It is too great a burden, I know. The children we might have together . . . they will never be able to claim a family from me. Even my name is a lie. It means nothing."

"Let me decide what I can and cannot bear. Brendan, look at me." I turned about to face her. "Never let me hear you say that again," she said. "You are the man I have chosen to spend my life with. You are strong, good, and honest. You are all a child needs in a father."

Tears burned in my eyes. I drew her close, and as I held her against me and breathed in her lavender scent, desire for her overwhelmed me. I longed to ravel my hands in her hair, uncoil it from the net at her nape to let it flow like dark honey over her naked shoulders. I longed to strip her of her clothes, to see her arch beneath me with breathless abandon, taking me deep inside her. I wanted none of the sordid intrigues and terrors of my past or the court to ever touch her again.

"I love you, Kate Stafford," I said. "I love you with all my heart. I only want to be yours, forever. If you ever find reason to doubt me, remember that."

She kissed me. "And I love you, Brendan Prescott, even if you hide too much."

After supper, Cecil and I retired to sit together before the fire.

Nursing a goblet of hot cider, his pale eyes turned strangely opaque in the flickering interplay of light and shadow, he said, "Will you do as I ask?"

In response, I extended the sheaf of reports, rebound with the cord.

"No questions?" he asked, with a hint of surprise.

"There isn't much to ask, is there? The bulk of those reports details events at court, as you said. They might be entries from the ledger of any master of ceremonies or clerk; there's nothing to question, at least not visibly. However, there is one thing I noticed besides the secret warnings." I took a moment, watching him. He was fully capable of omitting important details. He had done it before. I didn't want to consider that he might be engaged in one of his double ploys, not in this case, but my suspicion of him could not be quelled so easily. I had to be certain.

"Go ahead." He took a sip from his goblet. "I can see the doubt on your face. You'll have to master that trait. At court, everyone is an expert at reading others."

"Edward Courtenay," I said, "Earl of Devon. Your informant mentions him several times, in association with the princess. Why?"

Cecil smiled. "You are indeed a born intelligencer."

"It's hardly proof of my skill. Anyone who read those reports would ask the same. So, who is he?"

"A last survivor of the royal Plantagenet bloodline. Old King Henry—who could smell a foe at a hundred paces—imprisoned Courtenay as a boy in the Tower. He also beheaded Courtenay's father. Henry proclaimed it was because of the family's refusal to accept him as head of the church, but in truth he feared Courtenay's claim to the throne. One of Mary's first official acts as queen was to order Courtenay's release. She also gave him a title. In fact, she's shown him significant favor."

"Does that make him ally or threat?"

Cecil's brow lifted. "Denied so long his royal privileges, or what he believes are his privileges, I should think that royal favor or no, our earl must nurse plans of his own. Indeed, if rumor is to be believed, he was offered as a possible spouse for Mary, but she rejected him due to his inexperience and youth."

"Are you saying that he could be plotting against the Hapsburg marriage?"

"I'm saying he is one of the mysteries you need to investigate." Cecil's voice darkened. It was the first time he had let his frustration openly show that he was so removed from the undercurrents at court. Times past, he'd have put two or three agents on Courtenay's trail, to report on his every move. "If Courtenay is plotting, it will not be overt. Remember, Mary has yet to make official announcement of her intent to marry. Whatever Courtenay intends, he's planning it in secret."

"But Renard must be watching him." I had started to recline in my chair when I saw Cecil's hand tighten about his goblet. The movement was fleet, almost indiscernible, but the moment I gleaned it, I understood. "God," I breathed. "You're still testing me. You're sending me to court because you fear Renard's suspicions about Elizabeth could be true."

He let out a terse sigh. "The possibility has crossed my mind. I hope I'm wrong. In fact, I pray for it. But the fact that Elizabeth's name is linked to Courtenay is not an auspicious sign. Of course, it could mean nothing. Their friendship could be the natural outcome of two persons of import who have found themselves thrown into court together. They're not too far apart in age. He's twenty-six, six years older than she. It could all be perfectly innocent."

"Or it could not be," I countered. I hesitated, regarding him. Sometimes I forgot that few of us knew Elizabeth as well as we supposed. It was part of her charm; she could make anyone feel like her intimate, when in fact she hid her true nature in enigma. "Do you actually believe she's capable of plotting against her own sister?" I asked cautiously.

He gave a dry chuckle. "When it comes to Mary and Elizabeth, nothing would surprise me less. You'd be hard-pressed to find two women more disparate, let alone two who are sisters. I fear they're fated to become mortal enemies. Battle lines are being drawn even as we speak, with Mary on the one side, determined to wrest the realm from heresy and bind us to a foreign power, while Elizabeth is on the other as her heir, the last hope for an independent land beholden to the Protestant faith. Which one shall win?"

His voice quickened, imbued with urgency. "If Elizabeth is involved in Courtenay's plot, she must be stopped before it is too late. Like her, I've no wish for us to fall prey to Spain and the Inquisition, but unlike her, I've lost the impetuosity of youth. Elizabeth fails to realize that Mary nears her fortieth year. Even if Prince Philip manages to get her with child, she may never carry it to term. Without an heir of Mary's body, Elizabeth can be queen. We can guide her to her destiny—you and I. But first, we must keep her alive."

The echo of his words faded, until the crackling of the flames in the hearth was clearly heard. I stared into the fire, weighing his concerns in my mind.

I said quietly, "I will do it, then. I will go to court."

His entire posture sagged. All of a sudden, he revealed the profound weariness lurking behind his imperturbable facade, the insidious toll that years of toil in the arena of power, extracting bribes and favors, instigating plots and schemes, had taken on his spirit.

"Thank you," he said. "On the day she takes the throne, may it be sooner rather than later, God willing, I promise you'll be well compensated for your service."

I stood. "Don't promise anything quite yet. I said I'd go to court to help her, but I go on my terms. Understood? I'll brook no interference, no matter what course I take. If you have any men in London you're thinking of putting on my tail, warn them off now. If you don't, if I find out you're misleading me in any way, you will regret it."

His mouth twitched. "I believe we understand each other."

He reached into the satchel by his chair and took out a small leather purse. "For your expenses."

"I do this for the princess. I don't need payment from you."

He set the purse on my chair. "Consider it a loan, then." He came to his feet. I took satisfaction in it. I finally had gotten the upper hand when it came to William Cecil.

As he started to leave, I said, "What of this informant? Should I try to find him?"

"Absolutely not. If he wants to be found, he'll let us know."

It snowed in the next days—a light dusting that dissipated by the afternoon yet left a new and profound chill in the air. We were occupied from dawn till dusk, readying the animals and fields for the onslaught of winter, finishing the stocking of the larders and cellars, pruning the last of the fruit trees, and covering herb patches and other delicate plants to shelter them from the night's frost.

I sent word to Cecil and received his instructions in return. While I prepared, Kate and I did our best to not compound our impending separation. She set herself to purchasing cloth and making me the court doublets and shirts I required, sewing by the fire at night while I pored over Cecil's transcription of the warnings in the reports, seeking some other clue I might have missed. The heaviness between us thickened, so that even Mistress Ashley finally made comment of it on the morning of my departure as I packed my belongings.

The plump matron who'd overseen Elizabeth's household for years had become a stalwart presence in my life as well. Energetic and devoted to the princess's welfare, Kate Ashley had boundless optimism and an ability to make everyone around her feel at ease. I knew she'd not taken it well when Elizabeth refused to let her accompany her to London; they had quarreled, as was their wont, with Ash Kat, as Elizabeth dubbed her, wringing her hands as she watched the princess ride away.

"No good can come of it," she had said at the time. "She and that sister of hers should never be in the same city, much less under the same roof. I told her to stay put, feign an illness, but would she listen to me? No. There she goes, into the very jaws of the wolf."

Now Mistress Ashley bustled into my chamber to declare, "You're going to bring her home, yes? No shenanigans this time, no sneaking into forbidden rooms or jumping off leads into the Thames? You're going to pack her up and bring her here, where she belongs."

Clearly Kate had been confiding in her over the kitchen table at night, after I'd retired. "That would be the goal—if she'll let me," I added, with a rueful smile.

Kat Ashley snorted. "I warned you, serving her is no banquet. She demands more than she ever gives and rarely shows any gratitude. I hope you're prepared. The only thing she hates more than being told what to do is being told what she should *not* do."

"I'm aware of that." I latched my bag, then lifted it to test its weight. Cecil's loan had allowed me two new doublets, several changes of hose, and shoes suitable for court, all of which were heavy. I didn't want my horse Cinnabar to be overburdened. It would take a full day's ride to reach London, maybe more if the weather worsened.

Mistress Ashley reached into her apron pocket and took out an oil-paper bundle tied with twine. "For the road," she said. I accepted it in gratitude, knowing there'd be a chunk of fresh-dried venison, good cheese, and fresh-baked bread. Then she pressed another pouch into my palm, this one unmistakably filled with coin. "I've been saving for a day like this. A smaller cut of meat here, some extra butter sold there—it all adds up."

I started to protest that I had money left over from Cecil, but she held up a hand. "I insist. You cannot go to court like a pauper, not if you hope to impress the queen." Her keen eyes met mine. "The girl is beside herself," she said. I went still. "She won't say anything because you are doing your duty, but she fears you, too, are going into the mouth of danger."

"I know," I said softly. "But no one at court knows much about Daniel Beecham." As I spoke aloud the name of my alias, I touched my chin. I'd let my red-gold beard grow out as thick as I could, trimming it to the shape of my jaw, with a fashionable jutting prong at my chin. Between the beard and my long hair I hardly recognized myself. Would it be enough? Could I return to court and not give myself away as that callow squire who'd turned Northumberland's plans upside down?

"You could be any man," said Mistress Ashley, as if she read my thoughts. She took my face between her hands. "Kate needs you. Though she stays behind, her heart goes with you. All our hearts do. All we want is for you and Her Grace to return to us, safe and sound."

A lump clogged my throat. "You're not making this any easier," I muttered.

"I don't intend to." She patted my cheek. I embraced her, losing myself for a moment in her crisp scent of herbs and linseed oil and all the uncomplicated good things in life.

"There now," she muttered, drawing back. "Enough of that. Come, it's getting late and you've a long journey ahead. The boy can hardly contain his excitement."

I started. "Boy?"

She smiled. "Did you think we'd really let you go off on your own? Peregrine is going with you." She wagged a finger, again cutting off my protest. "It's not as if he'd stay, anyway. You know well that the moment you left, he'd be right behind you."

Chapter Three

As we went into the courtyard, I saw Peregrine holding the reins of his horse, swathed in a cloak, his thick curls shoved under a wool cap. Mistress Ashley was right: If I tried to leave him behind, he'd not stay. I loathed exposing him again to the dangers of court, but he had always served me well. He had even saved my life—twice, as he liked to remind me. I could do no better when it came to a loyal companion.

Kate turned from checking Cinnabar's harness. "Ready?" she asked, with brittle cheer.

"Except for him." I motioned to Peregrine. He started to open his mouth in protest, but I cut him off. "You're to do as I say at all times. No questions. No second-guessing me. You'll act as my squire, and a squire must be at his master's beck and call at all times. I don't need to be worrying about what kind of mischief you're getting yourself into. Do I make myself clear?"

"Yes, master," he said indignantly.

Kate tucked my cloak about me. "Be safe," she said. Her voice cracked.

"Kate." I reached out.

She took a step back. "No. No good-byes."

I gazed into her eyes. "I promise I'll send word as soon as I can."

"Don't." With that one word, she conveyed everything we dared not say aloud, the mere fact that by setting quill to paper I might betray myself. "Just come home," she said, and she pushed past Mistress Ashley, going under the archway back into the manor.

I started to go after her. Mistress Ashley stopped me. "Let her be. I'll look after her. You go now, before she changes her mind and orders her own horse saddled."

I turned back to Cinnabar. My horse snorted, eager to be off. Jumping onto a mounting block, Peregrine scrambled onto his dappled gelding.

We rode to the road. I glanced over my shoulder to see Mistress Ashley framed by the redbrick house, the tenacious ivy turning brown where it curled about the windows. She raised her hand in farewell. I kept looking back as she and Hatfield faded from view.

Though I did not see Kate, I knew she was at one of those windows, watching me.

The day was crisp, the sun an opaque halo in the bone white sky. Once we cleared the manor grounds, we took to a canter, the horses impatient to stretch their limbs. I didn't want to fill the silence with idle talk. Sensing my mood, Peregrine kept quiet, at least until we stopped to eat our midday meal. As I sliced the cheese, venison, and bread, he finally let loose the one question I was sure he'd been burning to ask since Cecil's visit. As usual he'd been listening in on every conversation he could, ferreting out the purpose for our trip.

"Is she in danger?" he asked, munching down his bread. He had an insatiable appetite but never seemed to gain weight. Whenever I saw him eat like this, I wondered how much hunger he had experienced in his short life.

"Chew your food. And yes, she might be. Or she might not be in any danger at all. I don't know yet. That is why I am going to court, to find out."

He looked doubtful. "But I heard Kate and Mistress Ashley talking. Kate said the imperial ambassador was trying to have the princess arrested for treason."

"Did you really? Those big ears of yours are going to get you into more trouble one day than you're worth. Have you already forgotten what I told you?"

He sighed. "No second-guessing you."

"That's right. I'm serious, Peregrine. This is not a game."

"Who said it was?" He sounded insulted. "But if she is in danger, you might as well tell me now. You wouldn't want me to wander about not knowing."

"You're not to wander at all. You're to do as I tell you or I swear, I'll send you back to Hatfield hog-tied, if need be."

"Yes, master." He snatched the last slice of venison and crammed it into his mouth. "Just answer me one thing," he said, chewing.

"What?"

"Tell me you're not planning on falling into the river again. Because sometimes the Thames freezes in the winter and it would be hard to rescue you—" He laughed, ducking from the hand I swiped at his head. He had a wonderful laugh, like a young boy's should be. For the first time since we left Hatfield I found myself smiling.

"You're impossible," I said. "Let's go. I want to reach the city before dark."

We resumed our journey. We passed few travelers on the road, an occasional farmer and band of merchants with carts of goods, trudging with heads down and wary greeting. Soon, however, the snow-flecked countryside of Hertfordshire began to give way to clusters of hamlets and lesser townships that indicated our proximity to London. The thoroughfare became more crowded; people were hustling to get through the city gates before curfew. As we passed a small stone church where bells tolled, I noted a recently repaired crucifix askew on its steeple, mortared clumsily back in place. Women with shawls draped about their heads clutched shivering children by the hand, answering the bells' summons.

Peregrine stared at the scene. I glanced at him. "Do you believe in the old faith?"

He shrugged. "I never much cared for religion. I don't think God does, either."

I was struck by how he had unwittingly described my own opinion. I, too, often wondered if one faith was any better than the other, considering how much blood had been spilled, but I kept my doubts hidden, for it was never safe to speculate aloud about religion.

Dusk fell, thick with snow flurries. Cinnabar snorted impatiently. I patted his neck. I, too, was tired, not to mention cold. My hands in their gauntlets felt frozen to my reins, and my buttocks and thighs were saddle-sore. In my mind, I fled back over the road we'd just traversed, back to Hatfield, where Kate must be lighting the candles for the evening meal—

"There's Cripplegate." Peregrine broke into my thoughts. "From there, we can take to the Strand and ride to the palace."

I brought myself to attention as we maneuvered our way through the horde pushing into the city before the gates closed for the night. As I paid the toll, I had a vivid memory of the first time I'd come to London. I had had no idea at the time, as I'd gazed in awe at the sprawling walls and the Thames's distant coil, of the adventure that awaited me. Just like then, I now felt an excited prickle in my belly.

There were people everywhere, closing up shops and hurrying home from last-minute errands while others, eager for the night, threw open doors to smoke-filled inns and raucous taverns. Already the ravaged doxies were patrolling the darker alleyways, garish in their paint, sidestepping the ubiquitous beggars, thieves, and skulking pickpockets. Emaciated dogs scurried underfoot, scavenging in the conduits that carried sewage to the river. Overhead, timber tenements leaned into each other, upper floors conjoining to form fetid vaults, from which denizens emptied chamber pots into the streets, showering unwary passersby with leavings.

At first, I didn't see much change. London appeared as dirty and unpredictable as it had been during the late King Edward's final days. Yet as we made our way toward King's Street and the palace, I began to notice graffiti scrawled on walls, declaiming, DEATH TO ALL PAPISTS! and SPANIARDS BE GONE! There were placards strewn on the ground, too, muddied now and illegible but no doubt offering equal dissent. It would appear the common people of London were not happy with the arrival of the Hapsburg delegation.

Whitehall reared into view. We rode into the courtyard and dismounted. Disgruntled officials trudged past us with cloaks yanked about their shoulders and caps shoved low on their heads. None paid us any mind. The snow was falling faster, whitening the flagstones. Cinnabar stamped his hooves.

"The horses will need feed and stabling," I said.

Peregrine gathered both pairs of reins. I gave him two angels from the purse Cecil had sent. He'd not been parsimonious. I had enough for a comfortable stay, providing I didn't stay too long. "Wait." I grasped Peregrine's wrist. "How will you find me?"

He scoffed. "I lived here, remember? And I warrant you'll not be lodged in the royal apartments."

"Fine, but don't tarry. After you see to the horses, come to me straightaway."

"Yes, master." With a mock flourish, he led the horses away.

Slinging my bag over my shoulder, I went to the nearest entranceway. Three sentries swathed in cloaks and bearing halberds blocked my way. Only after I reiterated that I was here to see Lord Rochester did one of them sneer, "Her Majesty's comptroller? Now, what would a common oaf like you want with an important lord like him?"

"Can you please tell him Master Beecham is here?" I asked wearily, using my alias and hoping Rochester would remember me. I was left shivering under the colonnade. It seemed hours had passed when I finally heard a blustering voice exclaim, "By the rood, if it isn't the very Master Beecham who saved us all from perdition!" and I turned to find Lord Rochester beaming at me.

I had last seen him in Norfolk, marshaling troops for Mary's defense as she prepared to fight Northumberland for her throne. He had been robust then; now he looked fat in his too-tight doublet of expensive mulberry velvet, his gold chain of office dangling about his meaty shoulders, his jowls reddened and breath hot with the odor of roast meat and mulled wine.

He pumped my hand. "Master Beecham! Who would have guessed? I never thought to see you again. After you came to us at Framlingham, you disappeared like a ghost."

I forced out a smile. "I regret to say, I had urgent business elsewhere."

Rochester chortled. "No doubt, what with all of Northumberland's men running for cover after the duke's head rolled. No matter. You're here now, and I'm glad of it, as will be Her Majesty." He whisked me past the sentries into the palace. Sensation painfully returned to my hands and feet as we moved through corridors hung with tapestries.

"How long has it been?" he asked. "Five months? Six? Ah, but so much has happened since then. You may not be aware of it"—he shot a look at me—"but Her Majesty has won the heart of the realm. It's a new England, Master Beecham, a new England indeed. Oh, but she'll be pleased to see you. Pleased and relieved. She wondered what happened to you."

I was heartened to hear it. I needed her to be pleased.

He came to a sudden halt. "Best not mention any of the past business, eh? Her Majesty will no doubt show gratitude for your services, but . . . well"—he coughed uneasily—"I'd not remind her of it. She'd rather forget what Northumberland and his sons nearly did to her."

"Naturally, I understand the need for discretion."

"Yes, a man in your position would. Are you here for work, then? If so, I daresay you'll find it. Her Majesty is always in need of able men, and you're as able as they come."

I could only hope Mary would feel the same. Of Elizabeth, I

dared not ask. But I did want to know of a friend I'd not heard from in some time. "Is Barnaby Fitzpatrick here?"

Rochester paused, frowning. Then his broad smile returned. "Ah, you must mean our late king's companion. No, he's in Ireland. Her Majesty honored his claim to the baronage of Upper Ossory. He left a few months ago."

I did not remark, recalling that Barnaby had feared Mary's accession because of her staunch Catholicism. Apparently he'd found a way to escape living directly under her rule.

We entered a gallery. Enormous double doors stood at the far end under a carved archway. As I caught the distant sound of music, my pulse quickened. The great hall lay beyond those doors. Instead of leading me there, however, Rochester steered me in the opposite direction, into another, darker gallery and through a narrow corridor, after which we started up a flight of cramped stairs.

Rochester panted, his girth taking a toll on his breath. "I've put you in one of the smaller rooms on the second floor. The Hapsburg delegation is here, and we're rather crowded at the moment. We can see later about something better for you, eh?"

We reached a low-ceilinged hallway punctuated by a series of plain doors. I recognized this section of the palace as well. This was where Robert Dudley and his brothers had lodged when their father the duke held sway. It felt strange to be here again, a free man in service to the princess, when just months before I'd been a Dudley squire with little hope of escaping my lot.

"Did you bring any servants?" Rochester sifted through keys on an iron ring he produced as if by magic from his voluminous breeches.

"Yes, one squire. He's gone to stable our horses."

"Oh, fine. The chamber is big enough for you and a squire."
As he unlocked the door before us, I braced myself. Had he actually brought me to the same room? One look inside showed
me he had not. While the chamber bore some resemblance to
that overturned sty where the Dudley boys had bedded, this
room was smaller, almost fully occupied by a utilitarian cot,
with a rush mat on the floor, a rickety-looking stool, and a battered chest, on which sat a pewter decanter, a warped candle-
stick, and two wooden cups. I saw no privy area save for a bucket
in a corner. A mean thick-glassed window set high in the wall
probably admitted little daylight. Now, tallow flares in oil dishes
cast a rancid glow.

"Hardly luxurious, but at least it's clean," said Rochester,
"and not damp like the rooms on the lower floor. At this time in
the year, you could catch an ague there overnight."

"It suits me." I set my bag on the floor. "I prefer my accommodations simple."

"Well, this is about as simple as it gets. You must be hungry.
There'll be some leftovers from tonight's feast. You can go to the
kitchens or have your squire fetch a platter. I'll see word is sent
to him. The stables are also full, and he may have trouble securing stalls. The Spaniards arrived with horses." He rolled his
eyes. "Can you believe it? Horses! Brought all the way from
Spain on ships, as if we didn't have anything to ride here."

"I've heard the Spanish breed some of the best horses in the
world," I said. I wasn't about to be drawn into criticism of for-
eigners, though I did find it noteworthy that he'd referred to the
Hapsburg delegation as "Spaniards." Recalling the graffiti I'd
seen, I added, "The people don't seem too pleased about their
visit, either. I saw placards in the city."

"Aye, that would be the apprentices." He shook his head. "Cheeky lot. Ought to mind their manners, lest Her Majesty claps all of them in the Fleet for their insolence." He turned solemn. "We had an incident at court not too long ago. Someone tossed a dead dog into the queen's chapel." He grimaced. "They'd tonsured the poor animal like a priest and tied a note about its neck calling for death to all Catholics. Since then, she's ordered the curfew strictly enforced. The apprentices are still posting placards, but they're wise enough to do it late at night to avoid our patrols. If any gets caught, he'll lose a hand."

I took a few moments to contemplate this. Evidently, the anti-Spanish faction was more overt than Cecil had supposed. I decided it couldn't hurt to ask. It wasn't as if the rumor were a secret, given the upset in London. "I've heard that Her Majesty is considering taking Philip of Spain as her husband. Could it have anything to do with the protest?"

Rochester's expression froze for a moment. Then he harrumphed. "Philip of Spain? Now, where did you hear that? I wouldn't put too much stock in rumors, if I were you. They're a dozen a groat these days." He tugged at his doublet. "Well, then, I'll leave you to rest. I'll advise Her Majesty and let you know as soon as she has time to see you."

I inclined my head. "I am indebted to your kindness."

"Oh, not at all! As I said, delighted you're here." He left, clicking the door shut behind him. In the silence, I moved to the coffer to touch the decanter.

It was hot. Lifting the lid, I found it full of mulled wine.

I had the distinct sense that Rochester had been expecting me.

After drinking half the jug, I collapsed on the hard bed. Despite the scratchy mattress and my best efforts to stay awake, I soon drifted to sleep. When I awoke hours later, my mouth was dry and the room so dark I couldn't see my hands in front of my face. I didn't recall dousing the tallow lights. As I struggled to get my bearings, I realized I wasn't alone. There was a warm weight by my feet.

I reached down. A warm lick on my hand and a soft muzzle told me Elizabeth's treasured greyhound, Urian, whom she had brought with her from Hatfield, was here. I eased my foot out from under the coarse blanket covering me and nudged Peregrine, who was, as I suspected, curled in his cloak on a reed mat on the floor.

"You'll catch your death of cold down there! And you took your time getting here."

"I found Urian, didn't I?" he asked. "I also befriended a groom who told me the princess goes riding in the mornings with her friend. I didn't know she had friends here."

I was suddenly wide awake. "Neither did I. Did this groom say who her friend was?"

"Edward Courtenay, Earl of Devon. Apparently he's her cousin."

"Did he say anything else?" I could barely restrain the impulse to bombard him with questions, recalling what Cecil had told me about Courtenay. I concentrated on breathing deep, pretending I was starting to fall back asleep before I muttered, "She's going to notice her dog is missing."

"That would be the point. Urian would only go with someone he trusts."

I smiled, crossing my arms behind my head as Elizabeth's hound settled between my legs. Peregrine's breathing deepened. The boy could sleep anywhere.

I now had confirmation of her association with Courtenay, whatever it was, and it didn't bode well, not if Renard was targeting them. Then I thought of the dead dog tossed into the queen's chapel, a placard denouncing Catholics knotted about its neck.

What perilous path did Elizabeth tread?

Chapter Four

𝕴 woke before dawn. As I hastily washed my face in the basin, after breaking a film of ice on the water, Peregrine lurched to his feet and insisted on attending me, staggering out the door with his hair askew and jug in hand to fetch fresh wash water.

He poured the jug over my head while I stood in the lumpy basin, the water so cold I was barely able to move my arms to wash myself. "You must find us a brazier, charcoal burner, anything, so long as it holds fire," I told him through chattering teeth. "I can't bathe like this every morning. I'll catch my death of cold!"

"Yes, master," he said, then ducked as I swiped at him with my hose. I dressed more quickly than I'd ever done in my life, not caring that I was still damp. As I stashed my poniard in my boot, Urian whined and scratched at the door.

"He needs to go out," said Peregrine, who clearly had no intention of repeating my bathing experience, though he'd slept in his clothes and looked a rumpled mess.

"Fine, take him out," I said. "While you're at it, see to our horses. I want them well fed and kept warm. I'll try to get there as soon as I can. I want to catch a look at this Courtenay. Oh, and if you see Her Grace before I do, try to detain her, but don't let anyone else see that you actually know each other."

"I'm sure she'll be delighted," Peregrine quipped, and, clipping a lead to Urian's red leather collar, he left.

I pushed my sword in its scabbard under the bed. Bearing weapons at court, at least visibly, was forbidden. Then I looked about for somewhere to hide my bag. I didn't have anything that could incriminate me except for a book Cecil and I had agreed to employ as a cipher in case I had need of it. I'd rather not leave it out in plain sight. None of the floorboards proved loose enough to pry up. I'd settled on stuffing the bag in the coffer when a knock came at the door. I found Rochester on the threshold, a self-satisfied grin on his face.

"Good morrow to you, Master Beecham. I trust you're well rested." He paused, scrutinizing me. "Are you ready?"

"Ready?" I echoed.

"Yes. Her Majesty has agreed to see you this morning. In fact, she insists on it."

Snow drifted outside the gallery windows, turning the courtyards into white-cushioned jewel boxes. Inside the palace, the chill was pervasive, despite the profusion of carpets and tapestries. Linked by numerous long galleries and passageways, with wide upholstered bays that reflected an emphasis on luxury instead of defensiveness, Whitehall remained unfinished. An elephantine undertaking, it had been under construction for years, its warren of ostentatious halls, chambers, servant's quarters, and official offices coexisting with tarpaulins and scaffolds parked beside unfinished walls, with gaps in the mortar where the wind whistled through.

My feet were chilled in my boots when we finally reached a gallery adorned with smoke-darkened paintings. Guards parted to allow us access into a world I had never seen before: a series of interconnected wainscoted chambers filled with sumptuous hangings, gold and silver plate and candelabra, and carved chairs big enough to fall asleep in. Dried lavender and rosemary were scattered underfoot on the carpets, so that each of our footsteps crushed the herbs and released a heady scent. Applewood fires crackled in every recessed hearth, heating the air to a summer's intensity. It was so warm, I suddenly felt sweat start to trickle under the tight fit of my new doublet. The drastic change in temperature was a sure breeding ground for disease, I thought, thinking of Kate's theory that weather affected our humors.

I removed my cap. As I dabbed at my brow, a burst of women's laughter was heard. Rochester motioned to the silver gauze curtain draped across an archway decorated with a lintel of plaster cherubs in midfrolic. He gave me a ribald grin. "You'll be the fox in the henhouse, but a young buck like you shouldn't mind the attention."

I smiled, adjusting my doublet. In the room beyond, the queen declared in her distinctly gruff voice, "Mistress Dormer, will you cease that infernal laughing at once! I can barely hear myself think. Now, is this the right headdress or not? We don't have all day."

Amid more high-pitched mirth, I stepped past the curtain.

The chamber before me was large, with two full windows overlooking the snowy parkland. It was also in utter disarray, every available surface—tabletops, chairs, sideboards, even parts of the floor—strewn with fabrics of different colors. A pack of small black- or brown-spotted dogs, all with fluffy ears and ornate jeweled collars, emitted high-pitched barks when they saw me. One bold and mostly black one raced over to nip the toe of my boot, to an accompanying explosion of feminine glee. A slim blond girl dressed in a silver satin gown rushed over to scoop up the offending pet. She glanced at me shyly. She had large blue-gray eyes and lovely skin tinged with the easy flush of youth. She couldn't have been more than seventeen.

"I'm sorry," she said, her voice identifying her as the breathy one whom I had heard laughing. "I just got him, and I'm afraid he's not very well trained. He hates strangers."

"What's his name?" I started to reach out to pet the creature in her arms, but it growled and showed me its teeth.

"Blackie." She gave me a timid smile. "I am Jane Dormer."

"Pleased to meet you, Mistress Dormer." I had just started to bow when a too-thin but otherwise handsome woman I recognized as the queen's favorite, Lady Susan Clarencieux, stepped forth. She gave me a welcoming smile; Lady Clarencieux and I had met before, during the time of Northumberland's coup, when I had helped her and Mary escape Robert Dudley's pursuit and reach the safety of Framlingham Castle.

She said to Jane Dormer, "I don't think this gentleman is here to see you. And you must muzzle that little dog of yours if it's going to keep nipping everyone it doesn't know."

A riot of choked giggles ensued from the other women. Jane Dormer turned bright red. With another shy smile at me, she returned to her seat. Though I didn't know most of the women staring in open curiosity at me, I noted at once that Elizabeth wasn't among them. Then I caught Lady Clarencieux's quick gesture at one of the matrons, who hastened to yank a linen sheet down over a large portrait propped in the corner. Before it was covered, I caught a glimpse of the image on the canvas—a fair, bearded man with a jutting chin and fine legs in white hose.

"Master Beecham, I am here."

I turned to where the queen stood before a looking glass. She peered at me in the reflection, her head swathed in a turbanlike confection.

I bowed low. "Majesty, I am honored you could receive me at such short notice."

The queen's lips pursed. She surveyed me from head to toe before she broke into a terse smile that revealed tarnished teeth. "Why, it is you. I wasn't sure at first."

Mary Tudor was not beautiful. Whatever physical appeal she'd once possessed had been spoiled by years of bitter antagonism, so that she looked older than her thirty-seven years, her close-set hazel eyes pleated by wrinkles and her sunken cheeks betraying a premature loss of teeth. Poor eyesight had carved a furrow between her near-invisible brows, and she was gaunt, her figure almost childlike in her rigid, gem-encrusted finery. What she lacked in beauty, however, she made up for with a regal presence and a generosity of heart that had engendered loyalty in many of those who served her.

"Someone, pray take this off me," she griped. Lady Clarencieux hastened to remove the turban. The queen's lank red-gold hair, liberally threaded with white, fell to her shoulders. With a sigh, she passed a ringed hand over her unkempt tresses before she peered at me again. "Something is different. I find you quite changed."

"Perhaps the beard, Your Majesty?" I suggested.

"No, you had a beard last time, though it wasn't as fancy." She startled me with her recollection. Feeling every woman's eyes in the room on me, I said gently, "I have grown out my hair and put on some weight, Your Majesty."

She brightened. "Yes, that's it. You're heavier." She looked inordinately pleased she'd deduced the change. Then, as if a cloud had passed over the sun, her expression darkened. If I was heavier, I could almost hear her think, where had I been? In whose pay? Under whose roof?

Her next words were barbed. "Perhaps we'd have recognized you earlier if you had deigned to attend us at court before today. We seem to recall issuing an invitation when we were still in Framlingham, offering you a post in our service."

"Yes, Majesty, I beg your pardon for my untimely delay. I thought it best to absent myself from court for a time." I lowered my voice and took a step closer, seeing her draw in a breath at my intimate tone. "I feared there might be some here who would not appreciate my having betrayed their trust. Though I would gladly put myself in jeopardy again for your cause, I had no desire to risk my life unnecessarily."

She went quiet, looking at me, before she took a small step back, restoring the proper distance between us. "We understand. And we assure you, you are completely safe. We've not forgotten how you rendered us valuable service." She held out her right hand to me, adorned with her coronation ring. As I leaned over to kiss it, I let out a sigh under my breath. Cecil had been right: I still had her trust.

Then I heard her say, "Though you should remember in the future, we do not like our invitations being ignored. Your former master learned that lesson the hard way."

A chill crept up my spine. I righted myself. She clapped her hands, eliciting another round of barking. As the ladies dug through the piles, Mary said to me, "We should discuss the reason for your visit. Rochester tells me you've come to seek employment?"

"If I may be so bold," I said. Lady Clarencieux handed her a bolt of canary yellow satin. I glanced to the window seat where young Mistress Dormer sat, caressing her dog. She blushed when I winked at her.

Mary held the yellow fabric to her chin. "Well? What do you think?"

I started. The queen tapped her foot. I caught Lady Clarencieux's amused regard. Was the queen offering me a post in her wardrobe? "It's . . . rather bright," I said helplessly.

"At last, someone who speaks the truth, Majesty," said a rough-silk voice, and a woman unlike any I had ever seen stepped forth.

She must have been sitting, hidden, in one of the window bays, for I would have noticed her. I couldn't have done otherwise; she was the kind of a woman I could not help but notice. She wasn't beautiful in the popular sense. Her figure was too slim, despite the shapeliness of her breast and hips, and her features too distinctive in their chiseled perfection. Her luminous skin enhanced deep-set eyes of startling violet-blue, a thin nose, and angular cheekbones that gave her face an almost feline cast. The overall effect of aristocratic frigidity was softened by her seductive, full-lipped mouth, which hinted of voluptuous promise just simmering under her surface. Hair the color of autumn gold was coiled into an elaborate coiffure under her small pearl-edged cap, showing off her fashionably plucked brow. As she glided to the queen's side I noted her elegance of movement, as well as her distinctive cap sleeves and stiff triangular skirts. She wore a fashion that set her apart from the other ladies present.

Mary groaned and let the sample drop at her feet. "What, then?" she asked. "It's been hours already and I'm weary of all this." She waved her hand at the mess in the room.

The woman turned to me. I heard a hint of challenge in her

voice. "Perhaps we can impose on Your Majesty's friend for a suggestion? He is a man, yes?"

The queen frowned. "I hardly think Master Beecham is in a position to . . ." Her voice faded as I moved assuredly to a nearby table heaped with samples. I scrutinized them, lifting and discarded several before I settled on a plum velvet shot with gold.

"This one," I said.

Mary took it from me. As she held it up to her face, the ladies *oohed* in chorus. It was, thankfully, a perfect choice, the rich purple hue distracting from Mary's wan skin while lending her faded hair luster. It didn't hurt that it was also the preferred color of royalty. When in doubt with a queen, always choose purple.

"All this time and all we needed, it seems, was a man." The woman laughed—a delicious throaty laugh that issued from low in her chest. She extended her hand to me. "Allow me to present myself. I am Mistress Sybilla Darrier."

I leaned over her extended fingers, detecting a unique scent. "A pleasure, my lady," I said. "Have you been in France? You smell of lilies."

Sybilla's eyes widened.

Mary said, "I see you are as perceptive as ever, Master Beecham. Indeed, Mistress Darrier has recently returned to England after many years abroad."

I assumed as much. Besides the unusual scent, it explained her distinctive apparel.

"She hails from Lincolnshire," added Mary, turning again to the looking glass to assess the sample against her complexion. "Master Beecham, weren't you also born there?"

I went still. She had not forgotten a thing about me, it seemed.

"Indeed." I smiled to hide my consternation. "But as Your Majesty may recall, I left following my parents' deaths. The

Sweat," I added, with a sad shake of my head in Sybilla's direction. "I was left an orphan while still a child."

"How terrible," she murmured. If I'd hoped to gain a revelation from her in return, I was disappointed, but I thought I caught a flash of interest in her eyes. My alias was one Cecil had assigned me, the persona of the sole surviving son of a client family of his. The real Daniel Beecham, like the rest of his kin, was dead. The family had been minor gentry, unlikely to have mingled with someone of Sybilla's evident rank, but I couldn't be too cautious. I didn't want this woman to see me as a fellow shire man, well versed in the area.

Then she said softly, "It has been many years since I, too, left Lincolnshire. I scarcely remember it."

She had indeed left quite young, as she appeared to be in her early twenties, not much older than me. I was relieved.

"And how do you find England," I asked, "after so long an absence?"

Her eyes met mine—piercing, like a cat's. "I hardly know. I am still a stranger here."

At that moment Rochester called from behind the room's curtain, "Majesty, His Excellency Simon Renard requests audience."

Sybilla cast another enigmatic smile at me before she curtsied and returned to the ladies. As she sat beside Mistress Dormer, I saw the girl clutch her spaniel closer. Sybilla reached out to caress the dog's ears. It did not snarl at her.

"Ah, Don Renard!" Mary beamed as a trim man in somber black came into the room. "Am I late for our appointment?"

"*Majestad.*" The Emperor Charles V's envoy, Simon Renard, raised her hand to his lips. "If you are not ready for me, then it is I who must be early."

As I saw Mary smile, I took a moment to gauge the ambassador. He had the effortless carriage of a career court official, with everything about him—from his perfect spade-shaped beard to his polished shoes and manicured doublet of expensive black velvet—denoting a man accustomed to moving in circles of high power. He was of moderate height, unimpressive physically, but his small brown eyes were discerning in his modestly handsome face, and I noticed how he scanned the room with expert dissimulation, taking note of each of its occupants, including me.

This was a man who might appear at ease but was always on his guard.

Mary pouted. "I've been looking at samples all morning and having quite a time of it. I do *so* want to look my best when the time comes. What do you think of this?" She thrust the plum velvet sample at him. "Master Beecham says it suits, and my ladies seem to agree. But will His Highness like it?"

Half-glancing at the cloth, Renard froze. Mary seemed utterly unaware of what she'd just said aloud, but as the ambassador shifted his hooded gaze to me, I understood. The portrait in the corner that the queen's lady had hastily covered: It was of Philip, the emperor's son, and this preoccupation about her apparel—it must have something do with the prince as well. Was Mary seeking the right hue for her wedding attire?

"Any shade would suit Your Majesty, though I find this one a bit dark." Renard straightened his shoulders. "You say this . . . gentleman here selected it for you?" He turned to me. "I don't believe I've had the pleasure."

Mary blinked in evident disappointment that he hadn't endorsed my choice, obliging her to return to the tedium of looking through more samples. She barely hid her dejection as she said, "Don Renard, this is Daniel Beecham. You recall my mentioning him to you before? He's the one Cecil sent with the warning that Robert Dudley was coming after me. Because of his message, I was able to escape to Framlingham Castle, gather my troops, and defeat Northumberland."

"Ah, yes." The ambassador's practiced smile did not touch his eyes. "So, this is the mysterious Master Beecham. I understand you undertook significant risk to assist Her Majesty in her time of need." He paused. "Do you still work for Secretary Cecil?"

Mary's terse look indicated she was as interested as Renard in my answer.

I shrugged with deliberate nonchalance. "I left his employ some time ago. Given his reduced circumstances, he could no longer afford my services."

"I see." Renard's stare bored at me. "And these services consisted of . . . ?"

I paused, glancing at the queen. As far as I was concerned, what had gone between us remained confidential. I had no idea how much she had told Renard.

"If Her Majesty would grant me leave, I'd be happy to elaborate," I said. "Though given our present company, I fear it would make for tedious conversation."

"I doubt that," said Renard sharply, but Mary let out a guffaw.

"Now, now, Don Renard," she chided. "Not everyone from the past is a potential enemy. Master Beecham may have served the duke's secretary, but so did many others, and with far less integrity, I might add. I have assured him he's welcome here." She went silent, her brow creasing. "Perhaps we might find him a position on your staff? You, of all men, are best positioned to appreciate his talents."

Renard's smile vanished. The opportunity was too perfect to pass up.

"I do have experience working for men of distinction, Excellency," I offered, "and I am literate in several languages, including Spanish."

I was, too, at least partially. I could only hope he'd not put me to the test.

"Is that so?" The ambassador's tone was icy. "As impressive as it sounds, I regret to say I've no need for another English clerk at this time."

No, I thought, clerks, especially English ones, tend to gossip; and it would not do for there to be more speculation concerning his dealings to betroth Mary to Philip.

"Begging Your Excellency's pardon, but I do not seek a post as a clerk. Unlike most men, I prefer to work outside confined spaces. Perhaps we could come to an arrangement?"

Renard regarded me with slitted eyes. He'd not expected me to press my suit so boldly.

Mary said, "Indeed. And I owe him a debt I wish to repay." Her insinuation was not lost on Renard. While he'd clearly rather see me cleaning cesspits, he could not gainsay the queen. He inclined his head to her. "I am your devoted servant."

"Good. I'll leave you to settle it." Mary motioned to her women. "Now, I must change for the council meeting. Don Renard, wait for me. We've business to discuss beforehand. Master Beecham," she said, as I bowed once more, "it's been a pleasure. I hope we'll have the chance to meet again. You must let me know how you get on in your new post."

Without awaiting my response, she swept through an opposite doorway, her women behind her, the little fleet of dogs yipping at their heels.

All of a sudden, I was alone with the ambassador.

"It seems you've more talents than I supposed," Renard remarked.

"And I hope to employ them all in Your Excellency's service," I replied.

"We'll see about that. Shall we say tomorrow, at around nine?" It was not a request. As I lowered my head, he abruptly crossed the space between us to seize my hand. He had an unexpectedly strong grip, more suited to a sportsman than one who made a living with his quill. "No need for that," he said. "We're just ordinary men who wish to serve, yes?"

I stepped back. His cordial words were anything but. He'd been maneuvered into a position of compliance, and he didn't like it. But I had achieved my aim. I now had the chance to infiltrate his office and discover his plans.

"Rochester can give you directions," he added, moving to the queen's sideboard. He poured himself a goblet from the wrought-silver decanter. He did not offer me one.

It was a dismissal. I had already turned to leave when a voice said, "Master Beecham?"

I looked over my shoulder. Sybilla stood in the doorway of the queen's private chambers, a folded paper in her hands. "Her Majesty is holding a banquet tonight for the Hapsburg delegation and hopes you can join us." She gave me the paper, stamped with the royal seal. "This invitation from her will secure you a seat," she explained.

As I took the note, I felt her fingertips graze mine.

Renard drew in an audible hiss of breath.

"Until tonight," murmured Sybilla, and she retreated.

I did not realize I was still looking at the empty doorway through which she'd disappeared until the ambassador said coldly,

"Are you also in the market for a noble-born wife, Master Bee-cham?"

I turned to him. "Alas, I cannot afford the privilege quite yet. But should my circumstances change . . ." I let my insinuation linger, gratified to see his eyes darken as he stared at me over his goblet.

"I suggest you look elsewhere," he snapped. "Mistress Darrier is already spoken for."

Though I didn't look at him again, I felt his stare follow me as I left the room, like the tip of a dagger poised between my shoulder blades.

It did not escape me that he had issued a warning.

Chapter Five

Rochester gave me directions to Renard's office—a series of turns and passages I hoped I'd remember—along with his effusive congratulations. "Well done! Don Renard is a fine man to work for, upright and devoted to Her Majesty's interests. You'd be hard-pressed to find a better post at court." He winked. "Or, I'll wager, one better suited to make your fortune. I hear these Hapsburg officials piss ducats."

Amused, I thanked him again for his kindness and took the staircase to the painting-hung gallery. Outside the mullioned bays, I saw the snow had stopped. A wan sun struggled to cast off winter's pall, shedding anemic light into the courtyards.

I ruminated on what I had learned thus far. I had seen a portrait of Philip of Spain in Mary's private rooms, a sure sign that she was seriously considering, if she had not already accepted, the Hapsburg offer of marriage. Elizabeth's absence from the queen's chambers was telling, too, suggesting a possible rift between the queen and her sister. Elizabeth went riding every morning with Courtenay; if he was supporting an anti-Hapsburg faction, might she be utilizing her friendship with him to indicate her own disfavor with a Spanish union for the queen? It would be typical of her: By not saying anything out loud, she was in fact stating her position quite clearly.

I turned my thoughts to Renard. He had no reason to trust me, a stranger who had arrived at court with nothing save my past actions on the queen's behalf to commend me. I had added to his suspicions by showing influence with Mary and coercing him to offer me a post. What awaited me tomorrow at our meeting?

I also wondered about Sybilla, an Englishwoman raised abroad, newly returned to England, and, according to Renard, "spoken for." I wasn't the most experienced when it came to women, but I knew jealousy when I heard it, and the ambassador spoke like a covetous man. Yet Sybilla had engaged me on purpose with her subtle flirtations, and she had done it before him. Why? What connection, if any, did she have with Renard?

I quickened my pace. It wasn't until I reached my room that I realized how fast I'd been walking, as if I were about to be detained at any moment. I had to smile. In less than a day, I'd managed to gain audience with the queen and secure an appointment with Simon Renard, the man whom Cecil believed was intent on destroying Elizabeth. I should be congratulating myself. I knew, though, how the court could enmesh one in its tendrils, how easy it was to fall prey to unseen traps. I had to watch my every step.

After checking that everything in my room was in order, I threw on my cloak and braved the maze of the palace. If my luck held up, I'd be able to get to the stables and chat with Peregrine's new groom-friend myself. I wanted to learn more about Courtenay and his relationship with Elizabeth, but I had just crossed the quadrangle and barely approached the long, painted stable block when Peregrine came running out, his cheeks flushed from the cold. When he saw me, he skidded to a halt.

"I saw her!" he burst out. "She spoke to me!"

I didn't need to ask whom he referred to. "Quiet!" I clamped a hand to his shoulder, looking about. A few ostlers idled nearby. "Not another word," I said, and I hustled him back to the palace. As soon as I closed our chamber door, I turned to him. "Tell me exactly what she said."

"Well, she came into the stables after her ride. I was tending to Cinnabar. He has a wound on his forelock; he must have been nicked by a stone on the road. Anyway, I was salving it when she walked in with a nobleman. They were laughing. He called for a groom to take his horse, and I volunteered to take it. She recognized me but pretended not to. When the lord left—she kept calling him 'sweet cousin'—she spoke to me. She was not pleased. She said we should not have come to court without her leave. "

Relief washed over me. That sounded like her. "Of course she'd say that, but at least now she knows we're here. Did she say anything else?"

"No, the lord was waiting for her outside. She said she had a headache from his endless chatter and was going to nap before she changed for the queen's feast. Oh, and she told me to take care of Urian, seeing as I stole him away."

It was a message: She wanted me to know she'd be in the hall tonight. The "sweet cousin" she had been with was Courtenay. I had just missed him. A few minutes earlier and I might have had the chance to gauge this man whose relationship with Elizabeth was starting to cause me grave concern.

"What was the nobleman like?" I asked.

Peregrine blew air out the side of his mouth. "Rude, like most of his ilk. He didn't tip me for taking his horse, though grooms survive on tips. And he looked at me as if I was going to steal something when Her Grace said she wanted a word with me about her dog."

I felt a prickle of alarm. Courtenay sounded mistrustful, not an encouraging sign.

"You did well," I said. "Now she knows we're here and won't be surprised if she sees me. But I want you to stay away from this Courtenay fellow. I don't like the sound of him."

Peregrine nodded. I went to the coffer, taking out my new vermilion doublet and the wrapped cloth protecting my shoulder chain. As I unfolded the cloth, exposing the thick gilded links, Peregrine whistled. "Nice! That must have cost a few angels."

"Don't get too excited. It's fake. I brought you a new jerkin and sleeves, too."

"But not of velvet. I wager I don't have a chain to go with it, either."

I laughed. "What a squire you're turning out to be!" I clapped him on the back. "Let's use wash water and soap. Tonight, we will feast with the court, my friend."

I made sure not to watch as he hand washed himself, concentrating on my own necessities until I heard him make an annoyed sound. I turned to find him standing stiff in his new garb, his unruly hair oiled and tamed to damp ringlets that fell to his shoulders, the green wool of the jerkin bringing out the emerald hue in his eyes.

"You clean up nicely," I remarked.

He scowled. "It itches. It feels like I have fleas."

"Well, you were in the stables all morning." I turned back to my small hand mirror, which I'd propped on the stool. As I adjusted the linked chain about my shoulders, I remembered my weapon. I was sheathing my poniard in my boot when Peregrine said suddenly, "Are we in danger, too?"

I paused.

"If you would just tell me what is happening, I might be able to help—"

I held up my hand. "You promised, remember? No questions." My tone softened. "I just need to speak to Her Grace in private. It may be that I'll need your help."

His face brightened, as I knew it would. I turned to my bag and removed quill, ink, and paper. Ripping off a section of paper, I wrote quickly.

The stables. Tomorrow at midday.

I didn't dare write more, in case my note should fall into the wrong hands. I folded the ripped paper into a small square that fit in my palm and slipped it into my doublet before turning to Peregrine. "Do you want me to deliver it?" he asked eagerly.

"We'll see," I said. "First, let's find out what this night has in store. Come. We don't want to be late for our first big event at court."

The cavernous great hall was large and surprisingly warm, boasting two enormous hearths fashioned of imported Caen stone, both of which glowed with scented fires. The vast hammer-beamed ceiling high above was barely visible, its painted vaulting clouded by a pall of smoke from the many gilded candelabras and torches set in cressets on the walls.

The black-and-white checkered floor was crowded, the air ringing with voices as courtiers sauntered about with goblets in hand, gathering to gossip and eye the dais, upon which sat a velvet-draped table and several upholstered chairs. I noted that many of the courtiers sported jeweled crucifixes and medallions of saints. Considering such idolatry had been abolished under our late king's reign, the goldsmiths of London must be enjoying an exceptionally busy season. I also espied a knot of somber men in tall black hats and short cloaks standing apart—bearded and hawk-eyed, without a smile to be seen among the lot; I guessed these must be the Spaniards of the Hapsburg delegation.

"Stay close," I told Peregrine, as we weaved past servitors carrying platters of goblets, making our way toward a series of trestle tables set in front of the dais. Already some early arrivals clamored for their seats; liveried stewards directed them to form a queue. I hoped for a place with a view of the entranceway, so I might spot Elizabeth when she arrived. My searching looks about the hall confirmed to me that she was not yet here.

As Peregrine and I waited in line, I had the sudden sensation that I was being watched. The feeling was so strong I actually felt the hair on my nape prickle. I swerved about, inspecting the crowd. Out of the corner of my eye, I noticed a sudden absence of color amid the swirl of peacock glamour—a swish of darkness, like the flare of an old cloak. A large figure nearby shifted, melting into the courtiers. Hard as I craned my vision, even rising up on my tiptoes to peer past the sea of bobbing heads, I couldn't discern who that shadow was or where it went. Nevertheless, I was certain it had been there, close to me.

At my side, Peregrine said, "What is it?"

"I don't know." I tried to push against the crowd, but the figure was gone. Then heralds announced the queen, and everyone started shoving forward. Angry words thrown in my direction alerted me I was holding up the line. I quickly made my way to the table indicated by a harried steward who snatched away my invitation. My seat was not far from the dais itself, close enough to gauge the activity without appearing conspicuous.

Peregrine eyed the lone chair assigned to me. "Am I supposed to stand?"

"It's what squires do. You'll hand me my napkin and refill my cup."

"Wonderful. And you can toss me bits of roast, like a dog."

"You'll eat as soon as I . . ." My voice faded as I caught sight of Simon Renard moving toward the dais, accompanying the queen. Mary had donned a heavy sienna-colored velvet gown with fur-trimmed sleeves, her hair parted under a hood. In her hands, she clutched a nosegay of silk violets. A sapphire crucifix swung from her narrow bodice as she strode past the bowing courtiers, accompanied by her female attendants. Jane Dormer guided her little dog, Blackie, who strained at his lead. Behind her was Sybilla Darrier, clad in striking crimson velvet, her peaked collar studded with garnets that caught the light.

The ladies took their seats at a nearby table. Several gentlemen of the Hapsburg delegation joined the queen on the dais, including Renard, who took the chair one remove from Mary. On Mary's left—a place of honor—sat a gaunt woman in old-fashioned patterned damask and a triangular gable hood. She had a prepossessing nose and piercing narrow blue eyes. Next to her was a handsome young man in flamboyant black-and-white satin, his short French-styled cloak strapped to one shoulder with elaborate braiding.

"That's him," Peregrine said in my ear. "That's the sweet cousin."

I took in my first sight of Edward Courtenay, Earl of Devon. He must be popular with the ladies, I thought: a well-built fellow, broad of shoulder and chest, with a full head of tawny hair that matched his well-groomed mustache and forked goatee. His appearance took me aback; I wouldn't have expected someone who'd spent so many years in the Tower to look quite so robust, though his appeal was marred by a petulant expression. As the long-nosed lady beside him lifted her goblet for wine, Courtenay said something of evident wit to her. She gave him a sour smile. They seemed to know each other, but then everyone at court did, especially at functions like these. Perfect strangers were not averse to feigning rapport if it might tender an advantage.

Pages bearing decanters circulated among us, filling our cups with ale. Renard suddenly leaned to the queen. As he murmured in her ear, Mary stared at the empty chair between them. Her face visibly darkened.

"What?" she said, in a displeased voice loud enough to carry into the hall. "Are we to endure her insufferable disobedience again?"

Taut silence fell. Renard exchanged a brief, conspiratorial look with the sour-faced lady as Mary swerved her attention to Courtenay. Her fist clenched, crushing the silk violets. "Did you not deliver our message to her as we instructed, my lord?"

Courtenay blanched. "Your Majesty, I assure you, I conveyed your request—"

Mary stabbed her finger at him. "It was not a request. Go to her apartments at once. Tell our sister the Lady Elizabeth that she *will* obey our order to attend our guests this evening, by our royal command!"

Courtenay had started to inch up from his chair when Mary went still, staring straight ahead. For a moment, it seemed as if the very hall sucked in its breath. I didn't need to look to know my mistress, Elizabeth Tudor, had finally made her appearance— late, as usual.

She wore an unadorned gown that sheathed her slim figure in black velvet, making her seem taller than she actually was.

Her coppery mane fell loose to her narrow waist, swaying like a curtain of fire as she moved past the tables of staring courtiers to the dais. The Spaniards actually crossed themselves and averted their eyes, as if she might cast a spell on them. I had time to take wary note of their reaction before I heard a frenzied burst of barking and saw Jane Dormer's dog leaping up, yanking at its lead as if it recognized Elizabeth. The princess had a special kinship with animals; even the wary stable cats at Hatfield responded to her. It gave me pause. That little dog might prove a useful distraction . . .

Then I focused on the queen as Elizabeth sank to a curtsy under her baleful gaze. The clench of Mary's jaw and the stony hardness that stole over her face were chilling.

Mary Tudor regarded her sister with undisguised hatred.

Elizabeth said quietly, "Forgive my delay, Your Majesty. I . . . I was unwell."

"Not so much that you refrained from riding with our cousin today," riposted Mary. "You were also invited to attend mass with us this afternoon, and once again, we waited for you in vain."

Elizabeth's reply was soft; only those who knew her intimately would have been able to tell how cautiously she was choosing her words. "Your Majesty, I thought I might have caught a chill after my morning ride. I didn't wish to expose you to—"

"Enough." Mary cut her off with an impatient wave of her hand. "I have heard it all before, too many times, in fact. It seems whenever the subject of attendance at mass comes up, you have a sudden ailment." She paused, staring at her sister as if she wished to make her vanish through the sheer force of her will. "Where is the blessed medal of the Holy Virgin I gave you?" she asked.

Elizabeth went still. Then her hand crept up to the high neckline of her gown. "I left it for safekeeping in my rooms." Her voice was guarded but remarkably steady. "It is so precious a gift to me, I fear that I may lose it."

"Or fear losing your heretic friends' support if you're seen wearing it." Mary leaned forward, glaring now. "You have an able tongue, madam, as always, but we are not so blind that we cannot see what is before us, though you may think otherwise. Do not think to defy us indefinitely. Your time of deception is fast coming to an end."

If she could feel the entire court's attention riveted to the sight of her, on her knees before the queen like a suppliant, Elizabeth did not show it. With a raise of her chin, she said, "I regret that I've given such cause for offense. Though it would cause me great sorrow, with Your Majesty's leave I would gladly return to my house of Hatfield—"

"You will not!" Mary banged her fist on the table, making the cutlery jump. "You will stay here, under our watch. Do not dare ask us again, lest you try our patience one time too many. There are worst places where we may yet send you." She gestured to the empty chair. "You will sit beside our cousin Lady Lennox, whose loyalty you'd do wise to emulate."

As if she trod on broken glass, Elizabeth mounted the dais. I now knew who that strong-nosed lady was: Margaret Douglas, Countess of Lennox. Like Edward Courtenay, she, too, bore a claim to the throne. To my disconcertion, I also realized we were related: My mother had been her mother's aunt.

Lady Lennox cast a barbed, sidelong glance at Elizabeth as a page hastened to pour wine into the princess's goblet. Elizabeth did not touch it. Having lived with her at Hatfield, I knew she rarely drank undiluted wine, for she was prone to headaches. A blue vein showed in her forehead, sole outward indication of her anxiety.

The feast began. I ate sparingly, watching Elizabeth likewise pick at her food. I was taken aback by her appalling slenderness, her cheekbones etched under her skin. These past months at court had taken their toll on her, and I had to clench my hands under the table. I couldn't let emotion get the better of me. I needed a keen mind and determination to extricate her from her predicament.

Still, I wondered if she had noticed me sitting a few tables away, a mere pebble's toss from her. If she did, she did not reveal it. Her gaze passed over the court as if she were looking across a murky pond, without any acknowledgment of the covert glances cast her way. The moment the feast ended and Peregrine leapt forth to wolf down the serving on my plate, Elizabeth rose. For a second, her eyes lifted and met mine, with a force that went through me like a dagger thrust. About us, servitors began to dismantle the tables, the courtiers leaving their plates behind, taking only their goblets as they cleared the floor for the evening's entertainment. In the minstrel gallery, instruments were tuned. I saw and heard all of it yet did not heed, struck by the hunted appeal in the princess's eyes.

Then she turned away to follow the queen and her guests to one of the massive hearths. Once there, she took a chair and sat alone, apart, like an exile. She and Mary each acted as if the other had ceased to exist, the queen regaled by Renard and the Spaniards, her laughter loud, overly ebullient.

"Remember, do as I told you," I said to Peregrine. He nodded, mouth and hands full.

I inched toward the royal company. Courtenay dallied with one of the ladies, ignoring Elizabeth as well, though she sat only steps away. I took note of his behavior, in light of what I knew so far. Apparently neither he nor the princess cared to advertise their association in public.

Seeking an opportunity, I paused by a group of gossiping courtiers. I finally gleaned it when Jane Dormer hastened to a stool, her black dog still straining on its lead. She was trying to get him to sit, shoving at his hindquarters and scolding him. He, in turn, let out a little yelp, his tail wagging furiously as he stared fixedly to where the princess sat. Moments later, Sybilla drifted to Jane and began to talk to her, though Mistress Dormer, intent on trying to wrestle her pet into obedience, barely glanced at her elegant companion.

I took a deep breath and sauntered over to them, swiping off my cap as I crouched down to pet the little dog. He leapt up to lick my face.

"Blackie," Jane exclaimed, "stop that!" She flushed, giving me an apologetic look. "I'm sorry. I don't know what to do with him! He won't listen to a word I say."

The dog lavished me with affection even as I examined the knot tying the lead to the collar. The knot was weak, as I had supposed, and easily loosened.

"Poor thing," I said. "All this noise and so many people—it must be terribly confusing for him."

"You have a way with dogs," Jane remarked.

"Yes," I replied with a smile. "I sometimes prefer them to people."

Jane frowned. "They warm our bed on a cold night and keep fleas at bay, but they are soulless creatures. How can you prefer them to us?" I heard a rustle of skirts as Sybilla turned to us.

"There are some who claim that those who prefer the company of animals are apt to be the most honest," she said. "Is that the case with you, Master Beecham? Her Majesty seems to think so. She has spoken rather highly of your integrity and valor."

I couldn't take my eyes from her. She was, if possible, even more beautiful in candlelight, the flickering shadows heightening the smoky lapis of her eyes and the carmine of her lips. Her mysterious half smile was also unmistakable. I knew that look. I'd seen it before on other women's faces—a seductive invitation.

I rose to my feet. "I am honored by Her Majesty's praise," I said carefully.

"As well you should be," she said. "And I hear you may soon be granted a post in Ambassador Renard's service. He, too, has been quite a favorite of the queen's."

I detected an undertone in her voice, alerting me to a motive I couldn't decipher. Was she warning me or merely making conversation? I sensed the latter possibility was unlikely. Sybilla Darrier struck me as a woman with a purpose for everything she did, and as I saw her gaze shift to where Elizabeth sat immobile on her chair, I tensed.

She said, "Differences of faith can tear apart even those who should be closest."

Her words caught me off guard, as did Jane's vehement response. "She hardly deserves our pity. Everyone knows she's a heretic who has refused to convert, though the queen has ordered her repeatedly to submit." She stared at Sybilla. "Were she not the queen's sister, I daresay she'd be in the Tower by now. And you, my lady, should be more careful, given your family's history. Surely you, of all people, would not wish to defy our sovereign."

I caught my breath at the malice lacing Jane's voice. Sybilla, however, seemed unperturbed. "My dear," she said, "you speak without thinking. Admirable as such fervor be, it ill becomes a maid, especially if one still has hopes to wed."

Jane's expression faltered. At her side, Blackie started barking again. I did not betray my curiosity as I leaned over to pet the dog. The contention between Jane and Sybilla intrigued me, as did the fact that Sybilla's time abroad could be due to a familial disgrace.

"Ah," said Sybilla, "and now it appears we've aroused Don Renard's interest." Following her glance to the group with the queen, I caught sight of the ambassador staring at us, his eyes smoldering as he took in Sybilla's and my proximity. Bent over Blackie, ruffling his ears with one hand, I lifted my gaze. This time, I found covert complicity in Sybilla's regard.

"*Audentes fortuna juvat,*" she whispered, and her eyes gleamed.

Fortune favors the bold.

She had seen my hand shift surreptitiously from Blackie's ears to his collar. Without looking away from her, I untied the lead. With a high-pitched bark, Blackie dashed forth. Jane came to her feet with a cry of dismay; I watched with my heart in my throat as the dog made his way directly toward Elizabeth, just as I hoped he might. Catching sight of the loose dog—something strictly forbidden at court and especially in the hall—the surrounding courtiers laughed and began stomping their feet. Frightened by the sudden pounding of their heels all around him, Blackie changed direction and swerved, his tail and ears tucked as he scampered in a full-blown panic toward the nobles idling by the hearth.

Jane screamed. "No! Stop him! The fire!"

Hearing her young lady-in-waiting's outburst, Mary frowned, half-rising from her chair to peer at the creature running past her. With her compromised eyesight, the queen seemed unable to identify the reason for the commotion and let out a startled gasp—"God save us, a rat!"—for with his small size, shadowy color, and furtive speed, Blackie was indeed rodentlike.

I started to regret having let him loose. Clearly I had overestimated Blackie's ability to get through the crowd to the princess and thus gain me the opportunity I needed to approach her. As I saw Renard make a disgusted moue and step aside, opening a path to the hearth, I ran forward to cut Blackie off before he reached the painted screen shielding the fire and found himself trapped between the hearth and the queen's company. He swerved again—and this time, to my relief, Elizabeth stood and called out to the dog.

His ears perked as if he'd heard the clarions of salvation, Blackie flew to her. She scooped him up, murmuring as he went limp in her arms, his tongue lolling. I moved rapidly to her through the guffawing courtiers, knowing Jane Dormer would be right behind me. I had only seconds. As I neared, I extracted the folded note from my doublet.

I held out my hands. Elizabeth extended the dog to me; our fingers touched. Her eyes widened slightly when she felt the note, and then she took it. Cradling the panting dog, I bowed to her and took a step back.

Jane hurried up to us. "Oh, thank you! I'm so sorry! I had no idea Blackie would slip his lead. If it hadn't been for Your Grace . . ." She seemed to have forgotten her prior disparagement of the princess, who regarded Jane with an impassive expression. I gave her Blackie. Jane clutched the dog, tears of relief spilling from her eyes. "Naughty dog!" she scolded softly in its ear. "You are a very naughty little dog! You scared me half to death."

Elizabeth did not speak. She shifted her regard to me with

the impersonal courtesy she might have shown any well-intentioned stranger before she turned to her chair.

Jane murmured to me, "I am indebted to you. If it is ever within my power to help you, I promise you need only ask."

"He was hardly in danger," I said. My heart's erratic hammer subsided. It had worked. Elizabeth had my note.

I did not hear the queen's approach until her voice startled me. "What is the meaning of this unseemly ruckus?" Jane and I reeled about, and I saw Mary lift her virulent stare past us to where Elizabeth stood, as if frozen, by her chair.

"You have our leave to retire, madam," the queen said coldly. "We'd not wish for such excitement to aggravate your already delicate constitution, nor, God forbid, induce another illness. And I suggest you think hard on what we have repeatedly asked of you. Remember, while we may be sisters, our patience is not without its limits."

Elizabeth's entire face hardened. For a second, I forgot to breathe. I half-expected her to retort something inflammatory enough to truly seal her doom. Instead, she performed a curt curtsy and, with her hand closed over my note, strode without a word toward the hall doors, her slim black figure scything through the whispering courtiers.

Beside me, Jane started to stammer out an apology.

"Mistress Dormer," cut in Mary, silencing her, "I'm not interested in your excuses. You are to make sure that lead is fastened henceforth. I only let you bring your dog into the hall tonight because you were so worried about leaving him alone. As both Mistress Darrier and I advised you when she gave you that dog, owning a pet is a responsibility. If you cannot care for it, then tell us now and we will find another person who can."

"Oh, no," said Jane, with genuine concern in her voice, "I

can care for him, Your Majesty. I promise you, it won't happen again."

"See that it doesn't." Mary eyed her. "Now, pray return to your seat."

Jane clutched Blackie to her chest. With another grateful look at me, she scurried back to her stool. I only had a moment to wonder why Sybilla Darrier would have given the dog to a girl who so clearly disliked her before Mary turned the full force of her gaze to me.

"I beg Your Majesty's forgiveness," I said. "I didn't mean to disturb you."

Her face was inscrutable. "Master Prescott, you're quick on your feet. It is an admirable quality I have come to appreciate, as it often averts disaster. But it seems to me that you need reminding of your proper station here. You are my servant. So take heed: I expect my servants to remain as far as they can from my sister. Do I make myself clear?"

She did not wait for my reply. With a lift of her chin, she returned to her chair, as if I had ceased to exist.

Chapter Six

Dwarves tumbled in. The entertainment had begun, and Mary's entire countenance lightened. She clapped her hands in delight as the dwarves, clad in spangled suits and belled caps, wrestled each other with abandon, slapping each other's buttocks and exchanging ribald jests. I'd not have thought she'd enjoy this rambunctious display, but she seemed thoroughly pleased, shouting encouragement and tossing coins from a purse held by Lady Clarencieux even as the knot of black-clad Spaniards gathered about her frowned at such undignified behavior.

I retreated to the cover of a shadow-drenched wall and seized a goblet from a passing wine server. I drank it down in a gulp, my hand trembling. Elizabeth had my note; now all I had to do was get through my appointment with Renard. It was clear to me that whatever was happening at court, the princess was indeed a prisoner. Mary had denied her leave to depart and treated her with a palpable disdain. I didn't know for certain that Renard was responsible for all of it, but I'd seen him whisper in the queen's ear moments before Elizabeth arrived. He'd alerted Mary to her sister's absence, knowing it would infuriate her.

Shifting my thoughts from the princess, I turned my attention to the company, focusing on Sybilla. She had glided to Lady Lennox's side to exchange polite conversation, leaving Jane with her dog, now fully leashed and curled, exhausted, under her stool. Sybilla seemed at ease with the sour-faced Lady Lennox, whose Tudor blood made her someone of importance at court. It stood to reason Sybilla was therefore in high favor with the queen herself, as Lady Lennox seemed unlikely to squander her time on menials.

Yet Sybilla had just helped me. *Audentes fortuna juvat,* she had said. Fortune favors the bold.

My curiosity burned. She had expressed compassion for Elizabeth's plight and somehow guessed what I was going to do, of that I was certain. She had known I needed to create a distraction so I could get close to Elizabeth, and it was why she had alerted me to Renard's jealous scrutiny, warning me I didn't have much time.

Did she know something of the ambassador's intent toward the princess?

Was she a potential ally?

My ruminations were interrupted by the sight of Courtenay. He had remained at the hearth, insolently leaning against the lintel, nursing a goblet, but now he was bowing low before the queen, as if requesting her leave to depart. I straightened up. I had deliberately stayed in the hall to ease any suspicions, but as the earl strode past me with a scowl plastered across his face, I realized the time had come for my next engagement.

I beckoned Peregrine. "Go back to our rooms. I've some business yet to conclude."

He gaped at me. "Business?"

"Yes. Now do as I say." I had started to move past him when

he suddenly grasped my arm. I stared at him. "I know what you're going to do," he said. "You're going to follow Courtenay, aren't you? Well, you shouldn't. It's not safe."

"Peregrine, let go of me—"

"You don't understand! While you chased after that stupid dog, I saw someone!"

I paused, lifting my gaze to see Courtenay vanish through the same doors that Elizabeth had gone through. "Who?" I asked, returning to Peregrine. "Who did you see?"

"There was a man watching you from that corner by the pillars. He's wearing a black cloak and hood. He's huge. I couldn't see his face, but he didn't seem friendly."

A shiver went through me. The shadow I'd glimpsed earlier: I *was* being watched. Was it someone in Renard's pay? Had he already sent an agent of his after me?

Had I been marked?

"Where is he now?" I pried his fingers from my arm. "Stop acting so alarmed or everyone will notice. Pretend to look around, as if you forgot something."

Peregrine glanced about us. "No, I don't see him. He's not there. But he was!" His voice quavered. "I swear to you, he was watching you the entire time."

"I believe you. I do. But this can't wait. So do as I say. Go back to our room and stay there. Don't answer the door. I'll be back as soon as I can." I pushed him toward the opposite entranceway. "Go. Now."

He left reluctantly, glancing at me over my shoulder. My night's intake of wine turned sour in my belly. Pulling my cap lower on my head, I plunged through the hall doors and into darkened corridors that smelled of stale perfume and candle smoke. By exposing myself to reach Elizabeth, I'd taken a significant risk and heightened Renard's suspicions even more, but I wasn't going to let that, or any henchman of his, stop me. On the dais, the queen herself had singled Courtenay out, about to send him like a lackey to fetch Elizabeth from her rooms, but then he and Elizabeth behaved as if they'd never met. The sheer distance they'd kept from each other in the hall was enough to confirm that he was more than a mere companion she went riding with. He and Elizabeth were involved in something, and I intended to find out exactly what that something was.

In the long gallery, bejeweled courtiers flittered past me. I feigned a drunken stagger that elicited a woman's giggle and a man's angry "Out of our way, sod!" As soon as the courtiers passed, I quickened my pace. Courtenay must have taken this gallery, but as I moved out of it, down a flight of stairs into a narrower passageway, I began to think I'd taken a wrong turn. Whitehall was a labyrinth I'd barely mastered, and I realized I was actually heading into the bowels of the palace, the damp rising off the stone flagstones.

I cursed under my breath. I started to turn back and retrace my steps. I had surely lost Courtenay by now, and—

The faint echo of voices reached me.

I inched back toward where the passage rounded a corner. Two figures stood partially illumined by icy light coming from a poorly fitted postern door. The taller of the figures had his back to me, but I identified at once the distinctive black-and-white-draped arm at his hip, dangling silver points. The other figure was lithe, shorter by a head and swathed in a black mantle. A jolt of recognition set my blood to racing when I saw the alabaster oval of her face, framed by her fur-trimmed hood.

I pulled out of sight, my heart pounding.

It was Elizabeth, alone with Courtenay.

"We must be careful," I heard her say, the passage's low vaulted roof amplifying her voice. "This game has become far too perilous."

"Game?" Courtenay gave a brusque laugh. "It's gone far beyond that. We're in a fight for our lives, now that your harridan sister means to set the Spaniard over us."

"You forget that my sister has not announced anything yet," she countered. "It may be that this betrothal to Philip of Spain will never come to pass. Such affairs take time. There are a hundred complications that could interfere and—"

"The only consideration is whether she'll take your head before or after the wedding," he cut in, with a callousness that chilled me. "Didn't you hear how she spoke to you in the hall? She warned you before her entire bloody court! Elizabeth, you cannot play both sides anymore. Mary will move against you. She'll see you to the scaffold even if she has to execute every Protestant from here to Dover to achieve it."

"Careful, cousin." Elizabeth's voice turned hard. "You speak of my sister. Besides, she has not done anything to me yet. I am still in the succession by our father's will."

Courtenay laughed. "Henry also named your aunts and their children after you. Mary will see you dead or disinherited, and put that sour bitch Lennox in your place, until she gets with child by Philip. You know it and so do I. Are you going to submit? Will you sacrifice your very right to be queen to Mary's unholy Hapsburg alliance?"

"God's teeth, I've heard enough!" Elizabeth exclaimed. She paused, lowering her voice to a hiss. "What would you have me do, eh? I'm watched day and night by her spies, by the ladies she's set in my chambers, by the very laundress who washes my linens! Since I came to court, I've been on the edge of an abyss.

I do not intend to submit. But neither do I mean to lose my head over it. If it comes to it, I'll do what I must to survive."

"Meaning what? You'll kiss the pope's arse, and Philip of Spain's, too?"

His tone was so taunting, I had to brave another look. I saw him reach for her, as if to take her hands, and she recoiled. "You would have me build my own scaffold."

"I do not force you to anything," he replied. "But you heard your sister: The time for prevarication is over. Trust in Dudley and me, if nothing else. Only we can see you safe."

My entire being froze. Dudley: He spoke of Robert Dudley, my former master, Northumberland's favored son and Elizabeth's childhood friend, whom Mary had confined in the Tower with his brothers—Robert Dudley, who stood condemned of treason.

Elizabeth had gone utterly still. The moments passed like years, weighted with her unspoken reflection. Then she said quietly, "Here it is." She parted her cloak. From within its pocket, she retrieved a small package and handed it to him. Drawing her cloak back about her figure, she gestured to the postern door. "Now call for your man to accompany me to my rooms. I feel a headache coming on. I need to rest."

My mind keeled as Courtenay avidly thrust the package into his own cloak. I stood as if paralyzed, trying to make sense of what I'd just seen, barely registering the figure that came through the postern door. It stepped forth purposefully, a gloved hand held up, detaining Elizabeth. Then it pointed that same hand to where I lurked. The princess turned to Courtenay, frowning. In that instant, I recalled what Peregrine had told me. *He's wearing a black cloak and hood. He's huge. I couldn't see his face, but he didn't seem friendly.*

I took one look at the man's bulk, at the shapeless cloak and cowl that concealed him from head to foot, and realized I had been mistaken. Renard hadn't set a man to trail me. The shadow watching me in the hall, the figure standing there now, pointing at me, was a hireling of Courtenay's. As I heard Courtenay curse and Elizabeth gasp, I spun around to race back the way I'd come, my footsteps like thunderclaps in my ears.

The long gallery was dark, a lone cresset sputtering oily flame high on a far wall, throwing more shadow than light. I was gasping for air, had to make myself breathe through my nose as I pitched myself headfirst into the nearest recessed window bay.

Moments later, Courtenay appeared, Elizabeth close behind him, her hood drawn up over her head. "Are you sure?" she asked anxiously.

"Yes, he was there!" Courtenay was turning to and fro, peering furiously into the gallery. "By all the devils in hell, he was eavesdropping on us, and now we've lost him!"

"Who are you talking about?" asked Elizabeth. "I didn't see anyone."

Courtenay's voice edged. "That nobody from the hall, who made such a show of rescuing Jane Dormer's dog, He must have followed us." Without awaiting the princess's response, he swung about to his henchman, who lumbered up with a distinctive limp, an unsheathed dagger in his fist. By the looks of it, the earl had hired a mercenary. "You idiot," spat Courtenay, "you were supposed to keep watch!" He lifted a hand as if to strike the man, but Elizabeth interposed herself between them.

"Enough," she declared. "You told him to wait behind the postern door for our privacy, remember? How could he have kept watch?"

"He's a miserable whoreson," snarled Courtenay. He stabbed his hand at the henchman. "Get back to the hall and find him.

If he overheard enough to tell Renard or, God forbid, the queen, we won't need Philip of Spain to come and burn us. Mary will do it for him." Courtenay's voice twisted, his lips drawn back to show his teeth. "I'll take Her Grace back to her chambers. You do what I pay you for and get rid of that mongrel-come-out-of-nowhere before he ruins everything!"

My breath shattered in my throat as I heard Elizabeth start to protest again; then her voice faded as Courtenay steered her away. In the silence that fell at their departure, I discerned footfalls starting toward me. I shouldn't have chosen the first place I saw to hide. The hall lay in my direction. The earl's man was going to walk right past me.

I eased my poniard from my boot, keeping it pointed inward so the blade wouldn't catch a stray reflection from the meager light. I had no illusions. He was big enough to smash me to splinters, even if I somehow managed to evade his dagger. Nevertheless, I was going to give it my best. Maybe if I put up enough of a fight and shouted loud enough, he'd not have time to kill me. The earl wouldn't want his man embroiled in a public murder at court.

My skin crawled as his shadow loomed, inches from where I crouched. He wasn't quite as large as he'd first seemed, though more than enough to make me wish I had my sword. I couldn't see anything of his face save for a misshapen nose peeking from his cowl. Time stopped. My heart thudded like an anvil. He paused, so close I might have reached out and touched his cloak. His head swiveled slowly toward me. My hand closed on the hilt of my poniard as I prepared to raise it and strike—

He moved on.

I held my breath, my body tense, braced for a lethal spring. I couldn't believe it. *How* had he not seen me? It wasn't that dark.

Was he night-blind? I didn't move, listening to his footsteps fade away. Maybe he thought to stalk his prey by pretending to let it go. The moment I slipped out, he'd charge me like a bull, seize me from behind to throttle me . . . but as the minutes passed with agonizing slowness, nothing happened. I heard only the cresset flame sizzling in its sconce, the clamor of music and laughter drifting from the hall.

Finally I dared to look. The gallery stretched into darkness. Empty.

I slipped from the window seat. Sheathing my poniard, I hurried to my room.

Peregrine was waiting for me, Urian on the bed. The tallow was lit. As I entered, Urian growled. When he recognized me, he thumped his tail.

"Good dog." I reached down to pet him. Only now that I was in my room did the impact of what I'd just been through hit me, tying such knots in my stomach that I felt I might be sick.

"Did you find the earl?" asked Peregrine. His eyes widened. "You look awful."

"Yes, well, it hasn't been an easy night." I started to unclasp my belt. "I found him, but then I nearly fell afoul of his hench-man."

"Henchman?"

"Yes. It seems that man watching me in the hall is a beast the earl hired as a bodyguard." I yanked off my doublet, raking a hand through my damp hair. Despite the cold, I was sweating, and, as usual, I had lost my cap somewhere. Peregrine was quiet, taking my doublet and folding it.

"I don't know what the hell is going on here. I saw Her Grace give Courtenay something, and judging by the way they spoke, the things he said—whatever is happening, he's knee-deep in it, and it's more dangerous than any of us thought." I paced to the coffer. "Maybe I should send you back."

"Back?" Peregrine gaped in dismay. "Back where? To Hatfield?"

"After what happened tonight, it would be safest. I won't put you in harm's way, and now it seems I am a target. Renard suspects me, and Courtenay wants me dead. The only saving grace in all this is that neither of them is likely to tell the other anything."

"Then let me help you!" He took an imploring step to me. "I know this palace like the back of my hand. I can find out things you need to know. You can't do it all, not if it's as dangerous as you say, and I . . ." His voice drifted off as he took in my expression. His mouth set in a stubborn line. "No."

I eyed him. "If I tell you to go, you will."

"And if I don't?"

"Then I'll strap you to your horse and send you back with an escort."

"To Hatfield?" He scoffed. "I don't think so, not unless you want them to know that's where you came from. Besides, I can't go back. I . . . I promised Kate."

My heart sank. "You *promised* her?"

"Yes. It was the only reason she let me accompany you. I told her I'd keep watch over you. But I can't do it, can I, if you won't let me?"

"You can't do it anyway. She should never have asked it of you."

"She didn't. I offered." He dragged his foot back and forth on the floor. "I heard her talking to Mistress Ashley one night. She sounded so worried. She said danger follows Elizabeth like a curse, but the princess in turn curses everyone who serves her with the need to save her. And you've got it worst of all, she said. You'll do anything to protect her."

"Kate said all that to you?"

"Not to me. She didn't know I was there. I was hiding in the pantry. Besides, what does it matter? She's right, isn't she? You love the princess more than anyone."

Urian whined from the bed, sensing the tension between us. I went to Peregrine and set my hand on his shoulder. He went still. "Peregrine, look at me." When he didn't, I cupped his chin. Tears brimmed in his eyes. "It's not true," I said. "Yes, I love Her Grace and I am sworn to serve her, but it's not the kind of love I bear for Kate or for you. You are my family." I resisted the guilt of my own deceit. I couldn't explain to him that my service to the princess was bound by more than a pledge; that we shared the same blood, though she didn't know it. Elizabeth was my kin.

"You . . . you see me as family?" he whispered.

"Like a brother." I ruffled his hair. "Now wipe your nose. Not with your sleeve. That's a new jerkin, remember?" He searched his bag and came up with a nose-cloth; I sat on the bed and scratched Urian's head as Peregrine dabbed his face.

"I slipped her that note, telling her we should meet tomorrow at the stables," I said, "but I had a sense tonight that she knew I was there. Hopefully she can tell me exactly what Courtenay is concocting."

"What if she doesn't?" said Peregrine. "She hasn't exactly made it easy thus far, has she? I mean, she didn't ask for anyone's help though she's been in danger."

I went quiet. He was right. Elizabeth had told Courtenay that she dwelled on the edge of an abyss, but none of us who cared for her—not I or Kate, Mistress Ashley or Cecil—had received a single request for help from her. I knew she was proud, and overly secretive, but now I also knew that Robert Dudley played a role here, and I did not trust Robert Dudley with anything.

Could Elizabeth be protecting the very man who could be her downfall?

"If she doesn't tell you the truth," Peregrine said, "I can get you Courtenay instead."

"What did you just say?"

His words tumbled out in haste. "After the princess left the stables this morning, my friend Toby—that stable boy who told me she goes riding with Courtenay, remember?—he said Courtenay pays him extra for one of the palace horses to be kept at his disposal at night. I could find out why. I mean, most noblemen don't take out anonymous horses for rides in the dead of night, do they?"

"No, they don't," I said. "This Toby is a veritable well of information. I suppose he knows how Courtenay likes his shirts hemmed, too?"

Peregrine gave me an exasperated look. "Did you think stable help survives on the mere pittance they're paid, *if* they get paid? Most of the lads take on additional work whenever they get the chance. I did it myself. Those extra coins can make the difference between a meal and scrounging in the ditches with the beggars."

I winced. All this time he'd endured my treating him as if he were an irresponsible adolescent, when he'd experienced more in his short lifetime than I could possibly imagine.

"God's teeth, I am an ass," I said.

He shrugged. "How can you know what it's like to be alone?" His remark stabbed through me, sharp with the memory of my own difficult childhood. Before I could say that actually I did know what it was like, he said, "So, are you going to let me help you? You need help, even if you won't admit it. You can't do all of this on your own."

I couldn't believe I was actually considering it after I'd just had a man the size of an ox come after me, but he was right. I had no idea when or how, but I had no doubt that given enough time, Courtenay's henchman would find me. I had to get to the earl first. This might be my only means. After tonight, I couldn't take anything for granted, including Elizabeth's cooperation, especially if she had something to hide. Moreover, I couldn't convince Peregrine to return to Hatfield. I'd have to gag and tether him, and he'd still worm his way back. I knew that look on his face. He was determined to be of service, and better I set the rules. At least I could keep my eye on him.

"I don't like it," I said begrudgingly, "but yes, for now you can help." I reached into my pouch and tossed him a few coins. "See what you can find out. Take this, too." I removed my poniard from my boot. "I don't want you going around without a weapon."

He nodded eagerly, stashing the dagger and coins in his bag.

"Just don't let the other grooms know. I wouldn't want . . ." My voice faded as he rolled his eyes. At that moment I was very glad to have Peregrine as my squire.

"Now let's get some rest," I said, chuckling. "I have to deal with Renard tomorrow while you arrange everything with Toby."

Peregrine grinned and started setting up his makeshift bed on the floor. As he stripped to his shirt and bundled up on the floor in his cloak, I said, "We need to get you a cot," and blew out the tallow. He grunted in response.

I had barely settled into my bed when I heard his soft snore.

He had fallen into deep sleep as only the truly young can, exhausted by the day's events.

I stared into the darkness. The day's events unspooled in my mind in disjointed fragments, along with Peregrine's words: *You'll do anything to protect her.*

Much as I wanted to deny it, I feared that I just might.

Chapter Seven

Simon Renard's office—if such it could be called—was located in the northernmost wing of the palace, crammed between a gloomy disused courtyard and outer gatehouse leading into the park. It wasn't sumptuous or even particularly well appointed, certainly not what I'd expect for the high-powered ambassador of Emperor Charles V, who represented Hapsburg interests at court. Rather, the antechamber where Renard's staff worked stank of cheap tallow, must, and mildew. Boxes crammed with papers were piled in every conceivable corner, precarious towers that looked unsteady enough to keel over at any moment. At two desks placed opposite each other hunched morose clerks who looked as if they'd not seen the sun in years; they had matching quills in their ink-splotched hands and the same resentful expressions on their faces when I informed them I had an appointment with the ambassador.

"Wait," one grumbled, pointing to what looked like a stool buried under a heap of ledgers. The other clerk rose slowly, almost indifferently, and trudged to the door, knocking twice before he entered and closed the creaking door behind him.

I remained standing, as far as I could from the leaning pillars of paper, smiling at the remaining clerk. He scowled and bent his head over his work. His slightly more rotund but equally ill-humored twin emerged from the room a few moments later and said to me, "Leave your weapon with us."

I unbuckled the scabbard from my waist and set it on his desk. "It's expensive," I added. "I expect you to take care of it." The clerk grunted. I wondered what he would think if he'd known the sword had once belonged to our late King Edward; crafted of Toledo steel, it was worth a small fortune. He might not have cared. I could have carried a harquebus under my cloak for all the attention he paid me.

I stepped through the door into a tidier chamber, boasting a mullioned window that offered a blurry view of the snow-speckled parkland beyond. The air here was sweet. Renard must enjoy beeswax candles for light. A brazier in the corner exuded heat.

"Ah, Master Beecham." Simon Renard stepped from behind his desk, hand extended. Once again I was struck by his self-assurance. "You're punctual. Good. I like that."

He wore unrelieved black, the wool of his doublet of high quality, the fine cambric shirt peeking above his collar edged in distinctive Spanish lacework. Without his cap, I saw his russet brown hair was thinning on top, his high unlined forehead adding distinction to his features. He'd seen a barber this morning: I could detect faint soap on his person, and his beard was cut closer to his chin.

He motioned to a chair. I declined his offer of wine. "Too early?" he remarked. "Punctual *and* abstentious. Most unusual for an Englishman, if I may be so candid."

"My lord is gracious," I said. My senses heightened as I

watched him pour a precise measure of red wine into a goblet, to which he added a portion of water. He acted as if our encounter yesterday were of no importance. It was an enviable quality—and a telling one.

Men like him were not the forgiving type.

He paced to his window. "Such a dreary winter." He sighed. "The snow reminds me of Castile, except here it's damper and lasts longer. The cold—it hurts my bones."

I kept my gaze steady. "Has my lord been in England long?"

"Sometimes it feels like forever." He returned to the desk. "It's been a little over eight months. Before this, I was stationed in Paris, but my wife and children reside in Brussels. I'd hoped to visit them this year, but alas"—he swept his hand over the broad leather-bound notebooks and other detritus on his desk—"an ambassador's work never ends."

I wasn't taken in by his complaint or casual imparting of personal information. He hadn't agreed to see me to discuss the weather or his official woes.

I said, "Winter can be harsh. This one may get worse."

"Yes. I'm told the Thames is close to freezing over. A rarity, I hear." His smile lingered as he resumed his seat. He had not yet tasted his wine.

He let the silence between us settle. Another trick of the trade, one Cecil had employed to significant effect. It induced a subtle anxiety that could compel a less patient man to initiate conversation. I was not susceptible to it. Not anymore.

His smile faded. "Her Majesty and I spoke at length about you after you left us. She assures me you are trustworthy." He set his goblet aside. So he, too, was abstentious. His offer of wine must have been either a test of my stated sobriety or a means to loosen my tongue. "She gave me a detailed account of your previous efforts on her behalf. It was all most impressive, particularly coming from someone with no apparent stake in the outcome."

"My stake may not have been apparent," I said, "but my payment depended on it."

"Oh, yes. Her Majesty told me you're a man for hire, with no personal affiliations of your own. Though it does raise the question of why you chose to undertake those errands in the first place. At the time, Northumberland had the realm in his grip; it must have been widely believed he'd succeed in putting his daughter-in-law Jane Grey on the throne."

"I wouldn't know," I said, and his gaze sharpened. "I wasn't privy to the duke's plans. I was hired to convey a letter from the council, which I did, and Her Majesty was gracious enough to hire me in return. But surely Your Excellency has verified all this by now."

He reclined in his chair. "Unfortunately, I could not. No one on the council seems to remember having seen you, much less hired you."

"That's because no one on the council did. I was hired by Cecil. Anyway, given the circumstances, I'm not the kind of person any of them would want to remember."

He let out a sudden laugh. "You are a fascinating fellow, most unexpected. I must confess, besides the comforts of home what I most miss about the Continent is stimulating conversation. In Paris, it's a staple of life, like good bread or wine. Alas, I've not found not much of either here; Englishmen are entirely too preoccupied with these tiresome matters of religion. No one has much inclination to cross swords, so to speak."

"Unless it concerns that tiresome matter of religion," I said, and he took up his goblet to sip. It reassured me. I'd gained enough confidence to precipitate his relaxation, if not his trust. Then he said, "Are you one to cross swords, Master Beecham?"

I allowed myself a smile. "Is it a condition of my employment?"

"Indulge me."

"If you're asking if I'm inclined to fight for one faith over the other, the answer is no."

He arched a brow. "You have no preference?"

"I didn't say that. I just prefer not to fight over it. I'm a man for hire, as the queen said. My motto is 'Whoever bids the highest. The soul can shift for itself.'"

He went quiet, observing me with a studied impartiality. It occurred to me that Simon Renard was testing my suitability for the task he'd already prepared for me.

"So we might say that for you, faith rests in the purse," he said at length.

"We might, though I wouldn't want to be quoted on it."

"Indeed. How is this, to start?" He inked a quill, wrote on a scrap of paper, and pushed it to me.

I looked at the sum, then allowed a few seconds to pass before I said, "Generous, to start. Though it depends on what it's for. I'm not accustomed to agreeing to a price before I know what I'm being paid for."

"Naturally." He took another sip. "As you may have surmised from those idiots in my antechamber, I am indeed in need of another clerk. Actually, several more, but as you made clear to me and Her Majesty yesterday in her apartments, an office position is not your preference. Nor, you will be satisfied to know, is it the job Her Majesty has chosen for you."

Under my jerkin, my stomach knotted. "Chosen for me? Could Your Excellency be more specific?"

"I can, though what I am about to say must be kept in the strictest confidence." He paused; when I assented, he went on. "Her Majesty and I believe there is a conspiracy afoot against her. She's made no secret of the fact that she deplores the heresy that has overtaken this realm, or of her determination to remedy it. However, not everyone on the council shares her aspirations. Those against her are in the minority, naturally, but they exist nonetheless. I've had an eye on this subversive element for some time now, but until recently Her Majesty has refused to accept that her own subjects may seek to do her harm."

I noted he made no mention of the emperor or Prince Philip, though there could be no doubt he was acting as much on their behalf as the queen's. Indeed, this so-called subversive element could be a direct result of the queen's consideration of a foreign Catholic prince as her spouse, only months into her own reign.

"But you believe her subjects do, in fact, seek her harm?" I said carefully.

"I *know* it." He set his hand on the desk. "The queen has enemies not only in the land but here, in this very court! They seek to destroy her peace of mind and overthrow her rule, if they can manage it. They would plunge England into chaos, to their own advantage."

"I see. May I ask who these enemies are, precisely?"

"Do you propose I give you names?" he retorted. "If I had them, we'd hardly have need of you, now would we?"

"Nevertheless, you mentioned you've had an eye on this subversive element for some time. Surely you must have some idea of who they are?"

He went quiet, regarding me as if he were contemplating throwing me out. Then he said tersely, "I have only suspicions, unfortunately." He paused again, drawing out the moment. I didn't reveal my apprehension, waiting patiently as if I had this whole day. Abruptly he came to his feet, moving to the window. Standing with his back to me, he said, "If you succeed in finding these traitors, Her Majesty will be generous. An official post at court is not out of the question; perhaps a title and grant of lands, if you prefer. But in return, the evidence must be unassailable. She will not be satisfied with less."

"It sounds as if my loyalty is in question," I said.

He turned around to me. Though nothing outward in his demeanor had changed, his tone now held unmistakable menace. "The queen has expressed confidence in you. Naturally, I must bow to her wisdom. Nevertheless, a man for hire, with no stated religious affiliation, who once worked for Cecil and is available to the highest bidder—well, surely you can appreciate my concern."

"I do." I inclined my head. "I thank you for your time. I'd not wish to be an impediment. I can seek my livelihood elsewhere and spare you this . . . concern."

He let me stand. I moved to the door and actually set my hand on the latch before he remarked, "Her Majesty wants you, and you alone, for this task. In fact, she commands it."

I swallowed and returned to my chair. My mind raced. It seemed I hadn't kept Mary's trust after all. I had stepped into the viper's nest. This time, she would have me prove myself in a job of her choosing, and everything told me I wasn't going to like it.

Renard let the moment settle. Then he said, "I would not hire you were it within my purview. You are not the sort of man to entrust with a matter of this gravity, and I protested as much to Her Majesty. Still, she gave me her order, and I must obey." He paused; his next words hit me like a bludgeon to the stomach.

"The suspects she wishes you to investigate," he said, "are Edward Courtenay, Earl of Devon, and the Lady Elizabeth."

I tasted bile. Though I'd expected this, to hear it said aloud was terrible, and it confirmed what Cecil had told me about Renard having Mary's ear.

"If you know who your suspects are," I said, my entire body tightening in the chair, as if braced for an assault, "why not simply arrest and question them?"

He made an impatient sound. "Her Majesty is a trusting woman. She does not want to think the worst of anyone, much less her own sister and her cousin. She'll not act before she has the proper evidence."

"And you expect me to . . . ?"

"Hardly. You'd never get any closer to Lady Elizabeth, for example, than you did last night with that dog. She hides her true self like no other; she is as cunning as she is wary. I daresay nothing short of the rack would break her." He smiled—actually smiled. "And we can hardly throw her on the rack, now can we? Nor do we dare arrest her yet; that would only alert her supporters, who would change whatever they plan to evade detection."

"Supporters?" I echoed. "You believe she has supporters?"

"Traitors invariably do. And while Lady Elizabeth and the Earl of Devon cannot be questioned directly, if they conspire to treason, as I believe they do, it stands to reason there must be some evidence of their conspiracy. We need any letters that may have gone between them and their accomplices, as well as dates and places of their meetings. This is what I require of you. And I require it *before* their conspiracy comes to pass." He paused, with emphasis. "The queen may be trusting, but I, Master Beecham, am not. A man in my position cannot afford to be."

I had to force myself to lean back in my chair, my hand at my beard. Elizabeth had once told me that Mary was incapable of trust, having inherited the worst of their father; now I understood what she meant. It wasn't that Mary could not trust; it was that she was easily persuaded to doubt—a doubt Renard now preyed on to his own ends.

Mary still had a conscience, though; she had insisted on hiring me because she was unwilling to condemn her sister on Renard's word alone. That had made him desperate. His secret plans for the queen's marriage could not stay secret for much longer; time was running out. The uproar against Mary's decision to wed the Spanish prince could be worse than he anticipated; should others at court vocalize their opposition, it would be difficult to single out Elizabeth as the cause. To succeed in destroying the princess, Renard needed proof of treason *before* any public announcement of the queen's betrothal was made.

That meant I could win. I could beat the ambassador at his own gambit.

"What if nothing can be found?" I asked. "Again, excuse me for stating the obvious, but with two such persons, well, surely you can appreciate *my* concerns. I value my reputation, my lord, such as it is, and the Lady Elizabeth is the queen's heir."

His face turned cold. "I'd not be so quick to consider her such. There is serious question as to her suitability. Some believe she is not the king's daughter at all. The queen herself has her doubts. She once told me she sees nothing of her father in Elizabeth and too much of her whore of a mother."

My fist clenched at my side. Had I not found myself in this position, I'd have knocked his teeth out for uttering such baseless filth.

"It is not in my purview to speculate on such matters," I managed to say. "But if evidence cannot be found against the Lady

Elizabeth, I've no desire to be singled out as the man who sought to incriminate her."

"You won't be," said Renard. "As I mentioned, this task is strictly confidential. Only the queen and I know of it. You can rest assured that Her Majesty would not have asked you to undertake it if she doubted the outcome. Do you understand?"

I did. I understood all too well. I understood I had no guarantee he wouldn't order me killed the moment I delivered what he requested. I also understood that while he might hide behind the queen's authority, this was his deed. He had orchestrated an invasion by a foreign power through the betrothal with Prince Philip and would not cease until he had Elizabeth on the block. He was ruthless and lethal.

To save the princess, he must be defeated.

"I understand perfectly, my lord," I said.

He remained motionless, his glacial stare fixed on me. Then his expression shifted with mercurial swiftness, that false air of camaraderie resurfacing in the blink of an eye.

"I'm pleased to hear it, as will be Her Majesty. I'm sure I needn't add that you must refrain from making yourself too visible about court, as you did last night. And if you provide me with a list of expenditures, I'll do my best to see them fulfilled. Though I must warn you, my resources are quite limited. However, I can spare an extra man if you . . . ?"

Either he toyed with me or he'd forgotten who he was dealing with. Did he actually think I'd ask him to set a spy on *me*?

I stifled the urge to smile. "I prefer to work on my own, given the delicate nature of this assignment. However, a third of my wage up front would be appreciated. Oh, and a new dagger, if at all possible. I seem to have misplaced mine."

He wrote on a paper, then rang a small silver bell on his

desk. The rotund clerk waddled in, wiping his hands on his breeches, spilling crumbs.

"Take care of this," Renard said, thrusting the paper at him, "*before* you resume your dinner." The clerk scowled and trudged out. Renard turned to me with an exasperated look. "Decent help is so difficult to find these days. I can't tell you how refreshing it is to finally be working with a professional. I'll expect a report from you in, say, three days? I trust that's sufficient time to compile . . . ?"

"I'll do my best," I said. I stood and shook his hand, resisting the revulsion I felt as I enclosed his dry palm briefly in mine.

Let the hunt begin.

Chapter Eight

I inhaled deep of the winter air, cleansing my mind and lungs as I strode across the base court toward the stable block, my new Spanish poniard of flexible Toledo steel secured in my boot, my sword at my side and my purse weighting my pocket.

The day was crisp; distant clouds clustered on the horizon, white as the snow on the ground. Urgency quickened my step. I prayed Elizabeth would keep our appointment; she had to be apprised that Renard was setting a trap for her. For the moment, I was a step ahead. I'd just been hired by the man I must thwart, but I still had Courtenay's henchman to worry about. She could tell the earl to get his man to back off, but until then I was exposed, and I kept looking over my shoulder, listening for the telltale crunch of feet on snow that would alert me I was being followed.

I covered my head with my hood as I neared the stables, avoiding several young grooms idling under an overhang by the courtyard, where they tossed dice on a mounting block and shared an illicit wineskin. Evidently there wasn't much call for horses today. I scanned them from under my hood, but I didn't see Peregrine among them. With any luck, he'd lured his friend Toby elsewhere to question him.

Within white-and-green-painted buildings that housed the court's horses and dogs, I was greeted by a startled black cat, which hissed and slunk away. The comforting smell of hide, manure, and hay brought back a sudden, vivid reminder of my boyhood, when I'd been charged with caring for the animals on the Dudley estate.

I almost didn't hear her approach. One moment I was breathing in the close, still air; the next I felt a shift and whirled about, my poniard drawn.

"Careful," she said, and as I lowered my weapon, my heart beating fast, I found myself staring into Elizabeth's leonine eyes, the black velvet of her hood framing her face. Her voice was icy. "I thought I told you that if I needed you, I would send word to Hatfield."

I replied cautiously, "Yes, you did. But I came anyway, to help you."

"Did you?" Her brow arched. "I had to bribe the grooms; luckily, it doesn't take much to entice them. You didn't think about that, did you, when you slipped me your note? That anyone could have seen us meeting here?"

I cursed under my breath. I hadn't, in truth. I had been so intent on speaking to her, I hadn't considered the possible consequences.

"We've still a little time," she went on. "I made up an excuse that I needed fresh air, a walk around the grounds and to check on my horse. I've sent Blanche Parry back for my gloves and muff, with that pack of witches my sister surrounded me with, but they'll return soon enough, so"—she fixed her gaze on me—"tell me why you are here."

I had a sudden moment of doubt. What was I doing? She'd been bred for this world; she'd long since learned to navigate its treacherous shoals. I hadn't. Still, I had no choice but to go on. As I recalled what Renard had told me and what he'd hired me to do, I said bluntly, "I've just had an appointment with Ambassador Renard. He's charged me to find evidence that you and the earl conspire against the queen." I lowered my voice, the restless horses in the stalls behind us nickering. "He seeks to arrest Your Grace for treason!"

The sparse color in her cheeks faded. When she spoke, her voice was tremulous. "So, it has finally happened. Mary has given that vile man leave to move against me."

"Yes, but she has doubts. Renard preys on her suspicions. He seeks your downfall to his own ends, and—"

She let out a mirthless laugh. "My sister hardly needs his persuasion to think the worst of me."

I searched her face. "Does she have reason to? I was in the passageway last night; I overheard everything. And Courtenay was very concerned that I might go to Renard or the queen with it." I took a step closer to her. "What are you involved in? What did you give Courtenay last night, and why did he mention Robert Dudley?"

"Not that I need to answer you," she said with a hint of asperity, "but I gave him a book. It's hardly evidence of anything." She paused, her voice turning grave. "I warn you now: You, too, could be in grave danger if you persist in this pursuit. I'll not have you risk yourself for my sake, not this time. Regardless of your loyalty, this is not your fight."

"Let me decide that on my own," I said. As she drew in a sharp gasp, I did something I had never done before: I took her hand. Her bare fingers were cold, and as she felt my touch, her expression faltered. I knew how difficult this was for her. She was daring, secure in her right to act as she saw fit. Few ever glimpsed the vulnerability she hid within.

"Who was that book for?" I asked softly, though I already knew.

She withdrew her hands. "For Robert." She lifted her chin, as if to preempt my outburst, and I recalled that volatile passion between her and Dudley, as inexplicable to me as it was terrifying. Their desire defied everything I thought I knew about Elizabeth, like a reckless tide that swept caution aside, though not, God willing, her instinct for self-preservation.

I appealed to this quality in her now. "Have you forgotten how Robert and his father did everything possible to force you, and your sister, into an impasse? They tried to set Jane Grey and Guilford Dudley on the throne. Had they succeeded, your sister would be dead or imprisoned; you'd have been obliged to do as they saw fit. Robert does not deserve your care for him. Were the situation reversed, I doubt he'd do the same for you."

Her eyes sparked. "You seem to forget that I know what Robert really desired."

"No, I remember all too well. He wanted to marry you and share your crown." We locked eyes. "But now, he and his brothers are condemned. Should Renard discover you've been communicating with Dudley, a traitor, he will use it against you."

Sudden pallor tightened her features. "It's more than a book," she said. "I put a letter inside it. Courtenay has a way to smuggle it into the Tower. He told me it was safe."

I felt as if my insides had turned to liquid. "A letter?"

"Yes," she said. "If my sister weds Philip of Spain, she will destroy everything—our faith, our future, our very lives. Robert must be forewarned. The betrothal could be his death warrant; Philip will demand it of her. He will demand that she execute every traitor in the Tower before he sets foot on these shores."

I found it difficult to draw a full breath. It was more than Cecil had feared, more than Renard could have hoped for: a letter from Elizabeth herself, to none other than Robert Dudley, a convicted traitor. I did not want to ask the question that burned on my lips; I did not want to confront some terrible truth about this woman I served. Yet I had to be sure. I had to know how far Elizabeth was willing to go before I committed myself.

"Do you know what Dudley and Courtenay plan?" I asked. "Tell me now, or so help me, I'll leave court this very hour. I cannot serve you if you will not place your trust in me."

I saw her teeth cut at her lower lip, hesitating. I turned on my heel and set off for the stable entranceway. I meant it. I would not be manipulated, not even by her.

"Brendan, wait." The unexpected tremor in her voice stopped me. I glanced over my shoulder. "I don't know anything else," she said. "I swear it to you."

I heard Cecil in my mind, *We can guide her to her destiny— you and I. But first, we must keep her alive,* and I had a vivid recollection of the queen in her fabric-strewn chamber, the complicit laughter of her women, that portrait half-covered by a sheet in the corner. In that moment, I faced a terrible choice. I could turn away now and disappear the way I had come. I could return to the life I'd left behind. I felt a sudden longing for that uncomplicated existence, where Kate and I could wed and have children; where I needn't watch for shadows at every corner; where there were no covert plans or lies within lies.

A simple life, without the burden of protecting Elizabeth.

Yet even as I imagined it, I knew I deluded myself. My choice had been made. I'd made it the hour I agreed to serve her. I'd done it willingly, knowing the price I might pay.

Elizabeth and I shared the same blood. My fate was now bound to hers.

"We still have time," I said, and she gave me a startled look. "To get your letter back," I explained, "and discover what Dudley and Courtenay plot before it is too late. Renard wants evidence; if I can, I will give it to him."

She took in my somber expression. "But it would mean their deaths . . ."

"It could mean yours if I do not," I replied. "You must survive this. Do nothing more, Your Grace; say nothing more. Let me retrieve your letter and do whatever is required, even if it means betraying Dudley and Courtenay."

Her hands clenched at her sides. "No. I cannot. There must be another way."

"There isn't. Your letter could be *your* death. You cannot rule from the grave."

Her conflict played upon her face, a tangled web of emotions that had no doubt haunted her since she arrived at court and realized the path her sister would take—a path that led to the abolishment of her faith and her right to be queen. She'd fought to save herself and those she loved; now she had to confront her own thorn-laden choice.

"It's the only way," I said. "You or Dudley. You cannot save both."

"Let me think!" She held up her hand, turning away. From outside the sound of voices reached us, along with the clack of wood pattens on cobblestone. As the grooms catcalled and women returned pert replies, Elizabeth straightened her shoulders. She turned back to me, her eyes remote.

"So be it," she said quietly. "Do what you must."

The women were almost at the doorway; we had no more time. I shifted into the nearest stall. As I dropped to my knees beside a startled mare, yanking my cloak about me to blend with the shadows, I heard Elizabeth say with staccato impatience, "Where have you been? I nearly froze to death here waiting for you. God's teeth, how long does it take to fetch a muff and gloves?" I heard the women's murmured apologies, followed by hurried footsteps as they walked out after the princess.

I let out a shuddering breath. Elizabeth had put herself in harm's way to save Dudley and her future right to be queen.

As I had suspected, however, when it came to choosing between them, she came first.

———◆◆◆———

Chapter Nine

𝕴 took a few moments to compose myself. I heard Elizabeth call out to the grooms, "Best get back to your chores before the stable master finds you squandering those coins I gave you. Don't forget, I want the best fodder, not the cheap hay you give the rest of the court's beasts. And plenty of blankets at night—my Cantila is a delicate creature bred for sunnier climes than ours. I'll take it amiss if something should happen to him."

As the grooms laughed and promised to do as she asked, I had to smile. Even in peril, Elizabeth would think of her horse, Cantila, an expensive Arabian she pampered like a child. She also wisely sowed allegiance where she could: Those grooms would be her willing slaves henceforth, after she'd paid them to gamble and drink during work hours.

The truant grooms tramped into the stables to go about their business. None paid me heed as I brushed straw from my hose and moved to where my Cinnabar was stalled. He snorted at my greeting, nuzzling my cloak for the bits of dried apple I usually carried. I'd forgotten to stop by the kitchens for some, so I apologized as he tossed his head in frustration and I checked his forelock for the wound Peregrine had mentioned. It was healing, a small nick. I could still ride him.

Urian came bounding up to me with an excited bark. I turned to see Peregrine holding the dog's lead, his gaze bright and hair unkempt. No matter how much he tried, a few hours on his own and he invariably looked as if he'd run into a windstorm.

"Well?" he said eagerly. "Did you see her? What did she say?"

"Never mind that." I eyed him. "Did you find out anything?"

He nodded, his voice lowering to a whisper. "That horse Toby keeps ready, Courtenay uses it to visit a brothel called the Hawk's Nest, across the river in Southwark near Bankside Street. He's smitten with a bawd there, and he's going again tonight. He paid Toby this morning."

I nodded grimly, reaching for Cinnabar's saddle blanket and bridle.

Peregrine's expression crumpled. "What? Are you not pleased?"

I began to saddle Cinnabar, making an effort to lighten my tone. "You did well, but you're not to ask anything more. Leave the rest to me."

He scowled. "I don't see why. I got the information you needed and—"

I wheeled about and pinched his ear, eliciting a stifled protest. I said softly, "Because I said so." I released him. He rubbed his ear. "No more working on your own. Understood?"

"Yes, master," he muttered.

I proceeded to ready Cinnabar. As I took his reins, Urian whined. "She's fond of this dog," I said. "Make sure you feed him before you put him in his kennel. I'll wait outside."

I led Cinnabar from the stall. During the time I'd been inside the stable block, the temperature had dropped even lower.

Snow had started to fall again. The wind nipped at my cheeks like teeth. Shivering, I walked Cinnabar around the courtyard to warm him, huddled in my cloak, my hood yanked up as far over my head as it could be. I desperately needed a new cap.

Peregrine emerged from the stables. I swung him into the saddle and mounted. "Let's go find this Hawk's Nest," I said.

With Peregrine's arms clasped about my waist, I turned Cinnabar past the parklands bordering the palace, bringing him to a slow canter as we left behind Whitehall's labyrinthine expanse. Barren trees bowed under the hush of new snow; I reveled in the sight of open land, its white tranquility reminding me of Hatfield.

Cecil had been wrong. Flair or not, being an intelligencer would never be my choice.

Taking Grace Church Street, we plunged into the city clustered by the Thames. The calcified spine of London Bridge reared into view, perched on its twenty vast stone piers. I'd never been on the bridge before and marveled that it could hold so much on its back. Below us, the glazed river was devoid of its habitual water traffic, the ice already so dense in the shallows that children were skating across it, using pieces of bone for their blades. I saw a skinny dog romping after them, couples roaming the serrated white shore hand in hand, and vendors hawking hot pies—an unexpectedly festive sight that brightened my mood.

At the northern gatehouse, crowds lined up to pay their toll and visit the hundreds of shops perched on either side of the bridge's span like teetering birds, the air clogged with the raucous shouts of peddlers and others going about their business. I maneuvered Cinnabar with a tight rein; he was not used to the near-deafening noise or masses of people. Mule- and ox-drawn carts laden with goods added to the clamor as they rumbled across with utter disregard for pedestrians. The bridge was the only way to transport merchandise across the river in winter, and the stink of animal ordure permeated the air.

I gazed up in awe as we passed under a gilded palatial structure that clambered several stories into the sky, its jutting balconies festooned with banners.

"Some people live and die without ever leaving the bridge," Peregrine said in my ear. "It's considered the safest place in the city after the palace, because the gates close at curfew and it has everything the people need, except for ale and beer. No cellars for it."

"Curfew?" I frowned. "That's inconvenient. How will I get across the bridge tonight? I'm not a nobleman who can flash his credentials whenever he needs to bypass something."

"You could always walk. The river should be frozen through by nightfall, and . . ." His voice faded as I glanced over my shoulder at him in disbelief.

"That's right," he muttered. "I forgot you're like a cat when it comes to water. But it would be safe, not to mention faster. You'll see. It's going to take an hour just to get across."

I didn't believe him at first, but as we progressed, I began to see that while there might not be official taverns, plenty of makeshift stalls offered beverages and food, inviting passersby to stop and peruse, sending those behind them into paroxysms of angry curses. Navigating the congested route between the edifices was like moving through a maze, for while the narrow central road was divided into designated lanes—one north and one south—nobody paid the directions any mind, sauntering to and fro whenever a shop display caught their fancy, ducking around and sometimes outright defying the passage of oncoming carts and wagons and horse riders with oblivious determination.

To Peregrine's glee, I kept ducking my head to avoid the painted signs in the shape of goods that hung overhead, proclaiming that shop's particular trade. The light grew dim. The top levels of many of the bridge's structures connected to each other across the road by soaring passageways, forming a web of vaults. Occasionally I glimpsed open space between the buildings, offering spectacular views of the partially frozen river and spires of London, but I didn't tarry, much as I might have liked to. I wanted to survive the crossing without trampling over some hapless pedestrian.

By the time we passed over the massive drawbridge at the southern end, I was breathless and Cinnabar quivered with distress. As we rode from under the fortified gatehouse, I glanced upward to its top; the tar-boiled heads of traitors were impaled there on spikes. A shiver went through me as I wondered if the Duke of Northumberland's head was among them.

I had started turning Cinnabar toward the din of Southwark when out of the corner of my eye I caught sight of a swish of telltale black. I reined in sharply, swiveling in my saddle to stare into the crowd. Peregrine clutched at my waist, my sudden movements nearly unseating him. "What is it?" he whispered.

"Ssh." I reached for my sword. A large, dark-clad figure was blending with the people emerging under the gatehouse; I was certain it was none other than Courtenay's man. As if he felt my stare, he went still. His cowl cast a deep shadow over his face, but I felt him meet my eyes before he wheeled about to disappear into the throngs going north onto the bridge.

I let out my breath. "We're being followed. No. Don't look."

"We are?" Peregrine's voice vibrated with excitement. "Is he still . . . ?"

"No, he saw me watching and turned around. But he must know what we're doing; he serves Courtenay. How far do you think it is to the brothel?"

"I don't know. It must be in the district." He paused. "Why didn't he come after us?"

"Perhaps he thinks it would be hard to kill anyone here, with so many witnesses," I said, though in fact the bridge offered a perfect spot for murder, if you were skilled enough. In all that bustle and commotion, a well-aimed knife could slice a victim open from sternum to gut and the body wouldn't be found until someone stumbled over it.

Anger surged at my own ineptness. I should have known Courtenay would have me tracked; he might have been lurking unseen near the stable block, seen Elizabeth emerge, and guessed we had met. That didn't trouble me for now; the princess now knew to keep her distance from Courtenay. My own safety was another matter altogether.

"Let's see how eager he is," I said. "We'll wet our throats in that tavern and wait."

Tethering Cinnabar outside, I hired an ostler to watch him, and we entered a seedy establishment smelling of dank and al-cohol, a convenient locale for passengers coming off or onto the bridge. After ordering two tankards of watered ale and a greasy pie from the hutch, I decided to try my luck and ask the server if he knew where the Hawk's Nest was. The man was an ugly piece of work, one eye covered in milky film, greasy strands of hair plastered to a skull like a rodent's; as he peered warily at me through his one good but bloodshot eye, I saw a louse skitter across his brow.

"Hawk's Nest?" he repeated. "Ye're that type, are ye?"

"Type?" I frowned. "I'm not sure I understand. I'm looking for—"

He cut me off with a leer that showed rotting gums. His breath alone could have felled an ox. "I know what ye look for," he leered. "Pretty boy-arse. Go into the district and find Dead Man's Lane. The Nest is nearby. Though it don't accept just anyone, I warn ye. Best be up to waitin', too, 'cause it's closed till dusk." He cackled at his own joke. "Up to waitin', now isn't that a riot? All ye fancy men are up to waitin', I wager."

I smiled through my gritted teeth. "Thank you." I went to the rickety table where Peregrine sat staring at me over his tankard as if he were about to bolt at any moment.

"Do you know what kind of place the Hawk's Nest is?" I growled.

He shook his head, too quickly.

"Are you sure?"

He shook his head again, this time with less assertion.

"Boy bum." I leaned to him. "It's a quean's custom house, isn't it?"

Peregrine said nervously, "Is that what you heard? Imagine that."

"Yes, imagine it. I also heard it doesn't allow everyone in. What does that mean?"

"It must be private. You'll probably need a password—" He avoided the swipe I aimed at his ear. "Would it have mattered if I told you before tonight?" he protested as I glowered at him. "You still have to get inside, no matter what!"

"I wish I didn't." I downed my tankard in a gulp. "And why a password? I thought the whole point of running a brothel was to attract as much custom as possible."

"Well," said Peregrine, "if their custom is, shall we say, not the usual kind, you'd have to be careful, right? You don't want the wrong sort getting in."

He had a point. Buggery was a crime in England, punishable by imprisonment, fines, even death, though I'd never heard of any man being executed for it. Then again, I didn't have experience. The most I'd gleaned was stories in my boyhood, lurid anecdotes about monks, one of the reasons cited for the closure of the abbeys. The way I looked at it, if the act was consensual, why should I care what anyone chose to do in private? There was more than enough evil in the world for it to rank as a minor vice, if that. Still, I'd never considered I might actually have to visit a place that catered to the predilection.

As if he could read my mind, Peregrine added, "You don't have to *do* anything, just get yourself through the door. It probably won't hurt to look the part, though."

"Great. And here I thought mastering the sword was my biggest challenge. Anything else you forgot to tell me? Best do it now. I don't want any more surprises."

He burst out laughing, his eyes gleaming as I dug into my pie with a decided ill humor. After we ate, we went outside. As I untied Cinnabar and paid the ostler, I gauged our environs. Courtenay's man could be hiding anywhere; there were still masses of people traveling over the bridge, but the cold was deepening to a bone-sapping chill as the sun started to ebb and I figured we might as well locate the damn brothel so I could return later without undue complications. The last thing I wanted was to lose myself in the crime-infested warren of baiting pits, whorehouses, and cheap inns and taverns of Southwark.

I clicked my tongue at Cinnabar, urging him to quicken his pace as we rode into the coiled heart of the district. I had never beheld such squalor. There was filth everywhere, festering in piles; skeletal dogs skulked past, every rib showing, and children dressed in rags, with open sores on their feet, sat listless in the frozen mud of the lanes while their mothers entertained custom inside seedy lean-tos fit only for rats—a significant quantity of which tripped over the rooftops and through the gutters, bold as day.

"This can't be right," I said. "Courtenay would never set foot here." I pulled out a coin, waving it. Five children immediately bounded to us, grubby hands extended, all eyes and knees and filthy hair. "Which way to Dead Man's Lane?" I asked, and I felt the tension in my shoulders ease when one of the boys pointed to one side, toward the river, and then caught the coin I pitched in midair. I saw feral cunning on the other children's faces and set my hand on my sword hilt, returning their stares. They retreated, like a pack of animals.

We rode down a rutted path that barely qualified as a lane, past a series of slightly less sordid establishments, and came up before a two-story, timber-framed building. I thought at first it must be a guesthouse until I saw the sign swinging above its stout oak door, depicting a bird of prey, crudely drawn wings stretched over a circle of twigs: THE HAWK'S NEST.

There were no lower windows or visible places to gain a foot-hold up to a narrow catwalk of a ledge that ran parallel under high upper windows, all of which were shuttered. Indeed, nothing about the place indicated easy access or a welcoming air. It was more a fortress than a den of illicit pleasure.

"Locked tight as a virgin's knees," I remarked, and Peregrine laughed. "How will we get inside?" I took another moment to memorize the house and its location before I surveyed our surroundings. I waited. After a few minutes, I turned Cinnabar around.

"We?" I said in response to Peregrine's question. "There is no 'we' tonight. You've had quite enough adventure for one day."

He sulked as we rode back to the bridge. Crossing north proved less arduous, the crowds thinning as dusk draped a cinder shroud over the horizon. Moving slowly through the waning populace, as shop vendors bolted their doors for the night, I kept my poniard unsheathed. I made a brief stop at a shop to purchase a new dark wool cap, lingering over the wares, but did not catch sight of Courtenay's man. His absence proved disquieting. It wasn't like a henchman to give up easily. He'd had plenty of opportunity to follow and engage, if he were so inclined, but he hadn't. Why?

The only reason I could think of did not ease my apprehension. Maybe he'd been paid to watch and report back.

If so, that could mean Courtenay *wanted* me to find him.

After seeing to Cinnabar's water and feed, we hurried into the palace. My fingers were so numb with cold by the time we reached my chamber, I could barely pull out the key from my doublet and unlock the door.

I went still. The room had been ransacked, the coffer flung open, my saddlebag overturned on the floor, its contents scattered, my cot pulled from the wall and upended. I released my sword, holding Peregrine back. "So much for giving up," I said. "While we were investigating the brothel, it looks like our friend came back to investigate me."

"What could he have wanted?" Peregrine slipped in front of me, gingerly stepping over the debris. "Doesn't look as if he stole anything; he didn't even take your fake chain. See? It's over there by the coffer."

"I don't know what he wanted," I said, but as I reached down for my bag I had the sudden thought that this overt display of theft seemed staged—a deliberate act intended to instill fear in me.

The skin of my nape crawled.

Peregrine started to pick up my chain. All of a sudden, he paused. He straightened up, a folded square of parchment in his hands. "What's this?" he asked, and before I could stop him he cracked apart the gray wax seal.

"You cannot save her," he read aloud. He looked at me, bewildered.

I lunged.

He recoiled instinctively, the note dropping from his hand. He gazed at me, his eyes widening. "It—it burns," he gasped. "My fingertips . . . they're burning . . ."

I took one look at the note, at the jagged edges of the broken seal. I tasted bile in my throat. Kicking the note aside, I seized Peregrine's hands. Welts were seared into his flesh, like burns.

Poison. The seal on the parchment had been poisoned.

He let out a startled cry and staggered against me. I dragged him to the nearby pitcher, overturning the water on his hands, rubbing them frantically against my doublet. His face drained white; blood-flecked foam bubbled from his lips. He clutched at me, his legs buckling.

The room swirled about me as I held him upright. He started to thrash, the greasy contents of our afternoon meal spewing from his mouth. As his eyes rolled back in his head, I hauled him up into my arms and flung open the chamber door, scrambling down the staircase, through the freezing courtyards, and into the torch-lit gallery. I couldn't hear anything except my own voice—like the cry of a wounded animal.

A group of figures paused at the gallery's end; as I staggered toward them, Peregrine draped in my arms, I heard urgent voices. A tall, thin man in black strode to me.

"My squire," I said haltingly, gasping. "He—he's been poisoned. Please . . . help me."

The man came to a halt, his hawkish bearded face closing like a trap. He was a Spaniard from the Hapsburg delegation; I recognized him from the night in the hall, one of the exalted lords who'd stood by the queen and frowned at everything. Behind him I saw the others staring. No one moved. Then, through a haze of despair, I caught sight of a familiar face, although it wasn't until she hastened forth that I recognized Sybilla. The Spaniard detained her. *"Dice que han envenenado al joven. No le toques."*

She shook his hand aside, moving to me. "I know some herbal lore," she said. "I can help him until we fetch a physician. Quickly, bring him to—"

Peregrine started thrashing again. As I tightened my grip, liquid seeped from his mouth, dark and putrid, staining his parched lips. Sybilla whirled about, her voice shredding, and the tall Spaniard barked at his companions. From among them, someone broke free, a slight figure I watched through a daze as she bolted down the opposite end of the gallery to the hall, her hood flying off to expose blond tresses, her frantic cry echoing as her little black dog bounded behind her, barking in excitement.

I crumbled to my knees. Clutching Peregrine, I rocked back and forth, over and over, whispering, "No, please God, no, not this, not him . . ."

Sybilla sank in a pool of skirts at my side. I felt her hand on my shoulder as Peregrine jerked, weakly. His eyes opened wide.

He looked at me. He was struggling to speak, but the liquid welled up again, thick and vile.

I heard a terrifying rattle in his throat.

His eyelids fluttered and closed.

He went still.

Chapter Ten

I couldn't move. I held him to my chest and felt my world disintegrate as the others arrived: Rochester with a napkin still tucked in his collar; two guards and several inquisitive courtiers come to see what all the fuss was about. Jane Dormer, who had run to alert Rochester in the hall, peered in anxious concern from behind them. When she saw Peregrine, she gave a cry of dismay and started weeping.

"Blessed saints, what is it?" Rochester bent to me. "Is the boy . . . ?"

"He's dead," I whispered. As I said the words, a chasm cracked open inside me, an awful endless void that threatened to pull me into its swirling vortex forever.

"Dead?" he echoed, and I nodded dully. I wanted to bellow at the immobile Spaniard with his aristocratic expression of distaste, at the others who had stood there gaping, watching from afar as an innocent perished in my arms, but I could not utter a sound.

Peregrine was gone. Nothing I did could bring him back.

"But how?" Rochester's voice quavered. "Did he eat something tainted? Drink something? What happened to him?'" He was looking around indignantly at the company, as though they were keeping the answer from him.

I heard Sybilla Darrier say quietly, "It doesn't matter now, does it? The child's body must be attended. Perhaps you can assist, my lord? Master Beecham has just suffered a terrible shock. He's clearly in no position to contend with this."

"Yes, yes." Rochester turned back to me. "I'm so sorry. I really have no idea what to say. I'm quite concerned that someone could have died thus in the palace. An inquest must be done. I'll notify Her Majesty and—"

"My lord," interrupted Sybilla. Her voice was calm, steady, but something in it, an indefinable hardness, brought Rochester to a halt. "I think it's best if you take charge of the boy while I see Master Beecham to his room, yes? These other details can be attended to once he gets his bearings."

Rochester fumbled at his collar, fingering his food-stained napkin. "Yes," he muttered. He snapped his hand at the guards, who stepped forth to take Peregrine from me.

I resisted for a moment. I clung to him as if he were the last upright thing in the crumbling edifice of my existence, and then I let them take him from me, his head dangling, his curls plastered with sweat. As they carried him away, I went numb.

Sybilla's hand felt cool as it enclosed mine. "Come," she said, and I followed her, still without speaking, moving as if through an impenetrable fog.

In the courtyard by the staircase, she paused, looking at me. "Which way?" she asked. I led her up the staircase, to my open door. I swayed. Her hand rested at the small of my back, steadying me. All of a sudden I could smell Peregrine's death all over me.

"I don't know if I can . . ." I whispered.

"You don't have to," she said. "If need be, we'll ask Rochester to put you in another room."

My eyes couldn't focus. I had to blink several times before I took in the chaos. None of it seemed real to me, as if I'd plunged into a nightmare from which there could be no escape.

"Let me go first." As Sybilla stepped inside, I caught sight of the note crumpled in a corner where I'd kicked it in my frantic attempt to save him.

"Don't," I said. "That seal on the paper—it's poisoned."

She blanched. "Did your squire . . . did he touch it . . . ?"

In response, I bent to the floor and retrieved my fallen gauntlets. Pulling them on, I took the note by its corner and went to the guttering tallow light. I looked at the message.

You cannot save her.

"This was meant for me." My voice sounded hollow, as if it came from someone else. "He found it, but it's me they wanted to kill."

Sybilla stood immobile. "Who are *they*? Why would anyone want to kill you?"

I swallowed. "I cannot tell you." I held the note over the tallow flame and watched it catch fire. A bluish flame curled upward, blackening the paper, devouring it. Before the flame touched my gloved fingers, I dropped the note and ground it into the floorboards with my heel, leaving a charred smear.

"They won't get away with it." I looked up to meet her gaze. "I will track them down if it takes the rest of my life, and I will make them pay for what they've done."

She took a step to me. "Where are you going? No, wait—" She brought up a hand against my chest, stopping me. "You can't. You're covered in . . . Come, let me help you."

She did not wait for my answer, taking the pitcher and departing. I began to right my belongings, my movements methodical, precise, the grieving rage burning behind my eyes. By the time I got the room in order, she had returned with the pitcher.

"Bathing water," she said, pouring it into the basin. "It's cold, but it will do. And you need fresh clothes—a new shirt, hose, linen. You can't go anywhere in that state."

I pointed to the articles I'd arranged on my cot. As she regarded my rumpled court doublet and only extra pair of hose, she said softly, "Let me help you. Tell me what you mean to do."

"I told you, it's not safe." Turning from her, I stripped off my soiled doublet and shirt. Using a cloth dipped in the basin, I briskly washed my torso. I didn't care that she stood a few paces away, watching. When she came to me and took the cloth to bathe my shoulders and back, I did not resist. She wrung the cloth out and turned me around to face her, cleansing my forehead, cheeks, and clotted beard. We were so close I could smell her intoxicating scent of lilies like an oasis in a desert. In the gloom, the blues of her eyes took on a near-turquoise hue, shaded by thick dusky lashes, as if she'd dipped them in soot.

"I know you are not who you seem," she said. "I knew it from the moment I saw you." Her hand slid the cloth downward, over my throat, past my collarbones to my chest. She was so close I could feel the heat of her breath on my skin. "Let me help you."

My hand came up, catching her wrist. "If you want to help me," I said, "we can talk later. But now, my lady, I fear I have an urgent appointment I must keep."

Her mouth parted, showing a hint of teeth. Then she dropped the washcloth in the basin and wiped her hands on her skirts. The moisture left damp stains on the silk.

"You mustn't let rage overcome your reason," she said. "Many a man has failed because he let his emotion get the better of him. Revenge is only satisfying if it is wielded with the full understanding of the havoc it will wreak."

I smiled coldly. "I'll take that into account, my lady."

As she turned to the door, I said, "Mistress Darrier," and she paused. "See that he is cared for." My voice caught. "See that he is veiled properly until I can say good-bye. Promise me. He—he was my friend. He did not deserve such a fate."

"No one does," she said, and she clicked the door shut as she left. I went to my mirror, took out my razor, and worked on my beard until it was trimmed close to my face. Then I buckled on my sword, thrust my poniard into my belt, and flung on my cloak.

A black flame smoldered in my heart.

Havoc or not, I would have my revenge.

Chapter Eleven

I stalked through London like a specter. The cold congealed my breath, emptying the streets of its habitual vagrants, pickpockets, and vermin. While curfew was supposed to secure the city and protect the citizenry, as I traversed the maze of tenements and taverns downriver from the palace, I knew the gates' closure only signaled the onset of a different sort of activity, most of it criminal.

But not tonight. Tonight, it was as if London itself mourned my dead squire.

I was heedless of my safety, taking shadowy alleyways as I made my way to the water steps, my hand on my sword. I would have welcomed an assault; I wanted to shed blood, to satiate the rage and disbelief I already knew would haunt me forever.

Soon I was standing at the river's edge, gazing upon a vast expanse of rippled viridian. The moon was veiled in the overcast sky, but its icy glow wasn't needed. The frozen Thames emitted its own luminescence, an eerie nimbus that captured tendrils of mist drifting like tattered silk over its motionless surface. On the far bank, I discerned errant firelight.

I forgot you're like a cat when it comes to water . . .

I spun about, with a stifled gasp. I had heard him so clearly, I expected to find him behind me, grinning, my faithful scamp who had refused to stay put in our room.

No one was there.

Returning my eyes to the embankment, resisting a surge of helpless tears, I gleaned rows of forlorn wherries, all useless now, the boatmen left to fend for themselves as best they could until the river thawed. Peregrine had assured me this way would be safest, faster, and I had no time to waste. As I stood there, though, I was gripped by a horrifying vision of getting halfway across and hearing a spidery crack, looking down to see the ice give way under my feet. I knew the river still flowed under its cold shield; its embrace would be swift, inescapable. I'd plunged into the Thames before. I had no desire to do it again, though death felt like a merciful respite at this moment.

I looked down at my boots. Taking my knife, I lightly scored the soles and took up handfuls of snow, rubbing them into the grooves. It might help stop me from slipping.

I sidled out onto the frosted edge. Fear cut off my breath. I told myself to focus, take slow steps, one foot in front of the next, as if I moved across a newly polished floor. As I progressed, the city disappeared behind me in the mist, but the noise of the south bank ahead did not yet intrude. The clouds parted for a glimpse of the moon; her silver halo dazzled, scattering diamond fragments across the river. With the black sky above me, embroidered with a thousand brilliant stars, and the Thames like a fantastical sea, bewitched in midmotion, I came to a halt. It struck me how cruel the world was; even as a child died in agony, nature could clothe herself with such majestic indifference.

Then I moved forward again, almost losing my balance, slipping and scrambling toward the shore. The cold I'd ceased to feel only moments earlier returned with vicious suddenness. I drew the hood of my cloak further over my head, my feet like blocks of ice in my boots as I clambered up the Southwark bank.

Sidestepping discarded drift nets, I stared at an odd tableau ahead: fire pits tossing sizzling embers into the air and the smell of bacon thick. I could see crowds; as I approached, to my amazement a night fair burgeoned before me.

Divided by meandering narrow dirt lanes were tables under sagging tarps held up by ropes, laden with piles of tarnished platters, pyramids of goblets, threadbare carpets, faded tapestries, splintered knives, and old cloths. In the tarry light of the fire pits, street vendors and alewives circulated offering meat pies, pastries, and other foods while crowds mingled—mostly men, from what I could discern under their layers of clothing, but also some women, bold and strutting, all perusing the displays. The vendors hawked their wares with tireless enthusiasm, though in subdued tones more suited to a graveyard than a market site. It seemed no one wanted to alert the authorities.

I was careful to not draw attention, keeping my head lowered as I blended with the crowd. At first I mistook the jumbled silver pieces on a nearby stall for looted goods, though it struck me that surely such wealth could not have gone unreported, much less unconfiscated. Then I saw an upholstered prayer bench, complete with gilded angels on its carved frontispiece and worn velvet cushion for the knees. I paused. Beside it were heaps of torn book clasps, many of which had chipped enamel iconography, and a wood trough such as pigs might use, filled to the rim with coiled rosaries.

The fair was selling rapine from the monasteries.

The stall owner lumbered up to me—a potbellied, bearded

man with pitted skin. He babbled at me in an incomprehensible language; it wasn't until he was jabbing his finger at my chest and repeating his words that I suddenly understood he spoke English.

"Buy or go," he said. "You no look here."

For a moment, I couldn't move. As I met the man's yellowed eyes I had an unbidden recollection of a time now gone, a time I had never witnessed but had only heard about, when these holy refuges for the sick, weary, and poor once dominated the realm, until they fell prey to King Henry and his break with Rome.

I felt a sudden rush of heat, a searing desire to grab this man by the scruff of his jerkin and remind him that what he so callously sold as scrap had once been revered by hundreds of monks and nuns, who'd been turned out of their ancestral homes. I knew in some remote part of me that it was my grief and I mustn't let it get the better of me. I could not indulge a meaningless altercation now, not when my real target lay ahead. Yet even as I fought to stay focused, I wrestled with my compassion for the queen. Mary had clung to her faith against all odds, unaware that what she sought to salvage had already been forsaken.

The man's hand dropped to his belt. Before he could draw his weapon, I strode off, leaving the fair behind for the rows of hovels clustered together like moldering mushrooms. The barking of dogs and agonized roar of a bear being taunted in a pit curdled the chill; on the thresholds I now passed lurked figures in tattered gowns, some no older than girls, their gaunt faces painted in a mockery of enticement. A lewd invitation floated to me, a cocked bony hip and beckoning finger . . .

I had reached the whorehouses.

I came to a halt, uncertain of which way to turn. In the night it all looked the same—filthy, decrepit, and corroded by suffering. The visceral pain of Peregrine's death collided with my understanding of the damage Renard brewed with Mary's marriage, which would pit her in a battle against her Protestant subjects, and all of a sudden I wanted this errand done with. I wanted to fulfill my mission and get as far from the court and London as I could.

When I finally espied Dead Man's Lane, I kept to pockets of shadows, my senses attuned. The Hawk's Nest came into view, a far different building from its daytime incarnation—the shutters of the upper story pulled back, candlelight winking in the mullioned glass, the faint sounds of music and laughter drifting on the cold air.

The front door opened. Two men staggered out, silhouetted by the light spilling from inside. I could see at least one of them wasn't from the neighborhood. He was tall and well built, with a fur-trimmed mantle tossed across his shoulders: a courtier by the looks of it, and of evident means. His companion was slender, smaller. As they careened down the alley where I lurked, the boy let out a lascivious giggle.

I palmed my blade. They came closer, tripping over each other and laughing. I could smell the alcohol wafting off them from where I hid in a doorway. All of a sudden, the boy yelped as the courtier swung him to the wall and began groping him with drunken urgency, the boy emitting squeaks of feigned protest.

I pounced.

The courtier froze when he felt my blade at his throat. "He's a little young, don't you think?" I hissed in his ear, and the boy pressed against the wall opened his mouth to shriek.

I glared. "I don't want you. Get, now!"

He didn't need to be told twice. Slipping around his companion, the boy ran off.

The courtier tried to elbow me. I pressed my poniard on his neck hard enough to give him pause. "Gutter rat thief," he slurred. "Kill me if you like, but I don't have anything to give you. That boy-cunny took all my coin."

"I don't want your money," I said. "Just tell me the password. Or would you prefer I turned you in to the night watch for consorting with an underage boy?"

He chortled, swaying. He could barely stand upright. If I hadn't had my arm about him from behind, he'd have impaled himself on my blade. "That's a fine one. They're all underage, you fool. That's the Nest's specialty."

"Password," I repeated. I pressed harder, enough to make him gasp.

"Fledgling," he said, and as I lessened my pressure on the blade, he abruptly whirled about, less drunkenly than I'd supposed. I had no choice but to slam him on the side of his head with my poniard hilt.

He dropped like stone.

Grabbing him by his sleeves, I dragged him into the doorway and yanked his mantle from him. It was expensive, a dark green damask lined in fleece, the outer edges trimmed in lynx. I threw it over my own cloak. Hopefully the bastard wouldn't freeze to death.

Tugging up the mantle's furred cowl, which almost covered my entire face, I shoved my knife in my boot and strode to the brothel door.

* * *

The clouds overhead had scattered, and the glacial moon now shed a colorless glow over the building. I rapped on the door and waited, counting the seconds under my breath.

A slot in the door slid open. "Fee," said a gruff voice.

"Fledgling," I replied.

The sound of bolts grinding preceded the door's opening. The smell of wood smoke and a blast of warmth greeted me; as I heard the clanking of tankards and laughter, I realized I faced a closed passageway lit by cressets on the walls. There was another door at the end of the short corridor, from which the sounds of entertainment reached me.

The front door slammed shut behind me. A hand yanked back my cowl. The voice barked, "Weapons, if ye please. And yer cloak, too."

He hadn't recognized the mantle had a previous owner. Nevertheless, he posed a problem—a titan with the crunched features of a pit mastiff and hands the size of hams. He also had a wheel-lock pistol shoved under his wide studded belt; despite my misgivings, I was impressed. One didn't see a weapon of that caliber every day.

The man glared at me. Slowly I unhooked my sword harness and wrapped it in both of my cloaks. "Be careful with it," I said. I had no intention of relinquishing my hidden poniard. He eyed me up and down, my fine Toledo-steel sword gripped in his fist.

"Fee," he said again.

I frowned, started reaching into my pouch for coin.

"*Fee!*" he roared.

God's teeth, were there *two* passwords? I said coyly, "I'm new, you see, and a friend recommended that I—"

He grasped me by the front of my doublet, thrusting his face at me. If he decided to start using his fists, I wouldn't stand a chance unless I could get my blade out.

"Who recommended ye?" he asked, and I replied softly, "His lordship the Earl of Devon. He suggested we meet here. He says it's the finest establishment of its kind."

"Earl, ye say?" He tightened his fist about my doublet, scrutinizing me. Just as I began to think I was going to have do something very unsavory to get myself out of this predicament, he grunted and let me go, signaling to the door at the end of the passage.

"Earl's man's in there. See ye report to him first. I don't like strangers who don't know the fee, and he don't like visitors who come lookin' for his master."

I bowed my head and stepped past him; without warning, I felt his hand shoot between my legs. He gripped my codpiece in a breath-quenching vise. "Nice," he said, his breath rank in my face. "Come see me later, if ye like, pretty man."

"I'll consider it," I managed to utter, feeling as if he had just castrated me. He gave me another breath-quenching squeeze. As I gulped against the urge to double over and cup my genitals, he reached up to a box above the shelves where a multitude of customer weapons and cloaks were stashed. He pulled out a thin cloth mask and thrust it into my hand.

"No faces in the common room. Rule of the house."

I muttered my gratitude, affixing the white lawn mask in place and tying its ribbons about my head. My groin throbbed; I feared I'd lost my ability to ever raise my yard again.

Apprehension coiled in me as I stepped through the far door and into the common room. Laid out like any well-to-do alehouse, it was ample, with herb-strewn rushes underfoot to reduce the chill of the plank flooring and tallow lights flickering on wide board tables, where men sat drinking, playing cards, or dicing.

All ordinary enough, until I realized the wavering figures by the hearth who swayed against each other were all men; the lithe servers weaving their way between tables carrying flagons or platters were male, too. There wasn't a woman in sight.

Every customer who turned to stare at me wore a mask.

Two men seated at a nearby table, both clad in open doublets of patterned cloth, expressed interest; one smiled invitingly at me while his companion whispered in his ear. I returned the smile but moved past them, scanning the room for the earl's man. I pondered how to contend with this complication. Courtenay had sent his man after me on the bridge; I didn't expect him to be exactly welcoming.

I spotted him seated at a table near a narrow staircase, hunched alone with a tallow wick floating in an oil dish and a tankard before him, his hood pulled over his head. Did the mask rule apply to him? I surmised the cloak and weapon policy did not.

He reared up his head as he sensed my approach, throwing his hood backward. I bit back a gasp. His left eye was a welted hole. It explained why he'd failed to see me in the gallery, huddled in the window alcove. The rest of him didn't look much better; his face was a mass of scar tissue that twisted his features from brow to jaw, the skin so puckered and knotted it no longer resembled flesh. There was damage visible even under his gray-flecked beard, as if someone had taken a mallet to him, followed by a cauterizing torch and crude sutures.

"What do you want?" he snarled in a raw voice. His speech was slurred, but not in the way men garbled when they were drunk. He didn't move a muscle. He didn't need to. I had no doubt this man had seen battle. He could be on his feet, with a dagger in my gut, before I had time to blink. Still, as I recalled the note he'd left in my room, and what it had done, I had to stop myself from lunging at him to carve out his rancid, black heart.

Yet he didn't appear to recognize me. With the mask covering my face, I could be anyone. I cocked my hip, affecting a playful tone. "I'm told you're the earl's man. I was hoping he might like company tonight?"

He didn't glance at me again, raising his goblet to slurp its contents. I could see why his enunciation was strange; his upper lip was gone, his mouth misshapen as if it had been spliced and put clumsily back together. He must have lost most of his teeth, too, I thought, as a trickle of ale dribbled into his beard.

"His lordship's not interested," he said. "Find some other custom, drudge."

Excellent. He'd taken the ruse. He thought I was one of the whores.

I said, "I'm very accomplished."

"Bah." He flicked his gloved hand toward the general vicinity of the room. "Save your tricks for someone who cares. The earl only likes them hairless as skinned squirrels." He let out a chortle, amused by his own joke. Again I controlled the urge to kill him and be done with it. He was only the messenger; he hadn't placed the order.

"Pity." I let out an exaggerated sigh, bending down as if to adjust my boot before I pivoted toward the staircase. As I'd hoped, he was quick as a lion, on his feet and yanking me about. "Not so fast, catamite. Don't I know you from somewhere?" Then he paused. "Is that a needle you've got in my gut? If so, I warn you I've a much bigger one and a mind to slit you open with it like a spring calf."

I stared into his eye. "Perhaps I'll slit you first." I pushed on the knife. "Don't think I won't." When I saw the sudden change in his expression as he realized who I was, I added, "Or we can go about our business as gentlemen and you can tell me where he is."

He could have yelled. Instead he said, amused, "Is that the way it is? Well, then, go ahead. I'll be here when you come down." He pointed up the stairs. "Last door to the left. Watch out for cats." He guffawed, turning back to his tankard.

I started up the creaking stairs, my knife in my hand. The ceiling sloped low. I hated enclosed spaces almost as much as I did deep water. When I reached the landing I glanced over my shoulder. He was no longer at the table. He wouldn't go far, though. He would be waiting for me, like a monster in a nightmare.

Yanking off the mask, I stuffed it in my breeches pocket. The passage before me was cramped and poorly lit, punctuated by narrow doors that couldn't be very thick, judging by the moans and slapping of skin I could hear from the rooms beyond. The air was fetid, a sour mixture of old rushes, cat piss, and sex.

I took a step forward. Something streaked past me in a dark blur down the passageway. A cat. As I eased past the doors, my eyes adjusting to the gloom, I began to see other cats, nestled by the walls, hissing or watching me with opaque eyes. The ceiling seemed to lower over me; I actually tiptoed past the animals as if they might attack.

By the time I reached the last door on the left, I was dripping sweat; it was hot as Hades from the rising heat of the hearth downstairs and God only knew how many illegal charcoal braziers in the rooms. The entire building was a firetrap; it explained why cats converged here, though I couldn't possibly imagine why anyone would keep so many indoors, except to keep the rats out.

Raking a hand through my damp hair, I put my ear to the door. I heard nothing within. I tried the latch. I was starting to turn it when the door flung open—"I've been waiting for hours!"—and the earl grabbed hold of me, trying to embrace me.

I threw him aside. Courtenay's eyes snapped wide. Slamming the door shut, he whirled to me. His chemise was unlaced, revealing a slim white chest; his features were twisted with rage and flushed with what I assumed was a liberal intake of wine. He started to come at me, his teeth bared, then stopped short when he saw my drawn poniard.

His eyes narrowed. "Who in bloody hell are you?"

Now that I was face-to-face with the earl of Devon, the man who I knew was plotting against the queen, and who I believed had tried to poison me and instead taken Peregrine's life, my desire for vengeance knotted like barbed iron about my heart. I took a moment to gauge him. He exuded the well-fed gloss of a noble, though I noted that without the extravagant padding of his finery, the effects of years of confinement in the Tower showed. Under his loose chemise and breeches, he was slender as an adolescent, his long-limbed body seemingly devoid of discernible musculature; despite his arrogant carriage, if it came down to a fight I had a feeling he'd have less physical strength than I.

"So you do recognize me," I said through my teeth.

He smiled coldly. "You're that no-name mongrel Renard has sent sniffing after me. You've a good nose, too, to have found me here. Pity you shan't be telling him about it."

"Oh? Are you going to try to kill me again?"

He let out a bray of laughter—until I stepped toward him and he saw the intent in my eyes. He went still as I said, "That surprise you left for me in my rooms killed my squire instead. He was just a lad. I *will* see you pay for it."

He blanched, glancing downward to the blade I aimed at him. "I assure you," he said slowly, "I've no idea what you are talking about."

In the silent wake of his words, I searched his eyes. Unless he was the best actor I'd come across, he seemed genuinely baffled by my accusation. My rage faltered. Had I made a mistake? Was he telling me the truth?

"Let me refresh your memory. You ordered me silenced the other night because I saw you meeting with the princess. You sent your manservant after me." He drew in a sharp breath as I stepped closer to him. The door was at his back; in order to get out he'd have to turn around to open it. "But he failed to catch me that night," I continued, "so you had him follow me. I saw him on the bridge; he didn't make himself inconspicuous. Though when he realized I'd seen him, he disappeared. Then I returned to the palace to find your note. Are you remembering any of this now? Because if you aren't, I suggest you start. Your life depends on it."

"Who are you to threaten me, you knave!" To my disconcertion, he reacted as any noble confronted by an inferior would. Heedless of my knife, he took a furious step at me, though he made the mistake of glancing at his discarded doublet on the bed. If he had a weapon, it was there. He'd have to come through me to get it. I gave him time to consider his options, even as I began to consider the possibility that his display of outrage was sincere. Not only would a guilty man have shown more caution, there was nothing in his demeanor to suggest any surprise that I was still alive.

If it had not been Courtenay, who had tried to poison me?

I shook my contemplations aside, lowering my blade.

Courtenay's expression shifted; with a lift of his brow, he pointed to a flagon on the side table. "May I? I'm parched."

I nodded, watching him move to the table and fill a goblet. He eyed me over its rim. "I am sorry to hear about your . . . squire, was it?" He took a sip. "But seeing as I had nothing to do with his death and you're still here, you must have another purpose in mind. Could it be blackmail, perhaps?"

"Now that you mention it," I said coldly.

"Then you're wasting your time. Contrary to how it appears, just because you found me in this disreputable establishment doesn't mean I swive boys." He gave me a languid smile. "But I know plenty of men at court who do. Shall I give you their names?"

I wasn't taken in by his flippant manner. "I don't care who or what you swive. I want answers, and you're going to give them to me."

"Oh, my. That almost sounds like a threat." He downed the contents of his goblet and set it back on the table with the exasperated air of a man obliged to engage in a tedious conversation. "Answers, you say? For whom? Your master, Renard, perhaps?"

"He does have the queen's ear," I replied, and before I had time to react, Courtenay flew at me, his hand closed about a long, slim dagger he'd lifted unseen from the side table. He aimed the blade at my stomach; as I swerved to avoid being stabbed, he kicked at my legs, knocking me to my knees. I dropped my poniard. I was trying to retrieve it while avoiding him and getting back on my feet when he leapt on top of me, yanking my head back by my hair. He slid his knife against my throat; I felt its bite abrade my skin.

"I don't like being accosted by common blackguards like you," he whispered, and the feral glee in his voice was more unnerving than the sudden warm seep of blood down my neck. "I'll ask you once, and if I don't like what I hear, I will slit your throat: *Who sent you?*"

Without hesitation, I whispered, "Elizabeth. She sent me."

Chapter Twelve

He still had me by the hair, but as I felt his grip ease at the sound of her name, I curbed my impulse to heave him off me and strike back. I had an entire childhood of experience to draw upon, years of being waylaid and thrashed by the Dudley brood. These men of so-called good birth were all the same: They assumed someone like me would always capitulate to their superior force.

I'd let Courtenay go on thinking that, at least for a short while.

"Elizabeth?" he echoed. "Come now, you'll have to do better than that. Why would our princess entrust her affairs to a grubby little street cur like you?"

I was finding it increasingly difficult to stay still. He'd drunk more than his fair share this evening; I could feel his grip quivering through his blade, and I didn't want to end up with my throat slashed in this godforsaken brothel because he let his knife slip. I told myself to wait, that the cut he'd inflicted was superficial, a mere nick; the throat always bled a lot. I'd been cut countless times while being shaved. This was no worse. Something ferocious was building inside me, though. He represented everything I'd come to detest—a fop who believed he had the right to bully his way through life with impunity, to treat with contempt anyone he deemed beneath him. If he hadn't left the poisoned note in my room, it was only because he lacked imagination, for he was perfectly capable of killing me without a second thought.

I'd had enough of men like him.

"That's the second time you've called me a cur. And I happen to like dogs," I said, and I slammed his rib cage with a backward jab of my elbow while simultaneously heaving up my back to knock him askew. Pivoting on my knees, I grasped him by the arm and wrenched it down, forcing his blade away from me. To my unpleasant surprise, he proved stronger than he looked, though I had caught him unawares. As he grappled with the sudden reversal in our positions, I yanked him to his feet with his arm up behind him, forcing him to release his dagger, which clattered at my feet.

"I can break it," I said in his ear, and I wrenched his arm higher. He cried out. I kicked his ankles apart, steadying his stance. "Or we can come to an arrangement. Your choice."

I yanked again. As I did, I pawed at the floor with my foot, dragging my poniard to me. I would have to release him in order to grab it, and I knew the moment I did he'd seize the advantage. Counting to four under my breath, I let him loose and leapt for the poniard, rearing up with it, slashing the air to stave him off. He backed away, cradling his wrist; he didn't even try to go for the other dagger. Apparently I'd inflicted damage.

He grimaced and jerked his chin at the side table. "I—I need wine. My arm hurts."

"This time," I said, "let me pour it." I yanked his doublet off the bed and threw it into a corner. Then I motioned him to sit on a stool by the bed, keeping my gaze on him as I poured from the flagon. He took the goblet gingerly, his wrist already starting to swell. In an hour at most, he'd be in severe discomfort.

"You'll need to get that treated," I told him. "Ice is best. Lucky for you, there's plenty of it." I paused. "Tell me about your friendship with Robert Dudley." I went tense, anticipating his reaction; all I received in return was a scowl.

"I have no idea who you're talking about."

"I'd reconsider if I were you. I overheard you, remember, in the passageway with the princess? I know you're working with Dudley. I also know the queen rejected your suit to marry her, which gives you plenty of motivation. What I want to know is what you plan."

Panic flashed across his face. "You're mad. We're not planning anything."

"No? Then perhaps you can explain why you're scheduled to deliver a book to Dudley with a letter from Princess Elizabeth hidden inside it?"

He couldn't contain his startled gasp. "How—how do you know about that?"

"She told me. Oh, and she wants her letter back. In fact, she insists on it."

He recoiled, even as his tone turned belligerent. "She insists, does she? She thinks she can change her mind and I'll get her letter back from Dudley, easy as that?"

I went still. "What do you mean by that?"

He gave me a malicious smile. "I mean it was delivered today. Dudley's been waiting for it, and he isn't going to change his course just because she's had a pang of regret. He knows what is coming. He knows the moment the queen announces her be-

trothal to Philip of Spain it'll be the end for him and his brothers. Renard will demand the head of every traitor in the Tower
as a wedding gift."

I went cold. "Why would he need a letter from her? *What* is
he planning?

Courtenay shrugged. "I couldn't say. I merely deliver—" I
lunged, leveling my blade under his chin with one hand as I
kicked his legs apart and grabbed hold of his injured wrist with
the other. I twisted hard enough to wring out an agonized cry.

"If you think that hurts," I said, "just imagine what the rack
must feel like. You're already marked, my lord, though you don't
know it. Though I secretly work for the princess, Don Renard
hired me not a day ago to find evidence that would put you back
in the Tower. And in my current mood, I'm thinking I just
might oblige him."

His eyes bulged. "Renard? He . . . he's marked *me*?"

"He believes you're behind a plot against the queen. But we
know better, don't we? We know your friend Dudley is the real
mastermind. So, my lord, help me and I'll help you."

His breathing turned shallow. Sweat beaded his ashen brow.
He looked frantically past me to the door, as if he awaited some
impromptu rescue. I was surprised myself that his beast of a manservant hadn't barged in by now, if only to see if his master was
still alive. Evidently Edward Courtenay didn't inspire much in
the way of loyalty.

I tightened my grip on his wrist. "I don't have all night."

"I already told you," he gasped through his teeth. "I don't
know anything—"

I twisted again; this time, he let out a piercing scream.

"Last time: What does Dudley plan?"

"No. God, please. Stop. I swear, I don't know." He was

panting, his legs thrashing between mine. "He doesn't confide in me. I just do as he asks."

"What does he ask?"

"To gain Elizabeth's confidence, that is all."

I eyed him. "You're lying."

"No. Don't!" Though I had his wrist and he was a mere half inch from being impaled under his chin by my knife, the pain must have grown bad enough for him to actually fling himself backward off the stool and go crashing to the floor. I had to let go and leap aside to avoid being tangled in his fall, looking down at him as he cowered at my feet. When he spoke, his tone was anything but repentant.

"You fool," he said. "Kill me if you want to, but I can't tell you anything more. Only Dudley knows what he's about. I just convey his letters!"

The undeniable desperation in his avowal gave me pause. I didn't trust him, not for a second. He could be lying through his teeth; he probably was, but he was my sole conduit to Dudley, and unless I was prepared to torture him, I had to strike a pact.

"Get up," I said.

He staggered to his feet, his wrist hanging at an odd angle.

"Tell me about these letters. I assume you meant you both send and receive them? How many are there? Who does Dudley write to? Who writes back?"

He swayed where he stood, his cheeks sucked in. He was colorless. I feared he might actually faint. "Not many," he managed to utter, a pinch in his voice. "Six or seven, back and forth, I think. I don't remember. We hide them in different things; my manservant, he delivers and retrieves the parcels. All the letters were sealed. No addresses, just the names of shires written on them. I didn't read any. I just did as he bade and waited here on the nights specified for the couriers to pick them up."

He hadn't read Dudley's letters? If he was telling the truth, I couldn't decide whether he was the biggest idiot I had ever met or the most naive.

"Which shires?" I asked tersely. "Think: Where did the letters go?"

His breathing was labored; the pain must be excruciating by now. "There was one for Sussex. Another for Surrey. Also Oxfordshire and Berkshire, I think. Suffolk, too. He arranged everything beforehand; I didn't ask questions. Why would I? The couriers paid me. I sent half the coin to Dudley and kept the other half. Living at court isn't cheap; my allowance from the queen barely covers my expenses."

I almost rolled my eyes. "I can imagine. So you have no idea who those letters went to, but if Dudley arranged the delivery without you, he must have someone else working for him, to alert his recipients that the letters were waiting with you. Who?"

Courtenay let out a moan and staggered to the bed. He sat, grimacing. "How would I know? Do you think he lacks for eager menials? Any lowly guard or urchin who cleans out the bilge pits in the Tower will oblige a noble prisoner if he pays enough."

I turned it all over in my mind, like the pieces of a disjointed jigsaw. Robert Dudley was not only receiving letters but sending letters out, to parties invested enough to ensure the earl's silence through bribes. Those payments Courtenay sent must also furnish Dudley with the means to pay whoever he used to advance word to his conspirators. Not that any of this made me feel reassured. All those shires Courtenay had mentioned surrounded London, from north to south; Dudley must be hatching a conspiracy. From the sound of it, it was something big.

But what? How did Elizabeth fit into it?

"I must speak to him," I said abruptly.

He gaped. "Are you mad? You're nobody to him! Why would he tell you anything?"

"I'm not as much of a nobody as you might think," I replied, and he flinched. "You're going to get me inside the Tower. Or would you rather I reported what you just told me?"

"No." He took a step to me. "I'll do it. I'll help you. Only I can't do it overnight. My manservant . . . he knows the right warders to bribe. He has to arrange it."

"You have twenty-four hours. Your man should be able to find me." I paused for a moment to let my words sink in. "If you even think of betraying me, believe me when I say Renard will get everything he needs. Do we understand each other, my lord?"

I turned to the door. He called out in a wavering voice, "Remember what you promised! If I do this, you'll not let Renard set his dogs on me."

I glanced at him. "Use ice. And refrain from riding for at least a week, lest that arm stiffens and you lose its use. I'll send your manservant up to assist you."

Wrenching open the door as he collapsed on the bed, I walked out.

His henchman waited at the bottom of the stairs. The common room was crowded now, a multitude of masked men in various stages of undress, dancing and kissing and cornering each other in the smoky shadows.

"That took longer than I thought," he remarked. He glanced at the bloodstains on my collar. "He must like you. He only cuts his favorites."

"You should attend to him," I retorted, and I strode past him, out of the common room. Retrieving my sword and cloak from the doorman, who gave me another knowing leer, I evaded his grab for my codpiece and plunged into the night.

Light snow was falling. I drew in drafts of the cold air, as if I could rinse the filth of the encounter with the earl from my person. As I trod back over the frozen river, whose surface felt decidedly less solid to me, I realized I was being followed and put my hand on my sword. However, as before on the bridge, Courtenay's manservant seemed content to remain a distance behind, making more noise on the ice-hardened snow than a professional should. As soon as I reached the shore, I whirled about with my sword in hand.

Swirling snow filled the empty, icy expanse I had just traversed.

I tossed the stolen mantle in King's Street and hastened, shivering, to the palace. Climbing the icy staircase to my room, I went still, a knot clogging my throat.

Then I forced myself to unlock the door.

Everything appeared the same as I had left it. Then, as I stepped inside and lit the tallow, I realized Sybilla had been here; she had returned to tidy my scattered belongings, setting the coffer and stool upright and folding Peregrine's cloak carefully on my cot.

My knees gave way underneath me. Sinking to the floor, I dragged the cloak from the bed, and, burying my face in folds that still smelled faintly of him, I wept.

Chapter Thirteen

I awoke with a profound sense of loss and, more prosaically, a rumble in my stomach. Belatedly, I recalled that I'd not eaten so much as a crumb of bread since that greasy meal in the tavern off the bridge.

I padded in my hose to the basin, cracked the layer of thin ice, and splashed water on my face. Catching my reflection in my hand mirror, I went still. My newly trimmed beard could not disguise my haggard appearance. There were dark smudges under my red-rimmed eyes; my skin was the hue of old parchment. I looked as if I'd aged years.

I turned to my bed. I had fallen asleep, clutching Peregrine's cloak. Now I had to fold it and put it aside, resisting my sorrow as I sniffed it and realized it was already losing his smell. I tucked it into the coffer, biting the inside of my mouth to stop my tears as I fished around for fresh hose and shirt. I'd brought few clothes in my stubborn refusal to admit I might be at court longer than I wanted to. Now I'd have to launder my soiled linens and—

Kate.

I rocked back on my heels. So much had happened in so

short a time, I'd not spared her a thought. What she was doing at this moment? Had she already been to the stables to see to the horses? Or gone to tend her winter herb garden, which she protected as tenderly as she would its eventual spring shoots? If I shut my eyes, I could see her wrapped in her mantle, reaching a gloved hand down toward the frosted earth . . .

She must be told. She loved Peregrine. Somehow, I had to get word to her.

Drawing out my writing utensils, I composed a letter with the simple but painstaking cipher Cecil had devised for me. Employing the manual on basic animal husbandry that I'd brought in my bag, the cipher consisted of the first and third letters of each line of the manual's odd-numbered pages. My note could only be read by someone with a matching book; in this case, Cecil himself. Once I was finished, I folded the paper. I had no seal.

A knock came at the door. I leapt for my sword, unsheathing it. Then I heard Rochester say, "Master Beecham? Are you awake?"

I set my sword aside. He stood outside, a pile of folded clothing in his arms. He gave me a forlorn smile. "Mistress Darrier mentioned you might have need of fresh clothes after . . ." He swallowed. "I trust these will fit. Her Majesty wishes you to join her in the chapel after you break your fast." He shook his head. "Such a terrible affair. She was most upset when I told her. She wants the matter looked into thoroughly. That a mere boy could have—"

"Her Majesty is too kind," I interrupted gently, "but there is no need for an inquest. Peregrine and I took our midday meal on the bridge yesterday. He must have eaten something tainted. He complained of stomach pains on the ride back."

"Ah." Though Rochester did his best to conceal it, I could see his relief. He had enough to contend with at court without a possible murder to investigate. "That is indeed unfortunate. It's never safe to eat at the stalls. The meat: You never know where it came from. Cats, dogs, rats—in times of need, people will cook anything. Poor lad."

I nodded. I needed him to go. I wasn't sure I could maintain my composure if he kept talking. "Shall I get dressed?" I suggested.

He nodded hastily. "I'll await you in the privy gallery."

As soon as he left, I pressed my knuckles to my temples, staving off a wave of utter despair. Unraveling the bundle of clothing, I found a plain but well-cut wool doublet, breeches, hose, and underlinens.

I washed thoroughly before I dressed and ran a comb through my tangled hair. I needed to see a barber, too. After rubbing the crust of snow and dirt from my boots, I slipped my letter to Kate into my doublet and went to the gallery. Rochester brought me to a side chamber to partake of bread, cheese, beer, and dried fruit. I was grateful he didn't mention Peregrine again, filling the awkward silence between us instead with chat of the weather and the rarity of the Thames freezing over, until the hour came to join the queen.

It was a long trajectory, through an upper loggia overlooking the barren gardens and several galleries where courtiers congregated to pass the time. As we walked, I asked Rochester about the Spaniard I'd encountered the previous day.

His mouth pursed. "That would be the Duke of Feria. He's a trusted noble and confidant of—" He stopped himself. "A hard man," he muttered, "as all these Spaniards are apt to be. I understand he wasn't helpful to you."

"He was taken aback." I realized Rochester had almost admitted aloud that Feria was a confidant of Prince Philip. "I'm not sure how I'd have reacted in his place."

"A sight better than he did, I'm sure," said Rochester. "Mistress Dormer was the one who fetched me from the hall, scared out of her wits, while he stood there as if . . ." He sighed. "I suppose there's no use stirring up what we can do nothing about."

"You're a good man," I said.

"Somebody has to be" was his reply. "I fear there are too few of us these days."

I debated for a moment. I had a sudden suspicion about Rochester that I needed to confirm. It was a calculated risk but worth the attempt. He could always refuse.

"I have a missive I must send." I removed the letter from my doublet. "A friend of mine should be told of my squire's passing. Could I impose on you to . . . ?"

He came to a halt. "I suppose you'll want it sealed and sent by courier?"

"If possible. Can you see it delivered to Theobalds House in Hertfordshire?" I did not elaborate; as color crept into his fleshy cheeks, I knew without a word spoken that he had recognized the name of Cecil's manor. I almost smiled, despite the circumstances.

Rochester looked at me. Still without speaking, he took the missive and tucked it into the large pouch at his belt. "Just this once," he said, turning to resume our walk. "I ask that you keep it between us. I'm not authorized to use our couriers without leave."

"I'm very grateful," I said softly.

In the spacious chamber where I'd selected plum velvet for Mary, the queen and her women sat before the hearth. I bowed on the threshold; the queen rose and came to me. She wore black, her high peaked collar framing her drawn features; she looked tired as she took my hands in hers in a maternal gesture and said, "I am deeply grieved by your loss, Master Beecham. No child should ever die thus." Her voice wavered. "No child should die."

"Majesty," I murmured. "I am deeply honored." As I spoke, I lifted my gaze to see Lady Clarencieux and young Jane Dormer in the background. They, too, were in black and regarded me sadly. Standing apart, the alabaster hue of her skin in striking contrast to her dark gown, was Sybilla. She inclined her head, as though we had only just met.

Mary said, "I've ordered that your squire be interred in All Hallows Church. His body is there; you may go and pay him your final respects later, if you wish. The burial is scheduled for the afternoon. This private mass is for us."

I recognized this singular privilege. Royalty never attended funerals, much less those of commoners; Mary's decision to hear a mass in honor of Peregrine was exceptional, a display both of the esteem in which she held me and of her innate kindness.

It brought a lump to my throat as we proceeded into the chapel. The scent of incense lay thick in the enclosed air, and while this private place of worship was not large, a deep sense of intimacy pervaded it. Frail winter light pierced the jeweled stained-glass windows set high in the stone walls, gilding the painted columns of the transept and carved angels entwined above the purple-velvet-draped altar.

I'd never heard a Catholic service before, but as I took my place in the pew and the priest began to recite the litany, the rhythmic cadence of his Latin brought me unexpected peace. I allowed myself to release the fury and sorrow for a few moments and pay homage to the boy I would always remember, my intrepid friend and companion whom I'd not valued as much as I should.

"God in heaven," said the priest, "those who die will live in your divine presence. We lift our prayers to you and your son, our savior, Jesus Christ, who died for our sins and now lives in eternity. May the souls of our beloved departed ones rejoice in your kingdom, where tears are wiped away and your praises are sung forever and ever. Amen."

I made the sign of the cross, startled by my instinctual memory of the act. Mistress Alice had taught me in my childhood; she had remained steadfast to the vanquished Roman practices of old, but it had been years since I had performed it. Though it was ingrained into the very weft of our world, the root of hatred and disorder, I'd rarely had the luxury of considering my place in the afterlife; I'd been too busy trying to protect my hide in this one. Still, as the queen rose from her pew and I marked the genuine devotion on her face, I envied her ability to seek solace in dusty, time-honored rituals. No matter how much faith I lacked, I would never forget what she had done for me this day.

Outside the chapel, I bowed again over her hand. "May your squire find swift passage through purgatory into the kingdom of heaven," Mary murmured and she returned with her ladies to her rooms. I stared after her for a long moment and was about to walk away when the apartment door reopened. Sybilla emerged. She quickly shut the door behind her, with a furtiveness that made me think she was slipping out unseen.

"Shall we walk?" she asked.

We moved into a gallery, where the chill seeping through the walls was smothered by ornamental tapestries, smoke-darkened paintings, and wrought-iron sconces festooned in melted cascades of wax. The evening tapers, now burned to nubs, were being collected by servants to be melted and recast, candles being one of the court's largest expenses. Icy sunlight filtered through window bays overlooking the gardens; beyond the mullioned panes arched a brilliant cloudless sky—one of those astonishing skies that turned the winter-bound landscape into a glittering wonder and almost made you forget the long, bitter months yet to come.

At length, Sybilla broke the quiet. "Did you keep your appointment?"

"Yes." I paused. "Although it did not go quite as I expected."

"Few things do." I met her violet-blue eyes. Her brow creased. "You seem perturbed. Did you discover something that troubles you?"

Now that we were alone together, I recalled how she had touched me in my chamber moments after Peregrine had died in my arms, how she had been concerned for me and offered to help. I'd just discovered that Rochester was more than he appeared; that while he loved and cared for the queen, he evidently didn't wish to see Elizabeth fall to Renard's wiles.

Might this enigmatic woman also be of value to me?

"I want to thank you for your assistance yesterday," I said. "It was very kind, considering I am a stranger to you." As I spoke, I could trace the stroke of her hand with the cloth over my bare skin, her throaty whisper: *Tell me who you are* . . .

"There's no need to thank me. I know what it is like to lose someone." She came to a halt before an alcove. "And I hope we're not strangers anymore. Indeed, I know far less of you than you do of me. No doubt you've already been apprised of my own misfortunes."

"No," I said, surprised. "I assure you, I have not."

"But Renard hired you. Surely he made some mention of me?"

"He did, but he didn't say anything . . . Well, he did say one thing. He told me you were spoken for. I assumed he meant to warn me away."

"Did you?" She gave a taut smile and sat on the window seat. As I perched beside her, she arranged her skirts. "Simon Renard is my benefactor," she said. "He took pity on my mother, sister, and me after we left England." She lifted her gaze to me. The impact was almost visceral; I'd never met any woman except Elizabeth who had such intense purpose in her expression. "My father and three brothers were executed for participating in the Pilgrimage of Grace. The king placed our family under attainder of treason."

I knew about the Pilgrimage of Grace. It started in Yorkshire as an initial demonstration to challenge King Henry's supremacy over the Church and his confiscation of its benefices. Anne Boleyn was dead and Henry had wed Jane Seymour, but it hadn't stopped his and Lord Cromwell's drive to accumulate ecclesiastic wealth. Henry placated the Yorkshire dissenters by promising to hear their grievances. Once he fulfilled his promise, he had Cromwell dispatch an army against them.

Over two hundred men and women in Yorkshire had died by the king's command.

"I was just a child," said Sybilla, "but I learned firsthand what defiance can bring. The king did not impose punishment directly on us because we were women, but the result was still the same. His attainder left us penniless, without hope of a future. So my mother took us abroad, first to France and later to Spain."

I recalled Jane Dormer's spiteful words the night of the feast: *And you, my lady, should be more careful, given your family's history . . .*

"Is that where you met Renard?" I asked. "He mentioned that he'd served as ambassador to the French court."

"Yes. He saw us settled in Spain." She paused, as if the memory pained her. "We had nothing to commend us, but he had heard of my father and brother's actions. Those who died in York were declared traitors here, but abroad, in Catholic courts, they were revered as martyrs. Renard found my mother a post in the Spanish Hapsburg court as lady-in-waiting to the empress; my sister and I became his wards. When the empress died a few years later, we attended Charles's daughters, the infantas. It was at Renard's behest that I came here to serve Her Majesty."

"I see." I did not betray my curiosity. She was Renard's ward: It explained his covetousness of her. Why, though, was she confiding in me?

I decided to opt for the direct approach. "I'm not sure why you're telling me this."

She tilted her head thoughtfully before she leaned close. Her distinctive perfume flooded my senses. "I told you, I want to help you."

I sat still. "I'm afraid I don't understand."

"Oh," she said softly, "I think you do. You were almost poisoned because of it. You must have considered by now that the man who left that note in your room is the same one who hired you. After all, Renard's ultimate goal is to—" She suddenly drew back as a burst of laughter preceded a group of courtiers entering the gallery.

In their midst, her hood crumpled about her shoulders, her hair like damp flame, walked Elizabeth.

Urian tugged on the lead in her hand. Her laughter rang out, high and effervescent. As she neared us, she twirled about to wag her finger at a tall man in dark damask, wearing a large feathered cap. "Enough of that, my lord. I vow, one day you'll go too far. Do you think me a hive to take in your honeyed words?"

It was then that I realized the man bore his arm in a black silk sling.

Edward Courtenay.

Disbelief kept me frozen to my seat. He did not look much worse for the arm-twisting I'd given him; that ridiculous sling seemed donned almost as an accessory as he made a move toward Elizabeth with his free hand and she tossed her head, dancing away. The others accompanying them were also young and privileged, strutting with costumed elegance. Elizabeth's ladies trailed behind, looking less enthusiastic.

Sybilla started to her feet. "Get up!" she hissed at me. As I rose, I bit back my fury. Gossip could spread faster than lice at court, but surely Elizabeth didn't yet know about Peregrine. She wouldn't be laughing and sauntering with Courtenay if she did. Nevertheless, I tasted iron in the back of my throat. Even if she didn't know, how could she continue to indulge Courtenay? Did she deliberately invoke disaster?

She acted as if she hadn't seen us like statues in the alcove, until Urian barked in joyous recognition and tore the lead from her hand, leaping toward me.

Elizabeth stopped. She turned to us. As I grappled with the dog, I murmured, "Your Grace," and at my side Sybilla dropped into a curtsy.

Courtenay strode up, saw me petting Urian, and swerved angrily to Elizabeth to hiss, "Is that him?" She gave a terse nod. Caressing the dog's chilled silvery fur, I braved a look at her. Her eyes had gone cold; I knew that look. She was warning me not to say a word.

"Fancy that," guffawed Courtenay. "So the dirty cur did not lie. But really, cousin Bess, you must choose your dogs more carefully next time. This one's a rogue."

Only her quick, probing glance at Sybilla betrayed Elizabeth's anxiety. I suddenly understood. Courtenay must have questioned her about me, demanding to know if I was her hireling before complying with my request. The man was bold; I had to give him that. I'd held a knife to his throat, nearly broken his arm, and threatened to report everything I knew if he didn't do as I bid, and still he'd taken the chance.

Now Elizabeth was doing what she must to protect me.

She yanked at the lead—"Urian, come!"—and proceeded down the gallery.

Courtenay turned to me with a sneer. "Fancy that. I had a mind to have you cut into pieces so small not even your mother would recognize you. Now it seems I must play along. Tomorrow at the stable gate, at the stroke of one." He cast an appraising look at Sybilla. "My lady Darrier," he purred, "if I were you, I'd be more circumspect in choosing those with whom I idle away my time. We wouldn't want anyone to think you're consorting with the enemy, now would we?"

He clucked his tongue in mock reproof before he strode after Elizabeth. As the princess's ladies moved past us, I caught sight of her favored matron, Blanche Parry, among them. She looked haggard.

My hands curled into fists. I almost forgot Sybilla was at my side until I heard her say, "She's as reckless as her mother Anne Boleyn ever was, and as heedless of danger. But if she continues to play this game, no amount of courage can save her. The earl is without scruple; he will lead her straight to disaster."

I drew in a shallow breath, mastering my emotion. I realized I, too, could be in acute peril now, seeing as I'd just been unmasked by the earl, callously revealed as Elizabeth's secret agent before a woman I hardly knew—a woman who, by her own admission, was beholden to Renard for her living.

"Why do you say that?" I looked at her. "Do you know the earl personally? He spoke as if you did."

She smiled. "I know *of* him; who at court does not? He was rather vociferous about his aspirations, declaring to all who cared to listen that he considered himself the most suitable candidate to wed the queen, encouraged by his ally on the council, Bishop Gardiner. I also know, though it's far less public, that Mary was amenable to the possibility until the Hapsburg delegation arrived. Then she rejected Courtenay outright. He's not apt to forgive the insult; I think he uses Princess Elizabeth to instill such fear of an uprising in her sister's name that Mary will return her consideration to him."

There was no avoiding her intimation now. She had divulged too much knowledge of matters that she should know nothing about.

"You are well informed," I said. "I understand now why you thought Renard might have told me about you. He's using you to spy on the queen, isn't he?"

She did not flinch, didn't even try to feign protest. "I'm not proud of it, but yes, I spy for him." She paused, meeting my stare. "The fact that he didn't tell you about me means more than you think. He must not trust you. Indeed, I believe he is the one who wants you dead."

I remembered the words on the paper: *You cannot save her.* Had it been Renard's message? Had he decided to hire me because the queen had ordered it, only to then do away with me? If so, then he probably suspected that I was, in fact, Elizabeth's man.

"I have no doubt someone wants me dead," I replied. "But at the moment, I'm more interested in why you are warning me against the very man you work for."

Though her tone didn't change, the tightening of her mouth betrayed a carefully contained vehemence. "Because I detest him. Since I was a child, I've been bound to his will. He made me spy for him at the Hapsburg court from the moment I shed my first blood; you have no idea what he's capable of. He'll ingratiate himself with the emperor at any cost, which is why he fears Courtenay. The earl would be a more popular choice for the queen's husband than any foreign prince, and if enough pressure is brought to bear, Mary could decide the same. Should that occur, Renard will lose the emperor's favor and be condemned to a lifetime of menial labor as an ambassador. Hence his order that I report everything I hear and see in the queen's apartments."

Her revelations sickened me, but I was not surprised. It was all part of Renard's drive to incriminate the earl—a rival for Mary's hand—as well as his seemingly preternatural influence over the queen herself. The royal apartments were her refuge; only there could she feel at ease. No doubt she'd discussed in the privacy of those rooms her fears concerning Philip, as well as her misgivings about Elizabeth and Courtenay.

Renard knew it all. Through Sybilla, he had bored his way into Mary's heart.

"I appreciate your candor," I said at length, "and I assure you, your confidences are safe with me. But if what you say is true, you mustn't risk yourself for my sake."

She gave a brief laugh. "You flatter me if you think I am that selfless. Renard spoke the truth when he told you I was spoken for. He would wed me to the Duke of Feria, that same grandee who watched your squire die in your arms. I'm to be sent to Spain to live out my days as Feria's wife—unless I act. I still have time, you see; my marriage is contingent on Renard fulfilling *all* of the emperor's demands. Only then will Feria consent to take me as his bride. I do not intend to waste whatever time I have left."

Dread coiled about me. "What demands must Renard fulfill?"

"You already know. His Imperial Majesty doesn't much care for his son to marry an older queen with a younger, heretic sister as her heir—not if said sister will wreck his plans for England if the queen dies without a child. Renard must do more than put Philip in Mary's bed; he must ensure that Elizabeth does not survive it."

I did not reply at first. I gauged her in silence, aware that she could be trying to mislead me, luring me into compliance so she could betray me to Renard. I found only a stark candor in her eyes, almost as if she were indifferent to the devastating truths she had just confessed. I knew she wasn't. Under her elegant fa-cade smoldered an ardor for vengeance more than capable of destroying anyone who came between her and her freedom. Ardor like hers could be a potent weapon.

"It seems you know everyone's secrets," I finally said.

"Not everyone's," she replied, "but I do know Renard's. I un-derstand how he operates. I will use whatever I can against him. I want him ruined. I want him chained to some backwater post for the rest of his days. I'll not be beholden to him or any man again, not if I can avoid it."

My wariness thawed into admiration. She might be a stranger to me in many respects, but I understood her, for I had felt the same helplessness myself. Ever since I'd been old enough to realize the world had no empathy for the powerless, I'd also fought to survive, just as Sybilla did. She sought freedom after years of living under Renard's heel, as I'd once lived under Robert Dudley's. Renard was cruel, calculating, and ruthless—like the man I'd served. He believed he deserved better and was willing to do anything to achieve it.

I felt the collapse of my brittle defense. As if she sensed it, Sybilla bridged the space between us with a single step. This time, I couldn't evade her touch, even as a fleeting image of Kate went through me. I was riveted by Sybilla's gaze, by the heat of her proximity . . .

"Don't you see?" she asked. "I must be free of him. You seek to protect the princess, and I seek to save myself, so let us work together. Let me help you find the proof you need."

"No," I said haltingly. I tried to step back. "I cannot ask this of—"

"You did not ask." She leaned to me and quenched my breath. Her lips were like scorched velvet; as they grazed mine, desire exploded in me, hot and fierce.

Without another word, she turned away and went back down the gallery, the hem of her black gown swirling about her feet. In minutes she'd rounded the corner and vanished, yet as I stood motionless, I felt as if she were still before me, as if she had branded her very presence onto my skin, and I had already began to surrender to the unthinkable.

* * *

I returned to my room, my mind in a whirlwind. Grabbing my cloak and cap, I went to the stables, saddled Cinnabar, and cantered from the palace. I kept seeing Sybilla in my head; I had to fight back the memory of what I had felt with her. I couldn't lose my self-control. Not now. Not with so much at stake. It was a momentary failing: I was grieving Peregrine and suffering the effects of living under prolonged tension at court. I was flesh and bone, beset by the frailties of any man; it did not mean I was faithless. I wouldn't lie to myself by denying my attraction to Sybilla, but I would never betray Kate, nor take advantage of a woman so clearly entrapped by her circumstances.

Still, I found myself riding through London in a haze, besieged by my own inner tumult, almost passing the church of All Hallows. I reined Cinnabar to an abrupt halt, causing him to snort in displeasure at my sharp pull on his mouth.

I could not think of it now. I had to focus on the heart-crushing task ahead.

Constructed of lichen-weathered stone, with its great turreted spire, the church was well appointed. It also offered an unsettling view of the nearby Tower. I stared toward that hulking fortress, like a closed fist behind its curtain wall, and wondered which of those tiny arrow slits marked the Dudleys' cell.

I would soon find out, I thought with a shudder, and I turned away to enter the cavernous church through a narrow doorway. I did not expect what I found. All Hallows was a burial place for those executed in the Tower; Sir Thomas More, martyr to King Henry's break with Rome, lay here. The echo of past cruelties permeated its ancient walls, but so did astonishing beauty, manifest in its painted archways, gilded statues, and glorious stained-glass windows. The glory of the Roman faith had never been fully erased here, and when I explained to the rotund priest who hastened to greet me why I'd come, he murmured platitudes and led me down worn stone steps into an icy crypt.

As I beheld the small wood coffin on its chipped dais, a lump filled my throat.

"Her Majesty paid for everything," the priest said with evident pride. "Though I understand the boy had no rank to commend him, she's insisted he be put to rest here until the ground thaws. A plot is set aside for him in the churchyard, away from the pit where common traitors go, all at her expense. She's been most generous to pay such honor to—"

I lifted my hand. "Please. Might I have a moment alone?"

With an offended pout, he nodded and retreated.

I stared upon Peregrine's waxen face, the only visible part of his body in its winding sheet. I had never seen him so still; as I reached out a trembling hand to touch the lifeless curls on his brow, I half-expected him to laugh and sit up. The faint tang of the herbs with which his body had been washed was the only sign of life in this place of stone. As I finally took it in and let myself accept that Peregrine was truly gone, a choked sob escaped me.

I stood over him for what seemed an eternity before I heard the priest shuffle in. He cleared his throat with begrudging respect. "The hour grows late; I must close my doors soon. If there is nothing more, the coffin will be sealed shut and left here till spring."

I nodded and made myself step aside, thinking I should have brought something to put in with him, some memento for him to have in the dark.

"Good-bye, sweet friend," I whispered. "I will avenge you."

Dusk hung over the city. I rode in silence back to Whitehall, stabled Cinnabar, and paid the groom extra to watch over him and Peregrine's horse. I tarried a while, trying to take comfort in the animals' tacit company, the horses sniffing at me as they sensed the bottomless well that had opened inside me.

That night, I could not sleep. I sat cross-legged on the floor of my room as the tallow guttered low in its oil, honing my sword with my whetstone until my fingers bled and every muscle ached, but I found no reprieve in the punishment of my body.

I could no longer control the stranger I was becoming.

Chapter Fourteen

Courtenay's manservant was waiting outside the postern gate when I rode out on Cinnabar at the stroke of one—a hulking figure seated on an enormous gray destrier, his black cloak enveloping him, its cowl drawn over his head to hide his ravaged face.

"Right on time," he said gruffly before he swerved onto the road that led to the Tower. Ice-hardened snow crunched under our horses' hooves. The day was clear, though a bracing wind made me glad of my layers of doublet and cloak, my scarf pulled up about my nose and mouth, and my cap shoved down about my ears.

I noted equal discomfort on the scowling faces of passing Londoners, the goodwives, merchants, and other citizens trudging over makeshift planks sunk in mires of slush, while vagabonds and beggars skulked, shivering, in doorways. I looked away from a cadaver, stripped naked and tossed on a midden, its limbs frozen solid, only to catch sight of a mange-ridden bitch herding four skeletal pups out of the way of an approaching cart. As the carter flayed his whip, the bitch yelped, grabbing two of the pups in her jaws and leaving the others to race into a nearby rookery of ramshackle edifices. I yanked Cinnabar aside to avoid trampling the cowering pups and was relieved when I looked over my shoulder and saw them darting, unharmed, after their mother.

"Lucky curs." The manservant swiveled his head in my direction. "By all accounts, they should be in somebody's stew pot by now."

I stared stonily at him. I had no doubt he'd have eaten those pups, too, straight out of the pot. I could see why Courtenay had hired him; with this beast at his side, the earl could prowl the most unsavory places in London and not fear for his life.

Though it was not the earl's life I was most concerned about.

Not forty-eight hours ago, this man had stalked me. I'd threatened him in the brothel and was blackmailing his master. Now we rode through the city, and while he'd kept his distance thus far, I was fully aware he might yet turn on me. Courtenay could have ordered him to make sure I never reached my destination.

He surprised me by grunting, "My name's Scarcliff. Hope you brought coin."

I nodded, resisting an urge to laugh. *That* was his name? I almost pitied the ugly oaf.

As if he read my thoughts, he gave me a disparaging grimace, his front teeth blackened and jagged. "You needn't worry. I have my orders. But you'll need to pay the yeomen at the gate and guards inside." He gestured to his saddlebag. "You'll take this in with you. Those who pay enough are allowed certain privileges, and the Dudleys get fresh linens every week, courtesy of his lordship. You'll deliver the bag to their quarters. I'll wait till the gates close at dusk. If you don't return by then, I'll see your horse back to the stables, but you're on your own."

His speech was less slurred than it had been at the brothel, no doubt because he was sober, but he still sounded as if he spat out pebbles instead of words. Nevertheless, I was slightly comforted that he did not harbor murderous intent. Of course, he might not need to. I was about to walk voluntarily into the most notorious and well-guarded prison in the realm, where countless men vanished, never to be seen again. If I didn't get out in time, it might do the job just as well as a blade between my ribs.

We approached the main causeway over the Tower moat. The Tower loomed before me, an enormous, forbidding sight, the domed turrets of its keep thrusting like the calcified fingers of a moribund giant from a surrounding warren of gatehouses, lesser towers, and impregnable walls.

My skin crawled. I'd never thought to set foot in this dreadful place again.

"I'd take off the scarf if I were you. Yeomen don't like visitors who hide their faces." As he spoke, Scarcliff shrugged back his own cowl, exposing his hideous, one-eyed visage. Seeing the destruction in daylight, I thought he must have survived some awful fiery battle.

I tore my gaze from him, unraveling the ice-flecked wool from my face. My cheeks were numb from the biting wind blowing off the river, though here the Thames ran deeper and had even started to thaw in parts, with chunks of broken ice bobbing in the dark water.

Various persons stood in line outside the gate, waiting to enter, their subdued chatter punctuated by an occasional mournful roar drifting from inside the crenellated barbican.

"Henry's old lions," said Scarcliff. "They don't much like being caged."

I shuddered. I couldn't imagine keeping a wild creature behind bars, though far worse happened every day in this city. I braced myself as we drew our horses to a halt. Scarcliff dismounted, trudged over the drawbridge with his lopsided gait, ignoring the startled glances in his direction from those in line. He reached the warder yeoman guarding the entrance. Two others checked the credentials of those seeking entrance; the warder appeared to recognize Scarcliff, heeding him attentively before giving a curt nod.

Scarcliff came back to me and unhooked the saddlebag. "You're the earl's man now, remember, so best act like it. The Dudleys are in the Beauchamp Tower off the inner ward. They like to take their exercise on the leads around this hour, but Lord Robert will be advised he has a visitor. I'll wait at the Griffin Tavern on Tower Street. Remember, I leave at dusk when the gates close—with or without you."

I clicked my tongue reassuringly as Scarcliff took my reins. I found it curious that while usually wary of strangers, Cinnabar did not seem averse to letting this particular stranger handle him. Then I hoisted the bag on my shoulder and moved to the portcullis, assaulted by a vivid memory of the last time I had seen it, slamming down like a fanged mouth on a crowd of frantic men. The Dudley steward Shelton had disappeared here that night, struggling in the crush, as guards galloped toward him, swinging maces and pikes . . .

I forced aside my ruminations, opening the bag for the yeoman to inspect. The scent of lavender rose from the wrapped parcel of linens. The yeoman stared at me. I thought he was going to question me before I remembered. As I fished coins from the purse at my belt, he said, "Through the Bell Tower and to your left into the ward." He let me pass. Behind me the waiting queue raised angry protest at my preferential treatment.

My boot heels struck hollow echoes upon the flagstones. Sentinels dressed in green uniforms sporting Tudor-rose badges, black-clad secretaries, and other official-looking persons moved around me, carving purposeful paths to various assignations. I recalled that the Tower was more than just a prison; within these walls were an armory, a treasury, a menagerie, and royal apartments. Like every royal fortress, it was governed by a strict bureaucracy, much like Whitehall itself, but as I passed the water gate through which the condemned entered by the river, I felt the walls close in on me, as if I were a rat in a maze.

I hurried up a flight of stairs to the inner ward. The massive White Keep stood to my right. Before me lay a cobblestone space hemmed in by towers and walls but open to the sky and festooned with stalls—an improvised marketplace where guild tradesmen took orders and vendors plied food, the air warmed by the odor of cooking fires. Livestock lowed in pens; everyone went about their business with brisk efficiency, circumventing an empty scaffold situated paces from the chapel, a grim reminder of the Tower's ultimate purpose.

I stopped in my tracks. Elizabeth's mother had died on that spot. Though there was no block, no hay to soak up the blood, in my imagination I saw it all, flashing in a tableau before me— Anne Boleyn's slim figure as she was blindfolded, the slow drop to her knees, and the swift, inescapable arc of the French executioner's sword . . .

Tearing my eyes away, I hastened to the Beauchamp Tower.

The guard at the entrance regarded me with the slovenly indifference of someone who needn't do much to earn his wage. His potbelly hung over his wide, studded belt as he slumped on a stool, a halberd propped against the wall. On the rickety table before him were the ruins of a meat pie and an open ledger. Ink-ing a pruned quill, he said in a toneless mumble, "Name. Occupation. Purpose."

Name. I hadn't thought of a name.

"Are ye daft?" He glared at me. "Name. Occupation. Purpose."

"Beecham," I said quickly, for it hardly mattered if I used another alias. "Body servant to his lordship, Edward Courtenay, Earl of Devon. By my lord's command, I bring linens for the prisoners."

"Oh. More linens, eh?" The guard snorted as he scrawled my information in the ledger. "Them Dudleys have the devil's own luck. We've got a hundred poor bastards rottin' underground and in the Ease, eaten by rats and drinking their own piss, but this lot dine like kings on the earl's purse, no matter that their father took the ax." He rummaged cursorily through the saddlebag, his fingers oily with pie grease. I suspected he did it on purpose, to soil the linens. He pushed the bag to me. "Their quarters are up the staircase," he said, but he didn't move out of my way until I doled out the requisite bribe.

As I climbed the stairs, the hilt of my hidden poniard dug into my calf. The Dudleys certainly enjoyed both privileges and risks, if this was all it took to get inside their quarters. I might have been a paid assassin, for all the guard knew. No wonder Courtenay found it easy to smuggle in books and letters. I could have carried a dozen on my person alone.

I also might have entered the hall in a manor, I thought, as I walked through a door on the landing into a vaulted room. The walls were adorned with thick, albeit faded, wool tapestries; there were carpets underfoot instead of the ubiquitous lousy rushes, and a fire crackled in the recessed hearth, staving off the chill. A low archway to the left led to sleeping chambers and a garderobe. Several chipped, high-backed chairs, stools, a reading lectern, and a long central table added to the illusion of domestic comfort, while a large mullioned embrasure admitted dusty light. Piles of books on the floor and a furry indent on a cushion by the hearth indicated the Dudleys had the means to keep boredom at bay; evidently it paid to be born on the right side of the blanket, even if one's family had a tendency to end up with their heads on spikes.

The room was empty. Unclasping my cloak, I draped it across a chair and set the bag on the table, eyeing the pile of books. I resisted the urge to search them for the one Elizabeth had given Courtenay. By now, her letter must have been taken.

I paced to the embrasure. Below me on a protected rampart, stretching between this tower and the next, moved a group of cloaked figures. I went still, recognizing Guilford Dudley's fair mop and the ginger coloring of his shorter and far less amiable brother Henry. Behind them trailed muscular Ambrose and the eldest of the Dudley brood, John, who bore the closest resemblance to their late father. Only Robert was missing, but I scarcely marked his absence, riveted by the unexpected sight of a slim female figure, her hood slipping from her head to reveal coiled gold-red tresses plaited about her head, a shade paler than her cousin Elizabeth's.

Lady Jane Grey, Guilford's wife, was with the four brothers.

John stumbled. As Jane put her hand to his back to steady him, a nearby servant holding a terrier on leash hurried to them. John leaned on the servant gratefully while Jane took the dog. Of the five boys, I knew John Dudley the least. The firstborn, he'd been educated at court, far from the castle where I'd been raised. I'd therefore rarely seen him and now recalled overhearing he was prone to fever, his lungs weakened from a bout of—

"Who are you?"

I spun around. Standing in the doorway was Lord Robert.

"Don't you recognize me, my lord?" I cast back my hood. "It hasn't been that long."

He paused, staring. Then he let out a hiss through his teeth, "Prescott!" and kicked the door shut behind him. He took a step toward me. The sight of him—taller than I recalled and much leaner, his raven-wing's hair shorn to his skull, accentuating the striking Dudley cheekbones and liquid black eyes—plunged me into the past, when I'd been an insignificant squire, unaware of my royal blood, dependent on him for my very survival.

"Well, well." He put a hand on his hip, eyeing me. "Imagine my surprise when I was told I had a visitor." His voice was tauntingly familiar, as if we'd only seen each other a few hours ago. "I've wondered what became of you and what it would be like to see you walk in here like a dog returning to its own vomit. But I never thought you'd actually do it. I never thought you'd be that stupid. Oh, and the guard downstairs? He isn't going to lift a finger to help you, so don't think of yelling. Whatever you paid him, I offered double."

I didn't doubt it. I refused to react to his threat, even as my heart started to pound. I pointed to the bag on the table. "I brought your linens."

"I see. Is that who you work for now? Are you Courtenay's latest bum-boy? You certainly move fast. They only let him out of here two months ago. Were you loitering outside the gates, waiting for the first pair of noble boots to lick?"

My anxiety faded. I should savor this moment. The wheel of fate had turned. Once, I'd been the defenseless one and he had all the power to strike against me at will, but I'd done him one better. I had won. It was time he knew it.

"I serve Princess Elizabeth now. I'm here to collect something of hers."

His lip curled, as if it meant little to him, but I sensed the violence lurking in his broad shoulders. If he decided to charge me, I'd have a time of it. He might look underfed, a shadow of the gorgeous favored son he'd once been, but he had the strength of a lifetime of privilege to draw upon, honed by years of horsemanship, archery, jousting, swordplay, and other costly recreations only the rich could afford. He'd always been gifted, both in his beauty and prowess. Six long months spent in this cage must have stoked his temper to a fiery pitch. After all the luxury and expectation, the aspirations of grandeur when his father ruled the realm, Robert Dudley had become a cornered man.

Cornered men were always dangerous.

His smile sliced across his lips. "So, you serve Elizabeth now. When did this occur, exactly? Before or after you betrayed me?"

"Does it matter?"

"It does to me. I should never have trusted you. I should have known a runt like you would have no concept of loyalty." He swerved to the sideboard and reached for a tarnished decanter. As he poured wine into a goblet, he kept his back to me. If he thought to lull me into lowering my guard, it wasn't going to work. I knew him too well.

"Let me get this clear." He turned around with a frown, as if I had presented a particularly vexing issue. "You work for her and she sent you here, to me? I find that odd, considering the last time she and I spoke she insulted me to my face. What were her words again?" He stared at me. "Surely you must remember. Though I didn't see you at the time, like the snake you are I'm sure you were hiding somewhere in the brush."

"I believe she said she'd rather die than let a lowborn Dudley rut in her bed," I replied, and I braced my entire body for his charge.

His face hardened, so that the bone structure under his taut skin seemed to show. "So, you *were* there. I'm impressed. You played me like a courtier. Just look"—he flung out his arm, sloshing wine from his goblet—"you're now free to hire yourself out to whomever you please, while I'm locked up waiting for the same ax that killed my father." His voice darkened. "And all because my family took pity on you, rather than throwing you down a well like you deserved."

"Are you blaming me for this?" I arched my brow. "Because if so, you do yourself a disservice. I didn't put you or your brothers in here. You did all that on your own."

His goblet froze halfway to his mouth. I had struck at his core; he could not refute that, more than greed or ambition, the Dudley belief in their infallibility had been their ruin.

"You speak the truth," he said at length, his voice dead quiet. "It's not as if you did anything but seek your advantage. Elizabeth always did have a weakness for subservience; she likes nothing better than to be fawned upon." He drank. "You said you came for something of hers. What is it?" He held up a hand. "No. Don't tell me." He smiled. "A letter."

The contempt in his tone enraged me. I had to stop myself from being the one who lunged first. "Because of that letter, she's in grave danger. Ambassador Renard seeks evidence against her. He suspects her and Courtenay of plotting against the queen. Your own head also stands to roll if you don't help me. I know very well that you're behind it."

"Oh? I fail to see how I can be suspect. Am I not a prisoner already?"

"Condemned men have the least to lose. Courtenay also told me everything." I watched his feigned indifference slip from his face like a poorly fitted mask. "I know about the other letters you've sent, to men throughout the kingdom. You made a mistake with Courtenay. He may cut a fine enough figure, but he's hardly heroic. How long do you think he'll hold out when Renard convinces the queen to order his arrest, as he will? I rather think the earl will take one look at the rack and spill his guts. And once he tells Renard what he wants to hear, they'll come here—for you."

The visible protruding of Robert's jaw muscles assured me I'd finally hit my target.

"But they'll need proof," I added. "The queen isn't given to signing death warrants without it. Give it to me and they'll never find it."

"You expect me to take your word for it," he snarled, "after what you've done? You betrayed my family!"

"If you don't, Renard will hire someone else. And if his next agent gets as far as I have, you won't survive." I returned his implacable stare. "Give me all your letters and they'll find nothing. No evidence. What can they accuse you of? Only the earl risks arrest."

He considered for a long moment. Then he raised his hands and began to clap slowly, in mocking applause. "Congratulations! You've become a man. But you've neglected to consider one thing." He showed me his teeth. "What if your precious Elizabeth isn't quite as innocent as you think? What if you seek to spare her from the very thing she herself helped set in motion?"

My hands coiled at my sides. "Speak plainly for once."

He chuckled. "I will. It would be my pleasure. Ambassador Renard is right about this much: There is a plot against the queen. It's the only way to save us from this infernal Spanish prince and Mary's deluded belief in her duty to return us all to popery and superstition. At the appointed date and time, men I have sent letters to will muster their armies; they will rise up to declare Queen Mary unfit to rule. She'll be given a choice: If she renounces her throne willingly, her life will be spared. Elizabeth insisted on it; she thinks that faced with an uprising, her sister will heed reason." His voice dropped to a whisper. "But we both know that Mary can't heed reason, don't we? We know she'll fight to the death, as she did against my father. And thus, death she will have, by my word. Her head will join my father's on the bridge, and then, my faithless friend, I *will* have my revenge."

I didn't speak. I stood silent and let his words absorb into me, like painful ink. It was difficult to hear but not a shock: Elizabeth had never been one to back down from a fight, and Mary had threatened her. The queen had even, according to Renard, questioned her legitimacy. She may have misled me as to her full involvement, but she didn't realize how far Dudley had preyed on her fears for his own twisted ends, not when she found herself in the midst of her own battle for her right to succeed. It was why she'd written to Dudley; why she risked her safety and Mary's eroding trust; why she indulged Courtenay even after she'd been warned. She thought she could still compel her sister to accept the sacrifice that being queen entailed, to turn away from her Hapsburg marriage for the good of her people.

She didn't know Mary at all, and regardless of her reasons, she had committed treason. It could cost her, and me, our lives. Not that I was going to let it stop me. I had my own fight to wage: my avenging of Peregrine, who had perished by Renard's hand.

I had to destroy the ambassador, come what may.

"Your life or death makes no difference to me," I said to Robert. I took a step toward him, my hand extended. "I want those letters, and you're going to give them to me."

He laughed. "I think not. Elizabeth didn't tell you the truth because, much as she may delight in sending you where you don't belong, in the end she understands that when a man has no lineage it's a stain that marks him for life. She knows you're just a nameless bastard who can't be trusted." He crossed his arms at his chest. "Now get back to whatever hole you crawled out of, Prescott, before I change my mind and make sure you regret coming here."

I didn't anticipate my reaction to these words. It wasn't as if he hadn't said worse, but as if all the memories of my tormented childhood surged up inside me, a violent wave that reduced my entire existence to this one moment, I lowered my head and rushed at him with all my strength, throwing him against the sideboard.

I heard a metallic crash as the decanter went flying. Then he let out a savage yell and started pounding me. I held fast to his waist, dragging him down onto the floor and swiping the poniard from my boot. As he tried to wrap his hands about my neck, I straddled him in one swift move and angled the blade at his throat.

"Last time," I said. "Give me the letters. Or would you rather bleed?"

"Bleed!" he hissed, and he twisted with brutal strength, bringing up his knees and ramming them into my groin. Stars exploded in my head. I lost my grip. I hit him as hard as I could in his face; he hit back, and then we were struggling, tumbling across the rug, fists ramming and fingers gouging as he sought to wrest the knife away or drive it into me. I felt nothing—no pain, no fear, not even when he slammed a fist into my temple and the world went dark. With a ferocious bellow I didn't recognize as my own, I started beating him, over and over, using my poniard hilt, hearing flesh give and bone crack.

Then my hands were about his throat; he flailed under me as I shut off his wind like a vise. He started to choke. My rage— that boundless, consuming rage, which I had kept tethered deep inside like some beast, fed on years of suffering, of doubt and yearning and helplessness—devoured all caution, all pity.

All reason.

"Stop! Please!"

A girl's frantic wail and the frenzied barking of a terrier barely penetrated my consciousness. A pounding sound echoed; Robert was kicking, his heels banging spasmodically against the floorboards as he fought for air. As I looked over my shoulder, past the blood seeping down my face, I saw figures rush into the room, coming toward me.

I thrust my blade at Robert's throat. "Any closer and I swear to God, I'll kill him."

His brothers slid to a halt. John was in the lead, ashen dismay spreading across his face as he took in our sprawled position, the contents from the sideboard spilled across the floor, the overturned chairs and stools strewn in our wake.

Guilford was the first to recognize me. He cried, "It's the foundling!" and Henry Dudley spat, "Whoreson. Let the dog loose on him. Then I'll kill him with my bare hands."

"You will do no such thing!" rang out a wavering voice; it came from the same girl who'd cried out at us to stop. As I tightened my hold on Robert, I stared through the ebbing haze of my anger to where Jane Grey stood as if petrified on the threshold.

She was looking at me in disbelief. "What . . . what are you doing here?"

"He's plotting treason," I told her. "You're in here because his father forced you to assume the queen's throne, and now he would send you all to the scaffold."

She lifted a hand to her chest, as though she lacked for breath. She said haltingly to John, "I believe he speaks the truth. I know him."

"So do we!" retorted Guilford. "We reared the worthless shit in our house and then he turned coat and betrayed us—"

I pushed the tip of my blade harder against Robert's neck. He let out a strangled cry. "He has letters to prove it," I said. "I want them. Now. Or he dies."

John Dudley shifted his gaze to Robert. I could see he was unwell, his face sunken and complexion sallow, like an invalid's. His voice was slow, measured, as if it cost him to formulate words. "Letters? Is this true, Robert?"

Robert tried to raise protest; I cut him off. "It's true, though he'll lie to his last breath if he can. Where are they? *Where are the letters?*"

John looked bewildered. "I don't—" Jane had already moved past him, evading her husband, Guilford, who stood clenching and unclenching his fists. Henry ripped the dog's lead from him and unleashed the terrier; it bounded at me, baring its teeth.

"Sirius, sit!" Jane snapped. The dog went to its haunches at once, a low growl in its throat as she proceeded to the hearth, groping under the lip of the chimney. She extracted a cylindrical oil-skin tube, which she held pensively before she turned around.

Guilford gasped. "How did you know?"

She gave him a bitter smile. "Do you still think me a complete fool? I've been coming here every week to walk and dine with you; I have eyes. I saw books arrive. I saw others leave. I counted them every day. I even tried to read one. But they are useless. The pages have been cut out." She kicked with her diminutive foot at the pile of books near the dog's cushion by the hearth, toppling them. "Your brother Robert would see us dead to satisfy his ambition. Even now, he refuses to recognize that our fate has always lain in God's hands."

"A pox on God!" snarled Henry Dudley. "And a pox on you, too, you righteous Grey bitch!" He started to lunge at Jane. John stepped in front of her with his hand held up.

"No." Though he was frail, in his voice reverberated an echo of that unquestionable authority his father had once commanded. "That is enough." He looked at me. "Let Robert go. You have my word you will not be harmed."

I hesitated. A room full of Dudleys and one exit: It was my worst nightmare come to life, but it was a risk I had to take. I released Robert, rising quickly to my feet and stepping away. He drew in gulps of air, his face a mass of contusions, his lip split and bleeding. I still couldn't feel anything, but I knew I would later. I must look almost as bad as he did.

"You can't let him leave," Henry was saying. "He knows everything now. He'll tell the queen. The bastard foundling will be the one who sends us all to the scaffold!"

John glared at him before he turned to me. "You once served our family. But you deceived us and, according to Robert, helped the queen put us in here. Will you now send us all to our deaths?"

I shook my head, trying not to look at Jane's thin figure behind him, the tube in her hands. "I want only to help my mistress, Princess Elizabeth."

Robert croaked from behind me, "Don't believe him. He's a

liar. He wants revenge. Give him those letters and he will use them against us. He'll take us down, every last one."

John hesitated. All of a sudden, fear seized me. I might not make it out of here alive.

"I promise on my own life," I said to John. "I will not use the letters against you." I clutched my knife tighter, sensing his brothers watching, waiting for his word to tear into me like hungry wolves.

Then John stepped aside. "Give him the letters."

Jane held out the tube. As I took it, I saw the stoic resignation in her blue-gray eyes. I had to resist the urge to clasp her to me, to gather her up and take her far from this awful place. She was so short she barely reached my chin, fragile as a child; the toll of her confinement showed in the hollows of her cheeks and in her shadowed, haunted gaze.

"I believe you to be a man of honor," she said. "I trust you'll honor your word."

"My lady," I whispered. "I would rather die than see you harmed." I bent over her hand. Then I tucked the tube into the saddlebag, grabbed it and my cloak off the table, and started for the door.

"Prescott!"

I paused, glancing over my shoulder. Robert had staggered to his feet with John's help. Leaning on his older brother's thin shoulder, he flung his words at me like a gauntlet.

"It's not over," he said. "Nothing you say or do can stop it. You may have won this day, but in the end I'll triumph. I will restore my name if it's the last thing I do. And remember this: On the day Elizabeth takes her throne, I will be at her side. I will be the one she turns to, in all things. And then, Prescott— then you'll regret this day. Her hour of glory will be your doom."

I didn't answer. I did not give him the satisfaction. I turned and walked out and left him there in his prison, where, if there was any justice left in the world, he would remain for the rest of his days.

It was the only way Elizabeth would ever be safe from him.

Chapter Fifteen

Outside, a cacophony of distant bells rang. It was late afternoon, and the winter sky had begun to darken. Pulling my cloak about me I hastened back through the ward, pausing briefly at a horse trough to wet my cloak and wash the blood from my face. The gates would close at dusk; I must be out before they did. Transferring the tube from my cloak to the safety of my doublet, I tried to look impervious as I made my way to the gatehouse.

The yeomen gave me a curious look. I yanked up my cloak's cowl, hurrying out. Only as I gained distance from the Tower did the knot in my chest start to dissolve.

I had done it. I had Dudley's letters. Renard couldn't use these against Elizabeth: The proof he required was now in my hands. All I had to do was to report whatever lies I must to keep him at bay, long enough to send word to her and—

I paused. And do what? Confront her? Demand to know why she'd acted so recklessly, why she had lied to me when she knew what Robert planned? Or should I simply destroy the letters and never mention that I had discovered she'd taken a stance against her sister, pretend she was as guiltless as she had feigned? As I considered this, though, I abruptly recalled with a jolt what she'd said to me in the stables. *I warn you now: You, too, could be in grave danger if you persist in this pursuit. I'll not have you risk yourself for my sake, not this time. Regardless of your loyalty, this is not your fight.*

I came to a stop in the middle of the road. She had warned me. In my zeal to protect her, I'd failed to hear her actual message. It was not my fight, she had said, and she meant it.

She had walked into Dudley's web willingly.

Around me, the light faded, lengthening the shadows. Veering into Tower Street, I began searching the painted signs hanging above doorways for the Griffin. People hustled about their errands, bundled to their ears and eager to finish with their day so they could get indoors before the night took hold. Everyone steered clear of me. I would have steered clear, too. My left cheek felt grossly swollen and was starting to throb. I had a wound on my temple and, no doubt, several nasty bruises on my face. Nevertheless, a burden of years had been lifted from my shoulders. I had stood up to Robert Dudley. No longer did I have to cower from my past, for this time I'd given as good as I got. Some might say I'd given better.

I espied the sign ahead, depicting a black-winged griffin. I pushed past the doorway inside, stamping my boots to get the blood back into my ice-numb feet. The tavern was choked with the smell of greasy food, cheap ale, and hearth and tallow smoke, and raucous with voices; it was also blessedly warm. I'd never been so happy to find myself among ordinary men doing ordinary things in my entire life. No one gave me a second glance as I weaved past the serving hutch and the crowded booths and tables. Apparently a bruised eye or two was common enough in taverns like these, close to the rough-and-tumble dockyards and riverside gaming houses.

Scarcliff lounged in apparent content by the smoking hearth, his legs stretched out before him, a tankard on the low table and a battered white mastiff at his feet. His chin drooped against his chest; he looked deep in slumber. I noticed his right boot had a wedged sole, as if he compensated for a disparity in the length of his legs, perhaps an old injury that had made one shorter than the other. I inched closer, transfixed by the sight of him in repose, but before I got within ten paces his head suddenly shot up, swerving to me with that uncanny precision he'd shown in the brothel, as if he could smell my approach.

He peered at me. "Christ on the cross," he muttered. "Looks like you had a time of it."

I broke into an unexpected grin, inexplicably relieved to see him. He might be a villain, as apt to drive a blade into my ribs and tumble me into a ditch as to escort me back to Whitehall, but at least he was a villain I could understand—a man for hire, who worked for his coin, not some treacherous noble whose corruption had permeated his very soul.

"Lord Robert and I had a disagreement," I said. "Guess who won?"

He snorted and hailed a passing tavern maid. "Nan, bring more ale!" Taking the flagon from her, he filled a tankard to its rim and shoved it, sloshing, at me. "Drink. You need it."

The ale was vile, a yeasty concoction that slid like wet flour down my throat, but the heat it generated helped clear my head. Scarcliff set his hand on the mastiff as it looked up at me with mild interest. He seemed quite familiar with the animal, which boasted nearly as many scars as he did—a fighting dog, no doubt, lucky enough to have survived the pit.

A survivor: like him.

"Thrashing aside, did you get what you wanted?" he asked, not sounding as if he much cared either way.

I nodded, downing the rest of my tankard. I couldn't keep from staring at him. The flickering dim light of the tavern made him appear even more sinister, shadowing his graying patchwork beard and misshapen mouth, but somehow emphasizing his empty eye socket and the fused lattice of mutilated skin on his face. I thought him brave for not covering his missing eye with a patch; I wanted to ask him what had happened, how he'd ended up looking like this, but as if he anticipated my curiosity he muttered, "You ought to put some food in your belly before we ride back," and he barked at Nan for pie and bread. He turned to me with sudden seriousness. "Few men leave the Tower unscathed. You're a lucky one; your injuries will heal." His chortle scraped my ears, like sand on cobblestone. "Unlike that Dudley lot, who I daresay can't grow new heads."

I was taken aback. The monster had a sense of humor. Who would have thought?

Nan arrived with the pie; it was steaming hot, with chunks of overcooked meat that I didn't examine closely. I was too famished to care, digging in with my blade and hands.

Scarcliff leaned back in his chair. It was a big tattered thing, with dirty flattened cushions and squat legs, but he presided upon it like a lord in his castle. After taking several loud sniffs at my pie, the dog curled back at his feet. It was definitely his. This was his spot. He must come here often. He probably felt comfortable among the foreign sailors and dockside workers, the pox-scarred whores and local thugs; certainly, it was more his style than that bizarre scenario Courtenay favored in Southwark.

He gave me a jagged-toothed sneer as I wiped my mouth. "That good, eh?"

"The worst pie I've ever eaten," I said. As the food settled in my belly, I began to feel the aftereffects of my encounter with Lord Robert; my every muscle was starting to ache. "I should get going before I'm too stiff to move," I added.

"What's the rush? Here, one more for the road. It's bitter as an old snatch out there; man's got to keep his bollocks warm." He poured again from the flagon. He seemed to have a limitless capacity for the stuff; he'd drunk three full tankards in the short time it had taken me to finish the pie. I'd already had one and normally wouldn't have indulged in more. The beverage was so fermented it guaranteed a temple-splitting headache, and the last thing I needed was to lose myself in drunkenness. We still had to ride together through the city at night; despite his genial manner, I wasn't entirely convinced Scarcliff didn't harbor nefarious motives. I wouldn't put it past Courtenay to have ordered that if I made it out of the Tower in one piece he was to make certain I didn't make it back to Whitehall. Nevertheless, I found myself clanking my tankard against his and joining him in four more rounds, until I felt the ale sloshing in my gut and the room whirled.

Finally I tossed some coin on the table for my share and he slapped his other half down. He gave Nan a pinch on her ample buttocks, and she slapped him playfully; then he threw on his cloak and oversized cap before he reached down to scratch the mastiff under its chin. I heard him mutter, "You be a good dog till I get back." Then he lifted his one good eye and said, "Night's not getting any warmer."

I followed him outside into the backyard stalls. Cinnabar whinnied in greeting, nuzzling me. I used a mounting block—my thighs were raw, as if I'd ripped every tendon—and checked for my sword in its scabbard. It was still there, hanging from my saddle. Scarcliff paid the urchin who had tended the horses and swung up onto his massive bay.

We rode out under a fog-wreathed moon, the cold gnawing at every bit of exposed skin. I wrapped my scarf tighter about my nose and mouth. The chill dissipated some of the fumes of the drink; I felt pleasantly soused, though not to the point of inebriation. Scarcliff ambled ahead, impervious, as if he'd been imbibing water all night. He glanced over his shoulder at me; in that moment, the winter fog parted and a spear of moonlight slashed down across his creviced face, catching the gleam of his eye.

I returned his stare. I reached for my sword.

That was when the others burst upon us.

There were two of them, both cloaked and masked, astride black steeds that gouged the hardened ice from the road. Cinnabar threw back his head in alarm as they came crashing toward us from the darkness. I grappled with the reins, nearly sliding off my saddle. Scarcliff swerved his bay in an expert maneuver, fending off one of the attackers as he lunged for the destrier's bridle. The horse proved impressively agile for its size. Then I heard shouting from the attacker riding toward me—"*No, ése no! El joven! Agárrelo!*"—and Scarcliff bellowed: "Go, lad! *Now!*"

I had thought he'd planned this, but as I heard him yank his sword from its scabbard—blades tended to stick in the cold, so he clearly kept his well oiled—I didn't wait to find out. I slammed my heels into Cinnabar, knocking my arm across my pursuer, backhanding him in his saddle long enough for me to gain a head start.

Cinnabar didn't need encouragement. He had been idling in a stable for days at Whitehall save for our occasional outings, and his eager bolt caught the man off guard, so that he barely had time to veer his own horse out of our way. Yet as I took flight down the road, I knew he would take up our pursuit, and I lifted my weight off the saddle to facilitate Cinnabar's stride. "Faster, my friend," I said in his flattened ear. "My life depends on it."

As indeed it did. The men had spoken in Spanish; they must be in Renard's employ and had no doubt been tracking me the entire time, waiting for the moment to seize what I had taken. I'd let my guard down, let myself get overly distracted by my suspicions of Scarcliff. I hadn't considered that Renard would have me followed.

The striking of hooves on the road behind me grew louder. I looked over my shoulder. Both men were gaining on me; the one I had backhanded was ahead, slighter of build than his companion, his dark cloak billowing like outstretched wings, the half-moon in the sky above capturing random glints of metal on his person, including the unsheathed sword he gripped in one gloved hand while he steered his horse with the other.

I strained to see ahead. I couldn't be too far away. A few more leagues at best and the torch-lit sprawl of Whitehall would appear before me. There would be sentries, courtiers, and officials; it wasn't that late. No Spaniard would dare harm me in view of the palace. Renard had chosen this moment because of the late hour, this lone stretch of road. He knew that with Peregrine's death, he could not afford to rouse the queen's suspicions. It had to appear as if I'd fallen prey to an unfortunate but all too common accident, waylaid and murdered outside the palace while I went about the task he had assigned—

All of a sudden, Cinnabar balked and swerved, throwing me sideways. Yanking on the reins, my right foot tangling in my twisted stirrup, I tried to steady him, but he had plunged off the road and was running toward the open fields of St. James. As hard as I pulled at his reins I couldn't get him to stop, and when I glanced over my shoulder I saw why.

The Spaniard was at our heels. As the moonlight caught a streak of dark wet on Cinnabar's hindquarters, I saw the wound that the tip of his sword had made.

Rage filled me. I wanted to stop and fight, but Cinnabar, maddened by the stinging pain and urgency emanating from me, galloped faster than before, so that it felt as though we were about to take wing. I kept looking back over my shoulder to gauge the distance between me and the Spaniard. It was widening, despite his frenzied heel-kicks into his own horse. I looked ahead. A copse of trees neared. Past it, flickering light indicated the palace of St. James. If I could only get past that copse, I might be able to—

My body lifted completely off my saddle as Cinnabar jumped, skirting a fallen bough. Then a low-lying branch hit me full in the face.

I tumbled onto stony ground, my skull ringing from the impact. My teeth cut into my lip, hard enough that I tasted blood. Looking up in a daze, I saw the Spaniard heel his mount, spraying up clods of frozen turf. He leapt off his saddle, his sword at the ready, his companion riding up close behind.

Struggling to my feet, my head pounding from the fall and the last, lingering effects of my ill-advised bout at the alehouse, I met his approach with my own sword brandished.

* * *

The Spaniard held up a hand to detain his companion. He was a narrow silhouette in head-to-toe black, not tall, though his lack of physical stature offered no comfort. He regarded me impassively from behind a full black face mask, as if he had all the time in the world, before he assumed his stance. This was a man of experience, with no fear of failure. He lunged at me with blinding speed, his sword arcing. As I parried his thrust, the impact of our blades shuddering through my arm and into my very bowels, I understood he wanted to play with me. As he assailed me, his polished moves forcing me backward, step by clumsy step, into the weaker position of defense, I realized just how bad my situation was. Setting aside that just hours before I'd grappled with Dudley and one of my eyes was now a swollen slit, I had only a few painstaking months of practice in the controlled environment of Hatfield's gallery to rely upon. I was an amateur; I didn't stand a chance against someone this highly trained.

I was sweating within minutes, breathing hard and fast as he attacked with almost nonchalant precision. Staggering over brittle twigs, stones, and broken branches littering the field, evading his swipes as he pushed me toward the deeper pocket of darkness under the trees, I began to consider that I might die tonight. If he hadn't delivered the fatal blow by now, it certainly wasn't because he couldn't. He was playing with me, biding his time and pushing me to my limits, until I either made a mistake that opened me to his killing thrust or surrendered voluntarily, in acknowledgment of his superiority. Either way, the outcome was bleak. The question was, did I want to die on my feet or on my knees?

Everything faded to insignificance. The knowledge that I still had the one thing that could save Elizabeth, and my fury that once again my own life was deemed forfeit by callous design, compelled me to fight as I had never fought before, even as my arm grew numb and my chest burned from deflecting his relentless assault. Only once did I catch him by surprise, nicking his sleeve with my sword tip.

His teeth gleamed as he smiled. Then he came at me with all his vigor, shedding any pretense of consideration for a savage display of professionalism. Before I knew it, the shocking smack of his blade on my wrist sent a flame of agony shooting up my arm, and my sword went flying as I desperately dodged his move to slice off my hand.

Panting like a winded foal, I scrambled to retrieve my sword. He leapt in front of me. I started to reach for the poniard stashed in my boot when I felt the tip of his sword at my throat, so close it pierced the matted wool of my scarf and bit into my flesh. I looked to where Cinnabar stood, quivering, his nostrils flared and reins dangling. I hoped that they wouldn't hurt or take him, that he'd be canny enough to elude them and find his own way back to the palace. His riderless arrival would alert the stable hands. They'd inform their betters; at some point word would reach Rochester, who'd dispatch a party to look for me. With any luck, I'd be buried with Peregrine—if anything of me was left to be found.

At this thought, a gust of laughter exploded from me, surprising me with its force, considering how winded I felt. What a way to end my not-so-illustrious career as a spy, skewered by an anonymous assassin after a visit to my former master in the Tower! Here lies Brendan Prescott, also known as the inept and short-lived Daniel Beecham.

"*Regístrele,*" ordered the Spaniard in a deep, almost too forceful voice. He did not take his eyes from me. Or what little I could see of them; under the mask I could only glean the glimmer of whites in the eyeholes, not enough to discern any expression or color.

"Don't move," said his companion in broken English as he marched to me and twisted my hands behind my back. He wrapped a cord about my wrists, binding them. Then he began to search me. The tube hidden inside my doublet revealed itself within seconds under his probing hands; it was futile to even try to stop him as he tore off one of my sleeves and wormed the tube out.

He waved it aloft. "*Aquí está,*" he said to the swordsman. "*Ahora mátale.* Kill him."

I braced myself, but the swordsman did not move, his stare intent, boring into me as he waved his companion back to his horse. He was clearly in charge; though the other man grumbled, he did as he was told. For what felt like an eternity, we faced each other, motionless. Then he took a step closer. I let out an unwilling gasp as he trailed his sword down my torso, slowly, until he poised it on my codpiece. Though I couldn't see it under the mask I knew he was smiling. He made a gesture with his other hand, ordering me to kneel. I suddenly couldn't breathe. I shook my head.

"No," I managed to whisper. "Not like this . . ."

He pushed on his blade. Fearing he'd emasculate me and leave me here to bleed to death, I dropped to my knees. He raised his sword. He's going to decapitate me, I thought in a burst of blinding terror. I was going to die like Anne Boleyn, by a foreigner's sword—

I closed my eyes. Urine leaked down my thigh. I felt a thud on the ground near me.

When I dared to look, I saw my sword lying a short distance away. The swordsman had turned away and was striding to his horse, his cloak swirling about him. After he leapt onto his saddle, he paused to look across the field at me. I was still kneeling, my hands behind my back, the sword a tantalizing glimmer, within reach.

With a kick of his heels, he galloped off with his companion.

Chapter Sixteen

T he cold finally encouraged me to attempt to stand—that and Cinnabar's concerned nuzzling. Drawing in a deep lungful of air, I hoisted myself as best as I could to my feet. The side of my temple where the branch had struck me throbbed; I could only imagine the sight I'd present when I finally made it to my room. I was having difficulty accepting I was still alive.

I went to my sword, lay down at an awkward angle, and maneuvered my bound wrists as best as I could against the edge of the blade. As I sawed back and forth clumsily—the tops of my palms rubbing on the blade with a sharp sting, I prayed I'd not end up shredding my hands or slicing open a vein—I considered my position. Clearly the swordsman had been hired to steal the letters; he had known what I carried. If he was Renard's man—and it seemed the likely explanation—then I must owe my life to the ambassador. Renard had what he sought; he had also neutralized my attempt to safeguard Elizabeth. My death could come later, after he'd sent the evidence to the queen and his prey to the Tower. I was not important. He could afford to dispense with me at his leisure.

When I felt a sudden loosening of the knot, I shifted away. With all my strength, I strained to pull my wrists apart. The leather cord frayed; with a gasp of painful relief, I slid one hand free. Unraveling the cord from my wrists, my skin smarting and bloodied, I picked up my sword and trudged to Cinnabar. Limping, I led him to a tree stump, where I balanced unsteadily to clamber onto my saddle. Cinnabar waited patiently; when he sensed I was seated, he ambled toward the road.

I searched the environs cautiously, though I already knew Scarcliff would not appear. He'd not come to my rescue. He must have bolted away the moment he realized who the men were after; there was no point in risking his life. By now he'd be back in the Griffin, slurping from his tankard and petting his ugly dog. He wasn't one to waste sentiment on circumstances beyond his control. As he had told me, he had his orders.

The palace appeared like a mirage out of the night. As we neared the postern gate, Cinnabar quickened his pace, eager for his well-earned rubdown and oats. I slid off him in the darkened stable yard. I'd barely started to unbuckle his harness when a groom hurried out of the shadows by the stalls.

My heart stopped. He reminded me of Peregrine. Then he paused, staring at me, and I saw he was an older boy, pimply and angular, with a thatch of unwashed hair. "Are you Peregrine's master?" he asked, hesitantly.

I replied hoarsely, "I am. You must be his friend, Toby."

He nodded. "I'm sorry about Peregrine. All the lads here are. He was nice. He gave us extra money and told us he was a friend of the princess. If we can do anything for you . . . ?"

"You can." I rummaged in my pouch, handing him a coin. "Please see that my horse is well attended. We've had a rough night."

He eagerly went to work, relieving Cinnabar of saddle, harness, and bridle while I took stock of myself. I was covered in muck, my cloak rumpled and torn from my fall. God only knew what the rest of me looked like. I couldn't walk into the palace in this state without attracting attention. I asked Toby for a pail of water. I washed up as best as I could, and once I saw Cinnabar to his stall, I stole through the back passageways to my room.

Undressing was a torment. As I peeled away the soiled layers, I clenched my teeth and reopened my cut lip. My chemise in particular proved torturous, the linen having mixed with my sweat to adhere to my contusions, like a hair shirt dipped in salt. Naked save for my sagging hose, I surveyed my shockingly bruised torso before I took up my small hand mirror. Catching one look at my face in the tallow light, I set the glass aside. No use dwelling on it. As terrible as it looked, as Scarcliff had said, I would heal.

The water in my basin was icy; I gasped as I carefully used a rag to wash away the worst of the filth and blood from my body. Despair lurked at the edges of my awareness. I'd have given anything to see Peregrine again, to hear him whistle in amazement and comment about how I couldn't go anywhere alone because I always ended up falling into a river or chased by ruffians. Blinking back tears—salt on my face was the last thing I needed—I went to the coffer and poured with a trembling hand from the decanter. I gulped the entire draft down, not caring that the beer was a day old and already souring.

As the drink hit my stomach, I sat on the bed.

Failure crashed over me.

I had lost the letters, and time was running out. Renard had sent his men to ambush me; he knew that without evidence, there was nothing I could do to stop him, short of murder. This possibility took root in my mind, even as I told myself that if his death were ever traced to me, I, too, would die. Somehow, though, my own life no longer mattered. I longed to see Renard's expression as he took his last breath; I wanted him to know that I was also capable of doing whatever was required. His henchman had not let me live tonight out of mercy; Renard had me spared because my demise was of no account for the moment. If he'd had his way, I'd be dead already. He'd come for me eventually, unless I got to him first.

I mapped out scenarios. I was scheduled to report to him tomorrow; I could meet him in his office and do it there, behind closed doors, but I'd have to contend with his secretaries afterward. It might be better to hide in the vicinity and catch Renard unaware as he made his way to the office, take him down in one of the remote courtyards, and make it look like a random assault, a botched robbery, as I had thought he'd have his men do to me on the road. However I did it, I had to act soon.

I had to kill him before he presented those letters to the queen.

Urgency brought me staggering to my feet. The room swam. I paused, choking back bile as I shrugged on my doublet, pulled on my boots, and, with my sword dangling at my belt, lurched to the door. I felt like I was moving underwater. I faintly acknowledged that in my current state I'd probably never make it down the stairs, let alone traverse the palace to his office in the dead of the night. I couldn't begin to think of how I'd actually wield my poniard with enough force to kill him, but I grasped the door latch anyway, determined to try.

I yanked the door open. Standing outside was a cloaked silhouette. I struggled backward, lifting the sword up. The figure resolved itself from the inky shadows; a warning hand came up, to silence my outburst. "*Ssh!* Don't shout."

I smelled lilies. I could only stare. In the guttering tallow glow, her eyes were huge, her face framed by a cascade of dark blond hair that caught the light like cloth of gold. She pulled back her hood; it crumpled softly about her shoulders. As she turned to close the door, the cloak parted to reveal her slim form, clad in a simple, high-necked black gown.

"What—what are you doing here?" I said in a hoarse whisper.

"Looking for you." Sybilla regarded me with a worried frown. "I knew something must have happened. I waited for hours, watching the staircase to your room."

"You—you waited?"

"Yes. I wanted to tell you something. Renard was with the queen all afternoon; they dined together in her apartments. As Lady Clarencieux and I served them, I overheard Renard telling her that you couldn't be trusted. She was not pleased; she said you'd yet to prove yourself either way. But he replied that he would soon deliver evidence to the contrary. So, as soon as I could, I came to find you. I waited in the gallery in an alcove, hidden from view; by nightfall, I started to fear the worst."

I stood immobile, as if cast in stone, my sword still clutched in my fist. "And did Renard . . . did he deliver this evidence?" The calm in my voice surprised me.

"No. I was returning to the queen's apartments when I happened to look out into the courtyard and saw two men hurrying toward his office. I recognized them; he employs them to fulfill whatever illicit deeds he needs doing. I also knew Renard wasn't in his office; after he left the queen, he went out. He rents a manor on the Strand he doesn't live in, but he visits often, so he must keep a mistress there. I followed the men. They gave Renard's secretary—the morose one, who never seems to sleep—a tube, like those used by couriers. They also told him they'd left the traitor hurt but alive, as ordered. The secretary promised to deliver the tube. I saw it all from the corridor. The door was wide open."

I could barely breathe, my entire being focused on her.

"Are you the traitor they were talking about?" she asked.

I nodded. "They took that tube from me. One of them, the slim one—he could have easily killed me. I see I was right in assuming Renard was behind it."

Her expression hardened. "He made a serious mistake with that poisoned note; he can't take another chance that something will go wrong." She reached into her cloak and pulled out the oilskin tube. "Is this it?"

My heart started to pound. I couldn't believe it. As I gazed at the seemingly innocuous object in her hand, stained with soot from the chimney and countless smudged fingers, I had to resist the urge to pounce on it.

Sybilla's gaze turned cold. "Do you still not trust me?"

"I'm not sure." I met her eyes. "This is almost too convenient."

"I see." Her smile cut across her mouth. "Do you think I'm deceiving you?"

"I didn't mean that—"

"Yes. You did." She made as if to leave; before I knew what I was doing, I gripped her by the wrist. It was thin but not frail; she possessed covert strength.

She went still. "Pray, unhand me."

I did. She didn't touch her wrist. "I told you, I would do whatever is necessary. If Renard wins, I'll be in his debt forever, like my mother before me."

I suddenly understood. "Your mother, she was Renard's . . . ?"

Sybilla's smile was bitter. "She didn't sell herself in a brothel,

but the result is the same. When we left England, we were penniless; she had nothing to offer save her services. Renard made
it clear those services would be his price for a position at the
Hapsburg court and the opportunity to give us, her daughters, a
future. My mother had no choice. But I do. So does my sister."
She tossed the tube on the cot. "Is this enough to stop him?"

"Bring me the light," I replied, setting my sword aside. Once
she fetched the tallow and set it by the bed, she shrugged off her
cloak to wait as I untied the tube's cord. It unfolded into two
compartments, a sturdy folder made to protect its contents and
withstand the rigors of travel. Within the compartments were
papers. My hands trembled as I removed them; I saw at once
they were letters—eight, to be precise. I didn't recognize Elizabeth's handwriting on any of them, however. None appeared to
be hers.

I read each one. When I was done, I sat in utter silence.

There was enough evidence here to send Edward Courtenay,
Earl of Devon, straight to the block. These letters were the re-
sponses of various important noblemen to the correspondence
the earl had seen delivered in Dudley's name, though I had to
wonder if Courtenay actually understood the extent of his own
complicity. He'd told me that he had never read what he so carelessly delivered; seeing these letters now, I was inclined to believe him. In his penurious greed and thwarted pride, Courtenay
had unwittingly let himself be named the figurehead for a coor-
dinated revolt ranging from the southwest of England to the
Marches, aimed at forcing the queen to retain the Protestant
faith and marry the earl, or forfeit her throne. Munitions had
been stockpiled in manors, routes selected for the march on
London. Each nobleman's responsibility in the rebellion had
been clearly outlined, as had that of their coconspirators. The

danger to Elizabeth was not explicit, but rather inferred; it stood to reason that if Mary denied the rebels' demands, as she would, Elizabeth would succeed her, with Courtenay as her consort.

I knew differently, though. I knew Dudley believed that Elizabeth would marry him instead, once he handed her the throne. He was using Courtenay as his pawn; that was why he'd taken such caution, why he wasn't mentioned anywhere. His role as the conspiracy's mastermind must remain invisible.

But why was Elizabeth's letter, which she'd entrusted to Courtenay, not here?

I had a sudden recollection of Jane Grey tumbling the pile of the books by the hearth—*I saw books arrive. I saw others leave. I counted them every day. I even tried to read one. But they are useless. The pages are cut out*—and Robert calling after me, *Nothing you say or do can stop it . . . In the end I'll triumph. I will restore my name if it's the last thing I do.*

I clenched my jaw. I now understood why Dudley had cajoled Courtenay to gain the princess's trust: Her letter was his insurance. He still had it, hidden elsewhere. Dudley anticipated interference, even betrayal, by someone dedicated to Elizabeth, who would realize the danger he posed to her. If anyone tried to expose him, he could in turn threaten to reveal the princess's letter as proof that she was his accomplice.

Sybilla's voice broke into my thoughts. "Can I assume by your lack of speech that those letters are the weapon you need?"

I looked up. "Yes," I said. I went silent for a moment. "How did you manage it?"

"With my wits, of course; it wasn't hard. I simply waited for his secretary to go to the courtyard to empty his bladder. The man was fit to burst. I saw a cup on the desk and two empty jugs. He must have been holed up drinking all day, as Renard insists someone must attend to his office at all hours. But he'll know by now that the tube is missing. He'll tear the office apart looking for it. It's likely he'll abandon his post and disappear once he realizes it was stolen." I heard a catch in her voice. "If Renard finds out I am to blame, he'll see me dead."

"You needn't fear him." I inserted the letters back in the folder's compartments, rolled it back into its tubular shape, and retied the cord. "When I show these to the queen, he'll have his hands full. He won't dare do anything to you or anyone else. He'll be too busy trying to explain how so much could have gone on under his nose without him being the wiser; how, despite all his resources, he had no inkling a conspiracy of this magnitude was brewing."

"He'll realize you were someone he didn't expect," she said softly.

I leaned against the wall. "Oh, he expected me, just not that I'd get this far. Despite the queen's stated trust in my abilities, he must have suspected from the start. So when Her Majesty ordered me to investigate his allegations concerning Elizabeth and Courtenay, he realized he had to eliminate the risk. He wasn't about to let anyone get in his way of entrapping the princess, which is why he left that poisoned note. Now he'll have to scramble to exculpate himself. You'll soon be free of him forever."

She gnawed at her lip, her hands twining in her lap. Her tears were so unexpected that as she lowered her head to choke back a sob, at first I didn't know what to do. Then I tentatively reached for her. Rising from the stool, she came into my arms.

"I'm so afraid," she whispered. "I've been afraid of him my entire life."

I caressed her hair, closing my eyes, trying to push back the heat she aroused in me. I acted as if I were comforting a disconsolate child, even as I felt her hands, so slim, so warm, reach upward to clasp at my shoulders like supple vines.

I made to pull away. "No," I murmured. "I cannot."

She lifted her face to me. In her eyes I saw oceans.

"I can," she said. She crushed her lips to mine. I let out a gasp. She whispered, "Does it hurt?" and grazed the broken cut on my lip with her fingertip, whipping desire through me. I heard myself moan; that one weak sound brought down whatever crumbling remnant was left of my resistance. I seized her closer, raveling my hands in her lush mane, and I no longer felt my bruises, the pain vanishing in the whirlpool of our mouths and the swift current of her touch as she yanked at my clothes, pulling down my hose to grasp at my hardness.

"I want to know something other than fear," I heard her say. "I want to feel desire, if only this once." She stepped back and unlaced the sides of her gown. I watched her with my heart in my throat, knowing in some dark recess of my soul that if I did this, I would never forget or escape it. I would live with the remorse for the rest of my days, with the betrayal of Kate, the woman I loved, who waited for me in Hatfield, unaware.

Then, as the dark velvet pooled at Sybilla's feet and I beheld the flawless breadth of her skin, her rose-tipped breasts arched high on her chest, her ribs woven like lyre strings under her pallor, and her lean belly, curving to the gilded shadow between her legs, I could think no more. Gathering her in my arms, I lowered her to the floor upon our cloaks and pushed inside her roughly, almost with anger, feeling myself engorge even more as I coaxed her pleasure from her, until she was bucking up her hips to meet my stride.

It seemed as though we merged forever, then my seed gushed

forth with breath-shattering suddenness. I did not have time to pull out. She clenched herself about me, making me cry out, heedless, as she shuddered.

I collapsed beside her, our heat subsiding like smoke from a doused fire.

My heartbeat slowed. As I looked at her profile and started to reach out to wipe the damp hair from her face, she said abruptly, "No. You do not owe me anything."

She rose to her feet, reaching for her discarded gown. I did not speak; I couldn't find the right words as I, too, stood and watched her in silence as she laced her dress. Now that it was over and I'd satiated my recklessness, I could take no satisfaction in it.

She bent to my discarded clothing and retrieved my sword. She gave it to me.

"If those letters don't work," she said, "use it."

Our eyes met for a moment. Then she turned and left without another word.

———◆◆◆———

Chapter Seventeen

𝕴 could not sleep.

I sat awake in the dark, facing the door, every sense attuned to the sound of any approach, until the window grate high in my wall lightened to a murky hue, indicating dawn had arrived. Then I stood, wincing at the stiff pain in my limbs, and prepared myself. I looked a fright, my eye blackened and half-shut, my lip swollen. Under my chemise, my bruises had ripened to a motley shade of yellow-blue. I did not tarry at my glass, however. I did not care to see guilt staring back at me.

In the long gallery leading to the royal wing, servants were already about their tasks, gathering burned candle stubs, stray goblets, and other objects left by inebriated courtiers from the night before. As I approached the double oak doors of the queen's apartments, one of the guards standing vigil stepped forth, his pike at the ready.

"Halt! What business do you have here?"

"Pray, inform Her Majesty that Master Beecham must see her," I said as he eyed me, obviously debating whether to order me away to take my place in the queue with the rest of those who gathered at midday as she made her way to the hall to dine. I added, "Tell her it concerns her betrothal."

The guard's eyes snapped wide. Turning to one of the others, he barked an order. I paced to a window and stared into a court-yard where a decorative fountain with a cherub on its tip dripped with melting ice. When the guard brusquely motioned to me, I followed him through the doors into the maze of corridors and chambers of Mary's private apartments.

She stood waiting for me, wearing a russet velvet gown with a jeweled belt, her hair gathered at her nape in a pearled snood. Her women were nearby, sewing. A quick glance showed Sybilla was not among them. Pulling off my cap, hearing their stifled gasps as they caught sight of my battered face, I bowed. "Forgive my intrusion. I bring news Your Majesty must hear at once."

"You've been brawling," Mary said coldly, and before I could reply, she stepped aside.

My stomach dropped when I saw Renard seated at the table behind her, a mass of papers strewn before him, quill in hand. His brow arched. "Up so early? I fear it's hardly the place or time for petty appointments. I suggest you return later today, when you will be heard—"

"No." Mary interrupted. "He's here now, and I will hear what he has to say. Judging by his appearance, it must indeed be ur-gent. Any other man in his state would be abed."

I returned my gaze to her. She, too, looked as if she could use more time in bed, her skin waxen and eyes ringed by shadows, as if she hadn't slept in days. I could also tell by the force of her regard that the guard had relayed exactly what I said at the doors, thereby revealing, as intended, that I knew something no one outside her intimate circle should know. She obviously was not pleased with my indiscretion.

"Begging your pardon," I said, "but what I have to say is for your ears only."

"Oh? You are among friends here. I have no secrets from them."

Panic knotted my throat; I had to clench my fist to stop myself from ripping out the tube of letters from my cloak. I couldn't simply hand them over; if she dismissed me without hearing what I had to say, I was doomed. Renard's terse stare warned me that he knew why I was here and if he could manage it I'd be dead before the day was done, the queen's suspicions be damned. I must explain to Mary personally what I had deduced before Renard spun his own take on the letters and she bayed for blood.

"It concerns your sister—" I started to say.

Renard leapt to his feet. "Majesty, please, do not indulge this man further! He is a liar. I told you, he cannot be—"

"I believe I'm perfectly capable of judging his ability to tell the truth," said Mary, her glance withering. "Come, Master Beecham." She motioned me to her study. As I passed her ladies, Jane Dormer gave me an apprehensive look, her dog growling on a lead at her feet.

I did not acknowledge Renard as he hastened to follow us into the wood-paneled study and closed the door, though I felt his stare boring into my back.

"Well?" Mary turned to face me, standing before her desk. "You have your privacy. Tell us this urgent news about my sister that cannot wait. Best be quick about it; my patience is sorely tried. I still have my council and the Hapsburg delegation to attend to, as well as my upcoming move to Hampton Court. The air here does not agree with me. I need a change of scenery."

With an incline of my head, I took the tube out.

She went still. "Pray, what is that?" she asked, and though she remained outwardly composed, I heard the tremor in her voice.

"More trickery!" Renard lunged to snatch the tube from my hand.

Holding it aloft from him, I said to the queen, "This is evidence of a conspiracy against Your Majesty—evidence Don Renard himself hired me to obtain."

Renard came to a halt, his face draining to a chalky hue. Mary regarded him for a lengthy moment before she held out her hand. She took the tube from me, turning to her cluttered desk to unfold it, perusing and discarding each letter in utter silence, until she'd let all eight fall from her ringed fingers to the blotter and had gone rigid, her gaze fixed on me. When she spoke, her voice was calm, which only increased my admiration for her.

"Are you certain of this?"

"I have been most diligent in my task." I paused, despising the fact that I had to protect Dudley and sacrifice the earl in his stead, even if it was for Elizabeth's sake. "I believe those letters prove my lord of Devon has been led into a rebellious plot aimed at forcing you to accede to his demands or suffer the consequences."

Her jaw tightened. "So it appears. Yet you said this matter concerned my sister. How?"

"When he hired me, Don Renard expressed belief that she, too, was involved," I replied. "I have found no evidence of it."

Mary swerved to Renard, her voice sharp. "You assured me otherwise."

"Your Majesty, I am as taken aback as you are," he replied. I almost envied his self-control. He seemed impervious, though his future hung in the balance. I wished I could tell Mary what kind of man he truly was—what he had done to Sybilla Darrier and her mother; what he might yet try to do to Elizabeth—but I, too, had secrets to hide. I could not risk being exposed as Elizabeth's agent until I was sure the princess was safe.

Sarcasm tinged Mary's tone. "I find that hard to believe, Don Renard, considering all your spies and expense. I cannot count the number of times I myself have provided funds for your endeavors through my own privy purse, so intent were on you on this theory of my sister and Courtenay's falsehood. Yet now you'd have me believe you had no idea that the earl was plotting to betray me with these other lords, many of whom I've received with honor at this court and forgiven past grievances?"

To my satisfaction, the ambassador was starting to look panicked. "Your Majesty must forgive me," he said warily, "but compelling as this so-called evidence may seem, we cannot yet be sure it offers proof of anything. We must verify the letters' authenticity. And even if they prove real, this rebellion must be disorganized at best, seeing as I indeed gleaned no rumor of it. Perhaps the earl has managed to rally a handful of malcontents, but it's hardly cause for—"

"Hardly cause!" Mary exclaimed. "It is treason, señor, treason of the highest order. And they shall pay for it, make no mistake. I will see every last one of them in the Tower."

Renard pursed his lips. In that chilling moment, I divined his ploy. He would dismiss the very proof before his eyes, delay even Courtenay's arrest if he could, if it meant Elizabeth might still be taken. A rebellion offered possibilities; something might yet be found to prove her involvement.

Mary was staring at him in astonishment, recognizing his diffidence, though she didn't understand the reason behind it. "I can hardly believe my ears! Time and time again you warned me of treachery in our midst, yet now you disregard the very man we hired to uncover it? Disorganized or not, it is still a planned uprising by nobles of this realm—subjects all, who'd dare arm themselves against me. They must be apprehended, an end put to their schemes." She suddenly faltered, reaching for the back of a chair. "God save us, should the emperor learn of it, he'll refuse to let Philip come here, for fear of his very life!"

As Renard's face turned thunderous at this, her open admission before me of her plan to wed the Spanish prince, I despised him even more. Despite what I knew of her religious intolerance, of her antipathy for Elizabeth and cherished dream of returning England to Rome, I couldn't find it in myself to dislike her. Mary Tudor wasn't a cruel woman, only a deeply misguided one. Renard was the serpent. Just as he'd assiduously worked toward Elizabeth's downfall, so had he preyed on Mary's innate lack of guile, stirring up the torments of the past and undermining her fragile confidence.

My sentiments had no place here, though. Only with the queen focused on Courtenay and his accomplices could I hope to fulfill my mission.

"We could question the earl," suggested Renard, as if the option had just occurred to him. "If it is your command, we can arrest him and obtain the information we need. This plot cannot have gone so far that we cannot stop it before we announce the betrothal at Hampton Court. By the time word reaches the emperor, it will be over. Your Majesty will have asserted your might, the conspirators will have been imprisoned, and neither the emperor nor Prince Philip will have anything to fear."

Mary released her grip on the chair. "Then do so. Have the warrant prepared this very hour; I will sign it before the council."

Renard bowed, curtly motioning to me to accompany him.

Mary said, "No. Master Beecham stays. I would have a word with him. Alone."

I couldn't have hoped for more. Renard knew it. For a telling fraction of a second, his gaze met mine in fury before he stalked out, closing the door on the anxious women in the antechamber, all of whom must have heard the queen's outcry, if not her actual words.

Mary dropped onto her chair. She didn't speak, regarding me with an opaque intensity that seeped under my skin. "Why do you defend my sister so unremittingly?" she finally asked. "Don Renard has been convinced from the start that she's had a hand in a plot against my person, indeed that she despises me and seeks my throne. He has many more years of intelligent judgment in such matters than you."

I cleared my throat, realizing I stood on a knife's edge. "I only did as I was bade, Majesty. Don Renard hired me to investigate both the earl and the Lady Elizabeth, and I found no evidence of her participation. She is innocent of any wrongdoing, though the ambassador may claim otherwise."

"Innocent, you say? Then I fear you do not know my sister at all. Elizabeth has never been innocent. From the day she entered this world, she has been steeped in sin."

Dread iced my veins. "I assure you, there is nothing to indicate she ever plotted—"

Her acrid laughter cut me off. "No, there isn't, is there? And there never will be." She stood. "Despite Renard's dedication, his copious bribes of my courtiers and payments to spies, riffraff, and the like, she has eluded him. She's too clever, like the viper you do not see until it bites. But she is not innocent. With or without evidence, I know it here, in my heart. I only need to take one look at her to know what it is she desires."

She turned to the window, her voice low, as though she spoke to herself. "I've watched her, day after day, ever since she came to my court. Flaunting her youth and witch's beauty, whispering, always whispering; luring others to do her deeds like her mother before her. Elizabeth wants me to suffer. She wants me to know that no matter what, I will never have peace. Without marriage, I cannot bear a child to supplant her in the succession; without a husband, I will die a virgin. *That* is what she desires. She lives for the hour when she can take my crown and call it her own."

When she turned back to me, I saw in her pale gray eyes the flickering ember of something horrible, unstoppable. Those eyes probed at me, seeking a flaw in the very texture of my face, so she might confirm the relentless hatred that had begun to consume her. "Who's to say she did not know of Courtenay's plot?" she asked in a dead-quiet voice. "Who's to say she knew and gave her consent, knowing my ruin would be her gain? She might have kept herself apart from the planning, knowing the risk her involvement would entail, but it would not stop her—no, not her, not the daughter of Anne Boleyn."

I stood silent, my throat dry as bone. In her expression and words, Mary revealed she had gone beyond reconciliation. Even if Elizabeth managed to escape with her life, there was no denying that she had lost her sister forever. Henceforth, they would be at odds until one of them breathed no more. Cecil's prediction had come true: They were destined to be mortal enemies.

Mary returned to her desk, composed again, resigned to what came next. "I want to believe you," she said, "and without proof of her guilt, I can do nothing else. But for now I do not want her near me; wherever I am, she must be elsewhere. Before she departs, however, I will look her in the eye. I will ask her to her face if she knew anything about"—she swept her hand over the letters—"this vile business. Go now. Bring her to me. Tell her the queen of England would see her."

I bowed and had started to retreat to the doors when she added, "You will continue to investigate every detail of this conspiracy. Courtenay may not confess to everything or he may not know. He was never a clever man; he couldn't have organized this alone. And I expect loyalty, Master Beecham. If you think to conceal anything from me, if you dare try to protect anyone to my detriment, remember that yours is the life which will be forfeit."

"Majesty," I murmured, and I left her.

I strode through the officials crowded outside the queen's apartments. In less than an hour, the gallery had filled to capacity, and all eyes marked me as I passed, gauging my importance now that I'd been closeted alone with the queen. I did not spot Renard; he must have gone to prepare Courtenay's arrest. I did see Rochester among those present, talking to an anxious-looking man in a bishop's robe, who I assumed was Courtenay's patron, Gardiner. I made to pause, catching Rochester's troubled glance.

He turned away pointedly, as if he did not recognize me.

I could hardly blame him. I moved onward, down the staircase into the lower gallery, where courtiers had converged to speculate. Already word had leaked out that something of importance had happened. By early afternoon at the latest, all Whitehall would be buzzing with news of the earl's fall.

I had a sudden pang as I thought of Courtenay. He would surely die for this; after having survived years of imprisonment in the Tower, his own actions had led him to the scaffold. Though he wasn't a pleasant man, nor, as the queen had surmised, a particularly clever one, I was relieved I could still feel pity for him, and angry regret that I'd had to expose his dealings, despite my promise to him. For all his misdeeds, he didn't deserve this.

Dudley did.

Then I came to a halt. I did not know where Elizabeth lodged. Raking a hand through my matted hair, I saw courtiers staring at me in unabashed disgust. All of a sudden, I was aware of my unkempt person. Must I approach one of these mincing peacocks to ask—

"Master Beecham! Master Beecham, wait a moment!"

I turned to see Mistress Dormer hastening down the staircase, holding up fistfuls of her skirts, exposing thin ankles in gray hose. "Her Majesty asked me to accompany you," she explained, breathless. "The rooms you seek are a distance away, and she thought you'd need help finding them, seeing as you've not been there before."

I smiled faintly in gratitude. With a toss of her pretty head, Jane Dormer led me past the courtiers, who immediately leaned to each other to whisper.

"Where did you leave Blackie?" I asked, hoping to distract her from uncomfortable questions concerning my meeting with the queen.

"With Lady Clarencieux. He'll have to learn sometime that I

can't be with him every minute. Though I'm quite fond of him now, I never wanted a dog. He was a gift—or so Mistress Darrier claimed." Jane grimaced. "As if that could excuse what she did."

Just as I'd been on the night of my arrival, I was struck by the spite in her voice. Though she seemed an otherwise unassuming girl, where Sybilla was concerned Jane Dormer was all claw.

"I did not see Mistress Darrier this morning," I remarked.

"No, you did not. Because Mistress Darrier comes and goes as she pleases." The silence turned taut before Jane added pointedly, "You'd be wise to stay far from her."

"Oh?" I kept my expression neutral, even as I took in the twist of her mouth, the slit-eyed jealousy that was too mature for someone of her age. Beautiful women often incited competition among their peers, I knew, but Jane Dormer was little more than a child. "What exactly has Mistress Darrier done to have provoked such dislike in you? She gave you that dog, which seems to me a kind gesture—"

"Does it?" she snapped. "Do you think it a fair exchange for stealing my betrothed?"

I almost stopped walking. "Your betrothed?" I echoed.

She glared. "Yes. You cannot know, naturally, having just arrived at court, but Her Majesty had arranged for *me* to wed the Duke of Feria. I was to be his bride and return with him to Spain, had Mistress Darrier not decided she wanted Feria for herself. Or rather, that toad Renard decided it for her."

A chill overcame me. "Perhaps she has no wish to wed Feria, then."

"No wish?" She gave a humorless laugh. "Women like her have *every* wish. Feria will make her a duchess, which is quite a step up from being the ambassador's whore."

An invisible noose coiled about my throat. "That's a strong accusation. I understood that he was her patron and moreover that she is of noble blood. Her father and brothers perished defending the Church during the Pilgrimage of Grace."

Jane sniffed. "Is that what she told you? I suppose it does carry a ring of truth, if you don't know the real story. But most do not, and those who do don't care to recall otherwise, given her proximity to Renard. But Lady Clarencieux certainly does; she remembers when Master Darrier, Sybilla's father, was one of those up-and-coming men who got rich under Lord Cromwell—a lawyer, like Cromwell himself, who inventoried the monasteries once they'd been slated for closure. He made his fortune pillaging like a pirate, building his estate with gold he never reported to the treasury. When Cromwell fell, so did Darrier. He was executed, yes, but not for defending our Church. He was drawn and quartered like a common criminal because he had stolen from the king."

I was finding it increasingly difficult to breathe. I saw Sybilla in my mind, her heavy tresses of hair draping over me, her body writhing . . .

"And her brothers?"

She shrugged. "Who knows if they even exist? If they do, they did not die in York, I can assure you. Of everything Mistress Darrier says, the only verifiable truth is that she, her mother, and her sister fled England to escape the king's wrath, no doubt with some of the Darrier wealth stashed in their underlinens. After all, they had to have something, to gain entrance to the Hapsburg court. Empresses don't take on paupers to be ladies-in-waiting."

I couldn't move another step, coming to an appalled halt.

Sybilla had lied to me. She had deliberately misrepresented her situation. What I didn't understand yet was why.

"She was actually telling Feria that same tragic tale when you came into the gallery with your dying squire," Jane went on, oblivious to my discomfort. "I tell you, she was not convincing and not pleased by your interruption. Oh, I'll give her this much: She's a fine feast for the eye, if you care for her sort, but Feria will regret having agreed to Renard's terms. A woman like her—all she can bring a man in the end is perdition."

I had to restrain myself from grabbing hold of her, bombarding her with questions she'd have no answers for.

"Do I offend?" Jane asked, taking note of my silence. "I merely thought you should be forewarned. She's not who you think she is. She is hardly a respectable person. To steal another woman's betrothed and give a dog as consolation is not a respectable thing to do."

She'd reverted to being a wronged adolescent, railing against the wiles of an older, more experienced woman. I gave her a vague nod, my mind awhirl. "Yes," I murmured. "I agree it is not respectable. I appreciate your candor. You've been very kind to me."

"I like you. I think it a pity you've nothing to commend you save the queen's favor."

I cleared my throat, turning my attention to the gallery we entered, the carved wainscoting and elaborate plaster decorations edging a coffered ceiling marred by damp stains. "I've never seen this part of the palace," I said, as I tried to get my mind around what she had told me, trying to fit the fragments into some cohesive design. Why would Sybilla mislead me? Had she hoped to incite my pity, perhaps? It could be that she still sought to escape Renard's hold on her; nothing Jane Dormer said had negated that. Maybe she thought the truth less compelling than a fabricated past, guaranteed to evoke sympathy in a man like me.

Jane said, "This part of Whitehall is rarely used." She paused. "Lady Elizabeth insisted on staying here, I'm told. Apparently the apartments used to be hers when her father was alive and she came to visit him at court."

Remote and empty, without the ubiquitous legions of courtiers or servants, the gallery before me offered a spectacular view of the river but little else. The cold was palpable as we came before a sturdy door adorned with faded gilt. There were no guards; as I rapped on the wood panel, the sound echoed. Scuffling on the door's other side preceded its tentative opening and a tremulous "Yes? Who is it?"

I recognized Blanche Parry. "Master Beecham. I bring word for the Lady Elizabeth."

There was a moment of hesitation. Blanche didn't know my alias, I suddenly thought, and as I heard her urgent inquiry of someone nearby, I turned to Jane. "Please inform Her Majesty that I'll escort Her Grace back as soon as she's ready."

She pouted. I recalled how she'd suggested that Elizabeth would do better to submit to the queen and realized she'd been looking forward to witnessing the princess's humiliation. It saddened me that a girl with so much to live for had already imbibed the venom of the court, where reveling in another's disgrace was a coveted pastime.

"Very well," she said unconvincingly, and she walked away, glancing over her shoulder as I waited for the door to be unbolted. When she was far enough away that she couldn't possibly overhear, I said, "Mistress Parry, it's Brendan. Open up."

The locks immediately slid back to reveal the haggard face of Elizabeth's trusted lady, the matron upon whom, after Mistress Ashley, she most relied. Mistress Parry had been in service to the princess since Elizabeth was a babe. Though not old—no more than forty-six—she looked ancient, her eyes hollowed from sleeplessness, graying hair escaping her hood. With a claw-like hand she yanked me into the room and slammed the door shut, bolting it again as if she feared an invasion.

"What is happening?" she asked anxiously. "Tell me. Are they going to arrest her?"

I shook my head. Urian dashed up to me, shoving his long muzzle into my hand, demanding to be petted. As I caressed him, I surveyed the chamber. It boasted a magnificent oriel window that let in plenty of light, floor-to-ceiling tapestries, carpets underfoot, and fine furniture. Scattered about were traveling chests, into which a perspiring young maid was emptying armfuls of clothing, candlesticks, and other possessions. Except for her and Mistress Parry, I saw no other women or attendants.

I turned back to Mistress Parry. "Where are her ladies?"

"Gone." She gave a fretful sigh. I could see the poor woman was about to leap out of her skin. "Her Grace is in her bedchamber; she was taking her exercise in the gallery, as she does every morning, when one of those insufferable women came to tell her that the Earl of Devon would be arrested. As soon as the others heard, they ran off, like rats from a ship, leaving Her Grace alone. She told us to start packing. Then she locked herself in her room. She thinks they're coming for her next. Are they?"

"Not yet," I said, and I moved to a narrow door I assumed led to the bedchamber, Urian at my heels. Mistress Parry warned, "She won't see anyone."

I knocked on the door. "Your Grace? It's me. Let me in."

No response. I knocked again. "You must open. I bring word from Her Majesty."

After a tense moment, I heard a key turn and pushed the door open onto a small bedchamber, suffused in darkness. There was no window or candles; only a rush light on a side table, which cast more smoke than illumination. As light from the outside seeped in, I saw an unmade tester bed and another coffer on the floor. Elizabeth crouched there, a heap of books at her side. She appeared to be looking through them, putting some in the coffer and discarding others. Another maid stood nearby with a frightened look; she must have unlocked the door.

I waved her out, keeping the door ajar. Urian padded over to Elizabeth and whimpered. She petted him absently, her hair tangled about her face; under the hem of her dark skirt, I glimpsed slim bare feet. The chamber was icy, yet she wore no shoes.

"Don't," she said, before I could open my mouth. "I don't want to hear it. I need to decide which of these books I can take with me into the Tower."

"You're not going to the Tower." I stepped to her, lowering my voice even as I heard Mistress Parry marshaling the two maids in the outer chamber.

Elizabeth turned to me, her eyes black in her ashen face. "Is she sending me to the scaffold instead?"

"She's sending you from court. I know not where. But before she does—"

"She'll question me. Am I to submit to her interrogation before the entire court?"

I did not answer. I returned her stare until she looked away. She pretended to go back to her books. Then I heard her say, "If she sent you, then I can assume you haven't lost her favor. Does that mean our other matter is resolved?"

"Yes. I delivered letters to Her Majesty. I am responsible for Courtenay's arrest." I paused. "But not Dudley. For the moment, he is safe—though he doesn't merit it."

She drew in a stifled breath and turned her sharp gaze back to me. "And my letter?"

"It was not there. Dudley must have kept it."

Her eyes narrowed. She searched my face. "Did he do that to you?"

"Among others. But he took the brunt of it."

Her mouth twitched; it was almost a smile. "I take it he wasn't pleased to see you."

"You might say that. He blames me for everything that has befallen him and his family. He vowed that when the time comes, he'll see me pay for it."

She nodded. "It's to be expected. Robert was never one to accept responsibility if he could blame someone else." She stood, her gown crinkled. "So," she said, "with all his threats and bluster, did he tell you everything?"

"Most of it, but I don't know how much to believe. That, too, I suppose, is to be expected." Then, before I could stop myself, I added, "Why? Why did you do this?"

This time, her smile crept across her lips. "I think you already know. Or if you don't, Cecil did. It's why he sent you. He could not have expected me to wait for Renard to put an end to me? I did what I had to. I don't regret it. I only regret that I put those I care about in harm's way." She brought a hand to her throat. "I was saddened to hear of Peregrine," she said. "I would never have allowed it to go so far had I known the price you would pay."

"He paid it. I wish it were otherwise." I met her eyes. "It's not over yet. Renard is enraged. He will do whatever he can to see you dead. You are still in danger."

Her gaze turned inward. She reached to her bed for her discarded slippers; their rose silk ribbons tangled about her slim fingers. "I've been in danger from the day my sister became queen. Our past is something she can never forgive or forget. If she does not harm me today, she will eventually. Nothing is more certain."

Differences of faith can tear apart even those who should be closest . . .

With the echo of Sybilla's words in my head, I watched Elizabeth move to her tarnished glass to gauge her appearance. "Is that all you want to ask of me? Speak now, for I'll not tolerate it later. Or have I so disillusioned that you wish to now serve my sister instead?"

"I pledged myself to you. After everything I've done, can you still doubt me?"

She turned from the glass. Though she didn't say a word, I saw in her eyes the momentary fracturing of her reserve.

"I will never leave you," I told her, "not willingly."

She bit her lip. "Mistress Parry," she called out. Her matron bustled in.

"It seems we've overstayed our welcome," Elizabeth said. "I must attend my sister the queen and request leave to depart court. I don't think she'll let us get as far as Hatfield," she added, glancing at me, "but perhaps my house at Ashridge will be acceptable." She gave a sudden shiver, sole indication of the fear she must harbor deep inside. "I'll implore on my knees, if need be. Fetch my white gown. I must look . . . penitent."

Mistress Parry nodded, hurrying back into the anteroom.

Elizabeth fixed her gaze on me. "We still have time. Robert wouldn't keep my letter, not because he cares anything for you but because he would not see me harmed. He has many faults, yes, and desires too much, but never my death. If my letter is missing, then someone else must have it."

I pivoted immediately to the door.

"Wait," she said. I looked over my shoulder. "Do whatever it takes," she whispered. "No matter the cost, Renard must never get hold of it. If he does, it will indeed be over—for all of us."

I strode through the outer chamber, startling Mistress Parry as she went to the princess with her gown. Only once I was alone in the gallery did I let myself pause, leaning against a wall to force out the air lodged like barbs in my chest.

A woman like her—all she can bring a man in the end is perdition . . .

I knew who had taken Elizabeth's letter.

A few moments later, the princess emerged. In silver-white satin, with her hair loose under a simple crescent headdress, she looked almost serene. I tried to focus only on escorting her through the palace to the queen's wing, even as urgency pounded in my blood, making it difficult not to abandon her and begin my frantic search for the woman I now believed had deceived me far more than I could have ever imagined.

Mary waited in her audience chamber, bedecked in a jewel-encrusted gown that swamped her thin figure, surrounded by terse black-robed councillors. After Elizabeth dropped to a curtsy, the queen motioned brusquely and turned without a word to march into the council room with the councillors behind her. Elizabeth did not look at me; she went into that room alone, her chin high, as if she truly had nothing to hide.

The door shut. Immediately, the queen's women began to whisper. I avoided their questioning gazes. I had already seen Sybilla was still not among them, but she must be somewhere. She couldn't have escaped yet, not from London. Where would she hide? She must have taken the letter from the folder before she brought it to me; perhaps she thought that as long as she had it, she'd have something to barter with, in case Renard discovered her ploy and her own life was placed in danger.

I had to find her first.

Then I saw Mistress Dormer watching me intently; turning to her without warning, I grabbed her dog's lead. "Blackie looks as if he needs to relieve himself," I declared, and I pulled the growling, snapping dog into the gallery, leaving her to hurry after me.

"What are you doing?" she demanded as I began to yank the dog down the gallery. He indeed had to go. At the first corner, he lifted his leg and pissed against the wall.

Jane gasped. "He's supposed to go outside! The queen warned me if he ever did that in the palace again, she'd make me give him up. She says Whitehall reeks of—"

I whirled to her. "Where is she? Where is Mistress Darrier?"

"How—how should I know?" She recoiled from me, glancing over her shoulder at a pair of courtiers strolling past. "I'm hardly in a position to—"

"Don't lie." I stepped closer, dragging Blackie with me. "You told me those things about her for a reason. You deliberately warned me against her." I paused. "You do realize the princess is still heir to the throne? She's not been disinherited yet, and the queen is her sister, her family. They might find accord. It would go better for both of us if we were seen to be on the winning side."

My intimation wasn't lost on her. "You . . . you serve *her*?"

"I serve the Tudors. And I must find Mistress Darrier before it's too late. It's a matter of life and death. Help me and I'll make sure you will not go unrewarded. You still want to marry Feria, yes? I'll put a word in with the queen, I promise you."

She arched her brow. I had gone beyond my bounds, and she knew it. I had no right to promise anything. With sudden determination, Jane snatched the lead from me. "I warned you about her because I like you. But I'm starting to like you rather less. You are indeed common as dirt, if you think this is how a gentleman behaves." She drew herself erect. "I do not know where she is. She does as she pleases. Why not ask Don Renard or the Earl of Devon, if you can find him? He seems to have gone missing as well, much like Mistress Darrier. Perhaps they're together. Surely one of those men ought to know where she gets to when she should be at her post in the queen's chambers."

"Together?" I whispered. "She and Courtenay . . . ?"

"You truly don't know anything, do you?" she asked. "Before you arrived, Mistress Darrier and the Earl of Devon were quite friendly. Some of us thought she hoped to have him as her spouse, until he was rejected by the queen and turned his attention to Elizabeth. But I daresay that didn't stop her. A woman who sleeps with an ambassador *and* an earl, while conspiring to steal another woman's betrothed, is truly capable of anything."

Horrified silence descended as I recalled the day in this very gallery when Sybilla had approached me and Elizabeth and Courtenay appeared. *My lady Darrier,* he had said, *if I were you, I'd be more circumspect in choosing those with whom I idle away my time. We wouldn't want your master to think you're consorting with the enemy, now would we?*

They knew each other. They were more than mere acquaintances.

Jane was regarding me impatiently. "You look rather shocked. I don't see why. As I told you, she's not respectable." She tugged on Blackie's lead. "Now, if there's nothing else, I must bid you good day, Master Beecham. I believe we've said all we need to say to each other." She turned about to return to the queen's chambers, Blackie trotting at her side.

I stood as if paralyzed. Courtenay had said in the brothel, *I don't swive men.*

He hadn't lied.

That night in the brothel, he had been waiting for Sybilla.

I raced back toward my room. I had no idea how long Elizabeth's interrogation might take, but I had to prepare. I had a feeling in my gut that Courtenay had gone into hiding in the brothel in Southwark; I had to reach him before they ran him to ground like a hare. If Sybilla had seduced the earl, chances were she'd uncovered his role in the conspiracy before me; she must have known that he was sending letters for Dudley and that Renard would try to intercept them. She'd stolen Elizabeth's letter from the tube for a reason, then provided me with the others to seal Courtenay's doom. Whomever she was working for, it wasn't the ambassador. She wanted the earl ensnared in his own trap, just as she had ensnared me, and she had to be stopped.

I had to stop her.

At the door, I was fishing in my doublet for my key when sudden footsteps came up behind me. Before I could yank my poniard from my boot, a fist slammed into my gut. It knocked the air out of my lungs. I doubled over, crumpling to my knees.

"Where is she?" Renard stepped from the shadows.

His henchman kicked me. I grunted, tasting blood.

"Again, where is she? I won't ask a third time."

I looked up. Renard regarded me impassively, his burly henchman standing over me with fists clenched. I eyed his man as I heaved myself into a seated position. He was the companion of the slim swordsman who'd taken the tube from me, and I saw again in my mind that polished figure in black, who'd fended off my clumsy swordplay as if he toyed with a child. I remembered the gleaming eyes under the mask, the deft speed.

Then I recalled gripping Sybilla's wrist and feeling her hidden strength.

The swordsman hadn't been a man at all.

It had been *her.*

"Did you think to best me?" Renard's voice slashed through my thoughts. "I've had a lifetime of practice at this game; I could see you dead this very hour and no one would question it."

"The queen might," I said, breathing through my nose. "Seeing as she ordered me to uncover everything else I can of the plot. If I go missing, she'll know who to ask."

His mouth twisted. "Is that a threat? Be very careful. The queen already mistrusts you; like me, she does not believe any man without a past can exist." He flicked his hand. "Enough. I tire of this affair. Where is Mistress Darrier? I know you've been working with her against me, just as I know that you managed to steal those infernal letters. She was supposed to get them for me, but she betrayed me instead."

I met his stare. "From what she told me, you earned it."

Anger distorted his face. "She will die," he snarled. Then he collected himself, allowing himself an icy smile. "Though I must admit, she played her part all too well. I even arranged a noble marriage with Feria for her, in exchange for her cooperation." He paused. "And you: You were unexpected indeed, disguising yourself as a man for hire so you could save that heretic Elizabeth. No one guessed your ploy. Except Sybilla. She has a taste for deception; she suspected you at once. It seems you charmed her, though. She's always been faithful to me until now. What did you promise her, eh? Safety in exchange for the letters? Money, perchance? Yes, I should think money would do the trick. She's a harlot, after all. I had her mother on her knees the hour we met, and when she failed to please, I took Sybilla instead. She depends on men like us for her survival. Your cock, mine: It doesn't matter, so long as she profits by it."

My fists clenched at my sides. I had to tell myself not to rise to his bait. If he'd resorted to this extreme, waiting outside my room to bully me, then he was desperate. Sybilla had struck a coup de grace to his plan against Elizabeth, and he was flailing. Without that letter, he truly had nothing. The princess was being questioned this very hour and would go free. Once she did, he'd never have another chance to destroy her.

With one eye on his scowling man, I came unsteadily to my feet. "I don't need to tell you anything. Lest you forget, I no longer work for you."

His smile vanished. He held up his hand, halting his henchman, who growled in Spanish and made a menacing advance toward me.

"You will regret this," Renard said. "I hold Her Majesty's trust, for all that you tried to make me a fool today. You and I can reach an understanding. Bring me Mistress Darrier and your life will be spared. You cannot win; no matter what you do, my master the emperor's son will wed the queen, and Philip will see Elizabeth beheaded like her mother before her. You'd be wise to change your allegiance now, while you still have the chance. If you do not, your days, like Elizabeth's, will be numbered."

"As they were when you left that poisoned note for me? I don't reach understandings with murderers. Because of you, my squire is dead."

He let out a sudden, cruel laugh. "Do you think I'm responsible for your squire's death?" He met my stare. "You're not as clever as I supposed. Poison was never my weapon of choice. Rest assured, had I chosen to dispose of you thus, you'd not still be here to reproach me." He stepped back. "I wish you luck. I do believe you're going to need it."

He walked away, his henchman throwing another mastiff glare at me.

I shoved my belongings into my bag, then threw on my cloak and sword. I left the room as I found it; I had no plans of returning. If I never saw the court again, it would be too soon.

As soon as I reached the gallery and heard the agitated clamor of voices, I made haste to the queen's wing. The doors were still shut, the sentries in place, but as I looked about, searching the crowd, I espied Mistress Parry, loitering at the edge of the throng as if she, too, searched for someone.

When she saw me, she turned on her heel. I followed, keeping my distance until we were in the empty corridor leading to the princess's apartments. Without looking at me, Mistress Parry said, "She's been granted leave to retire to Ashridge." Her voice quavered. "Thank God, we are finally delivered from this nest of papists."

Relief washed over me. "And the earl, has he been arrested?"

She shook her head. "The warrant has been issued. But no one knows where he is."

"Then I cannot leave yet. Her Grace knows why. Tell her I'll come to her as soon as I'm able."

She nodded. "God keep you," she said, and she continued to the apartments as fast as her legs could carry her.

Afternoon faded into premature dusk. Standing wrapped in my cloak in a shadowed recess of the courtyard, I watched Elizabeth bid farewell to the queen.

Snowflakes drifted down over the braided manes of the stamping horses, on harried pages loading the last of the coffers and chests into the wagon, and on the princess's red-gold tresses, coiled at her nape in a net, her slender figure enveloped in black velvet.

Not many had turned out to see her departure, though I could glimpse semiconcealed figures converging at the surrounding gallery windows, courtiers observing from the safety of their perches, waiting with bated breath for the queen's last-minute order for Elizabeth to return to her rooms, from which she'd emerge for the short trip to the Tower.

Mary stepped from among her ladies, the wind catching at her violet mantle. A jeweled rosary hung from her waist. She faced her sister as she might a combatant.

Elizabeth dropped practically to her knees, head bowed.

She'd come to court as the queen's cherished heir and sister; in less than six months she was leaving under a pall of hatred and suspicion. My heart went out to her as the queen extended her hand with its signet ring. There was no affection in the gesture, no sign of forgiveness or largesse; Mary was as remote as the clock tower looming above us.

In the silence broken only by the wind and sifting thaw of snow, with the queen's little hand trapped in hers, Elizabeth lifted her voice and said, loudly enough for everyone present to hear, "I depart from Your Majesty's presence with a heavy heart, though circumstances and my own delicate health require it. Yet I declare myself your most loyal subject, who loves you more than anyone. I beseech you not to believe those who spread evil reports about me without doing me the honor of letting me prove to you in person the malicious nature of such slanders, for on you alone do I depend for my honor."

It was a perfect speech, stamped with Elizabeth's signature flair for rhetoric. Mary reacted accordingly, her thin white lips seeming to disappear into the pressed crevice of her mouth. I held my own breath as everyone waited. Elizabeth glanced warily past her sister to Renard, who stood steps from the queen. Though his cap shaded his face, his eyes must have been directed at her with single-minded fervor. If he had had his way, this moment would have gone very differently.

Mary withdrew her hand. Something intangible, fleeting in its poignancy, moved across her face. Her attempt to smile came out as a bloodless grimace; she impulsively reached out without warning and clasped Elizabeth's hand again, as if in regret.

Then she called to her women.

Lady Clarencieux stepped forth, bearing what looked like a small animal. As the princess unraveled it, a length of lustrous sable flooded her arms—a cloak with inset sleeves and hood, fashioned of supple velvet and the exquisite Russian fur.

"It is cold in Hertfordshire," Mary said, "and, as you say, your health is delicate. We would not wish for you to take ill for lack of proper care."

Elizabeth started to speak, her gaze bright with unshed tears; before she could, the queen motioned again, and a friar in a Franciscan habit and cape, the knotted cord of his order about his waist, appeared. At the sight of him, Elizabeth's eyes dimmed.

"You assured us that you wished to become better acquainted with the ways of our true faith," Mary said. "This friar will go with you to Ashridge to instruct you. He brings with him the articles of our true faith, so you may see them every day and learn their solace. We pray that you'll soon realize that only by casting aside the heretic teachings of your youth can you prove this loyalty you so ardently declare."

She took a step back. The sable overflowed in Elizabeth's arms. Turning to Mistress Parry, she relieved herself of it and curtsied again before moving to her litter. She had a large entourage that included her women, an escort of men-at-arms, her Arabian jennet, Cantila, and Urian.

"We choose to believe you for now," Mary called out, freezing her in midstep. "Live quietly at Ashridge with no further upset, and we'll take note of your sincerity."

Elizabeth paused, casting her gaze over the assembly. Though she couldn't have seen me among the multitude, I hoped that somehow she felt my presence.

To the crack of whips and clangor of hooves, the procession

rode out under the palace archway. The crowd dispersed, the courtiers rushing to join the watchers in the galleries, to examine and dissect, to again place bets on Elizabeth's chances.

Shrouded in my cloak, I blended with them.

The time had come to embark on my own desperate gambit.

Chapter Eighteen

crossed the frosted gardens and tiltyard to the stables. Cinnabar whickered from his stall, happy to see me; I tarried a few moments, reassuring him. I did not want to risk riding over the bridge again or make myself too visible a target on horseback. If Renard was going to have me followed, this time let the chase be on foot.

After paying Toby a generous bribe, I gave him instructions as to what to do with Cinnabar if I did not return. "Send him to Ashridge, as a gift to Her Grace, Princess Elizabeth. She will reward you." As I left the stables, Cinnabar neighed, and I fought off a pang of fear. I didn't know if I'd ever see him or anyone I loved again.

Slipping into the frigid night, I headed for the river. Close to the water steps I suddenly heard someone behind me. I ducked into the nearest doorway, unsheathing my sword. The footsteps grew closer, an odd dragging sound that rasped in my ears. As I gripped my sword, ready to lunge, a beggar limped past the doorway, muttering to herself, her misshapen feet swathed in rags. She did not notice me lurking only inches away, my length of

blade bared. Warily, I searched the environs and continued onward.

The ice in the Thames had begun to break apart, the tepid
warmth of the past few days heaving it up in slabs. The river was
still dangerous to navigate, but I reasoned that with so many
boatmen facing starvation without their trade, a few must have
returned to work by now. I located one by the water steps, rubbing gnarled hands together to stave off the chill.

He avidly pocketed my coin, and I cautiously stepped into
his rickety skiff. Seated on the exposed bench, I repressed my
lifelong fear of dark water as the skiff bumped into the river. Ice
clunked against the sides; the wherry man maneuvered past it,
pushing larger pieces aside with his oar. I couldn't help but think
that if one of those sharp fragments struck the hull, we'd sink
like stone.

We made it across without incident, though I was frozen to
my toes from the wind. After paying the wherry man extra to
wait, I raced through the winding, filth-strewn streets to the
Hawk's Nest.

Its facade was shuttered against the inhospitable night.
Looking at it, I felt as though a lifetime had passed since I'd first
come to this place. I rapped on the door, thinking for no apparent reason that Scarcliff might be here.

"The earl's man," I said to the leering doorman, dumping the
last of my pouch's contents into his meaty paw. "Is he here?"

"Who?" He pocketed my coin. "No idea what you're bleatin'
about, pretty man."

They must have killed him on the road, dumped him somewhere he wouldn't be found until dogs or kites unearthed his
bones. Though he had done nothing to warrant my pity, I felt it
anyway. No man deserved such an end.

I was moving purposefully forward when the doorman grasped me by the sleeve. "Not so fast. I still need the fee and yer weapon."

My answer was to whirl about and slam my poniard's hilt into his face. Blood spewed from his nose. I hit him again, then again, in the groin. He groaned and dropped to the floor, cupping his parts. "Bastard," I heard him gasp. "You miserable arse-lickin'—"

I clubbed him again, silencing him. As I strode into the brothel, I hoped I hadn't killed him.

The main room was practically deserted. Only a few masked customers sat drinking or playing dice, attended by desultory boys who didn't even bother to sway their hips. Glancing at the booth near the staircase, where Scarcliff had his post, I found it empty.

Once up the staircase, I paused, listening for telltale sounds of customer entertainment. A few cats slinked into the shadows, but I heard nothing coming from behind the doors. Had news from the palace spread this far, so quickly?

I didn't bother to knock on Courtenay's door, kicking it open with my boot. He sat alone at the table, decanter and goblet before him. He looked up, startled; when he saw me, he scowled. "You faithless cur. You betrayed me."

I shut the door behind me and leaned against it with my arms crossed. Though I wanted to grab him by his shirt and shake him until he spilled his guts, I needed his cooperation, preferably without duress.

"Actually," I said, "I believe we've been both betrayed. Mistress Sybilla Darrier; she was the woman you'd been meeting here, wasn't she?"

He reached for the decanter. I strode across the room, swiping it from his grasp. "Drink yourself to death for all I care, but not before you tell me what I need to know."

Up close, I saw his eyes were bloodshot, rimmed in shadow. He was also halfway drunk by the looks of it, which wasn't going to make this any easier.

"The queen has issued a warrant for your arrest," I informed him. "They're searching for you as we speak."

He blanched. Staggering from his chair, he thrust his chin at me, his breath foul with wine. "Yes, and why is that? Because you lied! You promised to see me safe. You said, if I helped you, you'd not set their dogs on me. But you gave them those letters. Why should I trust anything you say now?"

"Because we've both been played false," I said. "She planned this. She stole Dudley's letters, only I didn't know it was her at the time. Then she brought them back, claiming she'd taken them from Renard. I had to give the queen something before Renard moved against the princess. It was your head or hers. That is what I believed."

The anger in his eyes faded. "She—she planned it?" he whispered.

I met his bewildered stare. "She made me believe she was helping me. But now I know she had something different in mind." I leaned to him. "She has another master. I must know where she is."

I was hoping for a revelation, but he turned away blindly, swaying. "She told me Renard had used her cruelly," he said, as if the act of admitting her duplicity aloud would somehow make it less true. "She said she was English, that she supported our cause. I believed her. She was so beautiful, so convincing . . . I told her everything about the conspiracy and Dudley's letters."

"About me," I said.

He nodded miserably. "She came to see me that same night. She must have seen you leaving the brothel. She asked who you were. I told her that you claimed to be working for Elizabeth and threatened me, so I had to help you get into the Tower. Later, when I saw you with her in the palace, I thought she would persuade you to see our point of view." He came to a halt, his eyes widening as he recognized the full import of his credulity. "God help me, she lied. She used me to her own ends. What am I going to do now?"

"Tell me where she is. You can still escape. But she has Elizabeth's letter; I have to get it back."

Tears spilled down his cheeks. "They'll torture me, won't they? Break me on the rack, in the Little Ease. They'll tear me apart with hooks; burn me with brands and whip my flesh from my bones, but nothing they do can stop it. The others will come. They will rise up against the queen. And Sybilla knows; she knows everything."

I felt as if a pit had cracked under my feet. "Others? What others?"

He went silent, his jaw clenching. Then he said, "The nobles Dudley wrote to—they're only the half of it. He didn't trust anyone, not entirely, so he had me recruit others."

"Who? When will they act?"

"When the queen's betrothal is announced," he muttered, lowering his gaze to his feet, "that will be their sign. Thomas Wyatt in Kent, he's rallied his supporters; he plans to join with the Duke of Suffolk's retainers to march on London."

The Duke of Suffolk: Jane Grey's father. God help her, Mary would kill her for it. She would end up paying for these men's treachery. I couldn't take any more. Seizing Courtenay by his chemise, I lifted him off the floor, ramming him against the wall. He moaned; glancing down, I saw his hose darken under his codpiece, the seep of piss trickling down his thigh.

"You fool," I hissed. "Do you realize what you and Dudley have done? Elizabeth could die because of you! So could her cousin Jane Grey. Sybilla sought information for someone else, and now, because of you, she has all the information she needs."

His eyes bulged. "I—I never meant to harm Elizabeth," he gasped. "I swear it."

My fist closed about his chemise, twisting the cloth, cutting off his very breath. "I need to find Sybilla. *Now.*"

"On the Strand." His voice broke. "In the old Dudley manor. She's there."

As I let him loose, his knees buckled underneath him. He slid down the wall, crumpling at my feet. I took a deliberate step back. Much as I wanted to feel compassion for him, all I felt was disgust. His pride and foolish ambition had cost him everything. He'd brought England to the brink of disaster because of it.

He slumped in a heap. It was then that I discerned a cacophony downstairs—terrified shrieks, the smash of cutlery and overturned furniture, and the stamp of booted feet punctuated by authoritative shouts. The queen's men were here.

Courtenay keened. I whirled about. There was nowhere to go, nowhere except—

I threw open the casement window and reached out my hand to him. "Come."

He cringed. "No. I—I can't. I'm . . . I'm afraid of heights."

I wasn't about to plead. Climbing onto the casement edge, I saw below me the stable yard and ramshackle stalls for horses. The commotion inside the brothel had roused an emaciated dog tied to a stump in the yard. It was barking, straining at its tether.

I looked to the left. Directly beyond the brothel lay a smaller dwelling, with a thatched roof that didn't appear too steep; to my right, a direct fall into the street. I stepped onto the outer ledge, balancing precariously. My breath came fast. I made myself take a deep breath. I wasn't fond of heights either, come to think of it.

Feeling with my foot past the ledge, I encountered a peeling beam that ran the length of the building, no wider than my hand. For a second, I froze. I couldn't do this. I couldn't skitter along the ledge like some damn cat—

Shouts boomed in the corridor. I glanced over my shoulder. Courtenay sat huddled in the corner, petrified. I couldn't wait anymore.

Step by step, I moved onto the ledge without looking down, gripping the outer wall, my hands splayed against moldering daub, my heels scraping icicles. In the room behind me, I heard Courtenay begin to pray, "Sweet Jesus, save me. Jesu, hear my plea," and the splintering of doors in the passageway being kicked in.

I crept onward. The dog was baying now.

An enormous crash came from the room. Courtenay let out a horrible wail.

They had found him.

I kept moving to the building's edge, assaulted by a vivid memory of the last time I'd found myself fleeing through a window in the dead of night . . .

I quickened my pace, just a little more to go.

The thatched rooftop was much farther down than I'd thought, slick with melted snow. I wondered if it would hold me or if I'd end up crashing through it.

"Someone's out the window!" a voice cried from behind me.

Unbuckling my sword in its scabbard, I tossed it into the street.

"You!" yelled the guard at the window. "Halt, by Her Majesty's command!"

I closed my eyes.

I leapt.

The fall felt eternal. Icy air whistled in my ears. Everything slowed to a crawl so that I had a dazzling, fleeting glimpse of the torch-lit maze of Southwark and heard the incredulous dismay of the guards leaning out the brothel window, watching me plummet to what they surely believed was my death.

I hit the thatch. Winter had frozen the bundled layers to mortarlike hardness. I tucked my knees, covering my head as I slid off the side. Sodden snow cushioned my fall; it was shorter in any event, a brief tumble, and then I sprawled on the ground.

Scrambling to my feet, too pummeled at this point to feel any pain, I grabbed up my sword. The stable-yard dog was yowling; any moment, the guards would come for me.

I ran as fast as I could into the labyrinth of clustered hovels and snaking back alleys. The guards' first priority would be to arrest Courtenay; with any luck, they'd assume I was a frightened boy-whore who'd made an intrepid escape and, after a cursory search of the vicinity, get on with the business at hand. Crouching in a recessed doorway to catch my breath, I listened for sounds of pursuit. Nothing.

I thought it unlikely the boatman would still be waiting, but there he was, right where I'd left him. He tucked a leather flask into his pocket. "Did you see 'em?" he lisped eagerly, through a paucity of teeth. "Queen's men, they were, searchin' for traitors. Heads on spikes—we'll be seein' heads on spikes come sunrise."

I muttered agreement as the inebriated sod angled the boat into the river, catching the current and swirling us round in a nauseating circle before he managed to direct us toward the city.

As the boat neared the steps, I unsheathed my sword. A dark shape stood on the quay, etched against inky night—large and cloaked, with a cowl over its head. Nearby was a massive gray destrier I recognized at once.

I half-rose off the bench, ignoring the boatman's shout that I'd tip the skiff, riveted to that figure as he grasped the rope tossed by the boatman and yanked the boat against the steps. From under his cowl, Scarcliff growled, "Put the blade down, lad. I don't bite." He tossed a coin at the boatman, who cackled in glee.

I hesitated. He was alive. He had been following me. Could he be trusted, though?

As if he read my doubt on my face, he shook back his cowl, revealing his ravaged countenance. "In case you're wondering, I'm a free man; I decide who I serve. I don't fancy serving a traitor."

"So you've come to help me out of the kindness of your heart?" I retorted, but much as I disliked it, I had to rely on him. The Strand was a distance away, and he had a horse, which meant I could gain time.

I thrust my sword into its scabbard. Scarcliff grunted, watching me approach his destrier. The horse stood nearly fourteen hands tall, with a thick neck and huge head, but when it whickered, nosing me gently, I took it as a good sign. A man who could keep a creature like this so even-tempered couldn't be all bad.

I had started to reach for the saddle pommel to haul myself up when Scarcliff said, "Cerberus is all I have that's worth anything. I expect to be compensated."

I swung into the saddle. "My horse is at Whitehall. Tell the groom Toby you've come to take him to Ashridge. He's yours until I return. Meet me at the Griffin."

Then I kicked my heels into his horse and galloped off.

Chapter Nineteen

I told her what I knew—about the letters, the conspiracy . . .
Courtenay's revelations tumbled in my mind as I rode at breakneck pace through the night-shrouded city. Sybilla knew about me; he had told her I was helping Elizabeth. She'd orchestrated our friendship so she could betray Courtenay to the queen with those letters and trounce Renard, but what did she want, ultimately? If she'd known the letters only exposed half of the plot, what did she achieve by hiding Elizabeth's letter? She was playing a mysterious game, and I had the sinking feeling that it wasn't to my benefit.

I couldn't stop to consider that while I raced to find her, Wyatt's rebels were arming themselves. As soon as the betrothal was announced, Courtenay had said, they would act. The betrothal wouldn't be officially declared until the queen went to Hampton Court, so I reasoned there was still time to stop Sybilla and report the rest of what I had discovered to the queen. If Wyatt joined with Suffolk as planned, Jane Grey could die for it. Months ago, her father had helped Northumberland put Lady Jane on Mary's throne, against Jane's will. The queen had promised her clemency, but Renard would cite Suffolk's treason as reason for her execution. If Jane, who shared Tudor blood, died, how long would it take before Renard convinced the queen to turn her wrath on Elizabeth?

I kicked the gray again. Skirting the city wall, I passed decrepit Ludgate and rode up the hill onto the graveled road of the Strand, which ran parallel with the Thames and was fronted by the nobility's riverside manors. It was another world here, where the misery and filth of London dissipated into affluence. Even the air smelled fresher than inside the city walls, with only a slight acrid tang wafting from the river. Copses of skeletal trees pocketed the road; I imagined leafy foliage at the height of summer, shading ladies out for evening strolls with their children and servants.

A flock of indignant swans scattered from the road. Each manor I passed resembled the next—ornate bastions of brick and timber framing, with expensive window bays and elegant chimneys in the new fashion, made to funnel smoke directly out of hearths. All were enclosed by high walls and protected by gates; each must have its own quay. No one of means rode through London if they could take to the river in a private barge.

Then I came up to a gate and reined Cerberus to a halt.

Silence pressed in around me.

I'd never been here before, though I had served the Dudley family. Still, I couldn't have mistaken the house. It exuded disgrace, clumps of dead vines festooning the gate, the courtyard beyond desolate. Above the doorway, stained by lichen and bird droppings, hung the Dudley badge: the bear and ragged staff. As I stared at it, a flood of memories threatened to engulf me. I'd seen that badge all my life, carved in wainscoting and window lintels, sewn into uniforms and cloaks. I'd worn it myself during my brief tenure as Robert's squire. It had been a symbol of pride and power; now it was the meaningless icon of a fallen dynasty.

I dismounted, tethering Cerberus to an iron rung in the wall. Well exercised, he began to munch on brittle weeds while I circled the front of the manor, seeking access. The gate was bolted, too high to scale. The walls looked equally insurmountable. However, at the edge of the surrounding wall abutting the river, I located a small gap where the stone had caved in from damp and neglect.

I crouched down to peer through the gap. It offered a circumscribed view of what must have once been a lavish garden, now barren. A parched lawn led to a set of water steps; a canopied barge bobbed there, anchored to the pier.

Scraping at the mortar with my poniard, I managed to widen the gap. Lying flat on my belly, my cloak over my head so it would not tangle between my legs, I crawled through, scraping against cold, stony ground.

Tension built in me as I stood. The manor was a short distance away—an ostentatious hulk, its windows dark. I crossed the flagstone terrace to a back door. I tried the latch, expecting to find it locked. It wasn't. Pushing the door open, I stepped inside and nearly tripped over something in the hallway. With one glance at the sprawled corpse, I recognized Renard's henchman. A pool of blood about his midsection attested to a recent and very precise sword thrust. He'd taken it as he came in, no doubt sent by Renard to find Sybilla. I suddenly remembered her telling me Renard rented a manor on the Strand for a mistress, only in the turmoil of the past twenty-four hours I had failed to recall it.

She had lured me here. Just as she'd waited for Renard's man to arrive, she was no doubt waiting for me.

Easing around the corpse, I proceeded warily into the manor. It was a ghost house, its vast emptiness returning the echo of my footsteps. The walls were bare.

When I caught sight of light flickering ahead, I gripped my sword. I half-anticipated Sybilla leaping from the shadows, but as I slowly approached I realized that the light was coming from a room, where a lantern sat on a side table before a reflective window.

Then I heard her. "You needn't be afraid. I am alone."

I stepped through a narrow door. The room before me might have been a private study or small library, perhaps, employed for personal business. The diamond-paned window overlooked the courtyard and front gate. On the floor under the window was a heap of old rushes, swept up with fragments of cloth. The air was dank, its mustiness tinged with an odd greasy smell I couldn't quite place.

The only furniture was the side table holding the lantern and a chipped oak desk, behind which stood Sybilla. She wore a loose-sleeved black shirt, a fitted leather tunic, and belted breeches: her swordsman garb. The only thing missing was the mask.

She smiled. "You took your time. I did mention Renard rented a manor, did I not? Though I suppose under the circumstances, your forgetfulness can be excused."

I had to make a conscious effort to resist her eyes—lustrous as moon-drenched violets, alluring as sin. My fist closed about my sword hilt, as though it were a talisman.

"You can put that away." She spread her arms. "As you can see, I bear no weapon."

"So you claim," I replied. "Not that it would stop me. Weapon or not, if you weren't a woman I'd kill you without hesitation."

"So my gender finally protects me? Pray, what have I done to merit such hostility?"

I stared at her. "You deceived me from the start. You said you spied on the queen for Renard, but in truth he set you to spy on Courtenay. You seduced the earl, got him to tell you all his secrets, but you didn't tell Renard what you discovered, about the conspiracy and about me. You knew I'd tracked the earl to that brothel and what I arranged with him. You made me think you were helping me, but all along you prepared a trap. Shall I go on?"

"Please do." Her eyes glittered. "I find this all . . . fascinating."

I took a menacing step toward her. "You left the poisoned note in my room. All this time, you led me to think Renard was the culprit when it was you, all along."

She reached for a decanter on the desk and poured ale into two goblets. She extended one to me. I ignored it. With a sigh, she set the cup within my reach. "I never intended to kill the boy. I merely sought to warn you away. I didn't expect you, you see; you were never part of the plan. I was at a loss as to how to contend with you. But I didn't put enough poison on that seal to do more than sicken you. Your squire must not have weighed much, for it to have worked so quickly. It was an unfortunate accident."

"Accident?" My voice rose in fury. "He died because of you!"

"I know. I . . . regret it." She spoke as though the sentiment were unfamiliar, difficult to enunciate. She was the same woman who had wept in my arms, shown me such concern and taken me inside her, and yet she was not, as if she'd shed her skin to reveal an equally beautiful but far deadlier persona.

"This elaborate deception of yours must have a reason," I went on. "You do not work for Renard, so whom do you serve?"

"Haven't you guessed by now? You've pieced the rest of it together with remarkable facility." She trailed her hand over the desk, forcing me to angle my blade to prevent her approach. She stopped at the edge of the desk, a few paces from where I stood. "Renard was always too unyielding," she said. "And he serves an equally unyielding master. Charles V may be emperor, but he's shackled to the past, much like Mary herself. He cannot forgive himself for what he did to Mary's mother, his aunt Catherine of Aragon. He promised to assist Catherine against King Henry's annulment of their marriage, but Catherine died alone in a remote manor, while Anne Boleyn, the witch-queen, assumed her place. For all his avowals, Charles did nothing." She paused, looking at me. "His conscience must have plagued him for years. Then Mary took the throne, and he saw a way to redeem himself. He'd wed his son Philip to her; they would return England to the Catholic faith and kill all the heretics, and the past would be put to right. Only one thing stood in his way."

"Elizabeth," I breathed.

"Yes. The witch-queen's daughter. She was dangerous. The heretics would fight for her; she had to be dealt with. The emperor sent Renard here with orders to negotiate the marriage and ensure Elizabeth did not survive it." She went quiet again, her expression pensive. "As I said, they are unyielding. My master, on the other hand, understands the need for compromise. He sees no reason to dispose of a potential asset."

"He . . . ?" My skin crawled. She spoke so matter-of-factly, as though these were matters that people discussed every day. Perhaps they did. Perhaps where she came from, conversations about whether or not to destroy a princess were part of daily life.

She tilted back her head, her laughter sultry. "How can it be that you still refuse to see what is right before you? The emperor views the world through eyes that grow old before their time. But Philip of Spain does not. He is still young, virile. He will only sacrifice himself on the altar of his father's guilt if he can reap the benefit."

"You—you serve Philip?" I asked in horror. "He is your master?"

"He hired me to be his special agent. He's known me for years; I grew up in his mother's court. He also knew I had spied for Renard, and he promised me freedom—a noble marriage and my own household, a dowry for my sister, refuge for my mother. All I had to do was use Renard's enmity to destroy Courtenay, a rival for Mary's hand, as well as any others who opposed the Hapsburg alliance. But Philip insisted that he mustn't be held responsible. Whatever blood is shed must be on Mary's hands alone."

"Dear God," I whispered. "Why . . . ?" Then, with sickening clarity, the final piece of the mystery slid into place. "It's been about Elizabeth, all this time. Philip wants her."

She smiled. "Does it surprise you? The prince is a modern man; he doesn't care about the past. His father is weary. When Charles abdicates, Philip stands to inherit half the empire. Why suffer the older sister's bed unless he has the assurance that in time, he can have the younger's? But Elizabeth must be brought to heel; all those who support her heretical leanings must die. And once Mary fails to bear a child and succumbs, as she must, Elizabeth will be his. Through her, he will sire heirs to make all Europe tremble—a Tudor-Hapsburg dynasty to rule the world."

I felt sick. "You are mad. *He* is mad. The very idea is monstrous. Elizabeth would never consent to him."

"Oh," replied Sybilla, with a lift of her chin, "she will, if she hopes to live. Her letter to Dudley confirms that she knew about the revolt." Her voice darkened. "The game is over. Not even you can save her."

I lunged forward, swiping my blade across the desk. I relished her swift inhale as she stepped back warily, her eyes on my sword. "Give it to me. Give me her letter."

She did not flinch. "Why do you insist on fighting for what is already lost? That letter belongs to Philip now. He owns the knowledge that Elizabeth consented to treason in her own hand. When Wyatt and his men reach London, the queen will order her arrest. Renard will make sure Elizabeth is blamed for everything and see her locked in the Tower. The only one who can save her is the husband Mary desires so fervently she'll do anything he asks, including spare her treacherous sister. Philip will be Elizabeth's savior. And in time, Elizabeth will be his."

"Not if I warn her first." I raised my blade. She flattened herself against the wall. As she gazed at me, at last I gleaned in her face what I craved.

Fear.

A spasm went through me. I despised her with every part of my being, but the memory of my desire for her still clung to me like chains. She was a woman. I had never killed anyone. I knew her death was necessary if I was to save Elizabeth. The letter had to be hidden somewhere, awaiting Philip's arrival. Sybilla would never entrust it to another. I might never find it, but if she was dead, neither would anyone else. I could gain Elizabeth valuable time before—

I hesitated too long. With a leap aside, she yanked a blade from within her sleeve and slashed it across my arm. Hot pain and a gush of blood broke my focus. I swerved away from her, flinging up my cloak to thwart her next stab.

Instead, she ran to the doorway.

I spun about. As I lunged toward her with my sword lifted, this time ready to cleave her in two, she kicked the side table holding the lantern. It fell onto the heap under the window and shattered. With terrifying suddenness, the piled rushes and rags burst into a flame, startling me and causing me to fling my hands up. She had doused the heap with tallow oil—that was the odor I had smelled and failed to identify.

"*No!*" I roared.

Sybilla slammed the door shut. I reached it in time to hear a key turn in the lock. I yanked at the latch, shouting at the top of my lungs, hammering with my sword hilt, oblivious to the spray of blood from my wounded arm.

Then I slowly turned back to the room. My heart capsized in my chest. The flames were leaping up the wall, feeding on the brittle pile and oil like a ravenous beast.

My eyes started to water. Forcing myself to stay calm, I moved as far as I could from the conflagration and scanned the room. There was no other way out except through that window. Sybilla had planned this; she had brought me here for this specific end.

I was going to die.

The smoke thickened, gusting up to the low ceiling like the clouds of an incoming storm. In seconds, it would fill the room and I'd suffocate. I'd lose consciousness; by the time the flames reached me, I wouldn't feel it. When it was done, when the manor had collapsed in smoldering ruins, there'd be nothing left save my charred bones.

A howl struggled in my throat. I looked about desperately, and my gaze fell on the decanter and untouched goblet. I yanked up my hood, sheathed my sword, and tore my gauntlets from my belt. Grabbing the goblet, I poured ale over my trembling gloved hands. Then I soaked my hood and threw the empty decanter aside. It wasn't enough; ten pitchers wouldn't have been enough, but as I turned resolutely to the fire, I knew I had no choice. I could feel the heat through my clothes, as if the flames already licked my flesh . . .

Hunching my shoulders, I stepped forward. The ground shifted under my feet. I looked down. The floorboards . . . they were moving . . .

A dull roar filled my head. I coughed, lurching forward. It was the smoke. I was being strangled by it, deluded into seeing things that weren't there. If I could just push through that writhing screen of flame to grab hold of the window latch—

I didn't think I was moving to my death or hear the section of floor creaking open behind me until rough hands grabbed hold of me, pulling me back, yanking me down into a hole. Only then did I realize the piercing sound in my ears was my own scream.

"Get moving, before it all comes down on top of us," an urgent voice said. I dragged myself after the hulking figure who'd rescued me, my smoke-singed nostrils detecting a faint trace of wet earth. I was in a tunnel under the manor, a secret escape passage. Slimy water sloshed underfoot; it was so dark I couldn't see anything. Gradually it began to lighten. A hatch above me was thrown back and I was again yanked, coughing and sputtering, into the garden. I lay on my back, gasping for air. In the distance, I glimpsed the river, shimmering like a dragon's tail in the sullen dawn.

The barge was gone.

I looked up into Scarcliff's twisted visage. "You're lucky I saw my horse bucking at his tether," he said, wrapping his cloak about me. It was soaking wet, foul with river-stink. "A little more time and you'd be roast meat."

"How—how did you know?" My voice was faint, hoarse.

"I told you. I saw poor Cerberus fit to slip his bridle and all that smoke—"

"No. The passageway. You knew it was there. You've been here before."

He went still. Then he said softly, "Don't you recognize me, lad?" and I felt as if I'd plunged into an endless void, falling and falling without reaching bottom.

"Shelton," I whispered. I couldn't believe I hadn't seen it until now.

It was there, beneath his ravaged face—the traces of the man I had known, the stern Dudley steward who had helped raise me and had brought me to court. As I met his one eye in recognition, I was swept back to that horrible night in the Tower when I'd pursued him. He'd been trapped in the crush at the portcullis. All those terrified souls, trying to escape the guards coming down on them with halberds and maces—skulls must have been cracked, limbs shattered, bodies scythed like chaff. Someone must have struck him, slashed his face to the bone. The wedged soles on his boots—his legs had been damaged, too. Yet somehow, he'd survived. He had dragged himself to safety and changed his name, his identity. He'd melted into London's underbelly, hired himself out as a strong-arm for the earl. He must have known who I was the moment he saw me, but he had not breathed a word. Had he intended to stay hidden from me forever, to take his secret with him to his grave? If so, he had betrayed himself to save me.

"I know I owe you an explanation," he said roughly, "but this isn't the place. If you want to catch that she-wolf, we'd best get moving. I've been tracking her since the ambush on the road. I didn't dare engage her"—he grimaced—"I'm not the man I was.

But I saw her take the barge toward the bridge. The current isn't strong, however. You still have time."

I struggled to get up, to get away. He tightened his grip on me. "We need to bind that wound." He tore a strip from the bottom of his chemise and tied it around my arm, stanching the blood. "It's not deep. It'll need curing, but that should suffice for now."

He let me go. I clambered to my feet, the taste of embers in my mouth. Looking past him to the manor, I saw smoke billowing from the rooftop, an eerie nectarine glow smearing the windows. The fire was spreading. It would consume the entire house.

We trudged into the river, the water coming to our waists as we waded out far enough to bypass the garden wall. Scarcliff had moved the horses away from the manor. As he helped me onto my saddle, Cinnabar pranced sideways, agitated by the scent of fire. My world shrank for a moment. What was I doing? How did I think I was I going to stop Sybilla with a wounded arm and the help of a man I'd believed was dead and barely trusted?

We bolted toward the city.

It was that preternatural hour before morning, when everything is softened by the waning of the night. The city was just awakening, grumbling goodwives still sweeping their doorsteps of refuse as peddlers and hawkers embarked on the trudge to the marketplace at Cheapside with their wares, and pigs and dogs rooted in the conduits for leavings.

We galloped past them, scarcely registering their presence.

There was still time, I kept telling myself. Still time . . .

The massive gateway leading to the bridge reared into view. Officials in cloaks clustered before it as liveried sentries and armored soldiers roamed the perimeter. People were lining up, herding livestock. I registered a cacophony that must be loud, though to me it sounded less intrusive than my heart's pounding in my ears.

Still time . . .

I slid off Cinnabar. "Too many people, and on horseback we're too visible."

He gave a grim nod. "I'll follow you. Be careful."

As I moved on foot to the gate, leading Cinnabar by the reins, I searched the crowd. Given the hour, most of those waiting to cross the bridge were tradesmen, but as I stepped into the line I suddenly spotted her near the front of the queue, swathed in a cape and with a cap pulled low on her head. She held a gelding by its bridle, the horse stamping nervously as it was jostled by those around it. She must have docked the barge and hired a horse. Under the bandage, my arm throbbed as I lowered my hand to my scabbard. The sentry waved her onward. She mounted and began to steer her horse through the crowd. She couldn't ride fast; once she was at a safe distance, I hauled myself onto Cinnabar, dodging the multitude of animals, carts, and wagons on the bridge, intent on not losing her.

She wasn't in a rush, nor did she appear to show concern that she might be followed. I saw her crack her whip, opening passage. I wondered where she was headed; wherever it was, she clearly wasn't returning to Whitehall. I glanced over my shoulder. To my relief, Scarcliff was a short distance away; he had left Cerberus in the stalls by the bridge, where grooms minded horses for a fee.

Sybilla abruptly reined to a halt outside a haberdashery. I slid from Cinnabar, watching her dismount through the ebb and flow of the bridge's denizens. She looped her horse's reins to a post and went to a door beside the shop, unlocking it. She disappeared inside. I lifted my gaze. The building was like all those cluttering the bridge—squeezed tight between its neighbors, precariously tall, its overhanging balconies festooned with sodden laundry, its peeling exterior pockmarked by small, thickpaned windows.

My blood quickened.

It must be a safe house. She had stashed the letter here. She had come for it.

Scarcliff neared. I motioned for him to see to Cinnabar and crossed the road. The haberdashery wasn't open; the building looming above me was quiet, even as the sounds of traffic on the bridge rumbled around me.

As at the manor, she had left the door unlocked. It put me on alert; cracking the door ajar, I found an empty parlor and a narrow staircase leading upward into gloom. I heard nothing as I took the stairs, wincing at every creak, knowing she was somewhere above me, perhaps already aware and ready for attack. That she'd shown no awareness of being followed was no solace. I'd underestimated her before. This time, I had to fight to the death.

Stepping onto the landing of the first story, I eased out my sword. There was movement in the room before me. Edging closer, reaching out with my free hand, I threw the door open and braced myself. I glimpsed a cot in a corner, a desk, and a stool; then, from the corner, she came to her feet swiftly, revealing an upended floorboard. Her expression faltered; she looked almost disconcerted to see me. My gaze riveted itself to that dislodged floorboard, seconds before she lunged at me with her sword in hand.

I ducked away, thrusting my blade. She pranced aside. "You should have let the fire take you," she said through her teeth. "I trained for years with a master in Toledo. After I kill you, I'll take your blade to him so he can see how far the steel of Spain has traveled."

I did not respond, saving my strength, concentrating on parrying her strikes and maneuvering her away from that upended board. My arm was aching; I could feel fresh blood welling through the makeshift bandage, but my rage was stronger, all-consuming, so that she was all I saw, all I felt and wanted. My doubt vanished; my sword seemed to anticipate my every move, and her expression hardened when I avoided one of her strikes and grazed her side with my blade, drawing blood and forcing her to pivot away from me to evade a deeper wound. She understood what I was trying to do, and she came at me with demonic fervor, lashing her sword, pushing me out of the room and toward the staircase, where she no doubt intended to put an end to me.

Our blades clashed with a merciless ring. Teetering on the edge of the stairs, I knew I had only moments before she broke through my defenses. I did not think, then; did not hesitate. I whirled about and leapt down the stairs, three at a time. As I hoped, like a wolf with its blood up, intent on fleeing prey, she came after me.

All of a sudden we were in the street, pitched in fierce battle, as passersby scrambled to avoid us. She moved so fast she was like quicksilver, her hair uncoiling from the knot at her nape to stream about her flushed features, so that even then, in that terrible moment as I fought for my very life, she was as beautiful as an avenging angel—and as cruel.

She failed to see Scarcliff. He had shifted Cinnabar to the other side of the street, a few doorways from the house, and hidden in the crowd. He suddenly barreled out toward her, his massive body poised like a ram. As he slammed into her with audible impact, she lost her footing on the uneven paving. Her blade flew from her hand. It was the opening I needed. As she whipped around to Scarcliff, snarling and jerking a knife from her boot, I ran at her with my sword brandished, determined to take her head. I missed by a hair's breadth, the very air quivering as she crouched and reeled away. For an instant that seemed to last an eternity, our eyes met. I was blocking her return to the house.

Her mouth curved in an icy smile.

She turned and began to run.

"Upstairs!" I yelled at Scarcliff as I bolted after her. "Under the floorboard!"

The congestion on the bridge had thickened; it was nearing midmorning, and hundreds of people were going about their business. She swerved to and fro, dodging shouting carters and angry mercers, her knife clutched in her hand, though it was no match for my sword and she knew it. She was heading for the southern gate; if she managed to escape the bridge and make it into the warren of Bankside, I'd be forced to hunt her down.

Chances were, she'd get me first.

Neither of us anticipated the additional sentries posted at the other end, a precautionary move prompted, no doubt, by Courtenay's arrest. As the hulking gateway with its massive barbican and spiked crown of rotting heads came into view, Sybilla's pace flagged. Everyone coming from London, be he a tinker with a shoulder pole or a fur-clad lady in a litter, was being stopped and questioned before they were permitted to pass. I heard snatches of agitated clamor from people standing nearby—"Rebels from Kent, they say, an army of traitors!"—and Sybilla spun around, knowing that those sentries would question her, that perhaps Renard had provided a description of her.

She came to a panting halt, facing me. Every sound and sight about me faded. Even as I started to rush to her, shouting, she leaped up onto a low parapet on the edge of the bridge— one of those rare openings between buildings that gave out onto the river and offered a stunning view of the city's breadth. She perched on that parapet like a gorgeous bird of prey, the wind catching at her cloak, silhouetting her slender figure, the cluttered spires of London erupting into gold as the sun emerged from its bed of mist.

"No," I heard myself whisper. I dropped my sword at my feet.

She cocked her head, as if disappointed. Then, to my disbelief and a communal gasp of horror from those watching, she flung out her arms and plunged off the parapet.

In the ensuing silence, something inside me cracked in two. A scream came from a woman nearby, piercing the hush, and then everyone was rushing to the parapet in a gaggle of morbid curiosity, peering down to the ice-clogged river far below.

I stood immobile. Then I picked up my sword and walked away.

Scarcliff was waiting by the house with Cinnabar. He reached into his jerkin, extending the leather cylinder containing Elizabeth's letter to me. He had Sybilla's sword in his other hand. "It's an expensive piece," he said, "worth saving."

"Keep it." I tucked the cylinder into my jerkin. "I have what I came for." I sheathed my own sword, taking Cinnabar's reins. We rode quietly back to the north gate. Scarcliff went to fetch Cerberus. As I waited for his return I noticed that the number of guards and officials near the gatehouse had increased; when I saw Rochester among them, his rotund person quivering as he spoke with the sentries, I called out, "My lord!"

He turned around, startled, and bustled over to me.

"What is it?" I asked. "What is happening?"

He glanced over his shoulder at the staring officials. "Word came before dawn of an army coming toward us from Kent. Scouts have been sent to verify. We await their report."

"But the queen's betrothal," I said, "it hasn't been announced . . ." Even as I spoke, I cursed my own blindness. I should have realized this, too, was part of Dudley's plan. He'd led Courtenay to believe the betrothal would be the sign, but it wasn't. Surprise attack: It was the only chance to catch the queen, and London, unprepared.

Rochester looked perplexed. "The official announcement will be made at Hampton Court, if you must know, though such matters have a way of leaking out. The earl is in the Tower; he was questioned at length and gave us names. Warrants are being issued for the other conspirators, though most, if not all, must have heard by now of the earl's arrest. If they're wise, they'll be fleeing the country as we speak." His voice lowered. "The earl did not mention the princess. He insisted over and over that she knew nothing."

I exhaled in relief. Despicable as he was, at least Courtenay had retained one last shred of honor. "You mustn't wait for the scouts," I told Rochester. "The uprising is real; it's being led by Wyatt of Kent. Those letters I delivered were only half the story. Wyatt plans to join with Suffolk's retainers. Whatever she does, Her Majesty mustn't tarry." I paused, seeing him turn pale. "Tell her for me. Tell her I did as she bade and uncovered this last detail of the conspiracy. But I must take my leave. Thank you, my lord, for everything you've done, for me and Her Grace. Your kindness won't be forgotten."

He flinched. "You must go to her," he whispered, "before they do. If this is true, if there is a rebellion upon us, I fear she'll have even greater need of you than ever before."

"I will do what I can," I said. "I promise."

Chapter Twenty

At Bishopsgate, Scarcliff drew to a halt. "This is as far as I go."

"What?" I stared at him. "You can't stay here. I have questions only you—"

He cut me off with a sigh. "I know. I owe you answers, but it will have to wait. London is my home; these thieves and whores and beggars, dregs no one ever gives a second thought to—they helped me when no one else would. If there's to be fighting in the streets, I must be here. Besides," he added, "there's my dog. I'm not leaving him."

I almost laughed. "The steward I knew never cared much for anything save duty."

"A dog can change a man." He turned somber. "Go now. Warn your princess. I will find you. Or if you return to the city first, come find me. If I'm still alive, I'll be at the Griffin. See that you cure that arm. You don't want to end up maimed, like me."

Without another word, he turned his horse about and rode back into the city.

I watched him vanish, wondering if I'd see him again. I

wanted to call him back, to demand a full accounting of his actions, the reason he'd assisted me and the reason he had vanished, all those months ago. No, he was right: It must wait. He had his path to follow, and I had mine. For now, they led in opposite directions.

I rode resolutely out of London.

It was a long ride, through a bleak landscape I barely registered, so weary I could have slept upright on my horse, though I did not.

In my mind, I kept seeing Sybilla balanced on that parapet, the curious look on her face before she soared to her death. I remembered her radiant smile, her breathtaking beauty, when she'd first approached me in the queen's chamber; her walk with me in the gallery and her solicitude when Peregrine died, and our searing, urgent communion in the darkness of my room.

Even now, knowing she was gone, knowing I needn't ever confess my transgression to Kate, my feelings were disturbing. Sybilla had deceived and manipulated everyone around her, connived to destroy everything I cared about. Peregrine was dead because of her; I should rejoice in her end, knowing her master, Philip of Spain, had nothing to wield against Elizabeth when he arrived. Without the letter, he'd be even more ardent in her defense, for only by saving her could he hope to earn her gratitude.

Yet as I rode through intermittent snow flurries, my head tucked to my chest as Cinnabar moved purposefully forward, I couldn't deny that despite everything she had done, despite the fact that never had I met another woman like her, and prayed I might never again, Sybilla had transformed me. She had roused something in me—a near-feral recognition of my own self.

You do not owe me anything.

She was mistaken. I owed her the knowledge that I understood. Like her, I had known the desperation of a fractured childhood, the helplessness of being prey to the callous whims of others. I, too, had burned with the fervent desire to prove my worth. She was my reflection, the dark twin of my soul. Only what I had sought to vanquish, to capture and tame by serving Elizabeth, she had embraced, honed to a lethal edge like the very blade she had brandished.

She was the person I might have been, had my fate not taken a different turn.

I reached Ashridge by nightfall.

Newly fallen snow draped over the Hertfordshire countryside. As I clattered into the courtyard, a groom came running out to assist me. I unhooked my saddlebag and dragged myself into the manor.

Mistress Parry greeted me from the torch-lit hall with a frightened gasp. "Sweet mercy, look at you!" Only then did I realize how I must present, covered in mud and mire from the road and crawling through gaps in stone walls and tunnels; my cloak bedraggled, my tunic torn, my arm blood-caked and my entire person stinking of sweat and horse.

"It's been a long day," I said, removing the cylinder with Elizabeth's letter and divesting myself of cloak and scabbard. She took them from me. "Where is Her Grace?"

"She's gone to her chamber to rest." Mistress Parry's voice quavered as she eyed the cylinder in my hand. "What is the news from London? Is she . . . are we still in danger?"

"I fear so. I've done all I can. But we should prepare; it is likely the queen will send men to question her. I must talk with her first."

She clutched my belongings as I turned to the staircase. "Should I send to Hatfield for Mistress Ashley and Mistress Stafford?" she suddenly asked.

I froze. Then I nodded. "Yes," I said, "I think you should." I continued up the stairs.

When Kate arrived, I would tell her everything.

The princess's bedchamber door was ajar; I knocked to announce my presence and entered. The room was small, wainscoted in linen-fold paneling and warmed by a fire burning in a recessed hearth. Strewn about were her open coffers and traveling chests. From what I could see, she'd unpacked her books and a few scattered articles of clothing.

She looked up. She was sitting on the edge of her bed, a lit candle by her side, an open book in her lap. Her hair hung loose over her shoulders, a red-gold sheen blending with the scarlet of her robe. She looked so young, so vulnerable, without the accoutrements of her court regalia: a mere girl. Not a princess at all.

A knot filled my throat.

I extended the cylinder I'd carried close to my heart the entire ride.

"You are a man of your word," she said. She set it unopened on the table next to her candle. "Is it done?"

"No. But there is no evidence against you."

She did not reach for the cylinder, did not react in any way as though she were interested in its contents, as I relayed what I had found out, about Sybilla and Philip of Spain and their plot to hold her hostage to the prince. She did not interrupt or ask a single question. She sat so still when I was done that she might have turned to stone, had it not been for the rapid rise and fall of her breast.

"I had no idea he considered me such a prize," she said at length. "I find cold comfort, considering it'll be yet another reason for Mary to despise me."

"She doesn't know—" I began, and the room keeled around me. My knees gave way; I almost fell as I reached for the nearest chair.

"You are wounded," said Elizabeth. "You must sit."

As I sank onto the chair, weak as a newborn foal, she went to one of her chests and extracted a painted casket. She pointed at my arm. "Let me see."

I shook my head. "It's nothing. There is no need—"

"Don't argue. Take off your doublet and shirt and let me see. If it festers, Kate will never let me hear the end of it." She opened the casket as I reluctantly shed my upper clothing. When I looked at her, she had set out a jar of salve and folded linen cloths. Taking up the pitcher of water from her sideboard, she bent over me and cleaned my wound. With the crust and dried blood washed away, I saw it was deep but not large.

Her fingertips felt cool as she probed the ragged skin. I winced.

"You're like a bear after a baiting," she said. "Stay still. This might sting. It is Kate's special salve; she made a batch for me before I left Hatfield. I always carry it with me."

Taken aback by her determination, I let her salve the wound with the rosemary and mint concoction, releasing the very aroma of Kate into the air. She worked efficiently, without revulsion. I'd forgotten that she had lived most of her life far from court, in a country setting where even princesses must learn rudimentary healing skills. The salve eased my pain, inducing a welcome numbness. I reached for my chemise immediately after, my breeches sagging perilously low on my hips.

"There. Better, yes?" She returned the items to the casket. "You should use the salve at least once a day, twice if you can manage it." She scrutinized my face. "That other wound on your temple should be tended, too. No matter what most physicians say, even such minor hurts can gather dirt. If corruption sets in, you will sicken."

She spoke matter-of-factly, as if I had not informed her that a revolt could at this very moment be upon London and that she was far from safe—indeed, that all of us were in danger.

"What are we going to do?" I finally asked.

"What can we do? We wait." She paced to the side table, her long fingers hovering over the cylinder. "Whether Wyatt succeeds or fails; whether my sister chooses to believe in my guilt or innocence; whether I'm left alone or taken—only time can tell now." She glanced at me. "Though if the situation is as dire as you say, I should think that we'll have our answer sooner rather than later."

She picked up the cylinder.

"What does that letter say?" Though I had told myself that I would not ask, I couldn't stop myself. All of a sudden, I had to know exactly what I had sacrificed so much for.

She paused. Cylinder in hand, she moved past me to stand for a long moment before the hearth. She pulled back the grate;

with a flick of her wrist, she tossed the cylinder into the fire. "I told you at court, you had one chance. Now, it is best if you do not know more than you already do. You've suffered enough for my sake."

Her rebuke did not surprise me. It had been presumptuous to assume she'd deign to confidence now. Her words to Robert Dudley would remain a secret between them, the evidence even now curling to ash in her hearth.

"Will you eat?" she asked. "You must be famished."

Holding on to the chair, I hauled myself to my feet. "No, I just want to sleep."

"Go, then. Mistress Parry will see to your chamber. We've hardly a full house here; there are several rooms to choose from." She remained at the hearth, the firelight limning her figure in a reddish glow. As I moved to the door, I felt her gaze follow me. My hand was on the latch when my question came out, unbidden. "Will you allow me one thing?"

She nodded. "If I can."

"Was it worth it?"

She sighed. "I have found it's always worth fighting for what we believe in, regardless of the outcome. Risk is never without consequence."

I inclined my head.

"And you?" she asked. "Would you have fought for me as you did, had you known the entire truth?"

I hesitated for only a moment. "Yes," I said. "No matter what you have done, I believe in your cause."

She gave me a dry smile. "I'd expect nothing less. Rest, my friend. You've earned it."

* * *

I feared that I might not be able to sleep, that the events of the past days would haunt me in the silence of unfamiliar quarters. In fact, as soon as I disrobed and climbed into the musty bed, I fell fast asleep, without dreams, for the first time since I had left Hatfield.

When I awoke, it was past midday. I could tell by the angle of light filtering through the window. Mistress Parry had sent someone up while I rested, who'd seen to my needs. Along with a fresh shirt, my breeches and hose were folded in a neat pile by my saddlebag, crinkled and stiff from having dried by a fire but blessedly clean and scented with lavender. After I washed and tended to my arm, I went to the hall. In the daylight, Ashridge was visibly as well appointed as the manor at Hatfield; it had the requisite furnishings and size, but the feel of disuse hung in the air, as in all places that are rarely inhabited.

I ate my fill, seated alone at a wide table, served by a blushing maid I didn't recognize but assumed had been the one who attended to my clothes. I was told Elizabeth remained in her chamber, so I went out to check on Cinnabar. I found him well stalled, with a warm blanket to cover him, and plenty of feed. Urian nosed the straw around his hooves; as the hound recognized me, he let out a joyous bark. Tears sprang in my eyes when I recalled Peregrine's love for this dog. I buried my face in Urian's fur as he licked my hands, whining low in his throat as though he could sense my sorrow, and let myself grieve.

Then I wiped away my tears and took Urian into the snowy courtyard to toss a stick, delighting in his eager retrieval, his lopsided gait, and his barks for more. It had been so long since I'd done anything so ordinary, so *normal*—it felt odd and wonderful at the same time.

Finally he was panting, his tongue lolling, and my hands felt like frozen mutton. Turning back toward the house with Urian at my heels, wondering if the princess was awake yet, I discerned the clangor of hooves. Even as I turned toward the road, I knew what I would see: men in cloaks and caps, galloping toward the manor.

I bolted into the house. Our answer had come.

Mistress Parry had also heard the approaching party. She was halfway down the staircase, kneading her skirts. She took one look at me and said, "Her Grace says you must hide. No one can see you here. You might be recognized."

"What of her?" Her anxiety was infectious; I found myself looking over my shoulder as I spoke, half-expecting the front door to burst open to reveal men at arms.

"She's staying in bed." Mistress Parry shook her head at my concern. "With a disposition like hers, she's prone to fever. She'll live, but she's too ill to rise or"—she set her jaw in a hard line—"greet any visitors. Those fine lords, whoever they are, will be in for a difficult time if they think they can come here to berate her."

It was a ploy, I knew it at once. A sick princess would be hard to move. I didn't comment as the other servants on the staff— the serving maid and kitchen personnel, a few idle grooms— crowded into the hall. To a person, they looked terrified.

"Get," Mistress Parry said with a wave of her hand, and the staff hurried back to their posts. She turned to me. "You, too. The last thing we need is one of them asking how the man who once served the queen is now in Her Grace's house."

She was right. I had to disappear. Fast.

I ran up to my room and started cramming everything I had

pulled from my saddlebag back into it. I was looking around to make sure I hadn't missed anything when I heard the men's horses cantering into the courtyard, followed by rough demands of the grooms as they dismounted.

They were inside the manor before I could reach my door; I could hear their booted heels, monstrously loud, and Mistress Parry's indignant protest. "My lady is abed! She has taken with fever. You cannot intrude on her—"

I hoisted my saddlebag to my shoulder, my other hand on my sword. Daring a glance into the passageway, I glimpsed men with caps bunched in fists as they came up the staircase and turned down the opposite corridor to the princess's apartment. The startled cry of one of her attendants preceded brusque rapping on her bedchamber door.

"Madam, open at once! We come in Her Majesty the queen's name!"

I inched backward into my room. My breath came fast. Maybe they wouldn't search the manor. Maybe they'd just question her, and when they discovered that she had been here all this time, abed, they'd—

Footsteps marched toward me.

Wildly, I started to move to the bed, thinking to hide under it. I was not fast enough. The door banged open. A sentry stood on the threshold. "You." He jabbed a gauntleted finger at me. "Downstairs. Now."

He accompanied me to the hall. The entire manor staff had been assembled, the maids openly weeping, the men white-faced. I was grateful Mistress Ashley and Kate were not here. With any luck, Mistress Parry hadn't yet sent their summons.

The queen's men milled about the hall, the central table cluttered with the detritus of their office: bags, weaponry, paper, quills and ink bottles. I recognized a few of the men from my time at court, though I didn't know their names; they were from the council. As the sentry pushed me into line with the other servants, one of the men—a lean, white-haired noble with a forked beard and the commanding stance of a man in charge— pivoted toward me and stared, hard, as if he were searching his mind for my identity.

Then he looked away and I sagged in relief, lowering my eyes and chin.

In a cold voice he announced, "I am Lord William Howard, Admiral of England. I am here by Her Majesty's command to search this house and inquire into the activities of said household as it pertains to the recent treasonous revolt against the queen's sovereign person. Thomas Wyatt and others have been appre- hended and are in the Tower. Her Majesty will show mercy to the innocent, if such can be proved, but none of you are to leave the manor or its grounds on penalty of immediate arrest." He treated us to a frigid stare that emphasized his authority before he motioned to the sentries, who herded the servants out.

I was turning to leave when Lord Howard's voice came at me. "Not you."

I looked over my shoulder. He *had* recognized me. I bowed. "My lord."

"Haven't I seen you at court?" He did not speak as if it were a question, but I decided to risk it, nevertheless. "You may have, my lord. I've been in Her Grace's employ and have occasionally run errands for her at—"

"Do you lie to me?" His voice did not raise a decibel, but the threat in his tone was unmistakable. "Because if you do, I warn you, we have ways to loosen the tongues of liars so that they learn to speak the truth."

I went quiet. As I considered my next move, I wondered who had betrayed me this time. Renard was the most likely culprit; after our confrontation outside my room, he had every reason to want to see me disappear. He had lost control of his own agent; Sybilla had turned rogue, stolen the evidence he sought, made him look the fool. Only he, too, had something to lose if I were to confess what I knew; I could certainly tell Lord Howard of how the Spanish ambassador had done his utmost to bring down the queen's sister, failing in the process to intercept the revolt brewing under his nose. It might not save me, but I was fairly certain Renard would rather his own sordid failings didn't come to light.

Lord Howard tilted his head. "What is your name?"

I hesitated for a second before I said, "Prescott, my lord. Squire Prescott." Again, it was a feeble attempt to gain time. Renard and Mary both knew me as Daniel Beecham; if Renard had told these men to look for me, Beecham was the name he'd cite.

"Prescott," mused Lord Howard. "Well, Prescott, you're not to leave the premises. I want you where I can find you, at all times. I may have reason to speak with you again."

"Yes, my lord," I murmured, inclining my head. He did not move, watching me turn to the door. I anticipated he'd call me back before I had the chance to step out, that he'd realize where exactly he had seen me at court, coming and going from the queen's own apartments, and then I'd find myself in boiling water, indeed.

A man without a past cannot exist . . .

Howard did not stop me.

* * *

Guards were placed at the princess's door; no one but Mistress Parry and members of the council was allowed to see her. I sat with the servants in the kitchens that night, listening with one ear to their hushed, anxious chatter while with the other I strained to overhear Lord Howard and his men deliberating over their dinner in the hall.

Mistress Parry came in with a tray, bearing Elizabeth's untouched meal; I drew her aside. "What is happening? What do you know?"

Clearly frightened despite her outward stance, she whispered, "Wyatt's rebellion failed. But it looked at first as though it might succeed; he had over two thousand men under his command, while the council refused to vote the queen so much as five hundred more guards. She marched straight to the Guildhall and gave such a speech that all London took to her defense. Wyatt's men deserted him when they saw the forces arrayed against them. Lord Howard was there; he barred the rebel entry at Ludgate. By nightfall, Wyatt surrendered. There've been deaths on both sides, but not many."

"And now?" I thought of Scarcliff. Had he fought for or against Wyatt?

"There'll be more," she replied grimly. "Every last man in that rebel army is being pursued. That's not the worst of it, either. I was in my lady's room today when Lord Howard informed her that a letter, purported to be from Wyatt, informing her of his plan, was found in a packet of secret missives being sent abroad. The queen is enraged. She's ordered that my lady be brought to court at once. I'm insisting she's too ill to travel, but Howard has sent for a physician. We've a few days, at best. When the physician arrives and examines her, he'll pronounce her fit. He can do nothing else."

I stood, stunned. Another letter, this time from the very man who had marched on London, found in a packet being sent abroad? It could seal Elizabeth's doom.

There could only be one explanation, and it made my blood run cold.

Renard. This was his deed. He'd found a way to falsify a letter from Wyatt, springing the snare that would bring Elizabeth to her knees.

I gnawed at my lower lip. If we only had a few days, it just might be enough. "Can we get word out? Is there a way to send a secret message?"

She stared at me, incredulous. "How, pray tell? They've surrounded the manor. Not even a flea in the stable can get out without their notice. Besides, who can we appeal to? No one will support her now, not even those who called themselves her friend."

"I know someone. A man highly regarded by the queen. If he could persuade her—"

"You don't understand. There is no persuading the queen. She's already agreed to execute Lady Jane Grey, Guilford Dudley, and Jane's father, the Duke of Suffolk. Lord Howard told the princess to her face. Oh, you should have seen the look she gave him! She might have struck him had she not been abed. It is too late for highly regarded friends now. The queen will see her to the Tower, and she"—Mistress Parry's voice caught—"she knows it. God save her, all she can think to do is to delay them, to continue to plead illness in the hope that somehow, some miracle can save her."

"Dear God," I whispered. I remembered them as I'd last seen them in the Tower, Jane kicking the pile of books before she handed me the folder, and Guilford, that petulant husband, to

whom she'd been wed against her will, cawing for my demise:
They were to be Renard's first victims. Would Robert and the
other Dudley brothers follow? Would Courtenay die as well?
How much blood would Renard make the queen spill?

How would Elizabeth survive it?

Mistress Parry's eyes were wet with unshed tears. "My lady
says if comes to it, she'll ask for a swordsman from Calais like her
mother. She says she'll not let them take her head with a hatchet,
like a beast in a barnyard. What can we do? What can any of us
do for her now?"

The servants had turned to look at us in dread. I took her by
the arm, silencing her. Her eyes widened as I leaned close. "Tell
her to write a letter to the queen. She must refute any knowledge of the revolt and Wyatt. If she can sow doubt in the queen's
mind, we may still save her. Tell her I will deliver the letter."

"You?" she whispered. "But how can you . . . ?"

"Never mind." I steered her to the kitchen door. "Tell her,
before it is too late."

We remained indoors as the snow fell outside, confined in the
manor as the councillors and Howard trudged up the stairs to
Elizabeth's chamber, once, twice, three times a day. Each time
they emerged flustered, their threats unheeded; each time Howard was heard debating angrily with them in the corridor as to
how to proceed. Mistress Parry told me he was related to the
princess through her maternal family; they were kin, and a little
of the burden I bore eased as I began to suspect Lord Howard
wasn't quite as sure of his mission as he appeared. Every inch of
the house and its grounds had been turned upside down; it was
clear they sought evidence that Elizabeth had been stockpiling

an arsenal to abet the rebellion and defend her position until she could be declared queen, as Mary had done before her in the struggle against Northumberland. They had found only frost-bitten hedges and a rusted old ax head in the orchard. Without concrete proof of Elizabeth's guilt, Lord Howard began to look more and more like a man who'd rather be anywhere but here, browbeating a sick girl and her parcel of frightened servants.

At night after supper, once the men had taken to their quarters, Mistress Parry came to tell me the news. Even as Elizabeth mounted a spirited defense from her sickbed, proclaiming she could not believe such terrible deeds could be ascribed to her, her past recklessness at court returned to haunt her. She had, Lord Howard reminded her, been seen indulging Courtenay, as well as his friends; it was also established that she'd resisted Mary's attempts to make her convert and indeed had sent away the very friar the queen had appointed to instruct her the moment she arrived at Ashridge. Nevertheless, as I repeatedly assured Mistress Parry, none of these acts was treason. Only rumor and innuendo linked Elizabeth to Wyatt's revolt, and neither was enough to kill her.

Yet while I spoke, I saw her again as she stood at the hearth in her room upstairs and threw her letter to Dudley onto the fire. If they were to search Dudley's prison, what might they find? What other secrets did he and Elizabeth hide?

On the fourth day, as the anemic sun struggled to penetrate a pall of cloud, the physician from court arrived—a self-important older gentleman in the peaked cap and black robe of his trade, who proceeded to shake the snow from his cloak and closet himself with Elizabeth. Mistress Parry was the only other person present; it was unthinkable, she declared, that her lady should be alone with a stranger, and a man, at that. When he emerged two hours later, his verdict was clear, just as Mistress Parry had feared: Her Grace the Lady Elizabeth suffered from a swelling sickness and fever, yes, but her condition was not grave enough to impede her from returning to court, providing precautions were taken.

Lord Howard ordered immediate departure. His men sprang into action, relieved to finally be doing something other than ogling the maids and drinking the cellars dry. As the servants went rushing to and fro, loading belongings into carts and setting up a litter in the courtyard, I slipped out to the stables to saddle Cinnabar. I was affixing his bridle when a familiar voice was heard exclaiming in the courtyard. I stepped out hastily into glittering daylight speckled by random snowflakes. My heart constricted. Standing beside two lathered mares were Mistress Ashley and my Kate, confronting the row of men-at-arms guarding the manor entrance and Lord Howard himself.

"I tell you, I must attend her," Mistress Ashley declared. "No one thought to inform me of her illness. It was only by coincidence that we heard of it at all. We made haste at once, but it took several days because of all the blockades and delays on the roads. Whatever has occurred, however lamentable, has nothing to do with us. I am Her Grace's governess, and you must let me pass!"

Howard appeared unsettled by this rotund, partridgelike woman wagging her finger in his face. He might have faced down Wyatt's rebels, but he had no experience with the tenacity personified by Mistress Kat Ashley. I walked toward them. As I approached, my boots crunched on the hard snow, and Kate glanced over her shoulder to me.

She went still. Then her hand came up to push back her hood, and I beheld the dark shadows under her eyes. I wanted to embrace her; she had come at the worst hour, after having braved days of arduous travel, but I could not show her intimacy. Since his initial query Howard had left me alone thus far, and I dared not rouse his suspicion now by demonstrating overt familiarity with the princess's women.

"My lord," I said, as Howard turned his gaze to me. "This is indeed Mistress Ashley and Her Grace's lady, Mistress Stafford. They serve her at her house at Hatfield."

"Yes," Howard said dryly. "So I'm told." His expression had softened, however. Without a word, Mistress Ashley took his compliance as permission and shoved past him into the manor. Kate hesitated. As if he could read the silent language between us, Howard turned pointedly away. "We leave within the hour," he said. "No excuses."

He retreated into the hall.

Kate moved to me. "Our sweet Peregrine . . ." I heard her whisper, and she started to reach for my hand. I pulled away, glancing at the guards, several of whom were eyeing Kate with appreciation. I said quietly, "I must return to my duties, Mistress Stafford. You should go inside. Her Grace will no doubt be relieved to see you."

"What?" She frowned. "No. I must talk to you. I want to ask—"

I took another deliberate step back, without giving her occasion to continue, turning about to return to the stable. I did not look back, though I knew she stood there, staring after me, bewildered. It was too dangerous. We couldn't risk it. I didn't care to explore the other reason, like a stain on my soul, which turned me into a coward, unwilling to face her.

Then I heard her footsteps coming behind me and suddenly she was at my side, her hood crumpled about her shoulders, her face flushed from the cold. "Do not avoid me," she said. "Not after all this time. I've been worried sick for you. When Cecil came to see me, with your letter about Peregrine—" She faltered. "Brendan, please. What happened to him? What has happened to you? It's something terrible, isn't it?"

"Yes, it is. And it hasn't ended." Again I resisted the urge to touch her, to feel her body press against mine and pretend that nothing would ever change between us, that no matter what, our love could overcome even my own weakness. "Howard suspects me," I said. "Do not question me anymore. Not now. Just do as I say."

The hurt showed on her face as she vacillated, torn between my warning and the unseen fissure she already sensed between us, though she didn't yet know its cause.

"What do you want me to do?" she finally asked.

Hoping our conversation would appear innocuous to the watching guards and fully aware it couldn't last much longer, I asked, "Do you wear my troth?"

"You know I do. I always keep it about my neck and—" She stifled a gasp. "I'm such a fool! I should have left it behind. If I am searched, they might find it."

"Take it off." I kept my expression neutral, as if we exchanged news such as two servants in our positions would.

She started to reach to her throat for the clasp. Then she stopped. "Why do you want it now? I offered it to you before in Hatfield and you refused it."

"Kate, please. There is no time to explain."

"You cannot do whatever it is you're thinking," she said. "It's a key to your past, your true identity; it could reveal that you have royal blood."

"No one would know that except the queen. It could be our

only chance. Kate, drop it and go. Don't ask me more questions; don't seek me out again. Whatever happens, you must stay with Her Grace. I am fighting for all our lives."

I started to turn away as she fumbled at her neckline, searching within her bodice. "I thought you trusted me," she whispered. She whirled about, her departure leaving me desolate. I could not think of it. I must focus only on what I had to do.

Bending down as if to check my boot, and taking advantage of the guards' catcalling distraction as Kate went past them to enter the manor, I retrieved the chain with its dangling ruby-tipped leaf, which she'd left on the snowy ground.

Chapter Twenty-one

T o the crack of whips, gusts of wind lifting snow in whirl-winds off the road, we departed Ashridge. A storm had rolled in; though the actual snowfall was light, the wind cut through our wool cloaks like teeth. Mistress Parry had tried in vain to gain us another day, cajoling Lord Howard that should anything befall the princess under such inclement weather it would be on his head. He remained adamant. Elizabeth had been pronounced fit to travel; barring a catastrophe, he'd rather risk the weather than the queen's wrath.

I'd scarcely caught a glimpse of Elizabeth when they brought her from her rooms, swathed in furs, her swollen face averted as they set her inside the cushioned litter. Guards surrounded her. The litter curtains were drawn. There wasn't a moment to ex-change a word with her, and even if there had been I was rele-gated to the vanguard with the carts and servants, while Mistress Ashley, Blanche Parry, and Kate rode beside her.

We proceeded in slow stages. The litter jostled on the pitted road, and Elizabeth called for several stops along the way, com-plaining of discomfort and forcing Lord Howard to attend her.

She prolonged the inevitable, determined to extend what should have been a daylong trip into as much time as she could. By dusk, with London still hours away, Howard had no choice but to order a halt. We would spend the night in a nearby manor, where the owners, apprised without warning of our arrival, arranged accommodations as best they could, giving up their own bedchamber for the princess.

The next morning, we took to the road at first light. This time, Elizabeth's litter curtains remained closed the entire way, and she did not raise a single protest. Lord Howard rode flinty-eyed beside her, her ladies behind him. From my position in the back, I strained to see Kate. She'd taken my advice to heart; not once did she turn to look at me.

Under a sunset that smeared crimson across the lead sky, we reached the city gates.

Everything was transformed, the poisonous suspicion of the past weeks having burst open to reveal its rotten fruit. On the gates hung the torn limbs of Wyatt's rebels. Their blood dripped onto the road, where dogs snarled at each other and lapped the congealed pools. Gibbets loomed like specters at every corner, adorned with gutted naked bodies, stiff and blackening. It was the expected punishment for treason, but as the smell of death invaded my senses, the impact of what we faced threatened to overwhelm me.

This time, I feared the queen would take all our heads.

Houses and businesses were closed tight, doors bolted and shutters drawn, though it was not yet dark. Only a few people roamed the streets, and as soon as they spotted our procession, hemmed by men-at-arms, they dashed indoors, furtive as mice. Yet as word somehow spread that it was none other than Princess Elizabeth making her entrance, a small, brave crowd gathered along the road to Whitehall—a sea of silent stares, their stunned expressions bearing testament to the unexpected violence that had swept through their city. I saw Howard tighten his grip on his reins, looking pointedly at the princess's litter, as if he expected an eruption.

All of a sudden, the curtains whisked back. Elizabeth revealed herself reclining on her bolster, her drawn features offset by a high-necked white gown. Her hair was unbound. In breathtaking symbolism, she wore a necklace of dark square-cut rubies about her throat. As she returned the crowd's stares with her impassive dark eyes, several women curtsied and one lone man called out, "God save Your Grace!"

Howard motioned to the guards. Before they surrounded the litter, impeding the view, Elizabeth shot him an amused look. Despite her fear, she had not lost her bite.

Kate finally dared a look at me as Whitehall appeared before us, protected by cordons of sentries, less a palace now than a fortress. Her gaze was questioning; though she rode only paces away, it felt as though an impassable chasm separated us.

We passed under the main archway. Elizabeth sat upright, stiffening as she looked ahead. The procession passed a knot of officials, watching warily from behind guards. We did not stop. We continued on, through a stout gateway, into an enclosed courtyard where yeomen with halberds, dressed in the green-and-white Tudor livery, waited.

Howard dismounted and assisted Elizabeth from her litter. As she yanked her furs about her, the guards' perfunctory bows brought an angry crease to her brow. "Is this to be my reception?" she demanded. "Where shall I lodge, pray tell? In a dungeon?"

"Your Grace will lodge in specially appointed apartments selected for you," Howard replied. "These yeomen are here to escort you. You're allowed the services of your three women; all others of your household are dismissed."

"Dismissed?" Her voice frayed. "Surely you can't mean to deprive me of these people on whom I depend?" Howard did not answer. Lifting her chin, Elizabeth said loudly, "I demand to see my sister the queen! I demand audience with Her Majesty, who cannot—"

The yeomen shifted to her. Taking in their stance, she went still. Mistress Ashley and Blanche Parry hastened to her; all of a sudden, the understanding that she was truly at Mary's mercy must have struck her, for she pivoted back to Howard. "I beg you, my lord, if only for the family ties between us." She set a gloved hand on his sleeve. "At least permit me the services of my squire. My travel chest is heavy. He must carry it for me."

It was an ineffectual excuse, concocted of sheer desperation; Howard must have realized it. Any one of those brawny yeomen could see to her traveling chest, but he looked as if he were actually considering it. His gaze lifted to where I stood by Cinnabar. Kate had also gone immobile by her mare, hooded and cloaked, as if uncertain what to do.

"No men," Howard intoned. "My orders are clear. Only Your Grace's women."

"Please, my lord," Elizabeth implored. "He's but a servant. What harm can he do?"

"Plenty," said Howard curtly, "if he's the same man I think he is."

He knew who I was. He had known all along. Could he actually be abetting me?

I dropped the reins and went to him. "My lord," I said, "Her Grace is ill. Surely she merits this consideration." My voice lowered. "It could be that one day she will find herself in a better position to reward your compassion."

His mouth worked. As I surmised, Lord William Howard was no sycophant. He had defended London, putting himself in harm's way to protect the throne. He had his honor to uphold. My appeal must have stirred his already conflicted conscience, for he nodded once, tersely. "He may assist. But after that, he must depart. I cannot," he added, a hint of apology in his tone, "gainsay the queen. If I earn her reproof, how can I be a friend to Your Grace?"

Elizabeth sighed. "Thank you, my lord." She drew herself erect. The yeomen closed in around her. She walked into the palace, Kate, Ashley, and Parry behind. Lifting the brass-banded leather chest from the cart, I caught Howard's gaze.

His impervious mask had slipped, revealing a troubled countenance.

"Whatever you plan," he muttered, "you'd best act fast."

I hurried after Elizabeth. The passage was clammy, the vaulted stone ceiling low above our heads. We were brought to closed chambers without any windows, furnished with only the essentials. It was freezing; there were no braziers. Stepping back through the antechamber without a word, the yeomen bowed and shut the door on us.

Mistress Parry gaped in dismay. Ashley stomped her foot. "This is an outrage! Does Her Majesty mean to murder us by ague?"

Elizabeth sank wearily onto a stool, as if her bones had turned to water.

I deposited the chest on the floor. "Your letter," I said. "I'll take it to someone who doesn't want to see you imprisoned any more than Howard does."

She regarded me blankly. "Letter?"

"Yes, your letter to the queen. The one I asked you to write. Please, Your Grace. We must hurry. There is little time."

Mistress Parry intervened. "I—I didn't believe you. And we had no means. They confiscated the ink, quills, and paper from her chamber at Ashridge. She couldn't write anything, so I . . . I didn't give her your message."

As Elizabeth whipped her stare to Parry, Kate knelt to rummage in her tapestry bag. She pulled out a sheaf of paper, a sharpened quill, and a small bottle of ink. Turning to the table, Elizabeth removed the stopper from the ink and dipped the quill. She paused, her hand poised over the paper. She looked at me. Then she leaned forward and started writing, her quill scratching furiously in the silence.

Kate watched me. I found it difficult to meet her eyes, to see the fear in them and know it was because I had failed to keep us safe. There was still time, though; if I could reach the queen and convince her, I might yet be able to avert the worst.

Elizabeth turned the page over, her tongue showing through her clenched teeth. Then she stopped writing as abruptly as she'd begun, perusing the page. She appeared to be deliberating, looking over her words for errors. Satisfied, she inked her quill again and slashed diagonal lines through the space at the bottom of the page before she signed it.

"Sand," she said. Kate searched her bag again. "I didn't bring any," she said. She cursed. "We were in such a rush when the news came that we—we—" As I saw her falter, overwhelmed by the emotion she had held in check, Elizabeth pulled her close.

"Not you," she murmured. "Not my brave Kate. Don't you dare. If you start crying, then so shall I, and we both know all the tears in the world will not avail us."

Over Kate's head, Elizabeth lifted her gaze to me. She couldn't know that I had betrayed Kate and taken another woman to my bed, but in that moment it was though she saw into the darkest part of me. In her regard I found the acceptance that I had denied myself, the understanding that she, too, had been prey to illicit desire. Yet her gaze also warned that those we loved must not suffer for it. There was no reason they should know how far we had trespassed.

"I must go." My voice was raw. Kate turned from the princess, a trembling hand at her mouth. I made myself return her frightened look, putting my hand on my chest over the inner pocket of my doublet, where I had hidden the jeweled leaf.

"The tide will soon turn," I told Elizabeth as she blew on the letter, drying the ink as best she could before folding it. I took it from her, stashed it in my cloak. "They can't take you by barge to the Tower then. Do whatever it takes to ensure you stay here overnight."

She nodded. "I will. God be with you, my friend."

Bowing low, I walked out, feeling Kate's gaze on me. I did not look back.

I did not deserve her, not anymore.

Nevertheless, I'd lay down my life to keep her and Elizabeth from further harm.

The palace was dark, torches sputtering on its facade scarcely illuminating the heavy winter night. Huddled in my cloak, I hurried along the courtyard, keeping to the pockets of shadow by the walls. Elizabeth's arrival could not have gone unnoticed. I had to evade detection for as long as I could.

Taking a side staircase to a gallery, I paused, looking about. The offices I sought must be near the queen's apartments. A discreet inquiry of a passing page set me in the right direction. I encountered more sentries than I'd seen in the palace before, but none displayed interest in me. I walked with purpose, adopting the gait of a menial with an important task to complete. Courtiers idled in alcoves, with a distinct lack of merriment. I assumed anyone with the means had fled London for the relative safety of the countryside, but I still saw evidence that the oiled machinery of the court remained in full motion, with secretaries and pages hurrying to assignations, bearing satchels and portfolios. No doubt the council would be up all night, debating a strategy for contending with the queen's sister.

I found Rochester directing a clerk as he hovered over a desk heaped with ledgers.

"My apologies if I disturb," I said from the threshold.

He looked up sharply, glowering at the interruption. He appeared exhausted, his habitual florid color drained. The events of the past days must have tired him beyond measure, leaving little time for wine or food, and less for sleep. When I tilted my hood back far enough for the candlelight to reveal my face, he barked at his clerk—"Go! Fetch those papers from the archives!"— and pretended to examine the open ledger before him as the clerk sidled out, with a glance at me. As soon as he was gone, Rochester breathed, "By the saints, are you insane? You're no longer welcome here. If they find out you've returned, you'll be arrested and thrown into a cell to rot."

I closed the door. The room was stifling from a lit brazier in the corner. "I must speak to her."

"Her?" he echoed, and then, as he realized my intent, he shook his head. "Out of the question. She will not see you. She refuses to see anyone, but she'll especially refuse you."

I removed the folded letter from my cloak. "I must deliver this to her. The princess's life depends on it. You care about Elizabeth, too. I know you don't want to see Renard win."

He swallowed. "What—what do you mean by that?"

"You know. Just as you knew from the moment I arrived why I had come. You were expecting me. You knew Cecil would send someone because you had warned him."

His aghast expression confirmed it: The anonymous informant at court was none other than Rochester, the queen's trusted comptroller. The warnings of the peril Elizabeth faced from Renard and the impending betrothal to Prince Philip—they had come from him. It must have tormented his conscience. He loved the queen; he'd stayed at Mary's side in her darkest hours, when Northumberland had the kingdom in his grip and no one believed she'd win the throne. Still, like many who served her, he also must believe she was about to commit a terrible mistake. English to his core, he couldn't stomach the thought of a foreign power coming upon these shores or the terror that would follow in its wake.

"I am Her Majesty's loyal servant," he quavered. "You cannot prove anything against me. And if you try, I'll deny it. All of it."

"You don't understand. I do not seek to—"

He came at me, seizing my wrist. "It is *you* who do not understand. Nothing can save her now. It is over. Finished. We have lost." His voice shook. "The queen will not be dissuaded. She had Lady Jane Grey and Guilford Dudley executed today. I was there; I had to bear official witness to their deaths."

Pain slashed through me. Jane and Guilford had been pawns

in other's designs; now, both were dead. Yet Robert Dudley lived. The man I had come to loathe and mistrust more than any other on this earth, who'd been behind the entire conspiracy, who had, by his very actions, compelled Elizabeth and me into this impasse—he was still alive.

So much for justice, I should have killed him when I had the chance.

"God assoil them," I murmured. "I pray Lady Jane did not suffer."

"It curdled my blood," Rochester said. "The poor lass couldn't find the block after they blindfolded her. She groped her way to it, begging those around her for help. I tell you, I'll never forget it, not as long as I live." He turned from me, wiping his sleeve across his face. "You must go. I cannot help you. It is over. Now every man must shift for himself."

"You do not believe that. You never believed that. You're one of the good men, remember? You must do as your heart dictates or you'll regret it the rest of your days. You'll always wonder, if you'd done as I asked, could you have saved the princess?"

He went still, his back to me, his shoulders hunched about his ears.

"Are you willing to let that devil Renard take her down?" I added. "Because I am not. I'll see him in hell first."

"Hell," said Rochester, "is where you'll undoubtedly end up. And I'll be there with you." He lumbered to his desk, yanked a ring of keys from its top, and took up one of the candles. Cupping the flame with his hand, he turned to me. "I can't very well parade you about court. You're a wanted man. I'll not risk my life for you. I have a wife and children. I need to keep my head on my shoulders." He jangled the keys, turning to the wainscoting. With a press of his hand on a decorative panel, he swung it open, revealing a narrow opening. "This passage leads to her apartments. I'll see you inside, but I warn you, that is as far as I go. After that, you are on your own."

"Fair enough." I ducked down, squeezing through the opening. The passage must be part of the older, underlying structure of the palace—a stone tunnel that scarcely accommodated Rochester's bulk, dark as a wolf's mouth, so that his candle cast a mere feeble circle of light.

I made myself take steady breaths. After deep water, there was nothing I liked less than enclosed spaces. I felt as if I couldn't get enough air into my lungs, my palms turning slick with sweat. The passage seemed to go on forever, a purgatory. Just as I feared I might have to turn back, Rochester rounded a corner, fumbling at his keys. He unlocked a mold-stained door and pushed it open on surprisingly well oiled hinges; as I gratefully stepped from the tunnel, I found myself in the royal chapel, close to the altar.

"Convenient," I remarked, trying to make light of the matter, even as sweat dripped from under my cap. "In case one is late for worship."

"An escape route," he said. "It's a secret passed down among a select few who serve the royal person, from the old days, when Cromwell sowed terror in every heart. Times past, this chapel used to be part of the monastery of York. This part of the palace is full of tunnels, some supposedly leading to the river." He sniffed. "The good friars must have liked a little contraband together with their communion wafers."

I took in the beatific silence of this jewel-box place, where I'd last heard the requiem mass for Peregrine. The stained-glass windows emitted a peculiar muted glow, catching the reflection of the outside torches and a hint of moon. As I inhaled the frigid smell of marble and fragrant wood impregnated by incense, I was struck again by how familiar, how intimate, it felt to me, as if I had been a Catholic once.

"You stay here." Rochester blew out the candle. "Renard has spies watching every nook and cranny; if it's not safe, we go back the way we came. No argument."

As he started to move down the aisle, I said, "Wait," and handed him the princess's letter.

He recoiled. "I'm not getting any more involved than I already am. If she agrees to see you, you can give it to her yourself."

I removed the jeweled leaf from my doublet, enfolded in a scrap of cloth I'd torn from the hem of my shirt before leaving Ashridge. "Then show her this."

"What is it?" He eyed me suspiciously. "A bribe? She'll not like it, I assure you."

"Just show it to her. Once she sees it, she will receive me."

He snorted. "Yes, trust and a groat will get me a tankard at Satan's table." But he pocketed the leaf and went on, grumbling under his breath.

I had to smile. If I ever needed a friend at my side, I'd want Lord Rochester.

I sat upon a pew and waited, the silence draping over me like velvet. I hadn't realized until this moment how frenetic my life had been, how driven; my entire existence, my every waking hour, had been subsumed by the struggle to safeguard Elizabeth. Now, in the solitude of this chapel, where by all rights I should not be, I suddenly felt the weight of the change that these past days had wrought in me.

I had crossed an invisible threshold. Come what may, I would never be the man I had been. Alone, without any more reason for pretense, I had to finally acknowledge that after all my denials, my painstaking efforts to lead a normal life, I had been deluding myself. I thought to escape the secret of my past, bury it deep within, and be a man like any other. I'd wanted so earnestly to believe it, I convinced myself that if only I married Kate and created a new existence with her, a refuge that was ours alone, where nothing and no one could touch us, I would find peace.

I had been wrong. Peace, it seemed, was not my destiny.

You have a flair for this work . . . You are a born intelligencer.

Cecil had been right. He had known all along what I had refused to see: I was fated for a different, far more dangerous path than the one I envisioned.

The susurration of skirts brought me to my feet. Turning to the chapel doorway, I saw Lady Clarencieux coming toward me. Her face was cold.

"Some would say you're too bold for your own good," she said without preamble. "Others would claim you're merely a man bent on finding his own death."

I inclined my head. "And others, that they are one and the same."

"For your sake, we pray not." She beckoned. "I don't know what Rochester said to her, but after an entire day in which she's not let any of us near her, she agrees to see you."

Chapter Twenty-two

I followed her into the royal apartments. The queen's other women had retired; though a fire burned in the large fireplace, and candles flickered high in sconces on the walls, there was no one else present.

The door to the study was closed. Lady Clarencieux started toward it, then came to an abrupt halt. "You mustn't think that because of your past endeavors on her behalf, she is inclined to mercy. Don Renard has been at her every hour since the revolt, assiduous in his advice, particularly concerning you. If you do this, you may regret it."

"I understand," I said. "But there are truths she must know."

"Must she? Sometimes, it's best to let the lie stand." She met my eyes before she knocked on the door. There was no reply. She moved aside anyway. "She's waiting for you."

My throat knotted as I turned the door latch and stepped inside.

The study was almost as dark as the tunnel I'd just traversed. I had to blink to adjust my vision, and then it swam into muted focus—the gilded desk, heaped with books and stacks of paper; the table where she met with her council; the upholstered chairs and large, mullioned bay of the far wall, its drapery drawn, turning the room into a cocoon that smelled of old smoke. A lone candle melted in a golden candelabrum.

I stood still, my heart banging against my ribs. I did not see her anywhere.

Her voice came at me from the shadows. "You *dare* show yourself to me?"

"Majesty." I dropped to one knee. A figure in the corner by the desk drew upright from its crouch. Laughter, brief and harsh, came at me. "Rather late for humility, is it not?"

I looked up. Mary Tudor's hair was unraveled about her face, its sandy white strands coiling to her shoulders. She wore the same purple gown I'd seen her in when she saw Elizabeth off to Ashridge, but it was crumpled now, misshapen somehow, as if she'd torn at it; the bodice gaped at her breast, revealing collarbones incised under her skin. Her fingers were bare; she appeared to have something coiled in one hand, but it was her face—her stark, hollowed face, in which her eyes burned like embers—that riveted me.

I could not look away. I could barely draw a breath.

She had also crossed a threshold, but whereas my passage would in time bring me to acceptance, for her there was only heartache and fear ahead.

"Majesty," I began, "I came to you because I know that you—"

"No." She flung up her hand. "I will not hear it. You always bring disaster."

Had Rochester failed to show her the leaf? I started to reach to my cloak, to remove Elizabeth's letter, when she opened her palm and revealed what she held—my ruby-tipped gold leaf, hanging from its chain.

"Where did you get this?" Her eyes bore into me. "*How* can you have it?"

The room swayed. For an instant, I saw and heard nothing. Then I said in a quiet voice, "It belonged to my mother."

"You have the effrontery to call a princess of my blood your *mother?*"

I felt as if I fled outside myself, watching from a safe distance as the world collapsed.

"Why would I lie?" I asked, and she moved so quickly, I did not have time to react. Her hand whipped out, striking me. The leaf cut into my cheek; I felt it draw blood.

"*Who are you?*"

Her rage spread a dark pool around us. I half-expected Lady Clarencieux to come rushing in, but as the hush returned, fraught with splintered echoes, I said, "I want you to know the truth. Your aunt Mary of Suffolk, sister of your father, King Henry—she gave birth to me. She had a gold artichoke, a gift from the French king upon her marriage to your father's friend, Brandon. Before her death, she ordered that artichoke broken apart, its leaves given to four women. You were one. You have a leaf just like it."

I could hear her breath coming in stifled pants through her teeth.

"The Suffolk steward who brought it to you," I went on, "later took up service in the Dudley household." I paused. "He did it for me. His name was Archie Shelton. He watched over me. He tried to keep the secret of my birth hidden, but he failed. Finally, during Northumberland's bid to steal your throne, I discovered it."

"Your secret?" Mary's voice trembled. "You come to me with this—this monstrous fabrication, this monumental lie, after what you've done? You don't want me to know the truth. You seek only to save my sister, whom you've protected all this time."

"Yes." I did not take my eyes from her. "But I never ceased to protect you as well. Trust this, even if you believe nothing else. I would never betray my own blood."

Her jaw clenched, the struggle against some terrible emotion distorting her features. I had the premonition it wouldn't be long before she lost her struggle, before the demon Renard had cultivated and unleashed, which had driven her to take Jane Grey and Guilford Dudley's lives, consumed her.

"What else?" she asked. "Best tell me now before I decide your fate."

"That is all I know, except that I . . . I do not believe I am legitimate. I think that is the reason my mother ordered me hidden away." My voice fractured as I fought against a dread I'd never admitted aloud. "I must have been a shame to her."

"In other words, you are a bastard." Her face set like stone. "Does Elizabeth know?"

"No. But she gave me refuge when I had nowhere else to turn."

She lifted her chin. "If she so cares for you, why did you not tell her?"

"I only have that jewel. Your Majesty has the other one. I saw no reason."

"Oh? Surely you must be aware that some claim Elizabeth is a bastard as well, yet she is considered my heir. Who's to say you'd not be granted the same, if you chose it?"

I had made a grave mistake. It would cost me my life. I should never have told her. By breaking my own vow, I had unleashed the unthinkable.

"I swear to you on my life," I said, "I only tell you this now because your sister's life is at stake. She, too, shares our blood. I thought that if I revealed my true self to you, you would see I have no desire other than to serve my queen and my princess."

"No desire?" she retorted. "Or no proof?"

Even as my breath froze in my lungs, the intransigence in her expression faded. All of a sudden, she became the woman I had first met, the valiant queen who had not let years of bitter antagonism destroy her. Somewhere in her heart, she understood. Like me, she knew what it meant to doubt who she was.

She twined the chain of my leaf around her fingers. "This means nothing. It's a fragment of a forgotten past, which you could have stolen to support your preposterous story." She paused. "But should you ever choose to act differently, you should know that I will not tolerate it. I will see you dead." She thrust the leaf into her skirt pocket and extended her hand. "Now, give me this letter Rochester told me you bring."

I reached into my doublet. She took the paper and turned to the desk.

I remained on my knee.

Unfolding the paper, she read in silence. She stood without moving for a long moment, holding the letter limply, before she let it drift from her hand to the floor. "Is it true?" she asked. "Does she revere me above all else? Or is she as much of a deceiver as you?" She looked over her shoulder at me. "I suspect not even you can say. After all, she's had far more experience."

"Majesty, she is innocent. I came to court to help her, yes, but I also investigated the conspiracy as ordered. And there is more you must know, about Don Renard and—"

She lifted her hand again, cutting me off. "Renard has told me already. I know all about Mistress Darrier and her scheme.

Even if he hadn't, I've had spies in my household since I was old enough to walk. I knew what kind of woman she was. I'm glad she paid the price for her treachery." Her smile was cold. "The Duke of Feria may now wed my Jane Dormer, as I first planned. And lest you doubt, I do intend to show clemency to my allegedly loyal sister. Enough blood has been shed—for the moment."

I exhaled. I was on the brink of allowing myself to believe I had succeeded when she said, "But she still goes to the Tower tomorrow. Evidently she cannot be left to her own devices. At least in the Tower, she'll be safe from these malcontents who foment rebellion in her name. Once my husband, Prince Philip, arrives, together he and I will decide what is to be done with her. I will follow his advice."

His advice . . .

I already knew what Prince Philip would say; unlike her, I knew exactly what he desired. Even so, I could venture no further. She would not kill Elizabeth. For now, it had to be enough. "Your Majesty is most merciful," I said, bowing my head.

"Yes," she replied, "so they say. Any other would have taken her head by now, but I must answer to God. I will not soil my hands with her blood without cause. As for you, while your tale is remarkable, I do not believe it. No princess would bear a bastard. You are mistaken; you have been misguided by others. Still, I spare your life because of past services, which, as you claim, you performed of your own free will. But you are henceforth banished from this court. I never want to see or hear of you again. Now you may go."

"Majesty." I stood and turned to the door. She spoke again, her tone rigid with devastating power. "Remember this, whoever you are: To me you no longer exist. You've achieved your aim. You are now truly a man without a past. See that you stay that way."

I turned to take one final look at her, erect with her head held high, every inch a queen despite her dishevelment. I bowed, with reverence, and I walked out.

Lady Clarencieux rose from her post by the fire. I saw relief wash over her face as I reached out and took her hand in mine.

"Watch over her," I said. "She'll need more care than she knows."

"I will care for her with my life." She left her hand in mine for a moment before she withdrew it. "Be safe, Master Beecham." She turned to the door of the chapel. She did not need to explain; a man who did not exist could no longer pass through Whitehall.

As the door closed behind me, I heard her say, "At the fork in the tunnel, turn right. It will bring you to the river."

Rochester had absconded, as I expected. As he'd said, he had a family to protect. He had left the chapel's secret door unlocked, but I knew the way back to his study was barred. Inhaling deep, I slipped on my gloves and entered the stone tunnel. This time, I had no light. I could scarcely see two feet in front of me, my heels crunching on rubble, the chatter and scamper of rats sending shivers through me. The farther I went into that airless darkness, the more I smelled the acrid tang of the river. I quickened my step, stumbling as I neared what appeared to be the fork.

The left tunnel stretched into nothingness; the right glimmered with faint light. Gripping my sword at my hip, I advanced carefully. More debris crunched underfoot; the moldering walls were slimy to the touch even through my gauntlets. I was so focused on reaching that distant pinprick of light that seemed to beckon like a mirage that at first, I thought I must be imagining the other scent wafting toward me—an insidious perfume, which clung to the air as if its wearer had just passed through.

I froze. Lilies.

A footstep came behind me. I whirled about, yanking at my blade.

No one was there.

I started to tremble. No, it couldn't be. It was impossible. I had seen her leap off the bridge. She had plunged to her death.

The perfume was everywhere now, swirling like a tenacious invisible mist until all I could smell was her. Inside my skin and out. Everywhere.

"Show yourself!" I cried, my voice reverberating wildly. I heard another footstep, the crush of powdered stone under a heel. I bolted forth, dashing toward that sound, my blade swinging before me as I kicked rats aside, my inchoate howl exploding from my lips.

I reached the fork. The tunnel that led to Rochester's office lay directly before me, the one to the chapel to my left. As I stood there breathless, terror erupting through my very pores, a door clicked open, and then there was the distinct clack of heeled footsteps.

Someone had entered the chapel.

God help me, she was alive. Sybilla still lived.

Muted voices in the chapel reached me: a murmur, a barked order, and then the singing of metal being drawn. I didn't wait to see the guards come charging through that door. Spinning back around, I raced the way I had come, careening like a drunkard in a labyrinth, my heart in my throat. The tunnel grew tighter, pitching to a slope. The ceiling lowered, so that I had to duck my head lest I scrape it, scrabbling into a rivulet that grew steadily deeper, until it reached to my waist and I was sloshing through it. The water was so cold it cramped my bowels. Light began to widen around me. I couldn't feel my own legs as I struggled through that fetid pool, almost wailing in fury when I saw the curved grate directly before me, set low in an impassable stone wall.

A sluice gate: I was in a sewer that carried waste from the palace.

Behind me, clamor approached. I heard the men splashing, coming closer. Sheathing my sword, I unhooked my cloak and threw it aside. With a whispered prayer, I shut my eyes and plunged underwater, groping at the underside of the gate, seeking an opening. If it went all the way down, I was doomed. Just as I began to despair, as my lungs screamed for air and I fought the impulse to open my mouth and let myself drown in the shit-filled bog, my hand encountered a serrated edge. Grabbing hold of it, I propelled myself under the gate, clawing with my hands across the putrid bottom. I felt a sharp tug at my shoulder, something snagging my doublet. I kicked hard, knowing whoever was behind me would see my floating cloak and know where I'd gone. The alarm would be sounded; guards would be sent from the palace. The queen would not protect me again if I were found.

With a talonlike scrape down my shoulder, I tore free of the grate and swam upward. The water carried me, tumbling, down an incline. I grappled with debris, clutching at anything I could, and then I was tumbling headlong into the conduit that spilled into the river, the sky wheeling above, scattered with stars, the moon remote in its cradle of cloud.

The sounds of pursuit faded; the far shore of Southwark winked with random torchlight. Dragging myself out of the conduit, I took a moment to catch my breath.

Then I scrambled to my feet and ran as fast as I could into the city.

* * *

I dragged myself toward the dockyards, sodden and shivering. Remembering Cinnabar in the stables, as well as Elizabeth's mount, Cantila, and Urian, I thought I'd have to find a way to retrieve them. I didn't dare return to the palace now, though. I had to find shelter in the only place I had left—in the crowded streets near the Tower.

I stumbled past evidence of Wyatt's aborted revolt: broken barricades, trampled standards, a bloodstained armband submerged in slush. Every house, shop, tavern, and inn was shut; when I reached the Griffin, I banged on the door with my bruised knuckles.

"Please, please answer," I whispered through chattering teeth. "Please, be here."

It seemed an eternity before a pair of shutters in an upper-story window flung open. "Who's there?" demanded a woman's voice. I craned my gaze to where she leaned out, a nightcap askew on her head, a work-roughened hand gripping the sill.

"Scarcliff," I said, and as she tilted her head, I repeated, louder, "Scarcliff! Is he here?"

She glared. "No one by that name here. Get from my door, beggar, or I've a mind to toss my chamber pot on you. Get, I say!"

"No, you don't understand . . ." My protest faded. I was fairly certain I addressed the buxom Nan, who served me the night I had met Scarcliff here. She must be the owner or his wife; proprietors usually dwelled above their place of business, as a safeguard against break-ins and theft. "Shelton," I suddenly thought to say. "I'm looking for Archie Shelton."

She hesitated. Then she vanished, banging the shutters behind her.

I groaned. I couldn't take another step. My clothes were lined in icicles; I could feel a stinging pain where the sluice gate had cut me. My knees wavered; just as I decided to drop on this threshold, as good a place as any to die, the bolt behind the door slid back and the woman was standing on the threshold, clutching a shawl to her plump shoulders.

Behind her, barrel-chested and clad only in his braies, was Scarcliff.

"I thought you might be here," I said, and he caught me in his arms as I collapsed.

Chapter Twenty-three

A fiery concoction being poured down my throat jolted me back to consciousness. Coughing, I tasted a sudden foul rise of bile and leaned over a tattered settle to heave up a horrifying quantity of vomit.

"You poor thing," exclaimed Nan, patting my mouth with a cloth as I groaned and lay back against a cushion. "Where in heaven's name have you been?"

"Smells like the river to me," Scarcliff rumbled.

"Worse," I croaked. I cracked open my eyes. "Much worse. You don't want to know."

"Aye, I'm sure I don't." He sat beside me on a stool, regarding me; they'd stirred up the hearth, and the fire's warmth slowly seeped into my chilled bones. I found myself staring at his bare chest, muscular as a wrestler's; he had few visible scars on that expanse of skin, compared to his face.

"Drink more." He shoved the cup at me. "It's brandy, imported from Seville, about the only damn thing the Spaniards are good for."

I resisted the offer, struggling to my elbows. I was in a small parlor, nothing fancy, but clean and neat. His battered dog lay on a reed mat by the fire, its eyes opaque as it watched me with cursory interest. "Do you live here?" I asked him.

"Most of the time; when Nan will have me."

From the sideboard where she wrung out the cloth in a basin, Nan harrumphed. She tramped back to me and set the cloth on my forehead. "There, now. You stay there and rest. I'll fetch some hot porridge from the kitchen." She cast a troubled look at Scarcliff as she left, closing the door behind her. I heard her descend a staircase.

"She worries," he explained. "She's always said her biggest fear is that one day we'll be woken at night by some Dudley hireling come to strangle us in our beds, though I keep telling her it's not bloody likely. That lot's got more important things to fret over than whether or not I'm still alive."

"She knows about you . . . about all of it?"

He shrugged. "A man can't be a stranger to everyone. Someone's got to know who you are." Seeing as I'd declined the brandy, he drank it down. "Besides, she helped me. She was a doxy in one of those rat-hovels on Bankside, growing long in the tooth; her customers weren't getting any younger, either. She found me washed on the shore that night I escaped the Tower, my legs all smashed up and my face—well, you can see what they did to my face. She and the other whores in the neighborhood fetched me indoors and tended to me. It took weeks before I could open my eyes or uttered a sound, Nan said. Had it not for that pack of cunnies, I'd have died."

"And now you two live together?"

"You could say that. After I healed—or healed as much as I ever would—I hired myself out as a strongman for the brothels; Nan and I tucked away every coin we earned. In time, we saved enough to buy this place from an uncle of hers, a drunken lout who barely kept it running. He died on that settle, from liver rot. Miserable bastard he was, but he did Nan a decent turn in the end. At least now, she needn't sell herself for bread."

My head reeled, as much from the aftereffects of my recent imbroglio as from the very idea that Archie Shelton, previously steward to the noble Dudley household, now ran a tavern with a former whore.

"Surprised?" His one eye gleamed. "I must admit, I was, too, at first. Didn't think I'd stay long. But I like it here. I'm thinking of taking up permanent residence and working full-time. After that ugly bit of trouble with the earl, I figure it's time for old Scarcliff to retire."

My throat tightened with emotion. "That's twice now you've saved my life."

"Yes, it is, isn't it? You certainly have a penchant for getting into trouble." He went silent for a spell, staring into the crackling hearth. "Did you do it?" he said at length. "Did you help her?"

I sighed. "She's going to the Tower, but I have assurance she'll not be killed."

Though his ravaged face could barely register an expression, I could tell he was incredulous. "Assurance from whom? The queen?" He snorted. "I'd not put much trust in her if I were you. Not if you've seen the dead hanging on every corner and those fresh heads on the bridge. She went to the Guildhall when Wyatt's men were spotted across the river; she swore up and down she'd never marry without her people's consent. She got the city all riled up so they'd march to her defense, like they did that time before, against the duke. But she lied. She'll marry the Hapsburg. Wyatt had the right idea; he just went about it wrong."

"I see your point," I said. "But it's not her word alone I'm counting on." I drew the blanket closer around me. I was naked under it, the discarded ruins of my clothing sitting in a dripping basket by the fire. The smell of herbs wafted from my shoulder; Nan must have tended the wound. It hurt, though it probably felt worse than it was.

"Do you want to tell me what happened?" he asked.

I didn't. I didn't want to relive it, not yet. I found myself telling him anyway, my voice remarkably calm as I related what had occurred, everything but what I'd confided to Mary about my secret. When I finished, he sat with his lower lip protruding, as though he were ruminating on a particularly vexing issue. "Are you sure it was her? It's a long fall off the bridge."

I considered. "It was very dark in the tunnel. I didn't see her."

"Then maybe it was your imagination. Maybe Renard found out you'd snuck into the palace to see the queen and sent someone after you. Or perhaps Rochester told him. It's the court, lad. Nothing is more important to a courtier than his own hide, and you've a lot of secrets to spill."

"Maybe," I conceded, reluctantly. "But that scent: Only she wore it. And it was everywhere. As if she'd doused herself in it, because she *wanted* me to know she was alive."

He looked doubtful. "In all that muck and mire, you could smell her?" He grunted. "I suppose it's possible. Hell, anything's possible. But if she survived that fall without breaking her neck, she's more experienced than anyone I've known. The way she handled her sword, and now this: She's had training. I've never heard of anyone jumping off the bridge in the middle of winter and living to tell the tale."

I had to agree. Sitting in his cramped parlor above the Griffin, after having nearly drowned in a sewer, I had to doubt my own experience. The tunnel had been suffocating, a nightmarish labyrinth. I must have lost my reason. It seemed utterly improbable that Sybilla could have plunged into the Thames and not died instantly. Mary had told me she had paid the price, but I had not thought to ask if her body had been recovered. I was glad I hadn't. It was better if I never knew. I had to believe she was dead. I didn't want to consider what I would do if I found out otherwise. The hunt for her would destroy my existence.

"I must be at the Tower tomorrow," I said at length. "I have to see it."

He turned to the door as Nan came trudging back up the stairs.

"Then we will," he said.

The next morning, he located old garb for me that had belonged to the dead uncle: a shirt, an itchy doublet that smelled faintly of lavender and more strongly of mold, mended hose, an oversized cap that flapped about my ears, and shoes too big for my feet. The dead uncle had been larger than me, I thought absently as I dressed, glancing at my contused arms, the purpling bruises on my torso, and the aching shoulder wound wrapped in a bandage; that, and I had lost too much weight. Shelton unearthed a worn belt from the clothes press to keep everything more or less in place. My other clothes were ruined. Nan had painstakingly tried to salvage them, but the taint of sewage was ineradicable, and I told her to give up. My boots could be salvaged, with care and loads of fat rubbed into the leather to restore its pliancy, after they dried out. I was most concerned for my sword, but while I slept Shelton had wiped away the moisture and filth and polished it to a bright hue.

We set out to an early morning that felt like spring, the sun breaking through the clouds in brilliant shafts that soaked into the frigid land. As we walked toward the Tower wharf on the west side of the fortress, I heard chirping in a beech tree and looked up, startled. A robin sat on bare twined limbs, where tiny buds were already visible—a welcome reminder that even this winter must pass, although it was hard to think that spring would find Elizabeth, Kate, and Mistresses Ashley and Parry behind prison walls.

It was a small crowd, not at all what I'd expect when a princess is sent into captivity. Today was Palm Sunday, Shelton told me, to my surprise, and official proclamations from the palace plastered on every wall encouraged the city's denizens to attend worship in the old tradition.

"Must be deliberate," Shelton said in my ear. "They don't want too many to see her going into the same place where her mother died. The people love her. They're starting to realize she truly is their last hope."

I stood with him among the handful who'd gathered on the side of the Tower entrance, the roars of the caged lions in the menagerie seeming to herald Elizabeth's arrival. At first, I thought she'd be brought by barge into the Tower via a water gate, but Shelton reminded me the tide ran too low at this early hour. They'd bring her to the wharf, as close as they could get, but she'd have to walk inside on her own two feet.

So it was that, hidden among curious onlookers, I saw her disembark from her barge and stand, utterly still, a hand at her brow as she gazed up at the looming bastion. She wore a black cloak, the hood drawn over her head, but as the guards cordoning the walkway shifted more tightly together and an audible murmur rose from the spectators, she cast back the hood to show her face.

She was very pale, yet appeared outwardly composed, escorted by five somber lords toward the same gateway through which I'd entered the Tower. Close behind her were Mistresses Parry and Ashley, holding bags stuffed with belongings, and a well-formed yeoman in the Tudor livery, carrying the traveling chest filled with her treasured books. My heart wrenched when Kate hastened from the barge to the princess's side, the last to disembark; as she joined Elizabeth, her hand dropped surreptitiously to clutch the princess's. Elizabeth turned nervously to her, as if Kate had murmured words of encouragement, and then redirected her gaze outward to the watching crowd.

"God keep Your Grace!" shouted a goodwife. As her shrill encouragement faded into the morning air, others lifted chorus, as if they'd been rehearsed: a fervent cry of good wishes that brought Elizabeth to a standstill. The lords, among whom I espied the tall, white-bearded figure of Lord Howard, exchanged concerned looks. Did they actually fear an impromptu rescue?

Elizabeth was looking directly at us, her eyes like black punctures in her pinched face; she could not acknowledge the greeting. Under suspicion of treason, about to enter the very place from which few ever emerged, she mustn't risk the accusation that she'd incited the mob. Yet even from a distance I could see how those cries moved her, how she gazed at us with heartrending intensity, as if she sought to engrave this sight in her memory as a talisman to carry with her during the ordeal yet to come. Her fear ebbed away; in its place, for the briefest of moments, like a glimpse of spring on a bare tree, she showed the strength that made her undeniably a Tudor.

I started to push forward, elbowing those around me. The people in front of me grumbled. Shelton chopped his hands at them; they took one look at his mutilated face and quickly shifted aside. All of a sudden, I found myself pressed against the barricade, peering past the row of guards. Howard had urged the princess forward. She took a step away from him, resisting. I yanked off my cap, heedless of the consequences, waving it as high above my head as I could. Everyone around me followed suit, whipping off their headgear—a flotilla of caps and veils and bonnets, swaying in the air like crude flags.

Elizabeth lifted her chin, searching; her gaze found me, wagging my cap as though everything in the world depended on it. For a fleeting second, our eyes met. They held.

She smiled.

We returned in silence to the Griffin. I couldn't speak. I had stood there and felt tears slip down my cheeks as they led her under the gateway. Metallic hatred almost choked me; all I could think of was that Robert Dudley had finally won. They were together at last, locked in a web of his making. What his lust for her, and the power she represented, had failed to accomplish, his treachery had.

I wished him the worst. I hoped the queen took his head next.

She wouldn't, though. She had told me as much. For now at least, the killing was done.

Mary Tudor had a wedding to plan.

Eventually Shelton broke the quiet. "Try not to worry, lad. If anyone can survive the Tower, it's her. She's old Henry's daughter, that one. She won't break easily."

I swallowed. It was the height of irony that Elizabeth must now rely on the goodwill of a prince she'd never met, a stranger come to wed her sister—and all because of the revelations of his double agent, a woman of vengeful mystery who would forever haunt my dreams.

"What now?" Shelton asked. I hesitated. I hadn't considered it. Since my arrival at court, I'd lived day by day, often hour by hour, never looking too far ahead. My future now stretched before me; exiled from court, with Peregrine gone, Elizabeth and Kate imprisoned, and my world in chaos, somehow I had to find a way to live. I had to prepare myself for the day when fate turned again in our favor.

"My horse and hers, and her dog, Urian," I said. "They're in the stables at Whitehall. I can't leave them there. But if I go back, I'll certainly be arrested. Even if I could get in unnoticed, I've nothing to bribe the grooms with."

"Leave it to me. You forget I was the earl's jack-of-all-trades. I can't count the number of times I saw to Courtenay's horse because he'd passed out in some den. Nan and I have some coin saved, too, enough to rescue the beasts."

I nodded gratefully. "I promise to repay you, for everything."

"No need," he replied. "After all, it is I who owes you the debt."

I stayed in the Griffin while Shelton went to Whitehall, after he retrieved a small purse from the parlor. Nan was not pleased, and I tried to make amends by assisting her and the urchin she'd taken in, who slept downstairs, to prepare the tavern for business.

"We've been closed days now, since Wyatt came," she told me. "Time to get back to work." She indicated a heap of stools. "Set those around the tables, if you please."

As I proceed to wrestle with the stools, I thought that in Nan, Shelton had found the perfect companion. Her no-nonsense manner suited him, and it was obvious they cared for each other. Again I marveled at the irony of life, that a man I'd always seen as cold and distant, even heartless in his sense of duty, had proved to be anything but.

"You'll not drag him back into all that court mess?" Nan abruptly asked. "He acts as if he's a bull, and, compared to most, he is. But he's had a rough time of it. He has pain still, in his legs. He can't be running about, looking after naughty earls and the like."

I managed to extricate the top stools without toppling the rest. "No," I said. "I don't expect so. Besides, there's no court mess anymore, not for me. I've been banished."

"Banished, were you?" She put her hands on her ample hips. "Well, now. What can a mite like you have done to piss off the queen?" She guffawed. "Count yourself fortunate, whatever it was. Court's no place for a sane man these days. Her Majesty's gone mad as a hare. She and her Spanish groom will be lighting the Smithfield pyres soon enough."

She spoke carelessly, turning to blare at the urchin to sweep the ashes out the door, not into the corner, but her words sent a shiver through me. Was this how the common people of London felt about their queen? How had Mary strayed so far, so quickly, from the jubilation she'd earned at her accession? In her zeal to save her people's souls and produce an heir to rule after her, she had alienated the one thing that no monarch who hoped to rule effectively could do without: the love of her subjects.

I sensed it was a lesson Elizabeth would never forget when her time came.

Chapter Twenty-four

Shelton returned by midafternoon, riding Cinnabar, Urian bounding beside him, spattered with mud from the road and leaping on me in excitement. As I petted him and endured his rapturous licks, Shelton told me he'd had a time of it getting the grooms to release the animals, though the overall chaos in the stables had helped.

"I had to empty my purse," he said, with an apologetic look at Nan. "They're getting ready to move to Hampton Court, so a few less animals were not to their disadvantage. But they wouldn't let me near the princess's Arabian. He's well cared for; apparently Her Majesty has decided to give him as a gift to Philip when he arrives."

"My lady's not going to like that," I muttered. I could imagine the roar when Elizabeth heard of it. Her rage would drown out the very lions in the Tower.

"The court leaves tomorrow," Shelton added. "Whole pack of 'em, headed off to get the palace ready for Philip and his entourage. Have you thought of what you're going to do next? I'm guessing you'll not want to stay here and serve quail pie to sailors."

"And why not?" demanded Nan. "It's a respectable trade. Not to mention a tad safer, I'll wager, than whatever it is he's been up to."

"Indeed," I said, repressing my laughter. I felt lighter all of a sudden, witnessing this domestic squabble. It was a relief to see some people could actually be normal. "I'll wager it would be. But I should leave London. I'm not a problem you need." I looked at Shelton. "I have only one option."

"Cecil," he said.

I nodded. "Yes. He'll be anxious for news, and he can hide me."

The flush in Nan's cheeks faded. "You're not thinking of . . . ?" she asked Shelton.

He cupped her chin, leaning over to kiss her. "Just for a little while, love. We can't let the lad go off on his own, now can we? With his luck, he's liable to end up in a ditch."

I was about to remind him that I certainly would not. I was one and twenty years old, a man grown, who'd faced more perilous ventures than an expedition to the countryside. Then I sensed his intent and kept quiet.

A trip to Cecil's manor was an opportunity we might never have again.

We departed the next day at dawn. It would be easier to evade unwanted inquiries, Shelton suggested, seeing as the court would be lumbering out of London, and everyone occupied watching the queen's procession.

I donned my borrowed clothes and kept my head lowered under my cap when we were detained at the gate, where Shelton spun a magnificent yarn about his time in the Scottish wars of

Henry VIII, claiming he'd thus earned his impressive facial badge of honor. The sentries were duly impressed. One of them—a gnarled old man whose uniform seemed to wear him, rather than the other way around—had fought in the same wars and proudly pushed up his sleeve to display a ragged scar on his arm. He waved us out, excusing us the exit fee. Soon we were cantering down the rutted road, the city behind us.

I took a long look at London over my shoulder. Though I could not see it, I conjured the Tower in my mind—its White Keep looming over the surrounding walls, the narrow parapets over the leads—and lifted a prayer for the safety of the four beloved women I had left there. I would be waiting when they were released. I would be waiting and I would be ready. Sybilla Darrier had imparted a lesson I would not squander; the time had come to embrace who I was: a spy for Elizabeth, devoted to her welfare. Next time when danger struck, I would not be caught unawares.

Then I cast my thoughts to the church where Peregrine lay.

"Farewell, my friend," I whispered. "I'll never forget you."

Shelton and I rode in quiet companionship through hamlets where people were recovering from the aftereffects of the rebellion, turning our faces from the gibbets where dead rebels swayed. Urian ran before us in delight, romping through woodlands and open meadows, splashing into streams fed by the thaw.

Finally I breached the silence. I'd had plenty of time as we rode to come up with an opening salvo; instead, I found myself asking hesitantly, "Was my mother beautiful?"

He let out a sigh. "Oh, she was. Like no other woman I'd ever seen. There was a reason her brother King Henry called her his Rose. She could bring his entire court to a halt just by walking into the hall. But it was more than that: She had a light in her.

It shone even when she was sad. And she was loyal to those she loved. She was never discourteous or demanding; she treated everyone as her equal."

I stared at him, fascinated. He had known her. He had known my mother.

"Were you . . . ?" My voice faltered; I couldn't say the words. I felt abruptly as if I were intruding on deeply cherished and private memories.

He kept his gaze fixed ahead, but recollection softened his face, so that I could envision the burly young steward he'd once been, all those years ago.

"Naturally I was," he said at length. "Any man who met her must have fallen in love with her. She invited desire, through no fault of her own." He paused and cleared his throat. "But it's not what you think. It wasn't a love affair like minstrels sing about."

The air about me seemed to solidify. "But you and she, you were . . . ?"

He finally turned his head to me. For what seemed an eternity he did not reply. Then he said, "Yes. It happened when her husband, my master the duke, Brandon of Suffolk, went to France with the king and Mistress Boleyn."

"Elizabeth's mother," I clarified. "Queen Anne."

"Yes. But she wasn't queen yet. Your mother wouldn't allow anyone in her presence to call her by any other name. She hated her, you see; she blamed her for stealing the king from Queen Catherine. She was mistaken. Henry wanted what he wanted and didn't care whom he trampled to get it. He obliged your mother to surrender her best jewels to adorn Mistress Boleyn for the French trip. Your mother was enraged; she and the duke quarreled bitterly over it. I was there. I heard them shouting at each other in the hall."

A muscle in his face twitched. "Mistress Boleyn had heard of the jeweled artichoke, and she wanted to show it off, to prove to the French king, in whose court she'd served, that she was worthy of being England's future queen. My lady would not hear of it. When the duke went to retrieve it she locked herself in her chamber and refused to come out. Later she sent me to court to deliver her other jewels. Mistress Boleyn understood the insult and turned her wrath on Queen Catherine, stripping her of every last jewel she possessed. My master, in turn, vented his wrath on me."

"On you? Why?" I began to understand his prior behavior, when he first brought me to court to serve the Dudleys, his taciturn attitude, his insistence that I obey my betters.

He shrugged. "He wasn't really angry at me; he was angry at himself. He had supported the king, though he privately disagreed. He did not think Anne Boleyn was worthy of anything more than a bedding, but he also knew telling Henry that wouldn't be wise. Your mother and he had been at odds for years over it; so much so, in the end it destroyed their marriage. She wouldn't attend the court, no matter how much Henry threatened. She stayed steadfast to Queen Catherine and made no bones about it. Her husband the duke, on the other hand, bowed to the strongest wind. And he was right. Before they left France, Mistress Boleyn gave in to the king and Elizabeth was conceived."

I bit my lip, caught between the past and the present. "You did not go to France."

"No. My master ordered me to his manor in Westhorpe." His tone lowered, as though even in the midst of these open fields, he might be overheard. "When I arrived, I found my lady, your mother, bereft. She, too, had realized that her brother the king was willing to plunge the realm into ruin for Anne Boleyn, and it caused her no end of despair. A few nights later, a great storm arose, as if God himself showed discontent. One of her women came running to summon me to her chambers. She was having trouble with one of her casements. The wind had thrown it open, and rain was drenching everything. My lady was soaked to her skin, but she kept yanking at that window as if her life depended on it. Her health had been precarious; the births of four children had taken their toll. She didn't show it outwardly, but I worried she'd catch her death of cold, so I . . . I tried to—"

He swallowed; all of a sudden, I heard a rupture in his voice. "I was a foolish young man then, lustful and proud, enamored of a woman so far above me in station she seemed unattainable. But that night she was so alone, so lost. She dismissed her maid, and I stayed with her as she sat before the fire. I served her mulled wine, tried to comfort her. She spoke of the past, when she'd been sought after as a royal bride. She told me of how François of France himself had pursued her and why she could never give up that artichoke jewel, because it was all she had left of a time when she risked everything to marry Brandon, the love of her life. Then she smiled and said, 'And look at me now, Shelton: I'm a sad old lady. No one remembers the girl I was.'"

Heat prickled behind my eyes. I reached over the space between our horses as if to touch his hand on his reins. He jerked away, disdaining my reassurance.

"No," he said hoarsely. "Let me finish. Let me get this out. I haven't spoken of it to anyone. I need to tell you as much as you need to hear it."

He drew Cerberus to a stop beside a stream. As our horses bowed their heads to drink, he dismounted and moved with heavy steps toward an oak. He stood there, staring at it. I slipped from Cinnabar to go to his side. In the distance Urian rolled in a patch of field.

"It was only a few times." Shelton's voice turned impersonal, as though he sought to put distance between himself and the man he had been. "That night was the first. I couldn't help my-self. She must have seen it in my eyes. I'd thought myself so clever, keeping my feelings to myself and acting the loyal squire, but she knew what desire looked like. Perhaps it gave her solace, to know she could still rouse such passion, to be young again . . . but to me—oh, to me, it was paradise on earth! I had never felt anything like it. I pledged my undying love to her, vowed I'd never have another. She laughed, said all men utter such nonsense in the heat of the moment, but I meant it. In a way, I still do."

His broken mouth creased in a smile. "It's why I tried to pro-tect you after I found you in the Dudley household, why I sought to keep you hidden from those who might do you harm. It was my promise to her, though I never had the chance to tell her. I know I was hard on you at times, but I believed it was necessary to keep you safe. She wouldn't have wanted you to suffer."

I couldn't move as he swiveled to me, looking at me with his one eye, which could no longer shed tears, though his entire countenance bore testament to his grief. "I returned to court when the duke came back from France. Mistress Boleyn an-nounced she was with child; her coronation was planned in haste. I left your mother at Westhorpe, not knowing she, too, had conceived. She didn't tell a soul except her herbalist, Mis-tress Alice, letting out that she had a swelling sickness. I never saw her again."

"She died because of me." I sank to my haunches, my head in my hands.

He knelt beside me. "No. Not because of you. She loved her children; she would have loved you, too." He cupped my chin, turning my face to him. "You have her eyes, the same pale gray that can turn blue or sea green depending on your mood."

"How did you find me?" I whispered. "How did you know where I'd been taken?"

"That damn artichoke again," he said, "the one Anne Boleyn had coveted. Your mother stated in her will that it was to be broken apart, a leaf given to each of the women she named. The duke didn't care. Anne Boleyn had given birth to a daughter, and Brandon had to contend with the king. Your mother was scarcely in her grave before Brandon wed his ward, a girl of fifteen. He wouldn't have troubled himself with his late duchess's request had I not offered to distribute the leaves in her honor."

"But you didn't know about me? You did not suspect?"

"Not at first. Then I learned that one of the women named in your mother's will was the herbalist, and it sparked my suspicion. Alice vanished after your mother's death; no one knew where she'd gone. I believed the bequeathing of those leaves was a sign, a message meant for me. So I did my duty. I delivered one leaf to Princess Mary and returned to court to serve the duke, to watch and wait. I had the leaf for Lady Dudley as well, but there was something about her I mistrusted; I didn't approach her yet. By the time the duke died," he added, "I'd discovered that Mistress Alice lived in the Dudley home in Warwickshire. When I went to Lady Dudley for a post, she hired me as her steward because of my service to the duke. Alice couldn't believe it when I walked into her kitchen. Neither could I. When I saw you sitting there with her, the spitting image of your mother, I almost wished you didn't exist. I feared for the life you'd face, a secret son with royal blood in your veins."

I knew the rest of the story; I had lived it. I'd barely survived it. Even so, the final question had to be asked, though it seemed unnecessary now, almost irrelevant.

"Are you my father?"

He did not answer at once. The wind rustled through the branches above us, a flock of birds scattered overhead. Our mounts stamped their hooves, ears upright to the sounds of awakening nature. Urian trotted back to us, panting and covered in mud.

"Yes," he finally said. "I suppose I must be." He rubbed his chin, as though the thought perturbed him. "I should never have kept the truth from you. I suspected you had returned the night you were eavesdropping on the earl and the princess, but I wasn't sure. Then you appeared in the brothel, and I recognized you immediately. I thought, here he is. Here is my second chance. But I'd never expected to see you again, and you thought I was dead. I'd changed so much; I didn't want to do what I knew I must."

"So instead you followed me," I said. "You still tried to protect me."

He chuckled. "Didn't do a very good job of it, did I? I'd seen the earl exchanging missives with couriers; I knew he'd become involved in something dangerous, helping Robert Dudley in the Tower. I figured, whatever had brought you back to court, you'd soon be in over your head. Old habits never die: I wanted to keep you safe." He reached into his jerkin and extracted a small silk-cloth packet, tied with a frayed ribbon. "This belongs to you." He put it in my palm. "I've kept it all these years."

I closed my fingers over it. I didn't need to open it to know what the packet contained: the jeweled leaf meant for Lady Dudley, which he never gave her.

"Thank you," I said softly. I shifted nearer to him. He stayed immobile as I slowly put my arms around him. I held him close; though I didn't look up, I heard him choke back a sob.

"Ah, lad," he murmured, and his hand came up to caress my hair.

I finally had my past.

Now I could look to my future.

AUTHOR'S NOTE

Like *The Tudor Secret,* my first book in the Elizabeth I Spymaster Chronicles, this story is first and foremost a work of fiction. While I've endeavored to stay true to factual events, in order to facilitate the plot I admit to taking liberties, particularly with the historical timeline, which I have compressed. Likewise, while each historical character has been carefully researched, I present them with fictional motivations and traits, while keeping at the forefront what we do know about their personalities.

This book is based on events leading to a pivotal and often overlooked event in Tudor history: the Wyatt Revolt. Had it succeeded, the future of England might have been quite different. Carefully planned yet betrayed at the last moment, the revolt failed. For centuries since, historians have debated Elizabeth's knowledge of, and possible involvement in, this conspiracy against her sister, Queen Mary I.

Not surprisingly, as with much concerning Elizabeth, the verdict is divided. I've chosen to depict one possible scenario. While it may be challenging in retrospect to believe Elizabeth ever took such a risk—she is famous for her caution as much as for the brilliance of her reign—we tend to forget that at the time, her coronation was hardly assured. Most Catholics believed she was illegitimate; certainly her own sister had cause to wonder if Elizabeth was their father's child, given the trauma Mary had endured during her parents' acrimonious separation and her hatred of Anne Boleyn, who was beheaded for treason and adultery. Ludicrous as it may seem to us, Mary must have certainly believed in Anne's guilt.

Mary's determination to wed Philip of Spain proved a fatal mistake; it nearly cost her the realm and contributed to her death. She ascended her throne to popular acclaim; within two years she'd earned the sobriquet of "Bloody Mary" because of the marriage. In her zeal to please Philip and restore England from heresy she ordered the deaths of hundreds of Protestants. Elizabeth became a beacon of hope in these dark days, and a focal point for intrigue. Yet bizarrely, it was Philip of Spain— hardly a tolerant man by any standard, especially in matters of religion—who interceded on Elizabeth's behalf with Mary. It is also known that upon her accession, Philip paid suit for Elizabeth's hand in marriage. These few facts were the inspiration for my fictional character Sybilla Darrier.

Edward Courtenay, Earl of Devon, was implicated in the Wyatt Revolt. History is unclear as to how exactly he was made to confess, derailing what could have been a far graver threat. The accepted version is that he broke down under interrogation by his ally and mentor Bishop Gardiner, who'd championed Courtenay as a consort for Mary. Many on the queen's council would have preferred the handsome, if sybaritic, Courtenay to the Catholic foreigner, Prince Philip. Some even espoused a union between the earl and Elizabeth herself.

Courtenay survived the ordeal. In 1555, he was released from the Tower and exiled. Though he kept his title and estate, he was forbidden to return to England, and both Mary and Elizabeth refused to have anything more to do with him. He died in Italy at the age of thirty-nine, unwed and childless.

Simon Renard exercised significant influence over Mary and was a trusted confidant of Charles V. Historians agree that he also became Elizabeth's most fervent foe, repeatedly urging Mary to execute her before and after the Wyatt Revolt. He died in 1573, after a long and distinguished career in service to the Hapsburgs.

The executions of Jane Grey, Guilford Dudley, and Jane's father, the Duke of Suffolk, as well as approximately one hundred rebels and Wyatt himself, marked the tragic end of the uprising—a blood offering to the emperor, thus securing Philip's marriage to Mary.

Brendan's adventures will continue . . .

I'm indebted as always to my fabulous, hardworking agent, Jennifer Weltz, whose unflagging enthusiasm and guidance are my lodestone. Her colleagues at the Jean V. Naggar Literary Agency are my cheering squad, never wavering in their encouragement. My editor Charlie Spicer not only helped shape a stronger book but left me alone to do it, a supreme vote of confidence. My assistant editor April Osborn, copy editor, India Cooper, and the entire creative team at St. Martin's Press support me with vigor and expertise. In the United Kingdom, my editor Suzie Dooré and her team at Hodder & Stoughton continue to champion me and I'm so appreciative. I also wish to give special thanks to my friend Sarah Johnson, who took time out of her schedule to read a draft of this book and provide invaluable suggestions for improvement.

At home, my partner constantly adjusts to the demands of living with a working writer, taking trips with me, nurturing my obsession for research, and promoting my books to everyone he meets. Writing can be compulsive and lonely; I am blessed to have him in my life. Our late dog, Paris, was my loyal daily companion, always reminding me that it was unacceptable to skip meals or walks. She is deeply missed. The addition of two new cats to our household has brought additional love and mirth to my life, as well as much-needed solace.

Independent bookstores are my heroes; in this complex time of digital revolution and myriad entertainment choices, they continue to promote the importance of the printed word. I especially wish to thank Bookshop West Portal and Orinda Books for hand selling my books, recommending me to their book groups, and supporting local authors.

In that vein, I am also grateful to all the bloggers who participate in my tours, as well as those who discover my books and take the time and effort to review or mention them. Bloggers are authors' unsung partners; though most have busy lives and cares of their own, their dedication to raising awareness of books is unswerving.

Friends are a joy and respite. My author friends, in particular, are always there to help me off various ledges of vacillation or panic, and those not in the business remind me that nonbook-related talk can never be overestimated. To all of you who share this journey with me and have not yet fled for the hills, thank you.

Lastly, I owe everything to you, my readers. Your e-mails,

social media messages, comments on book-related sites, and ongoing support are why I keep writing. Without readers, a writer is mute. You are my voice. I hope to continue to entertain you for many years to come.

To learn more about me and my work, and to schedule book group chats with me, please visit www.cwgortner.com.

1. *The Tudor Conspiracy* takes place in the winter leading up to the Wyatt Revolt of 1554. What did you discover about this event? Who were the major players and what were their motivations? Did you agree with the rebel's goals? If so, why? If not, why not?

2. Religion plays a crucial role in this story's conflicts. How do Mary and Elizabeth Tudor embody their faiths' aspirations? Were their conflicts based on actual religious differences or on a larger power struggle? Do you see any parallels in today's religious divides?

3. Brendan Prescott is a fictional character with a secret. He comes to Mary's court to safeguard Elizabeth by becoming a double agent. What were some of the challenges he faced in his dual role? Do you think he acted as he should have?

4. Illicit correspondence is a method of communication in the book, based on actual ways that prisoners in the Tower communicated with the outside. Why do you think Edward Courtney became involved with the schemes? Do you think he was a pawn or did he act out of choice? What are your impressions of Edward versus Robert Dudley? Which of them did you like or dislike more?

5. Sybilla is an enigmatic character who carries secrets of her own. Did you understand her reasons for doing what she did? What does her character tell us about the role of religious exiles and survivors of treason in the Tudor world?

6. Brendan sacrifices his secret and puts himself at risk for it. Why do you think he felt he had to confess? What were your impressions of his relationship with the queen? Do you think he liked her? What are some of his conflicts in terms of his service to Elizabeth and his own faith?

Discussion Questions

St. Martin's
Griffin

7. Whitehall, London Bridge, the Tower, taverns and brothels feature in the novel. What did you learn about these areas of Tudor London? What are some of the differences in how people lived? If you had to choose, where would you prefer to live and how would you make a living?

8. Elizabeth Tudor is one of history's most enduring figures but in this novel we see a different side of her. Did you agree with the author's depiction of her? Did you find her sympathetic? Would you have behaved as she had, given the choice?

9. Shocking revelations and events happen in the course of this story. Which did you find most unexpected? How do you think you would have reacted if you faced similar situations?

10. Who was your favorite character in the book, and why?

For more reading group suggestions,
visit www.readinggroupgold.com.

"A fast-moving tale of espionage and suspense . . .
the velvet peril of Tudor England comes alive
in this haunting look at Elizabeth I's secret spy."
—Margaret George, author of
The Autobiography of Henry VIII

St. Martin's Griffin